S:
Th
F

Loving Geordie

Also by Andrea Badenoch

MORTAL

DRIVEN

BLINK

Andrea Badenoch

Loving Geordie

MACMILLAN

First published 2002 by Macmillan
an imprint of Pan Macmillan Ltd
Pan Macmillan, 20 New Wharf Road, London N1 9RR
Basingstoke and Oxford
Associated companies throughout the world
www.panmacmillan.com

ISBN 0 333 78169 4

1 3 5 7 9 8 6 4 2

A CIP catalogue record for this book is available from
the British Library.

Typeset by SetSystems Ltd, Saffron Walden, Essex
Printed and bound in Great Britain by
Mackays of Chatham plc, Chatham, Kent

For the people of Elswick and Benwell,
past and present

And fear not them which kill the body,
but are not able to kill the soul:
but rather fear him which is able to destroy
both body and soul in hell

Matthew: chapter 10 verse 28

Acknowledgements

I would like to thank Northern Arts for assistance under the Year of the Artist programme. The grant enabled me to finance the time I spent researching the backdrop for this novel. More importantly, the associated residency scheme placed me with West Newcastle Local Studies. This proved to be immeasurable good fortune, as the group consists of indefatigable enthusiasts whose knowledge was matched only by their generosity. They remained helpful, patient and inspiring, allowing me access to their photographic archive, which contains many hundreds of images, including the work of the celebrated amateur photographer Jimmy Forsyth. Their collection is an astonishing and unique record of a working community in both ascendancy and decline. I am indebted to Harry Bennett, Barbara Bravey, John Hinds, Liz Michael, Fred Millican, Terry Quinn, Warren Thompson, Des Walton and Ian Whillis.

Thanks also to members of the Havelock Community Centre's lunch club, Benwell Local History Society and a group of retired employees from Vickers Armstrong, formed to produce their own publication *Vickers: The Worker's Story*. In addition, many other west end residents were interviewed. These include Mick Bell, Tom Charlton, Billie Cummings, Joyce and Jim Cruse, Tommy Robson, Thomas Tuff, Lily White and Derek Wall. I am grateful to Barry Redfern for his advice on police procedure, to Rebecca Mellor for her information on choral singing and to Sam Rigby and Murray Martin of Amber

Films for insights into the social legacy of T. Dan Smith. So many people helped me during my west end residency, some names have surely been forgotten. I apologize for any omissions but would like to assure everyone that their contribution has found its way into these pages.

Cuillen Sound, Scotland, February 1945

It was described afterwards as the stormiest night on Scotland's western seaboard for years and years and the most violent in living memory. An unspeakable wind battered down from Iceland like some resurrected, avenging warrior god from pre-Christian times, slicing off roofs, flattening barns, stunning livestock, swamping and sinking moored vessels, lifting the sea into black peaks of surging rage. It grew stronger and more vicious. The day gave up, and there was no respite for the coastal communities, no safety, nowhere to hide. They were crouched against the assault, helpless and marooned.

The grim, forbearing little settlement below Arisaig clung like a limpet to the rocky shoreline as its lights went out, as the radios failed, as the roads south and west became flooded and impassable as a result of mountainous waves. Beyond assistance, people covered their ears, held hands, quoted the scriptures and waited for deliverance.

Iris MacDonald, the city woman, leant against the metal railing above the harbour, her hair whipping her face, her cheeks lashed with salt and rain. Her thin coat flapped in the gale, her swollen belly strained against its too-tight buttons and she held her first-born, Leslie, in a blanket, in her arms. The babe whimpered anxiously, snatched as he had been from his warm cot next to the kitchen fire, but his cry was entirely drowned by the tempest, the furious

1

roaring sea. She could feel her second child turn inside her. A few other villagers appeared, pessimistic and stoical, unable to stay indoors, but she refused to acknowledge them. These were her husband's friends and neighbours huddled together, yards behind the barrier. They clutched oilskins and lanterns, prayed a bit and sang a dispirited hymn, which sounded only weak and ineffectual against the ravages of the night. Despite their presence, despite the nearness of her two sons, one recently born, one unborn, Iris felt completely alone. She shifted her bundle to one arm and with the other reached out, grasping the tumult of air, the boiling spume from the waves. Soaked to the flesh, she found it almost impossible to see, to breathe, to stay upright against the wind. She knew that to lean one more inch would mean toppling into the water, falling, flailing, giving up her life to the weather. At that moment she felt she was leaning out over the edge of the world, over the edge of the universe, about to fling herself into nothingness. She was alone in a cataclysm of wind, darkness and war. It was 1945, the Allies were winning, she was only twenty-one, she had two babies and her man was out there somewhere in a fishing coble, a craft as light and flimsy as matchwood. 'Help me!' she shouted at the warrior-god blackness, at the invisible horizon, and the boiling waves, already knowing, intuitively and without doubt, that he wouldn't return and that everything she had ever wanted and loved was lost. Irrevocably lost. 'Help me!'

Suddenly, behind her, from the half-shelter of a doorway, there was a woman's scream and a deep male cheer. The villagers, arms around each other, joined her at the barrier. She looked and looked, rubbing her smarting eyes, pushing back her salty strings of hair. There was a boat! It

2

bobbed and struggled, tossed this way and that but it seemed determined. It seemed brave and sure. There was another louder cheer and men swung their lights in welcome, women waved and shrieked and at once the lifeboat was readied. Apparently secure, the bedraggled fishing coble bearing six of the village's sons and husbands advanced towards the harbour. There was excitement and rejoicing but Iris did not cheer or wave. She knew.

Suddenly there was a shocking, dazzling flash – white at first, then yellow, then orange, followed by soaring flames. There was a noise, an explosion that made the warrior-god weather seem as nothing. Pieces of the boat were sent soaring skywards and the sea was lifted higher, far higher than anything managed by the elements. Seconds later there was a hot feeling. This is how it was described, afterwards – a hot feeling, almost reassuring. Then there was steam, spatters of warm water, debris and smoke. Then there was realization. Finally there was a blast, a force that knocked some onlookers backwards on to the concrete of the harbour floor. The fish yard clock cracked and stopped for ever. It was midnight. The boat had hit a mine. The Germans had vanquished the fishermen minutes before they could claim victory over the storm.

Newcastle Post, 28 August 1960

ANGEL TWINS SHOCK ARREST

Youth in Custody

A POLICE SPOKESMAN today confirmed that a youth is being held for questioning in connection with the savage killing of the Newcastle 'Angel Twins' over a week ago. George MacDonald (14) of Elswick, Newcastle, is at present helping police with their inquiries at Scotswood Road police station.

Attack

It is believed that MacDonald, a talented child artist, is mentally handicapped. Living at home with his mother, blonde Iris MacDonald (35), at the time of the attack, it is claimed he has never attended school. She was today unavailable for comment. Neighbourhood representatives are said to be concerned. A resident of the area who did not wish to be named commented today: 'This lad should have been locked up long ago. It's all wrong that people like him are free to wander the streets. Someone's to blame for this.'

Councillor

Tragic twins Muriel and Maureen Robson (13) were found murdered in an empty half-demolished slum property in Elswick last Tuesday. Official sources have not revealed whether or not there was evidence of molestation. The cowardly attack has caused citywide outrage. Council boss T. Dan Smith expressed his horror in an interview in this newspaper yesterday. Dubbed by the media as the 'Angel Twins' because of their fair hair and pretty faces, the girls were the daughters of city councillor Mickey Robson, a divorcee and a leading member of the planning committee. Councillor Robson is rumoured to be under sedation and at present is being comforted by friends at an unknown address.

1

Elswick, Newcastle upon Tyne, August 1960

It was a hot day and Leslie was looking for his brother. Sweaty and a little exasperated, he crossed a road near his home on Glue Terrace where the uniform rows of houses basked in the heat of the late afternoon. He paused. Shining in a strip between the rooftops was the clearest sky he'd ever seen. There wasn't a cloud disturbing the rarest of rare blues. He rubbed his eyes and took in the otherwise familiar surroundings. He was worried. Where is that Geordie? he wondered. I hope he's not getting into any more trouble. Where *has* he gone and got to? Glancing along the side streets he expected to see the smaller boy, possibly teetering on a kerbstone, clutching his oversized sketchpad and pencil-case, but there was no one about. Everywhere was deserted, with only the repetitive terraces clinging to their slope. Greyish red and regimented, on a steep hill above the River Tyne, they were ranked like an army of soldiers. Here, all the roads were cobbled, without gardens, without any greenery at all, divided by a grid of back lanes and walled yards.

Leslie always felt some anxiety about his brother but at present he was shocked by something that had happened the previous evening. Everything had been normal at first – they'd both been sitting upstairs in Auntie Ada's flat on Glue Terrace. She'd already given them their supper of tinned oranges with evaporated milk, and a glass of lemonade. Despite the warmth of the evening a small fire burned cheerfully in the grate. Geordie was wearing his monkey pyjamas, and his old monkey slippers, his silky hair hanging over his eyes. He was filling in pages of his colouring book with wax crayons, and he'd looked, Leslie remembered, very young, and very beautiful.

It was late and Leslie was just about to suggest going back downstairs. Their mother was out but it was dark outside and past their bedtime. At that moment there was a knock at the street entrance and the clump-clump of heavy boots on the stairs.

'Who's that?' exclaimed Leslie, startled. 'Uncle Jack?'

Auntie Ada grasped the sides of her deep chair and struggled to her feet. 'Sounds like the polis,' she muttered.

A police helmet appeared round the door and underneath it the ruddy face of Constable Henderson. He entered and loomed above them, massive and official, a truncheon swinging from his belt. He pulled out a chair from under the table and sat down, legs apart. He seemed to fill the room. He took off his helmet.

Below, from his place on the hearthrug, Geordie stared, wide-eyed. The Constable was not an unfamiliar visitor but it was too late for this to be a social call. Somewhat flustered, Ada went into the scullery to make tea.

'It's these two lads I've come to see,' the officer said, importantly.

Leslie stepped between his brother and the newcomer.

'Sit down, son.' The policeman sounded stern but kind.

Leslie perched on Auntie Ada's armchair, his protective hand on Geordie's shoulder.

Ada fussed with the best china and a plate of home-made gingerbread.

Constable Henderson was hungry. He devoured two crumbling squares. 'There's been allegations.'

'Oh dear,' whispered Ada to herself. 'Oh dear.'

'Serious allegations down at the station, which I've volunteered to investigate.' He pointed at Geordie. 'Concerning *this* laddie here.' He blew into his teacup then swallowed.

'Our mam's not in,' Leslie offered, a little desperate, trying to forestall any unpleasantness. 'Don't you think you should talk to our mam?' His heart was beating in an unnatural way. He wanted this intruder to go away. 'Tomorrow?'

'It's the Robson twins again. Those two girls. Muriel and Maureen.'

'Those *buggers*!' Leslie expostulated.

'You shush, now!' said Auntie Ada. 'Mind your language!'

The policeman straightened. His uniform creaked. He looked straight at Geordie. 'Where were you at two p.m. this afternoon?'

Geordie gazed at him unblinking, his mouth open, his tongue protruding slightly, but he said not a word. He waggled his feet, the monkey heads colliding.

'He was with me,' Leslie interjected. 'He's been with me all day. We've been downstairs and ... and ... up here ...'

'I'm speaking to your brother.'

Leslie was desperate. 'We've been in all day. He hasn't been out of my sight. He's been here ...'

The policeman raised his voice a little. 'Where have you been, George?'

Geordie looked completely blank.

'He won't say anything,' said Auntie Ada, gently. She poured more tea. 'What's it all about, any road?'

Constable Henderson coughed into his serge sleeve. He turned to the woman. 'The complainants have alleged . . .'

'Those minxes!' Ada was dismissive. 'They've been more than unkind to this little laddie here before. They're nasty girls.'

'Well. That's as maybe. But they're saying he exposed himself.' The words emerged in a rush. 'That's it, in effect. Today. Out the back here. Exposed himself at two o'clock this afternoon.' He was embarrassed.

'That's what they said?' Ada was aghast.

Leslie's bottom lip trembled as if he were on the point of tears. He leaned forwards and encircled his brother in his arms. 'Those . . . those awful twins!' he almost sobbed.

Geordie neither moved nor registered any emotion. A drop of saliva gathered in the corner of his mouth.

Ada took a deep, decisive breath. 'He's been up here with me all day long,' she lied. '*All day*! And he's no more than a little bairn, even if he is fourteen.' She paused. 'Those girls are mischievous young devils. They're running completely wild with no one there to check them or mind them. And they'll say or do anything to bring trouble to decent people's doors.' She hesitated. 'It's their *dad* you ought to be paying a visit to. Tell him to wash their dirty little mouths out. With Lifebuoy soap.'

Relieved, the policeman stood up and prepared to go. 'There's been no independent corroboration . . .' he muttered.

'What are you going to do?' asked Ada. Having gained the upper hand, she sounded stern.

He put on his helmet. 'I'll make sure it's noted in the station's Occurrence Log. Say I've spoken to the lad.' He directed his attention back to Geordie. He spoke slowly. 'You stay away from those girls, mind. Keep well away.'

Geordie stared. Leslie hugged him and buried his face in his hair. He made a big effort not to burst into tears. I hate those girls, he thought. I hate them to pieces.

*

Now perspiring in the heat from the unrelenting sun, Leslie chinked his basket of empty lemonade bottles. With the same rhythm, he rattled pennies in his trouser pocket. Four threepences for these bottles makes one shilling, he thought. Added to the coppers that Auntie Ada had given him this morning for doing her messages, this meant he could buy fish and chips for Geordie's tea. Everything's going to be all right, he told himself, dismissing last night's memory and wiping sweat from his brow.

However, despite his best efforts, an uneasy feeling remained buried in his heart. Whichever way he looked at it, he couldn't deny that within these familiar streets where all was named, paved, built upon and knowable, everything was about to change. This summer, made curiously vibrant by the brightness of the heatwave, his down-at-heel, smoke-stained, denatured and utilitarian world was on the point of disappearing. It was being demolished.

He continued his search. In the next row the windows were all missing, but not because they were flung open joyfully, welcoming the warm and beautiful day. Instead they had a hopeless, ruined look about them. Most of the houses were empty. Doors hung like gaping teeth, and too-big-to-move furniture was visible from the street, alongside a muddle of abandoned belongings that was the detritus of people's former lives. These residents, Leslie knew, had recently been shifted by the authorities. They'd piled up their sad handcarts and departed to new addresses supplied by the council. In one flat he could see a vacuum cleaner. I'll come back for that, he thought. In another, a jacket hung on a coat hanger, dangling from a broken picture-rail.

Leslie shielded his eyes from the glare, moving slowly, as if tired. Untidy, even scruffy, he was dressed in a duffel-coat and canvas plimsolls, which he wore whatever the weather. His mop of bright ginger hair was uncombed and he looked poor, almost ragged, his white arms protruding from his frayed cuffs. However, he was unaware of his clothes. Unlike other boys his age, he was still innocent, and like a child he was indifferent to his appearance. Leslie lacked guile and sophistication. Not handsome, his wide open, freckled and trusting face had been, until recently, habitually cheerful, his mouth usually ready to break into a gap-toothed grin. But now he was troubled. His fingers clutched the handles of his shopping basket much more tightly than was necessary. Where *is* that Geordie? he thought. I haven't seen him for hours. Constable Henderson patrolled offstage in his imagination and he was doing his best to keep him at bay.

In the next street, things were worse. Here the buildings on all sides were stripped of their lead, slates and cast-iron drainpipes, with their roofs open to the sky. The place resembled a bombsite from the war. At the top corner, the terrace was half-gone, the walls bashed down in places, revealing desolate bedroom wallpaper, fireplaces hanging in space, pipes, wires, semi-detached floorboards.

Leslie saw that two girls were playing here, jumping off a ceiling joist on to a pile of old mattresses below. He stopped and watched them. Taking turns, they ran laughing up the smashed staircase, edged out on to the beam, then leapt, their skirts flying up to their heads, screaming. As they hit the soft floor a cloud of dust rose and they rolled over, first their feet, then their bottoms poking up into the air. Leslie rubbed his eyes. Their knickers were flowery and trimmed with bows. He was wary of all girls and girlish things, particularly underwear. It's them! He suddenly realized who they were. Oh no! He'd always been in the habit of avoiding these twins but now, after the terrible things they'd said about his Geordie yesterday, he wondered if he should confront them and tell them off. for spreading spiteful tales. Leslie hated confrontation. Maybe he had a better idea. Maybe he should try to befriend them, get them on his side. Perhaps he could win them over.

The twins, Maureen and Muriel Robson, were identical. They were thirteen, but for reasons inexplicable to anyone but themselves they dressed and even behaved like ten-year-olds. They lived, Leslie knew, in a nice, decent house, a mile away, right up past the park, which had both an upstairs and a downstairs joined together, and, it was rumoured, a proper bathroom. Despite this luxury, during these summer holidays they'd forsaken their own neigh-bourhood and the ravaged byways of Elswick had become their daily playground.

'Hello there.' He struggled to summon his most win-ning smile. 'You better be careful. Those stairs might give way, or something.' He fingered the pack in his pocket, wondering whether or not they'd like to join in a card trick. He decided against asking them if they'd seen Geor-die that day.

The twins moved into a hole that had been a down-stairs window. Framed like a picture, their blonde pony-tails were woven with ribbons and their filthy dresses fashioned with broderie anglaise. Their too-small bodices strained against the mounds that were their breasts. Leslie had often wondered why they liked pretending to be younger than they were, but their motives had always eluded him. They never mixed with the other children, happy with each other's company. Now their smudged faces were cynical. They looked at each other and giggled, unpleasantly.

He sensed their hostility. He was good-natured and avoided conflict. Befriending these two immediately seemed unlikely, if not impossible. Feeling himself blushing, he turned to go.

'Watch out, dottle-face!' one of the twins called.

He hurried away. He touched his cheeks, where he knew his smooth and so far hairless skin was blotchy with summer freckles.

The girls started one of their childish chants, to the tune of 'Davy Crockett'. 'Spot-ty, spot-ty *Les-leee*, freak from the wild fron-tier! Spot-ty, spot-ty *Les-leee*, freak from the wild frontier!'

'Germolene!' one of them called for good measure.

'Valderma!'

'Dip your head in turpentine!' They shrieked and hollered and threw pieces of brick.

Leslie was unaccustomed to abuse. His face burning, he fought back more unmanly tears. His eyes brimmed and he rubbed them hard with his coat sleeve. There's no need to be like that, he thought. There's no need to be *horrible*. These aren't real spots. They're only freckles. He departed, blushing, ungainly and humiliated. He walked as quickly as he could, without running.

Around another corner, thankfully, the next terrace was safe, occupied and normal, as it had always been. A hula hoop was suspended from a railing. A kitten rolled on a doorstep, ecstatic with warmth. A naked toddler sat on a front step and poured water from a jam jar into a toy bucket. Everywhere was quiet. Leslie felt the sun prick the skin of his face, saw the heat rise up from the pavement, shimmering and strange. He took a plastic cowboy from his pocket and handed it to the small child, who smiled and dunked it into her bucket. He breathed a deep breath. The weather was releasing different odours. Combined with the usual industrial taint, there was softening tar and stagnant drains and warm brick. He forced himself to half-smile at the cat and the infant. He sniffed again. Above all else, he could sense the sunshine. It's the summer holidays, he thought, and it's a lovely day. His spirits failed to rise. Squinting into the sunlight as the shadows lengthened, still searching for the diminutive figure of his brother, his problems welled up. Despite his best efforts, the twins' taunts made his eyes blurry with tears

Since leaving school in July, Leslie's boyish, easy-going life had become complicated. Now, admitting the sensations brewing inside his heart, he realized he was being forced, unwillingly, to jettison his childhood. The narrow perimeters of his existence were being stretched and strained in disconcerting ways. He raised one finger and stared at it. Firstly, he decided, there's the job. He had no idea what he wanted to do. School was over for him now. He wasn't really on holiday. Because he was fifteen, long summer holidays were a thing of the past. But the idea of starting work seemed impossible.

He raised another finger. Second problem, he thought, I'm useless. He often tried to picture himself in a factory all day doing an important, masculine job, wearing proper overalls, but he felt too inexperienced, too much like a young boy. He felt useless and inept and no matter how hard he tried he just couldn't see himself with a man's cap, a haversack and *skills*.

On top of this, at home, behind the clock on the mantelpiece, there were wedged an unpaid electric bill, a red demand for gas, the water rates, and a nasty threatening letter from the coalman. This had never happened before. A third finger joined the other two. I've got to get a job in order to provide. I've got to be a breadwinner.

He paused. His fourth concern was his little brother's growing independence. This was creating all kinds of problems, which he was uncertain how to resolve.

Finally, he raised his hand, all digits spread, and stared at it sadly. I wish she'd stop it, he thought. I wish she'd be like she used to be. He was thinking about his mother, because worst of all, by far the worst thing happening this summer, were the little pills she swallowed like Smarties. She called them her purple hearts. In the last few weeks, his mother had become his biggest worry of all. Something's the matter with her, he told himself. She's changed. Now, every day, Leslie felt that *he* was in charge at home. Despite the fact that she was still living and sleeping in the front room of the flat, just like she'd always done, it was as if his mother wasn't really *there*.

The sun slanted over the rooftops, casting luxurious shadows. He swallowed, took a deep breath, and without thinking, sang a few notes. His boy's voice rather than his man's voice emerged and the sound was clear and pure, filling the windless, warm air. Pleased with the sound, his voice climbed higher and higher, the scale soaring like a bird above the chimney-pots of the close-packed terraces. It was incongruous and beautiful.

Continuing his search, peering along all the lanes, he

deliberately brought a happy occasion into his mind. He'd been at school, at sports day. It was two, maybe three summers ago and his teacher had entered him in the sack race. He'd stood at the start, enveloped in his sack, per-spiring and nervous, with lots of keener, more confident children on either side. Just as the starting pistol was fired he saw his mother by the finishing tape. She was pretty in a blue dress with a lemon cardigan around her shoulders, her sunglasses pushed up on to her head. She's the pretti-est mother of all, he'd thought. Geordie sat at her feet, picking dandelions. She smiled and waved and made the thumbs-up sign. As the gun went off Leslie felt his feet gain the corners of the sack, which seemed straight away to fit like soft slippers. He didn't run down the course, he just walked quickly, following the marked lane, his sack like a rough baggy skirt, hardly impeding his pro-gress at all. His exuberant competitors tumbled, tripped and sprawled, but he just kept on going, determined and focused. Right left, right left, right left, his mother's face came nearer. She was cheering and jumping up and down with excitement. 'Come on, son!' he'd heard her shout enthusiastically. 'Come on, son!' He crossed the finish way ahead of the rest. His mam hugged him and Geordie showered him with dandelions. He'd won a silver cup. He'd been allowed to keep it by his bed for a whole year.

Leslie smiled at the memory but it faded as he approached the police box on the corner of Gloucester Road. The policeman was inside. The boy hesitated but then decided to stop for a moment. Constable Henderson was only doing his job, he reasoned. He had to follow things up even if they were just dirty lies from those buggers, those horrible twins. 'Hello,' he called out, his tone conciliatory.

The officer at once realized that this was a truce. 'Are you going to show me one of your tricks, laddie?' He winked appreciatively. He was resting his large boots on a stool and enjoying a cup of tea.

The boy put down his basket, ever ready to oblige. From his coat pocket he took out a well-thumbed pack of playing cards. 'Choose a card, any card . . .'

The policeman joined in the game, displaying appropriate astonishment when, after shuffling, Leslie was able to produce the chosen king. He laughed and patted the boy on the shoulder. 'Keep at it, son,' he said as he turned to lock up. 'You keep at it.'

Leslie swallowed. He knew that deep down, the policeman was tolerant of his brother and knew he was harmless. 'Have you seen my Geordie?'

'I can't say I have,' was the reply. 'No, not today.'

Leslie turned to go. A new burnt smell was now detectable on the air. In the near distance there was a rumble like approaching thunder and he thought he felt the ground shake. It was as if a bomb had just dropped out of the sky. He picked up the basket and set off in the direction of the disturbance. That's where he is, he told himself. That's where he's hiding himself. He looked about anxiously, but couldn't see the twins.

That morning the postman had delivered two envelopes, addressed to his mother. Leslie had opened them and taken them into his bedroom. One had come from the Council, telling his mother, Scotch Iris, that her house, which was in fact a lower flat, his home and most importantly *Geordie's* home, was scheduled for demolition. The street, the whole area, was in something called a clearance programme. Leslie had painstakingly looked up these long words in his dictionary. Despite being a poor reader, their meaning eventually became clear to him and sitting on his bed he'd felt panic grip his heart. He was afraid. The letter said that his mother must report to the housing office on Amen Corner, down by the cathedral, in the town and that she should register for new accommodation. In other words *shift*. Leslie had sat for a long time, worrying. He felt certain about one thing. He didn't want to shift. He wanted to stay put, stay here, stay at home where everything up until recently had been reliable, predictable and almost happy. He didn't want to go to some unknown place on the edge of the city, in the country. He especially didn't want to move to the peculiar houses in the sky which were at this very moment rising miraculously upwards from among the old neighbourhood terraces. Piece by rectangular piece, inside a giant skeleton of steel, they were already dwarfing everything, absolutely everything with their sharp, modern lines, even the old church steeple. More importantly, he understood that Geordie hated disruption. Geordie hated change to his routine more than anything in the world. Shifting was out of the question, he'd told himself, replacing the heavy dictionary on top of his wardrobe. Shifting, it was clear, was impossible.

Now, passing the building where the twins had been playing, Leslie heard in the near distance a second loud rumble and warning shouts, which thankfully drowned out all memory of their voices. A whitish cloud hung above the next terrace, entirely blocking out the sky. As he approached, two members of the demolition gang ran clear, dragging shovels and a mallet. Stripped to the waist, their bodies glistened with sweat and dirt. They stopped, then turned, hands on hips, apparently masterful and in control.

Leslie stopped and looked upwards. Slowly and with cautious surprise, the centre of this row of houses leaned inwards. Then, more hastily, the brickwork cracked, and the window-frames split, shattering the glass. All decorum lost, the roof beams collapsed with a roar and the entire façade crumpled back, collapsing into a heap of rubble, dust rising like smoke. Leslie forgot his humiliation, his worry and his tears. He was at once strangely excited. He was reminded of the Blitz on newsreels at the cinema. To see a substantial structure succumb and be obliterated in a few moments was awesome. His heart pounded. For a moment he considered asking the foreman for a job. He looked at the workmen who were now leaning against their wagon, sharing a bottle of brown ale. He realized they were everything he was not. He turned away, and it was then that he saw Geordie.

The boy stood alone, holding his sketchpad. Only a year younger than Leslie, he was smaller and thinner and he looked nothing at all like his untidy, shambling, ginger-headed older brother. He had a sensitive, bony face, white skin, and over-long heavy black hair. His body was elegant and slender. However, belying his slight stature, his self-possession was total. Oblivious to everyone, he was absorbed in making pencil marks, glancing along the half-demolished terrace, his concentration fixed. He ignored the workmen. Leslie reached down and gently pushed his black hair away from his eyes. 'All right?' he asked, tenderly.

Geordie was sketching intricate brickwork, coping-stones, a misaligned window. He was engaged in his favourite activity: recording buildings. One of the gang walked over, interested. He was a stranger, a burly fellow, wearing a dusty cloth cap.

'All right?' enquired Leslie in his usual friendly manner. He felt cheerful again, now that he knew his brother was safe.

Geordie didn't speak but turned back a page, revealing a representation of the newsagent's on the corner of Clumber Street and Scotswood Road. It was a magnificent drawing, with perfect perspective and attention to detail. The peeling paint and the grain of the wood were meticulous. The billboards with their scrawled headlines were represented and every advertising sign was shown: Condor, St Bruno, Woodbines, Players Please, Senior Service Satisfy. Every brick, every roof tile, the wooden carving along the upper edge of the door; all were executed with precision and artistry.

The workman whistled with amazement. However, the boy seemed scarcely aware of him or his approval.

'That's the paper shop!' exclaimed the labourer. 'Where I've been getting my baccy! That's grand!'

Geordie lifted his gaze and regarded the workman with his extraordinary large green eyes. 'Where I've been getting my baccy,' he echoed. 'That's grand.' He appeared neither pleased nor displeased by the compliment.

The man looked uncomfortable, as if the boy might be mocking him.

'He's good,' murmured Leslie, his breaking voice suddenly low and croaky and grown-up. 'He's my *brother*.' He touched Geordie's arm. 'Come on, let's go.'

Wordlessly, they set off back towards the main road. Geordie walked with a strange stiff-legged gait. He was like a beautiful little doll. Leslie knew that he rarely showed any sign of emotion, although his mood could be unpredictable. Today, from long experience, he guessed that Geordie was calm, which meant his drawing had gone well that day.

Andrea Badenoch

'Those girls are in boxes,' said Geordie suddenly. He stopped, suddenly tense like a taut wire.

'What?'

Leslie noticed that his brother was staring into the distance with a faraway expression.

'Boxes. With gold handles. Those girls.'

Leslie tried to continue. He wanted to get Geordie home where it was safe. 'Come on.' He knew that his brother sometimes saw things, understood things that other people didn't. But he rarely listened to his predictions. They were always peculiar and unhelpful. They usually didn't make sense and long ago he'd decided they were best ignored. Everyone else who'd heard them had assumed they were meaningless ramblings.

The younger boy persisted. 'Those girls are in boxes in St Stephen's church and there's big bunches of flowers on top of them. Shop flowers. Who's put those shop flowers on top of them, Leslie? They can't get out of there.'

'Come *on*.' Leslie chinked his basket of bottles, indicating his intention to collect the threepences. He began to hurry, wanting to get back to the normal streets where as yet there were no signs of all this disconcerting upheaval. Letting the matter drop, Geordie accompanied him. After a while the older boy explained his plan for the rest of the evening. 'I want you to stay inside,' he insisted. 'Until I get back from choir.'

'Geordie's a good boy,' came the agreement. He repeated his brother's words, 'I want you to stay inside.'

'That's right. In the house. Draw or play the piano. Or go upstairs with Auntie Ada.' Leslie was relieved.

'That's right. In the house. Play the piano. Or go upstairs with Auntie Ada.'

'I've got choir. I'll get fish and chips afterwards.'

'Get fish and chips afterwards.'

Leslie placed his free hand around Geordie's shoulders and hugged him. 'I'm glad I found you,' he confided. 'I was getting scared. Have you had a nice day?'

At that moment a sharp spattering of pebbles rained down on them, followed by half-bricks. Leslie glanced in horror at the empty, derelict buildings on either side. Those twins! He could see no one.

'Freck-ly, freck-ly Les-*lee*, freak of the wild fron-*tier*!'

Leslie took his brother's arm in a firm grip and tried to hurry him forward but Geordie froze, resisting.

Another couple of handfuls of small gravel rained down like hailstones.

'Spot-ty, spot-ty Les-*lee*, freak of the Elswick fron-*tier*!'

'I don't know where you are, you two,' called out Leslie, 'but you can just bugger off!' His breaking voice was high with emotion, like the sound a young boy makes. His adult tones had deserted him. He swallowed hard. 'Bugger off!' he repeated, sounding even more squeaky.

'Bugger off yourself, babby!' squeaked one of the twins in a high falsetto.

'Bugger off, you scabby-face, titty-bottle babby,' added the other. 'Boo-hoo!' She pretended to sob like an infant. The twins jumped out from a doorless passage, blocking the pavement. 'Leslie's a spotty cry-*babby*!'

Geordie's pixie face registered alarm. His teeth chattered a little and he clutched his sketchpad to his chest like a shield. He stared at the twins, from one to the other, his face vacant, his green eyes wide.

Leslie felt a wave of panic. He put his arm back around his brother's shoulders. He didn't want Geordie to get upset. He didn't want him to fall to the ground and take a fit.

The twins had smudged each other's filthy faces with wet fingers, creating an effect that resembled war paint. Their hair was undone and their ribbons dangled. They each poked out a pink tongue. One of them had torn her dress. The other carried a staircase spindle like a weapon.

I can't hit them or anything, Leslie thought desperately. They're just stupid girls. He had never hit anyone in his life. He called out to them, trying to sound in some way confident. 'Hey! Let us past, man.'

'Make us, stinky bum,' came the reply.

'Make us, dottle-face.'

Leslie pulled his brother out into the road. He noticed, not for the first time, that the girls each had discoloured teeth. Everyone always said that their indulgent father bought them far too many sweets. 'Come on,' he muttered.

'That's George MacDonald,' said one of the twins. 'We know him.'

'No you don't,' said Leslie. 'You don't know anything. You know *nothing*.'

Her sister chimed in. 'We know that George MacDonald. Everyone says that George's a real dafty.'

'He does things to himself down your back lane. We've seen him. He shows his thing to anybody. We saw it yesterday. It's all big and red.'

'No he doesn't.'

'He wets the bed.'

'No he doesn't.'

'He wears nappies.'

'He doesn't.'

'He should be in a *home*.'

'Shut up!' shouted Leslie. All at once he sounded out of control. 'It's not true. You're *making* all that *up*!' He felt his brother's terror. He tried to drag him away, pulling at his sleeve.

The girls followed. 'George is a dafty! George is a dafty!' They started a steady chant. 'George is a dafty!'

To Leslie's relief, Geordie allowed himself to be guided forwards but he began muttering and his knees knocked. A fleck of foam appeared at the side of his mouth. His pale face was parchment white. Leslie took the sketchpad and pencil-case from his shaking fingers. 'Come on,' he murmured, 'they're just stupid. They're not going to hurt you.'

Geordie began grimacing and wringing his hands and his walk became even stiffer than usual, more puppet-like. His meaningless words became louder.

The girls stared. They seemed alarmed. Despite their assertions, they barely knew Geordie at all. They decided he looked scary. They dropped behind, leaning against the crumbling corner of a dead grocery. They were silent for a moment, then as their victims hurried away and there was distance between them, they called out in unison, 'George is a *dafty*!' once more, for good measure.

*

At the bottom of the hill, on Scotswood Road, the shops had closed. All was now quiet except for a plodding horse pulling a cart, a few small children swinging around a lamp-post and a group of tired-looking workmen returning home, the last stragglers from the day shift at the riverside factory. These were Vickers men, the men of the neighbourhood. Breadwinners and rent-payers, they laboured long hours and they were skilled and loyal. Free for the rest of the day, enjoying the relief of the outside

23

world, they moved slowly and with rhythmic dignity, carrying their jackets and haversacks. Their caps were pushed right back from their brows because of the clemency of the weather. Theirs was a serious world of noise and fire, of metals and machines, of mechanical parts, of shifts, timesheets and pay-packets.

Suddenly, as pretty as a budgerigar, a woman clack-clacked through them on her exaggerated high heels, her hips wiggling in her tight skirt, her nose in the air. She was self-conscious, pretending to be unaware of their collective gaze. Each workman touched his brow without speaking and smiled and nodded shyly in a half-salute as she passed by. 'Hello, Iris,' the bravest one of them called.

Scotch Iris made out she'd not heard. She too was on her way home, to the flat she shared with her sons, Leslie and Geordie. She strutted towards Glue Terrace. Her small breasts were pushed up high and together on a black raft of underwiring and lace and their smooth mounds peeked from the vee of her blouse. The fading light made her bleached beehive hair-do shine like a beacon. She always moved like a Hollywood starlet. As she turned into the smashed street where earlier the demolition men had been working, it formed an incongruous backdrop to her unsubtle brand of eye-catching glamour.

She suddenly stopped. One hand tightened on her bag, the other was raised to her lips in dismay. She swore quietly, both transfixed and horrified. Below, visible for the very first time from this place, high on the hill, was the River Tyne. It was revealed by a sudden gap in the houses. Here, several dwellings had tumbled to the ground earlier that day, creating a brand new window on the valley. Glittering and grey, the water stretched beyond the steep terraces, beyond the factory, over and away to the shores of a different county. Iris stared. For generations invisible from this point, the Tyne bisected the floor of its polluted valley and a large ship glided over its wide surface like a dream. Her eyes took in the steep drop, the depths of shining water, then the green haze of Durham in the distance. It was extraordinary. She felt dizzy and afraid.

Iris truly, truly hated open spaces. With her memory of the wild, inhuman night that had claimed her husband's body, when his fishing boat had fallen out of the sea, she always tried to avoid the long view and shunned emptiness. What are they *doing* here? she thought. What do the council think they're *doing*? Shaken, she wanted to lie down on the rubble-strewn cobbles of the road to stop herself tumbling forwards and downwards into an unknown expanse, into newness, into thin air. She wanted to catch hold, to cling on. She wanted home, with the security of everything familiar, the low narrow lanes, communal washing-lines, neighbours, cooking smells, out-door netties in back yards ... she wanted to be *enclosed*. She averted her eyes from the dramatic alteration in the vista, clenched her jaw and walked on.

She heard humming. Turning a corner, she came across a familiar figure. It was Sammy Schnitzler, the barber. He was sitting on a chair outside his shop mending an umbrella. An unopened newspaper was folded at his feet. When he saw her he winked, but did not smile. He continued to drone the tune of Strauss's 'Gypsy Baron Waltz' in a mournful way. Iris heard the melody, aware that it was one of a few he always carried in his head. She knew this proved he was a stranger here, like herself. It was a sign of his many years of exile. Without being able to articulate it, she understood that he too was haunted by the past. Shadowy wraiths from his European youth

25

never ceased their uneasy dance on the surface of his unconscious.

'What are they *doing* here?' Iris demanded. 'The whole damned place is *falling to bits*. Down around our fucking ears.' She leaned in the doorway behind Sammy, lethargic and sexy. She took off a shoe and examined the slingback, the thin heel, its loosened metal tip. She offered it to him. 'You can put a nail in this, if you like.' The sandal was so flimsy, so feminine, so impractical, the suggestion sounded almost indecent.

Sammy stopped humming. He was about to complain that he was a skilled hairdresser, not a cobbler, but because he was doing his best to ignore her, he said nothing. Fresh in his memory, their last encounter had been very unsatisfactory. He was trying to demonstrate the fact that he was displeased, very displeased – that he was, in effect, not speaking to her.

Business was slack and he'd stayed open beyond seven o'clock hoping to catch one or two pitmen at the close of their shift at the Montague Colliery, or the Monty as it was known locally. He had two more umbrellas to mend but throughout this day he'd only cut one Tony Curtis and tidied the necks of three pensioners. He sighed. The sun had sunk below the rooftops but the light was still golden, the air warm. He laid down his work, leaned back and rested a hand on his heart. His eyes were moist. 'These authorities are ruining me,' he agreed, sadly, whispering not to Scotch Iris, but to the dying afternoon. '*A brokh tsu dir*. A curse on them!'

Sammy Schnitzler had come to England from Austria during the war. He'd opened this business on Cannon Street and then another on Buddle Road in Benwell and for a long time he prospered. His combs, semi-combs and scissors were always sterilized, his floors well swept. He made his own brand of hair oil, Schnitzler's Brilliant. After a while he bought several pairs of Tyneside flats in Elswick that he let out to tenants. After a few more years he bought many more. He had good properties at the top of the hill, where he'd even taken the trouble to put in electricity at one or two of the best addresses. These included his own. In addition, he had medium-quality properties in the middle of the hill, with some amenities such as indoor plumbing. He also had deplorable buildings at the bottom of the hill where single mothers existed alongside the feckless, the workshy and those too sick to earn a wage. Here things were somewhat ramshackle. However, he considered himself to be a fair landlord; fair but strict. He didn't tolerate defaulters, backsliders or lice. He occasionally had to 'put people out' but he always saw to the dry rot and the glazing. But now this crazy council was taking everything from him, hell-bent as they all were on modernization and change. Madmen, he called them. Vandals. Communists. As the old houses were pulled down he was losing both tenants and customers. The whole area was starting to look like the aftermath of an air raid. For the first time since before Mr Churchill had sorted out the Germans he was facing uncertainty and insecurity. I don't know what's to become of me, he thought to himself now. 'Dear, oh dear, oh dear.'

'Gloucester Street's half down,' offered Iris. 'Jimmy Dawson's pork shop's down.' She replaced her shoe. A little calmer now, she took out a compact from her bag and inspected her face, pursing her rosebud lips.

Sammy pressed his left chest, where his heart regularly ached. His other business, his Benwell salon, or saloon as he'd called it, was now pulled down and soon he would

be eating into his capital, even though he subsisted on
biscuits, hot water and bicarbonate of soda. The future
of this establishment was also in doubt. He knew that
when the time came there was little point in resisting. He
knew there'd been one or two businessmen in the area
who'd refused to go. There'd also been a couple of long-
term tenants who'd declared their intention to stay put as
their neighbours' dwellings tumbled around them. Before
too long, their properties had mysteriously caught fire, or
their windows had been broken and dog-dirt had found
its way inside their letterboxes. Those who were unwilling
were forced to go. He stood up and wordlessly went
inside. Iris, delaying the short walk to her flat, sat down
on his chair and yawned. She picked up the newspaper
and began reading it.

Sammy was a music-lover. He kept his second-best
gramophone in his barber's shop. Now, determined not to
speak to Iris, he removed a black bakelite disc from its
cardboard cover, blew on it and polished it lovingly with
a special duster. Carefully, he placed it on the turntable
and set it in motion. At once the animated pizzicato of
Pachelbel's 'Canon' broke the silence of the evening, as
delicate as fairy footsteps pursued by the rise and rise of
tender strings. He listened, moving a finger up and down
like a conductor. After a minute he started tidying up.
He was a heavy man but he moved lightly on his feet. He
sighed. 'I don't know what's to become of me,' he said
aloud. He took off his white coat and put on a shiny old
jacket that was part of a pre-war suit, which he always
wore for work. He knew that Iris would go home soon
and leave him by himself. He had nothing to look forward
to tonight except another lonely evening. *'Oy gevalt!'*

There was a roar in the street. Sammy glanced out,

irritated by the disturbance. Beside his entrance a motor-bike and sidecar had pulled up. A young man in army uniform sat astride the machine and his friend, Sammy's only son, Ratty, climbed out from within.

Here they are again, he thought, money, money, money. What's mine is theirs.

'Evening, Iris!' exclaimed Ratty with a jocular air, easing his thin, angular body into an upright position. He shrugged his drapecoat and smoothed his quiff.

Scotch Iris lowered the newspaper and regarded him without warmth. 'Have you got . . . what I asked you to get?'

Muttering, he said, 'Yeah, doll, no worries.' He jerked his head towards the shop interior, warning her to say no more.

She gave him a hard stare. 'Bring them round to the flat later, will you? And don't piss me about. Right?' She raised the newspaper, disappearing behind it.

Ratty took a deep breath and entered the shop. 'Evening, Pops!' His cheerfulness seemed designed to hide unease.

Sammy ignored him.

'Pops, listen to me. We'll sort out Beaumont Street and Rendel Street tonight. Or should I say, what's left of them.'

Slowly and fussily Sammy turned over some documents in a drawer at the back of the shop. The gramophone played on melodiously to the end of the piece, then stopped. He handed his son a ledger. These two layabouts, as he privately described them, were responsible for rent collection. Also, they were tallymen, which meant they collected credit payments for the local department store. They called themselves *financiers*. However, Sammy was convinced that all they were really interested in was getting their percentage and spending it straight away in public houses.

'Money buys everything except brains!' Sammy shook his head and handed over the ledger, unwillingly.

Ratty grabbed it. 'Ta, Pops!' He leapt out and dived back inside the sidecar, catching his canary yellow drape-coat in the door. The uniformed youth kick-started the bike and with a mechanical cough and a roar they were gone.

Iris stood up and stared into the haze of exhaust. Unlike the young men, she was reluctant to leave.

Sammy raised his awning, brought in his chair, newspaper and broken umbrellas and switched off his revolving electric red and white pole, which he'd been so proud to install outside, above the door, not so very long ago. He went into the back and stirred his vat of Schnitzler's Brilliant.

Iris followed him inside. 'Lend us a twenty, will you?' Affecting nonchalance, she spun a barber's chair first one way, then the other.

Sammy came out and stared at her, his expression even more mournful. He looked both disappointed and unsurprised.

There was another voice from the doorway. 'Hello, Mr Schnitzler.'

'Are you there, Mr Shit?' a second visitor enquired. It was the two girls, the twins.

Iris looked displeased. 'It's like a fucking railway station here tonight.' She disappeared into the back of the shop.

Sammy's face had lit up. He smiled for the first time that day. 'Come inside, my dears! Come inside!'

Muriel and Maureen entered. They were now smartly

dressed in their Girl Guide outfits, their hair was tied back under their berets and their hands and faces were clean. 'Is Ratty here?' said one.

'We thought Ratty was here,' echoed the other.

'He was here. He's gone.'

The twins stared. 'Bob-a-job, mister?'

'*Oy vey*, Bobby job?' Sammy was mystified.

'Bob-a-job? Support the world-wide Scout and Guide movement?' Muriel gave him her best smile, revealing her discoloured teeth. They held hands. Both girls had perfected a saccharine little-girl charm that they felt it best to retain, despite the fact that they had now reached puberty. As usual, they were giving the impression of being much younger than they actually were.

'Ah, so, bob-a-job.' Sammy opened the till and took out a half-crown. He handed it to Maureen. He smiled. He liked these girls, he thought they were pretty and it amused him that he couldn't tell them apart. However, it concerned him that they ran about all day and evening, unsupervised.

'What job do you want us to do?' asked Muriel.

'We do a job for you in return,' explained Maureen.

Sammy considered. He went into the back and emerged with three bottles of his hair oil. 'You can deliver these to my customers. You are very good little girls.' He gave the twins the names and addresses. 'Then afterwards you go to the church hall, yes? To the Girl Guides and say your prayers?'

'That's right,' agreed Maureen, sweetly.

'A Guide's duty is to her God and to her Queen,' offered Muriel.

'Yes,' conceded her sister, 'that's the First Guide Law.'

Sammy smiled, indulgently. 'Off you go then.'

Outside, the twins clutched each other and sniggered. Holding hands, they ran down the hill towards Scotswood Road. Pausing outside an empty house, they threw the bottles inside and heard them smash on to the rubble that had been the front room floor.

'He'll believe anything!'

'He doesn't even know it's not bob-a-job week!'

'Fancy not knowing. Fancy not knowing that bob-a-job's at Easter!'

Muriel twirled around and around, lightly, her arms outstretched, her sandals pitter-pattering on and off the kerb. She stopped, a little dizzy. 'It's because he's a darkie.'

'Mr Shit's not a darkie, silly.' Maureen polished the half-crown on her tie.

'He's a *sort* of a darkie. That's what Dad said.'

'No he's not! He's not!'

'Well, he's not from round here. That's for sure.'

At the top of the slope, unseen by the giggling twins, Sammy and Scotch Iris watched. He shook his head sadly. 'It's not right,' he said. 'It's not right at all. Their mother can't help them. Their father's lost all control. It's terrible. What's to become of them?'

The woman shrugged, dismissive. Her expression suggested that she couldn't care less. She held out a hand, palm up. Sammy felt for his wallet then gave her a note. She turned on one spindly heel, tottered a little on the rough cobbles and then, with her perfectly rounded backside tipping provocatively from side to side, she minced away in the direction of Glue Terrace.

*

Much later, after the sky had turned inky black, lit by a moon and a small sprinkling of stars, Leslie walked homewards from choir practice, clutching a mouth-watering meal wrapped in newspapers. The haunting words and melody of 'Panis Angelicus' still resounded in his ears and in his heart.

Panis angelicus
fit panis hominum;
dat panis caelicus
figuris terminum;

He pictured the stained-glass window in the church glowing like jewels in the last rays of the evening sun. He was not a religious boy, but the Virgin Mary had held out her hands to him, as if inviting him to climb up into her arms. This had made him happy. And not only that, his voice hadn't started cracking or plummeting in its new, alarming way. His pitch had been perfect on each new phrase. Mr Green the choirmaster had said, 'That was splendid, Leslie.' Splendid, he thought to himself. I was splendid.

A cool wind blew up from the invisible river. He was tempted to open the parcel and take a few bites but he stopped himself. Instead, he sniffed it, appreciatively. He'd been cheerful at choir practice, managing to forget both the summer's worries and responsibilities and the upset of recent events. I hope things have quietened down at home, he thought. When he'd left there'd been a party going on in the front room and he'd taken Geordie upstairs, to Auntie Ada's. Even though she wasn't their real auntie, just a kind neighbour, he knew he could always trust her to be patient with his brother. She always praised his drawings and if necessary helped him to sharpen his pencils with his special little penknife. 'He's had a fright,' he'd said, as he surrendered his precious burden into her comforting arms. 'Some nasty children frightened him.' He refrained from mentioning that it was the same girls who had, the night before, brought the police to her door.

Leslie reflected on today's ugly scene with the twins and then replayed in his mind the disquieting episode with Constable Henderson the previous evening. It was no longer possible to guard and monitor his brother, keeping him safe, all the time. People have always been nasty about him, he told himself, calling him a dafty and suchlike, but not . . . not . . . *this* nasty. He remembered the twins' name-calling antics in the past. This had been nothing more than a nuisance. However, because Geordie was now out and about on his own, he was potentially the subject of much more serious persecution and he couldn't defend himself.

Leslie was sophisticated enough to understand that the allegation of 'flashing', if it became known, would cause all sorts of trouble with the mothers of the neighbourhood. They'll all get together and stand outside our house, he decided. He pictured them in tight groups, tight-lipped, arms tightly folded, keeping watch. He saw unknown, unfriendly officers following Geordie around in squad cars, speaking into their walkie-talkies. He rubbed his face with his sleeve. He imagined worse things, like bricks through the front window, jeers, demonstrations. The twins' persecution of Geordie could become very, very serious and he could see no way of protecting him. He felt at a loss. There was absolutely nothing he could do.

A smell of burning wafted up on the breeze. Leslie turned a corner near where the demolition gang had been active earlier in the day. Several bonfires flickered and glowed, illuminating the eerie skeletons of roofless properties, collapsed chimneys, a sleepy bulldozer. Smoke climbed towards him, as insubstantial as the ghosts of those families who'd shifted, moved their furniture away in vans or on handcarts to . . . goodness knows where. He sighed. It looks like a bomb's dropped, he thought again.

*

Leslie and Geordie's mother, Iris, or Scotch Iris as she was known, had moved to Newcastle after the death of her young husband in the final months of the war. She was unwilling to return to Glasgow, where she had been brought up, although she never said why. She brought with her Leslie, her plump and mild first-born son, and very soon afterwards gave birth to George, in the downstairs flat she rented from Sammy Schnitzler. It was a difficult labour and the newly fatherless baby took a long time to emerge, as if he feared a world that had already caused his mother so much pain and grief. He had black hair like his dad and big unusually coloured eyes. The midwife said he was a beautiful boy, which in fact, he was.

Ever since, for all of his young life, Geordie had ignored Scotch Iris. This was a mystery. He'd turned away from her when he was born and it had been left to the midwife to force the bottle's teat between his resisting lips. Later when he was old enough to take notice he wouldn't speak or meet her eye. Despite all her efforts to mother him, he'd consistently shut her out. Now, he treated her with what she interpreted as glassy-eyed contempt. He stared through her like he stared through everybody. Everybody, that is, except Leslie and Auntie Ada, both of whom he trusted and needed and clung to like a child.

Scotch Iris had several men-friends when the boys were small. They paid her bills and bought her dresses but she didn't care for any of them at all. She was perpetually and privately mourning her young fisherman, who had been blown apart so badly by Adolf Hitler that there was nothing of his body found for her to bury. Soon she dropped all pretences and began exchanging sex for money. She entertained men in the front room of the flat and dyed her hair. Recently, she'd been very unhappy. She'd just turned thirty-five and the limits of her way of life had all at once come into sharp and irresolvable focus. There seemed to be only one way to make a change. She'd decided it was imperative that she remarry. To this end she'd started taking amphetamines in order to stay slim and desirable. They'd also helped her mood, she'd discovered, so she began taking more and more. As well as these, every night and sometimes during the day too, she swallowed prescription sleeping-pills to calm her and to stop the nightmares. Inevitably, the drug cocktail and the depression had started feeding off one another in a vicious downward spiral. Her fear of open spaces had become a neurosis. This summer she'd become distant and unreachable, or she was a false and desperate party girl, but often, for more than fourteen hours every day, she was tossing uneasily in a pharmaceutical sleep, imprisoned in her airless, curtained boudoir.

In the last month or so, because of the way she'd become, Leslie had tried to follow Geordie's example by closing his mind to his mother, but he found he loved her still. He worried about her. He wanted her to return to her happy-go-lucky, chaotic, immoral but cheerful self. He wanted her back. Hiding her pills hadn't worked. She'd simply got some more. Now, tonight, he turned down his own street hoping that the noise of the gramophone had ceased as well as the beery laughter and the thump-thump of Iris trying to jive with someone in the too-small front-room space between the furniture. He paused. There was a motorbike and sidecar parked outside his door. He stood in a shadow as Ratty Schnitzler and his soldier-mate slammed the front door of his mother's flat then, laughing to themselves about something, slouched under a lamp-post smoking cigarettes.

Leslie hesitated. He thought of Ratty as a friend and he quite liked 'Desperate Dan the Army man' but he didn't want to talk to them tonight. Not if they'd just been to his mother's party. He considered. Not if they're *drunk* and talking *dirty*. He turned down the back lane. I'll just walk around the block, he thought to himself. He didn't want the fish and chips to get cold so he pushed the fragrant parcel inside his duffel-coat and fastened the toggles. It felt hot on his chest and soft belly. I'll just walk around the block and by the time I get back to our house, Ratty and Desperate will have gone.

The moon had come out from behind a whisper of cloud and the rising smoke from the demolition gangs' fires. It shone bravely on to the cobbles, the back yards, the rooftops and the chimney-pots. A couple of cooped-up dogs barked as he passed by. The rise and fall of 'Panis Angelicus' echoed in his mind. He thought about the two letters that had arrived, addressed to his mother. He'd hidden them in one of Iris's old shoeboxes, underneath his bed. He recalled their typed, official words. One letter had been about shifting. It said there would be an offer of rehousing in a one-bedroom unit in an unspecified location. The other single sheet had come from a hospital in Prudhoe. Leslie shuddered at the thought of it and despite everything he was momentarily cold to his bones. Prudhoe, or Prudda, as it was pronounced in these parts, was a byword for incarceration. Prudda, Leslie knew, was where they put loonies, axe murderers, unmarried mothers, mongols and people who had no one to look after them, like old women who'd gone completely mental. And someone at Prudda, some *clinical psychiatrist*, said in this letter that he would assess George MacDonald, with a view to admission.

Leslie forced himself, at that moment, to look into the future and he shuddered. The words of the choirmaster, the prospect of a delicious meal, ebbed away. Geordie might be taken, he might be locked up in a home. With nutcases, maniacs, dafties and the rest. And our mam's shifting out to the far country or maybe right up in the sky in a one-bedroom unit and *she's not taking either of us*.

Leslie stopped and sniffed his fragrant parcel again. Everything's going to be all right, he repeated several times, like a prayer. Everything's going to be all right. He allowed the words of 'Panis Angelicus' to soar again in his head and in his heart. I'm not going to let it happen, he thought. We'll all stay here. I'll get a job. I'll work hard. I'll work shifts.

Suddenly there was a roar which cut through the night air and was then immediately extinguished. It was a motorbike. This was followed by giggles, male laughter, the noise of the sidecar door closing. Someone whistled 'Apache', which, Leslie knew, was Ratty's favourite tune. The bike rumbled again and accelerated. It thundered off into the distance. Leslie hesitated then continued. At the end of the lane was a pile of rubble, heaped up by the diggers ready to be carried away in a lorry. It was like a rounded hill, taller than the yard walls but smaller than the rooftops. The street light was smashed here, but the moon lit the mound with a silvery glow, making it look precious and magical, like a fairy castle. Leslie heard familiar, girlish voices. He turned to stare. It can't be, he thought. What are those two doing out with Ratty and Desperate all the way down here, at this time of night, a mile away from home?

The twins appeared from up the back of the pile and stood on its peak. They held hands as usual and one of them pointed up towards the star-spangled blackness. They were now wearing white Confirmation dresses, white veils, white lace-trimmed ankle socks and white pumps. They seemed young and somehow holy. Their faces were partially hidden and their voices tinkling and subdued. The breeze lifted their gauzy headgear and their skirts fluttered a little.

They look like angels, Leslie mused. Even though they're not nice. Even though they're dangerous. They still look like pretty little angels, ready to fly up to heaven.

2

Scotch Iris's music was now turned low, but standing outside, Leslie could hear drunken voices. The party wasn't over. He pushed open the unlocked adjacent door and went up to the first floor to collect his brother from Auntie Ada's.

Auntie Ada was middle-aged and warm-hearted. She had been a reliable presence for as long as Leslie could remember. She smiled at him now, her creased face doughy and serene. 'Good choir practice?' She was sitting quietly, reading the newspaper, with Geordie at her feet. He was wearing his monkey pyjamas again, and he was busy with his pot of wax crayons, his child's colouring-book. Leslie reflected, for the second night running, how small and young he looked for his fourteen years. The occasional loud guffaw could be heard from below and the door slammed a couple of times as visitors stepped out noisily into the night. Ada and Geordie seemed unaware of these disturbances.

As was usual upstairs, Leslie felt straight away more relaxed. He took off his plimsolls on the hooky mat just inside the door. He acknowledged the comforting glint of the fire, always lit, whatever the weather, the Toby jugs grinning on the dresser, the egg-timer shaped like a dog, the grandfather clock in the corner with its swaying pendulum, the soft glow and hiss from the gas mantle. Everything was as it should be. Geordie was safe. He put his package on the table. 'Geordie. Come and eat these fish and chips before they get cold.'

The younger boy showed the page he had been working

on. It was a picture of an idealized farmyard but Geordie had given it a curious abstract quality. The child and the farmer in the foreground he'd almost erased with black wax. The animals and chickens were orange blobs. Behind, the tractor and the farmhouse were carefully coloured, their details meticulously picked out, the outlines clear. He'd added extra embellishments like roof tiles and tyre treads.

'Look at his lovely picture,' murmured Ada, approvingly. She always spoke to Geordie as if he were about six years old. She stroked his head. 'He's just had a nice hot bath in front of the fire. You can both sleep up here if your mam's got company.'

'It's all right,' replied Leslie, hungrily shoving chips into his mouth. 'We'll go down when it's quiet.'

Geordie joined him at the table. Suddenly he became tense, his green, peculiar eyes staring through the wall, out beyond the yard, the lane, up and over the hill, all the way to the local cemetery. 'Those horrible girls are both in holes in the ground,' he said, lucidly. 'They're still in those wooden boxes, but they're in the ground with their eyes shut.' He paused. 'Men are shovelling soil on top of them.' He laughed harshly, without amusement. 'Where are their fine shop flowers *now*, Leslie?'

Neither Leslie nor Ada responded. Auntie Ada always ignored Geordie's predictions, as if they were somehow indecent. Leslie tonight felt more than uncomfortable about the obvious inference of his brother's remarks. 'Shush!' he said. 'Don't talk like that. It's not nice.' He waited until he felt his brother was back in the present. 'It's not nice, is it Geordie?'

'Not nice,' the younger boy agreed.

*

The following morning some of Scotch Iris's friends were still in her room. They'd been there all night. They came back to life around ten o'clock when they were noisy once more. Iris had electricity in the downstairs flat and the Dansette record player was turned up loud, spinning an LP by Shirley Bassey. This was her third favourite artiste, after Frank Sinatra and Nat King Cole. However, despite the emotional ballads and the brass and the wail of the backing strings, it was still possible to discern the shrieks of immoderate female laughter.

Leslie tried not to notice. He'd made breakfast for himself and his brother, then cleared away. Now he sat at the battered old Scottish piano in the kitchen, running through his vocal exercises and scales. He managed to reach high B. His breaking voice was under control once more and the pure, ethereal sounds coming from his mouth seemed mismatched with his untidy appearance, his grubby neck, his bitten fingernails. Leslie couldn't play the instrument properly but he could pick out the notes well enough. He tapped them out on the chipped, discoloured ivories and trilled as melodiously and effortlessly as a songbird. He knew this was his father's piano. His father had had a good voice. He had been in the village chapel choir. These were three details out of a mere half-dozen facts that he knew about his dead parent. Not that he ever wondered much or looked back. He wasn't a curious person, nor did he feel bitter. His father was dead and that was that. But there was a talent competition about to take place at the local youth club. Leslie knew that his father had won two such contests in his teens in Scotland and he wanted to follow his example. He wanted to repeat his success.

Leslie was the boy soprano at St Stephen's Elswick, but

he was sure that by Christmas he would no longer be able to reach the top notes. He would be croaky and gruff all the time and might not even have a decent voice at all. Mr Green would move him from the front row of the choir stalls to the back with the grown-ups, where he would be inconspicuous, ignored and probably inaudible. He might even have to leave altogether. If he thought about it, the inevitability of this change and his own powerlessness made him sad. He merely hoped his voice would hold out long enough to see him through the competition.

The kitchen was dim and shabby, with worn linoleum on the floor, ancient wallpaper and a curtain dividing it from the back scullery, which contained the sink, pantry and gas stove. It was comfortless and small. The fire in the range was unlit, even though summer was drawing to a close.

Geordie sat at the table lost in his own world. A narrow ray of weak sunlight penetrated the rear yard, shone through the window and fell on to his stooped back, his longish, pretty hair which flopped like spun silk over his eyes, his sculpted, perfectly formed childish hands and the sheet of paper on which he was drawing Tulloch Street. Here, with minute accuracy, he detailed the terrace. His photographic memory enabled him to represent every brick, every splinter, every misaligned roof tile, every cracked window-pane from the row of condemned, semi-abandoned properties that were within days of the demolition gang's mallets. He laboured with pen and ink, swiftly and confidently. He was totally absorbed.

Leslie watched him for a moment, glad that he was calm. That's all that'll be left of this place soon, he reflected. My brother's drawings. He pictured an empty desolate hillside above the river, with loose sketchbook pages blowing through windy open space. Here there was nothing to impede the sight of the water and instead of buildings there was just scorched earth and piles of bricks, cinders and stones. The people were all gone. He took a deep breath and sat straight, bravely facing the piano. He plonked out another couple of scales on the piano keys. Everything's going to be all right. He glanced again at Geordie's jabbing pen. *He* isn't letting things get him down.

Leslie understood that his brother never felt anything beyond the stimulus of the present. He had no emotions other than his reactions to the immediate situation. He had a phenomenal memory but no imagination. He had no abstract thoughts and recognized only that which was perceivable, tangible and real. Except for the instances when he could see into the future. At these moments he seemed to transcend the conceivable, becoming a visionary. Geordie had predicted many things including, last year, the crushing of a toddler from number six Ramsey Street under a runaway coal wagon. He'd foreseen the birth of a prince, an explosion at the colliery and old Mrs Lee's chimney fire. However, these were isolated successes. Mostly, his perceptions into the unknown appeared to make no sense at all and Leslie found it convenient to disregard them. Moreover, the local community didn't listen to or value his prophecies, however accurate they might prove to be. They were not superstitious people in Elswick, rather they were practical and rational in all ways. Geordie's ability to make predictions was one of the reasons he was treated with suspicion. He wasn't heeded, while his trances and his forecasts were regarded as shameful. People turned away from him, but not because he was a Jeremiah. It was simply because he was the local dafty and that, as far as they were concerned, was the end of that.

Leslie struck another chord. I'll get a job, he told himself. I'll find a way we can all stay here, somehow or other. Everything will be the same as it used to be. Our mam will get better. She'll be her funny old self. Everything's going to be all right.

His mother appeared from the front room into the hallway. She seemed annoyed about something. Her face had the pinched expression it always assumed when she was displeased. She was lightly tying on a pink chiffon headscarf over her backcombed beehive hair-do. She smelled strongly of 'Evening in Paris' and wore a cerise floral sleeveless shift dress, which was new, with matching high heels. She seemed unaware of her sons, who regarded her from the kitchen. Without speaking, she left the flat, slamming the door behind her.

Shirley Bassey reached her loud and final crescendo and there was silence. Without the strident competition from the record player, Leslie ran two fingers through another tinkling octave, sang it, then closed the piano lid with a thump. There was a brief silence, then girlish voices and giggling from the front room. 'That cack-faced Les-lee's singing!' someone said. There was more laughter. 'He's singing like a girly-girl!'

Leslie was aware of Geordie laying down his pen, freezing with fear. Pushing aside his own dislike of the twins, he quit the piano and went into the passage. They emerged from Iris's front room, hand in hand and still dressed in white.

They've been here all night, Leslie realized, horrified. 'What're *you* two doing here?' He sounded squeaky and high.

'What are you two doing here?' one of the twins mimicked in a baby voice.

'What's it to you, poo-face?'

'Dottle-heed, freckle-bum!' Maureen sniffed noisily. 'Washed your stinky armpits lately? Phew!'

'Where's that dafty? Don't let that damned dafty anywhere near me, that's all.'

'He's in there! Help!'

'Save us from the dafty!'

Leslie's mother's friend Betty joined them, pulling Iris's door shut behind her but not before the boy glimpsed strewn clothing, record sleeves, empty bottles. There was a smell of stale cigarettes and cosmetics. 'Hello, pet,' the woman said to him, pausing and smiling. She gestured the girls towards the front door and they left, going outside to the street. Catching sight of her reflection in the hallstand mirror, Betty rummaged in her handbag for a panstick. She applied it liberally, rubbing orange smears over her cheeks. Outside, the girls were already disappearing down the road.

'Hello,' said Leslie automatically. He wanted to ask what the twins were doing in the flat, but the words got stuck in his throat. He felt he'd failed to protect his brother in a vital way, but what could he do if even their own mother was against them?

Betty glanced into the kitchen and her eyes fell on Geordie, who was still frozen, immobile, holding his pencil. 'I hear this laddie's been in trouble,' she said in a matter-of-fact way.

'No, no, he hasn't,' Leslie insisted.

'That's not what I've heard.'

'It's all lies. All made up. Just ask our Auntie Ada upstairs.'

'I've heard he's been flashing young girls in the lanes.'

'It's not true!'

Betty stepped outside. 'Your poor mam's got enough on her plate . . .' she suggested.

'Nothing happened!'

The woman turned and set off after Maureen and Muriel.

Leslie fingered his face. Some of his freckles were raised, as if they might be spots. He smelled under one of his armpits. Those awful twins! What *were* they doing here? And all night! What was their dad doing, letting them stay out all night? And what had been going on in the front room? As soon as he had this thought, he tried to push it aside. He refused to let his mind dwell for long on his mother's abstracted air, her silences, her frequent, inappropriate parties as well as everything else that went on in the front room. Instead he went and stood by Geordie, trying to imitate his detachment. He loved his mother, but at present he envied Geordie's ability to shut her out. 'It's all right. There's no one here now,' he murmured reassuringly. 'Those nasty girls have gone.'

'No one here now,' Geordie repeated, at ease again, resuming his quick, deft representation of the army of Tulloch Street chimney-pots, which retreated along his perfectly realized terrace, becoming smaller in the diminishing perspective. Leslie brushed his lips across the top of his brother's head. His newly washed hair smelled of roses.

After a moment, Geordie looked up at his brother. His green eyes, Leslie noticed, were like deep pools. Seriously, he pointed to his drawing. 'Apron and stepped cover flashings,' he said, his pencil aside, his little finger now rubbing and smudging an eaves gutter in the foreground of the drawing, creating depth within the outline. 'Hog-back clay tile ridge.'

'I can see,' Leslie agreed, unaware of these meanings, but sure the terms were correct. 'Yes, I can see those all right.' He laid a protective hand on Geordie's shoulder. The younger boy felt relaxed, but suddenly he became rigid, tense. He stared straight ahead. 'Tulloch Street's down,' he said, responding to a vision in front of him. 'I can see. It's down. Herbert Street's down. And *our street's* down. Our house is . . . our house is . . .' There was a long silence. 'You'll never guess what. Our house is . . . gone!'

*

Later the brothers left home. It was warm and sunny again, a cool breeze blowing up the valley. 'Will you be all right?' Leslie questioned Geordie, with his habitual concern. He straightened his brother's collar, pushed back his heavy hair. 'Here.' He deposited two custard creams into his trouser pocket. He was trying to resign himself to the fact that Geordie wanted to do things on his own. He wasn't a baby. He couldn't stay mollycoddled for ever. 'If you see those twins, cross over the road. Don't go near them. And don't go in any back lanes. Stick to the main streets where there's plenty of people.'

'Cross over the road. Stick to the main streets.'

'That's right.' Leslie was worried.

'Don't go near them.' He squeezed his arm. 'Geordie's a good boy.'

Some distance up the hill, they stood together on the kerb of Elswick Road. Like the Scotswood Road below them, the morning street was busy with shopping house-wives, queues, gossips, delivery vans and old men waiting for the pubs to open. Unlike Scotswood Road, however, here for Geordie, on this thoroughfare, were the exciting benefit of trolley-buses. These were big, bright, chrome and yellow vehicles, powered by electricity. They were frequent and rather silent apart from the dull whine of their motors. These were Geordie's second passion, after buildings. He leaned against a traction pole, his drawing pad ready. A bus approached and his pencil immediately started etching in the overhead wires and the trolley-heads, which poked from its gaudy roof like a pair of surprised antennae.

'Fleet number six, one, four,' insisted Geordie know-ledgeably, his voice now a low monotone. 'Metropolitan Cammell Carriage and Wagon Company, registration N, B, B, six, one, four.' He paused. Obsessive, his face was expressionless.

'I'm going now,' replied Leslie.

'Length thirty foot, width seven foot six,' replied Geordie, 'short front wings.' He carried on drawing, oblivious of everything except his scurrying pencil and the large vision bearing down, with its gorgeous, improbable colour, the satisfying symmetry of its four front windows and its rectangular destination blinds. A couple of people stopped on the pavement to try and peer down at his pad, but he ignored them. He was unaware of their interest. He was unaware of their very presence.

'Go straight home when you've finished,' Leslie advised. 'Are you listening? Straight home, mind.'

Geordie said nothing, his concentration total.

Leslie hesitated.

'Straight home,' the younger boy eventually agreed.

Still Leslie was unwilling to leave him. The worst that could happen was that he'd take a fit, although this hadn't happened for more than a year. He stepped into

Andrea Badenoch

the nearest doorway. It was a greengrocer's. 'Will you watch out for my brother?' he asked. He didn't know the shopkeeper but he gave him his best smile.

The man looked out at Geordie and his eyes narrowed, suspiciously. He was a big person with bushy sideburns and full red lips. He shook his head. 'I've seen that lad before,' he muttered. 'That lad's not all there.'

Leslie was undeterred. 'Will you, mister? Please.'

The greengrocer's wife emerged from the back, dragging a sack of potatoes. 'I'll keep an eye on him, pet,' she said, tersely.

*

Leslie went back down the hill towards the invisible river. He was on his way to Adamsez, a factory that made toilet bowls and washbasins for people who had proper bathrooms. Ratty Schnitzler had told him that they were laying on new men. 'The pay's lousy,' he'd added. 'But at least try to look decent.' He'd shaken his head in despair. 'Look at your shoes! You nicked those plimsolls from school, didn't you? They're school plimsolls, pinched from the gym. I know they are. Haven't you got any proper shoes?'

Disregarding this advice, Leslie now headed along Scotswood Road past the Vickers works. As usual, he felt dwarfed by the place. It was huge, seventy acres at least, stretching all along the bank of the river. Leslie knew the factory was the main employer in the area and its scale terrified him. He feared the Vickers cranes, the jetties, the hooting ships on the concealed Tyne that carried away their products; engines to Africa, trains to India, presses to the Americas, weapons to the Middle and Far East. He had been told at school that it was all the creation of someone called Lord Armstrong, who turned out to be an old-fashioned-looking person with a wing collar and white hair. This gent had made the factory into the heavy engineering capital of the world.

Leslie pictured smelting and moulding, fire and brimstone, oil and metal, pulleys and machines. Vickers supplied the means to keep the world running, turning, producing, expanding, not only here but *everywhere*. He knew this and he feared the Vickers noise, the smog, the rank industrial smell. He feared their terrifying tanks that were driven around his Elswick terraces on test, gouging up the roads with their caterpillar wheels. He knew it was a place where time-serving apprentices wielded efficient spanners, and compared with them he was just a ginger, freckled-faced kid with a girl's singing voice. He knew that inside there would be a lot of swearing, dirt and heavy lifting. The factory contained the rituals, the codes, the unknown mysteries of the world of men. The thought of it made him feel useless.

Young and inconsequential under the high brick wall, Leslie remembered a film that he'd recently taken Geordie to see at the Majestic. It was called *Spartacus*. In it, the slaves were muscled and brown and seemed bonded by their common masculinity. Leslie had sat watching, impressed but feeling excluded. He knew he would never be like them – not now, not when he was twenty, not when he was thirty, not ever. He also knew that all work, whether it was in Vickers or ancient Rome, wherever it might be . . . it went on without a break for years. It went on and on and on until you were too old and finished to do anything apart from hang around somewhere, like a pub on the Scotswood Road, probably in a worn-out raincoat and cap, coughing phlegm into a stained handkerchief and playing listless dominoes.

Now he walked as quickly as he could, a little late, unkempt and sweaty, an almost comical figure against the factory's dirty brick. He passed the Elswick works, then, afterwards, the Scotswood works. A single white cloud floated in the improbable blue of the sky. That's the ghost of Lord Armstrong, Leslie decided.

He knew he had to get a job in one of these places along the river. He had no choice. Despite himself, he could picture no alternative, for his mind never carried him beyond the boundaries of Elswick, Benwell, or possibly Scotswood. He accepted that he had to earn money, the same as everyone else. Despite his cowardly, cold dread of the back of the cupboard at home with its toolbox, hammer, string, torch, paint-pots and brushes and all the rest of the household jumble . . . he *had* to be practical. He had to be a breadwinner. He had to sort out the bills that his mam was neglecting to pay. Geordie was depending on him. He took a deep breath. He had to protect Geordie from the twins, this was the most pressing concern, but over and beyond this he had to see to *everything*. He had to make a living with his hands.

He slowed down for a while, catching his breath. I'm hot, he thought. He could hear the tinkle of an ice-cream van. He stopped, feeling in his pocket for coins. The vehicle pulled out on to the main road and he raised his hand. Suddenly he had a vision of Geordie on the beach, a few summers ago when they'd gone on a trip to the seaside. Iris had bought ice-creams and Leslie held them aloft, dripping and cold. Geordie had run towards him, all excited, coming from the shallows, his feet splashing up rainbow droplets. He'd been so happy, so changed, he was even laughing, and because this was so rare Leslie had laughed too. At this exact moment their mam had taken a photograph and captured the scene for ever.

Leslie bought a raspberry-flavoured ice lolly. He was late, but the frozen sweetness stopped him in his tracks. He felt in his shirt pocket, took out the precious photo that showed a unique grin on the beloved face that was normally so sad and serious. He smiled back at his brother. Adamsez will be friendly, he decided, trying to be cheerful. Basins and toilet bowls seemed to him at that moment to be very ordinary things. They'll be easy, he reasoned. Compared to Vickers, they'll be easy to understand. There's nothing to worry about, with sanitary ware.

Finally, a mile and a half from home, way outside his normal range and after Leslie had passed the famous hydraulic crane, one of the great marvels of the western world, the Vickers works finally came to an end. Their heavy steam hammer still thump-thumped back in Elswick, where he'd come from. He had never strayed so far in this direction before. The sun was climbing now and the temperature was getting hotter. Behind the high wall, a train rattled by. On the other side of the road, unknown terraces climbed steeply upwards, just as they did at home, but so far these were too far west to be touched by the demolition men. Their days, Leslie realized, were probably numbered. The people here too would be told to shift, just like at home. He trudged slowly now, tired and anxious in his duffel-coat and plimsolls. He tried to tidy his bright, unruly hair with his fingers. He rubbed his face with his sleeve. His final school report was in his coat pocket. This described him as 'responsible, friendly, willing and good-hearted'. It didn't mention his singing or his card tricks.

He was glad that it didn't say he was bewildered in woodwork or that he struggled to read and write.

Adamsez was comfortingly small and ramshackle. Inside the gates of the Low yard, Leslie found Mr Brewis, the foreman. He smiled. 'Have you been eating an ice lolly,' he asked, 'or have you been kissing the girls?'

Leslie was reassured, but when he looked around this brief moment of confidence deserted him. Outside the sheds there were stacks of bathtubs and basins, protective wrinkly cardboard poking from each. Leslie paused. His mouth went dry. The sanitary ware looked at once important and intimidating. The ground, the walls, even the air seemed pale with clay. He felt overwhelmed.

Mr Brewis was a large man and wore a white overall and a bowler hat. His moustache bristled like a walrus. They stood together in the doorway of a building. Inside it was gloomy, dusty and cramped. The foreman explained that the shadowy workers within were casting and glazing and that it was a skilled job requiring strength to lift the materials and heavy moulds. 'Have the dole sent you?'

Leslie shook his head and handed over his school report. This is hopeless, he thought.

The foreman glanced over it, indifferently. 'How old are you, lad?'

'Fifteen.'

He folded the paper and handed it back. 'And what're you good at?'

Leslie considered. He swallowed hard. 'Singing,' he replied.

Mr Brewis's lips twitched. 'There's not much call for singers in this yard, son.'

Leslie felt the colour rise to his cheeks. 'I didn't mean . . .'

The foreman smiled. 'You start at the bottom here and you work up. It's a canny job. You learn by watching and doing.' He placed both hands on his round belly, over his watch-chain. 'We're one big happy family here. You can sing if you like.'

Leslie swallowed. 'Is there . . . is there an opening?'

Mr Brewis pushed back his hat and scratched his bald head. He looked Leslie up and down.

Leslie shifted from one foot to the other, feeling scrawny and weak.

There was a silence. 'You're a healthy enough lad.' He sounded doubtful. 'Could you put basins on the bogies, stack them?' The man frowned. 'You strong enough for that? Apprenticeships don't start till you're sixteen.'

Leslie stared at him. His normal good humour deserted him. He could think of nothing to say.

The foreman became even more unsure. 'There's always cleaning the sheds up.'

The boy said nothing. Suddenly, on impulse, he took out his playing cards and separated the first few from the pack. 'See these?' he said enthusiastically. 'You choose one and make sure you remember it.' He showed the foreman six cards, all kings, queens or jacks.

The man looked a little bemused. He scratched his cheek.

Leslie was insistent. 'You chosen one? Are you ready?'

'Aye, I have.'

'You remembered it?'

The man nodded.

Leslie made a show of returning the cards to the pack. Meanwhile, surreptitiously, he slipped an alternative five from the bottom, which he produced. Again they were all kings, queens and jacks, but different ones. Leslie was confident the man would only remember one card, the one he'd chosen. 'Yours isn't here,' he said, smiling. 'Is it? Where's yours? Yours has gone missing.' He made a show of looking on the ground, and on his own person, slapping at his coat. 'Where's *yours* gone?' Meanwhile, he put the rest of the pack in his pocket.

The foreman stared. 'No ... How did you know ... Mine was the queen of clubs! It's gone!'

Immediately, Leslie's hand counted off two cards from the top of the pack. He knew the next was the chosen card. He secreted it up his sleeve then with a swift and deft gesture pretended to pluck it from inside the man's waistcoat. 'Here it is! The queen of clubs! You had it all the time!' He held it up triumphantly.

The foreman looked baffled then he let out a hearty laugh. 'Well, I'll be darned!' He clutched his belly and guffawed. He wiped his eyes. 'I'll tell you what, son,' he offered, recovering his composure. 'I know there's nowt doing over at the kilns. But you could try the mine. If not, come back here and I'll get you started with your sweeping brush.'

'Thank you, mister,' Leslie croaked, his voice suddenly deep and hoarse.

'There's demand,' the man offered, as he turned to go. 'Since the war. Since everyone's started wanting proper bathrooms. Proper *inside* bathrooms. They're the thing of the future.'

Relieved, Leslie departed, his rubber soles creating little eddies of dust as he tramped away. He walked out on to the road and up the hill. He knew he would never go back. What's the matter with me? he thought.

At the fireclay mine the gate was broken, hanging to one side. An abandoned lorry sat idle, its tyres flat, its bonnet open. It was a desolate, leafless scene with rickety corrugated iron shelters covering piles of mud or segger, as it was known. As he watched, a miner in a stained singlet and a helmet emerged listlessly from the pit entrance leading a small pony, dragging a laden tub. Both pitman and animal regarded him steadily, without acknowledgement.

Leslie took several steps backwards, turned on his heel and returned down the hill. At the bottom he stopped, discouraged. He was dismayed and uncertain about his reaction, except that the mine, like all of Adamsez Sanitary Wares, seemed as alien as the moon. He was afraid. Not only that, he was wasting their time. He took out his school report, read it, then returned it to his pocket. He felt close to tears. Everything was all right when I was still at school, he remembered. I was safe there. But I've got to get something. I can't go on like this. I've got to grow up and be willing and face my responsibilities. I've got to look after Geordie. I've got to *provide*.

He deliberately thought of Mr Green. 'That was splendid, Leslie!' he'd said at choir practice. That was splendid, Leslie, he repeated in his mind. Splendid, Leslie. He tried to sing. The words of 'Panis Angelicus' stuck in his throat.

*

Back at home on Glue Terrace, when he reached his front door, Leslie's heart somersaulted in his chest. He stood on his own step, wide-eyed with both amazement and dread. Two words were scraped on to the wall with a piece of broken plaster. They were chalked in big wobbly letters but they were not uncertain or indefinite. Rather they were aggressive and determined. One of them was 'FLASHER'. The other was 'WANKER'.

Leslie pushed open the door then took the unusual step of locking it behind him. He took a couple of deep breaths, because he felt sick. Hurrying into the back bedroom he was relieved to find Geordie lying on their big double bed, studying his trolley-bus timetables, calm and engrossed. Thank goodness, Leslie thought. He's home. He's all right. He checked the rest of the flat. Their mam was nowhere to be seen. He went into the back yard and stood in the nettie, wondering if he might vomit, but after a while the nausea faded away.

Back in the bedroom he asked, 'You didn't see those girls did you?'

Geordie now faced the wall. He was tense and pale. His eyes were green, fathomless and farsighted. He was in the future. 'Those girls are both in the ground,' he said in an unemotional way. 'Fat worms are eating their bodies. Their faces have almost gone and their teeth are sticking out. They're turning to slimy mush.'

The older boy shuddered. His stomach was once again uneasy. 'Have you seen those girls this morning?'

There was no response. Geordie picked up his time-tables and began studying them again. He appeared calm.

In the scullery, offended by the stained sink, the grimy cooker, the unwashed dishes Leslie boiled a kettle and rubbed things over with Vim sprinkled on a dishcloth. It didn't seem to make much difference. Everything still looked worn out and old-fashioned. In the kitchen he ran the carpet-sweeper over the rug and picked up discarded dirty clothing. He tidied Geordie's drawing equipment on the table. 'I'm just popping upstairs,' he called out to his brother. 'Mind you stay here, now. I'm locking you in.' He passed by the offending words with his eyes averted. It's those twins, he thought. Those twins have written this up here for everyone to see. Soon everyone's going to be pointing at Geordie and whispering these nasty words. He imagined jeers and catcalls. He thought about groups of children throwing stones.

Auntie Ada was in the kitchen as usual, reclining in her big, old armchair, reading a newspaper with a magnifying glass. Immediately above her head, on the wall, was a framed black and white photograph of Sir Winston Churchill, seated at his desk. To the left, one by one, the spent days of the month were crossed off in pencil on a calendar. This showed Princess Margaret in colour. She was wearing a red hat and coat and holding aloft a bottle of champagne on a string, preparing to launch a ship on the Tyne. She was glamorous and rich, with jewels around her neck, and various men stood about, clapping and looking honoured.

Ada was an extremely large woman, not tall, but wide, with a commodious lap and several middle-aged chins. 'Come and sit yourself down,' she said, smiling and unsurprised.

Despite the sunshine outside, today there was a sizeable fire burning in the range. From the bread oven at the side of the blaze there came a smell of baking scones. 'I'm just resting my old bones,' she added cheerfully, folding the paper and pushing it temporarily behind the cushion on her armchair. 'And having a look at the notices.'

Auntie Ada was very keen on reading the Births, Marriages and Deaths columns in the *Newcastle Post*. She perused them avidly, every day, searching for mention of friends, distant relatives or people connected in some way to those she knew. If she found a familiar name, she ringed the entry with a pencil kept behind her ear for the purpose.

Leslie sat on a hard chair, some distance from the heat.

He smiled. 'Been to Adamsez,' he admitted, trying to appear unconcerned.

'Any luck?'

'No.'

'I'll have a word with our Jack. Take your coat and shoes off and put the kettle on for me, pet. Wash your hands. Get yourself some pop. Some bread and butter. Or would you like a nice hot scone?' She heaved herself up with difficulty and opened the oven door. The smell that filled the room was heavenly. Using the hem of her apron she pulled out the tray. Lumbering, she carried the scones through into the scullery and tipped them on to a rack to cool. 'Here you are.'

Ada's husband had been a miner but he'd died of black lung when he was only forty-seven. She had no children of her own. Her baby had lived for only three days. This was a great sadness to her and sometimes her soft face became creased with lines of regret. She lived on her widow's pension and a small income gleaned from the preparation of honey cakes, rock buns, fruit scones and toffee apples, which she sold to three or four corner shops nearby. Her brother Jack was a foreman at Vickers. He too was widowed and he came to visit twice a week for his tea.

Ada had taught Leslie how to bake. The two of them often laboured in her spotless scullery, mixing and weighing. Here dirty hands, plimsolls and duffel-coats were not allowed. He helped her fulfil her orders from the local shopkeepers, turning out fairy cakes as light as thistledown. His pastry, Ada admitted, was even more melt-in-the-mouth than her own.

Now Leslie moved his chair further away from the fire, placing it next to the open window. He bit into a scone, the melted butter running down his chin and fingers. He realized he was hungry. 'Can I have another one?' For a moment, Leslie almost forgot his worries.

'Of course you can. There's some nice jam in the pantry.'

Leslie sat down again with a second scone and a glass of home-made lemonade. 'Auntie Ada?' he asked tentatively.

'Yes, pet?'

'Can you show me how to bake a big cake? You know, a proper one, with icing and everything?'

'If you like.' Ada had returned to her paper and was now studying the page of wedding photographs.

'You know, with words and stuff on. Like "Happy Birthday" made of sugar.' He paused. 'Will you show me how to make meringues?'

Ada looked at him for a moment and nodded. She returned to her paper. 'That's Polly Taylor's lass, young Deborah.' She smiled. 'Mind, she's very like her dad.'

'Will you show me how to make a wedding cake with silver bells on?'

Ada held the picture close to her eyes. 'She's gone and wed a lad from down Prudhoe. Can't say I know the family.' She turned the paper towards the light of the window and studied it through the magnifying glass. 'Mind, she looks real bonny. Those Taylor lasses were all fair. Not bottle blondes. No, they were *proper* blondes, all of them. And lovely manners too.' She sighed with pleasure.

'Prudhoe?' Leslie was at once reminded of the envelope from the psychiatrist that had come from the hospital about Geordie. He licked the jam from his hands and drained his glass. That's why he was here. He'd brought it up to show her. He took the letter from his trouser pocket and handed it to Auntie Ada. 'Have a look at *this*.'

She unfolded the page and studied it for some time. She examined it both with and without the glass. 'Well, I don't know,' she said eventually. Her doughy face subsided into an expression of melancholy resignation. She took a handkerchief from her sleeve and blew her nose. 'I don't know what the world is coming to.' She began reading the letter for the third time.

Leslie regarded her, waiting for an expression of outrage, a declaration that taking Geordie away was out of the question. He looked at her white hair, her puffy ankles which spilled over her slippers, her gold ring almost lost in the soft flesh of her marriage finger. She shook her head sadly and said nothing.

'He's not going,' Leslie insisted quietly. 'I won't let them take him. It's my job to look after him and that's what I'm going to do. Doctors or no doctors.' He paused, then added, as an afterthought, 'Twins or no twins.'

Auntie Ada looked at him, folded the letter, handed it back, then stared solemnly into the fire. She shook her head.

'He's staying here with me.'

'You can't argue with doctors,' Ada said eventually.

Leslie felt a surge of an unusual emotion. 'Yes you can!'

'If the doctor says he has to go, then he has to go. Doctors know what they're doing.'

'No he won't! He won't!' Leslie stood up, stuffing the jam-stained letter back into his trouser pocket.

Ada looked concerned, but also aggrieved. 'Listen, pet. If that's what they've decided, then that's what they've decided.'

Leslie walked towards the door. He struggled into his coat and plimsolls. He was both furious and disappointed. Auntie Ada, his old ally and friend, was saying the last thing he wanted to hear. He walked out without saying thank you or goodbye. He clumped down the dark stairs and out into the blinding sun of the street. She's just like everyone around here, he thought, kicking a stone into the gutter. He stood squinting up the road. She just does as she's told. He took a deep, steadying breath. We're all expected to do just what we're told, for our whole *lives*. They say pack up and shift, we all shift. They say go and live in the sky with the birds *and we do it*! They say Geordie's a dafty and should be locked up and we're all supposed to go along with *that* too. Well, I'm not going along with it because they're all buggers. I love my brother and he needs me. My brother's staying here with me and that's the beginning and the end of it. He took a deep breath. His eyes were full of tears. Rebellion was a previously unknown sensation. It was strangely liberating and it made him feel reckless and strong. He went into the downstairs flat, got a bucket of water and a brush and rubbed furiously at the horrible words written on the wall. He imagined the chalked letters were the faces of the twins and he scrubbed and scrubbed, washing them clean away. In a minute or two, they were completely gone.

*

Later, Leslie decided to walk up to De Grey Street to see if Ratty Schnitzler was at home. Ratty lived with his father in a smartish-looking terraced house near the top of the hill. It was small, but unlike most it had an upstairs, a downstairs and a dormer window in the roof. Leslie had never been inside but it was commonly believed that the Schnitzlers had the luxury of modern plastic furniture and electric fires.

As he drew near Leslie waved to his friend Constable Henderson, who was patrolling his beat. He'd forgiven him for the treachery of the other evening, but felt unable to tell him about the bad words written on the wall. He might not be too sympathetic, Leslie decided. Although good-natured, he wasn't sure that the policeman really believed one hundred per cent in his brother's innocence.

Leslie felt dwarfed by the skeleton framework of the high flats and their crane that loomed behind the houses. The block was being erected on top of the ruins of Cruddas Park, a former grassy space where he had once played. There was also a pile-driver and a vast hole where foundations had been poured for a second tower. There would be more of these going up elsewhere, just as soon as the demolition men had created enough room.

Leslie tried to imagine living somewhere that reached into the clouds, but the thought made him dizzy. He imagined birds flying past, underneath the window sill. *'Oh for the wings, for the wings of a dove . . .'* He remembered the words of a solo he'd sung in the choir and in his mind's eye he saw white birds fluttering against a pure blue sky. They were like prayers. Inexplicably, they then became the twins, dressed as angels, winging their way to heaven. He shrugged and shook his head and successfully dismissed them. He was quite certain that he had no desire to fly like a dove or live up in the sky in a little box. Elswick's going to become New York, he thought, remembering newsreels he'd seen at the cinema. It'll be like the Empire State Building. It'll be like that film, *King Kong*. I don't *like* it. I don't want it. Not in this neighbourhood. No, not ever.

*

Scotch Iris sat on a high bar stool in the Royal Station Hotel. She sipped a dry Martini but grimaced and pushed it aside. 'This is fucking horrible,' she said to the white-jacketed barman. 'Get me something nice. Get me a lemonade with plenty of blackcurrant.' She pretended to inhale on a Rothman's Filter Tip then stubbed it out. Iris wasn't too keen on smoking or drinking.

Well away from her usual beat, she was waiting for Mickey Robson, her new lover. He was talking on a public telephone in a booth on the other side of the room. She stared at his back, his gesticulating hand. He was tall, broad-shouldered and slim-hipped. Nicely dressed, he was wearing an Italian-style jacket, tapered trousers and elastic-sided Chelsea boots. Iris thought he looked like a film star. He turned and smiled at her, holding up three fingers, indicating that he wouldn't be long. His face was chiselled and handsome, his teeth good, his brown hair thick and combed back from his high brow. He was thirty-six or thereabouts, but could pass for twenty-eight. He's a catch, she thought to herself. He's a smasher. He's a real hunk.

She took out a mirror and inspected her make-up. She looked pretty, as usual, with her high cheekbones, plucked brows, tiny upturned nose, pink-painted rosebud mouth and big, darkened eyes. Her skin was pale and matte and without a blemish. She snapped the compact shut with confidence. She smiled at him and waved. Mickey, she knew, was unaware of her line of work although he knew that she had 'a reputation'. This meant that he considered her fast, probably too easy but not entirely unrespectable. He lived more than a mile from her Elswick flat, beyond even the top of the hill, in an outer realm of breathtaking affluence that consisted of thirties-built semi-detached houses with gardens. As well as this, his business and council duties took him day and night into the city. He was, she was sure, well away from any rumours and scandal connected with her lifestyle. It was her ambition to secure an engagement ring from Mickey Robson, to marry him and move into his posh house and make a fresh start. He was the best chance she'd ever had in this rotten town and the thought of the future with him could make her faint with expectation and happiness.

Iris opened her bag, put away the compact and took out a bottle of tablets. She washed one of them down with a swig of lemonade. This, she knew, would help her to be chatty and amusing, it would make her feel in control. Thank Christ for *these* little bastards, she thought. They're just like a miracle, so they are. And I hardly need eat anything as long as I take these. She glanced down at her lap, her slender thighs. And I know he likes slim women.

Mickey put down the phone but then immediately picked it up again and pushed more money into the slot. He gave her a thumbs-up sign, then turned away, talking rapidly. He tapped his foot and raised his voice, but it wasn't possible to hear what he was saying. It sounded as if he might be giving orders.

Iris crossed her legs, hitching up her skirt slightly to show them off to their best advantage. She allowed one of her spindly high-heeled shoes to dangle, seductively. She pushed and poked at her blonde beehive hair-do, puffing it up and pushing the ends under. He's my best chance,

she thought again. He's my only bloody chance. She ran
through the few facts she knew about Mickey Robson.
He had a modern job installing telephones in offices. He
wasn't rich but he was 'comfortable'. He was a Newcastle
city councillor and went to a lot of meetings. He lived in
his mother's house, way up on the 'right' side of Elswick
Road, but the old lady was ga-ga and he'd got her into a
home, somewhere in Whitley Bay. His wife had left him
but he was glad because she was a nagging bitch and
she'd got fat and let herself go. He had twin daughters,
Muriel and Maureen, who were wild and conniving and
potentially a bit of a problem. Iris frowned into her glass
and looked at her watch. On the one occasion she'd
been to her lover's house, he'd bolted both outside doors
but the girls had climbed up a drainpipe and come in
through the bathroom. She'd sat up in bed, horrified, the
sheet clutched round her naked body as the terrible two
had hammered on the locked bedroom door. Iris had
used some colourful swear words. Mickey had apologized
and laughed and told them to 'get lost'. He'd pushed
a pound note under the door and they'd run off, shrieking like Red Indians. She hadn't been back to the house
since. She sighed. Those girls were the only flies in the
ointment. She really, really could do without those girls.
Perhaps they'll run away. Perhaps their stupid mother will
have them, she pondered. I wish they'd just *disappear*.

Mickey finished his second phone call and returned to
the bar. His strides were long and manly and he rattled
the change in his pocket. He picked up his pint glass and
drained it. He lit a cigarette and wedged it in the corner of
his mouth. 'Come on, flower,' he said happily. 'Let's get
you upstairs. I've only got an hour.'

Excited by each other's bodies, these two parents were

Andrea Badenoch

oblivious of their children. They were uninvolved and
unaware. It well suited them, at the moment, never to
mention each other's parental responsibilities. This wasn't
too difficult, as they rarely allowed themselves experience
of the burden.

*

A short distance from the skeleton of the new, towering
flats, Leslie approached the normal, more comforting
dimensions of the Schnitzlers' front window, where a little
cage was visible above the respectable half-nets. It was
hooked on to a special stand and contained a budgerigar,
which regarded him quizzically. Instead of knocking on
the door, which would have seemed impertinent, he went
around the back. The gate to the yard was open as usual
and he stepped inside.

Two walls on either side of the Schnitzlers' yard were
lined with aviaries. They held dozens of brightly coloured
birds: finches, canaries and cockatoos that fluttered,
preened and chirruped. On the floors were special chickens
with ruffs and fancy leg feathers. The aviaries also contained sparrows and starlings, which had forced their way
under the netting, preferring the meal ticket that accompanied captivity to taking their chances in the world
outside.

Ratty loved his birds. He had long ago worn down his
father's objections to their lack of freedom. He also loved
dogs and cats. He had three Siamese cats and an ancient
dog that was now blind and deaf, which he cared for
like an infirm elderly relative. He often said he'd like to
keep a horse in the yard and a sheep, but was aware that
this was unrealistic. His main ambition was to make
enough money to move to Gosforth, where the houses

had proper gardens. Here he intended to turn his sub-urban back plot into an animal sanctuary where people would bring injured and mistreated creatures into his care and where he would devote himself to nursing them back to full health.

Leslie regarded the pretty feathered birds for some time. *'Oh for the wings, for the wings of a dove ...'* He couldn't get the song out of his mind. He remembered the talent competition. He'd put his name down. Experi-mentally, he tried the high notes, singing aloud. His voice stayed in tune. It sounded perfect.

The little caged creatures seemed cheerful and lively. One or two whistled beautifully in response. Maybe I could live in there with them, he thought, irrationally. When our house gets pulled down. But it's a bit small. It's no good. There wouldn't be enough room for both of us.

Ratty appeared. He was wearing his everyday outfit, which consisted of a modest maroon drapecoat, dark green drainpipes, fawn suede crêpe-soled shoes with buckles and an open-necked shirt. His hair was slicked back into an approximation of its regular Teddy-boy quiff. He was tall and thin, but as swarthy as his father, and he had a mournful, foreign, long-faced look. He was not good-looking. He tried to overcome this with mannerisms such as an Elvis Presley sneer, a slouch, a particular way of raising and lowering his shoulders, and a style of holding a cigarette that involved cupping it under his palm.

Ratty placed his transistor radio on the ground. It was red plastic with a white dial and had a special carry-ing handle. Leslie knew no one else who owned such a marvel. He couldn't understand how it worked without wires. How did the sounds *get into it*, he wondered, with-out wires to travel along?

Leslie admired Ratty because he always had plenty of money and seemed unafraid of anything. He smiled.

'Hello there, bonny lad,' Ratty greeted him. 'Was that you singing?'

Leslie shrugged. 'Nothing doing at Adamsez,' he lied. His voice had sunk low again, making him sound like a man.

Ratty opened a hatch in an aviary and tipped in some seed. He changed the drinking water, refilling the dishes from the outside tap. 'No?' He appeared surprised. One of his cats came out from the house and rubbed itself against his legs.

'No.'

Ratty fed the cat then swept up some spilled bird-seed. He sat down in a battered old armchair, which he'd moved outside at the beginning of the summer in order, he explained, to catch some rays. He turned on his radio. 'You tried Vickers? You must've tried Vickers.' He bent down and turned up the volume. 'Listen,' he said. There was the jaunty rhythm of electric guitars. 'It's "Apache"!'

Leslie listened obediently. He pretended interest by tapping his foot. He was not a fan of popular music. Whenever his mother had visitors, or recently, when she was holding one of her noisy front-room parties, he'd hated all the blowzy records which he heard her play. Not only this, his choirmaster said all pop music was the devil's own rubbish. Leslie didn't believe in the devil and outside of choir practice he was even uncertain about the existence of God, but he'd nevertheless managed to absorb this prejudice.

Ratty was a big fan of the Shadows, particularly their instrumental numbers. He'd been to school with Hank Marvin, or Brian Rankin as he had once been known.

Because of this association, he didn't share the common Teddy-boy jealousy of Cliff Richard that had resulted in demolished theatre seats and missiles such as eggs and light bulbs being hurled on to stages across the land. Ratty said this was 'infantile'. Now he nodded his head and shook his shoulders in time to the beat, adopting a mean, rock 'n' roll expression. He struck some chords on an invisible guitar. When the tune finished he asked again, 'Did you try Vickers?'

Leslie looked uncomfortable. He shifted from one foot to the other. 'Er, no.'

'Everybody works at Vickers.' Ratty grinned. 'Well, nearly everybody.'

'You don't.'

Ratty stretched lazily and sighed. 'Yeah, well, I've got plans, me.'

'Plans?'

'One-armed bandits.'

Leslie had a cinematic vision of a Mexican cowboy with one missing limb, galloping across a desert, somewhere in the Wild West. He thought Ratty was talking about going abroad. He stared. His friend had sometimes mentioned a desire to go to London, but he'd never before suggested leaving the *country*.

'Fruit machines.' Ratty yawned. He was a modern man who had turned his back on the past.

'Fruit machines? They like bubblegum machines? For fruit?'

'Nah. They're for gambling. You put money in, pull a lever and you either win or lose. Mostly you lose. That's why they're called bandits. 'Cos they rob you blind. Unless you're the one *emptying* the machines, of course. Then you get rich. Very rich.'

'You got some of those machines, Ratty?'

'I know someone who knows someone.'

'Can I get a job emptying those machines?'

'You're too young.'

'No I'm not, me. I'm responsible. Responsible and willing.'

'You *are*, kid. The machines are in pubs and clubs. That's where we'll put them. All the pubs and clubs. You're too young. You have to be eighteen to go in.'

'Can I do it when I'm eighteen?'

'Why not? Of course you can.'

Leslie smiled. 'Right then.' He was at once serious again. 'I need to get a job now. I have to look after my brother. He's depending on me.'

'I've told you. Try Vickers. They'll start you as a messenger boy or a teaboy. Then you'll get an apprenticeship next year.' He grinned. 'It'll be steady. It'll be grand. If you don't like it you can always come in with me on the one-armed bandit racket when you're older. Yes?' He sighed, lifting a leg, regarding one of his own shoes appreciatively. 'Cheer up, misery-guts!'

Leslie said nothing. He watched a pair of canaries peck at the floor of the aviary. It's all right for *them*, he thought. He remembered why he'd come. 'I've got this letter,' he said, his erratic voice suddenly plunging very low. He took the envelope from his trouser pocket and handed it to Ratty.

The youth read the typed page slowly. 'This might be for the best,' he said, sadly, shaking his head.

'No,' answered Leslie, his voice high again. 'I'm not letting them take him away. They'll lock him up. Put him in a straitjacket. Shave his head.'

'No, they won't. They might make him better. You never know, do you? Modern science and all that jazz.'

Leslie hesitated. He reached out and retrieved the letter, folding it.

Ratty shrugged. 'They might give him treatment.' He hesitated. 'He's ... he's ...' he rushed out a few words. 'He's cruel to animals.'

Leslie said nothing. He was used to criticisms of his brother. He heard them all the time and he knew they weren't true.

Ratty was suddenly very sad. 'I've heard he hung a cat then cut it open.'

Leslie raised his eyes to heaven. 'That's just stupid.'

'He steals kids' pet guinea pigs and boils them alive.' Ratty clenched his fists. His voice wavered. 'Hey, it's not on, is that. Is that on or isn't it on? It's bloody criminal, that.'

'It's *not true*.' Leslie shook his head. 'None of it.' There was an awkward silence. 'People say all sorts of things. And now some stupid girls have been saying ... they've just been saying ... that he's a flasher!' He gulped. 'And it's not true. Geordie wouldn't do nowt like that. He's just a little kid. He doesn't know nowt about ... about ... all *that*.' His voice was beseeching. 'The thing about my brother is ... he's just different, that's all.' He hesitated. 'But pills won't make him better.'

Ratty coughed. He was uncomfortable with the conversation. 'You never know. He might be better off in there. He'd be with his own kind.'

'No ...'

There was a loud roar in the lane, which grew louder before being suddenly quashed. It was Desperate Dan on his motorcycle. He stepped into the yard in full khaki, his battledress immaculate, trousers folded into gaiters, boots as shiny as glass.

*

Desperate had loved the army. He said he'd taken to National Service like a duck to water and he had been made a lance-corporal in no time. He loved parades and he loved drill. He loved marching everywhere, bulling floors, blanco-ing and brasso-ing his kit. He loved saluting. He said his demob was the worst day of his life. Now he wanted to sign up to be a professional soldier with the Northumberland Fusiliers but his slatternly, down-at-heel mam was against the idea. She wanted to keep him at home. She said she didn't want him going off to some far-away jungle where he might be captured and tortured by slant-eyes. She was adamant. She wouldn't even agree to him joining the Territorials. So every night he said a special prayer asking God to stir up an even bigger conflict in Malaya or somewhere, so he'd be called up into the Reserves. If this happened he would have no choice but to go because it was his duty. He would be able to escape the run-down filthy pair of rooms at the bottom of the hill that were on the worst street in Elswick. The government would send papers, ten shillings and a transport pass to base, overruling his unreasonable, clinging, hopeless mother.

*

Desperate duffed Ratty on the shoulder and gave Leslie a wink. He had a flat, friendly face and a punched-in nose from a NATO under-twenty-ones boxing match. 'Hello there, our kid,' he said, warmly.

'Hello, Desperate,' replied Leslie, shyly. He put away the letter.

The two older youths began discussing rent collection for Sammy and their other job working as tallymen for a department store on Scotswood Road. This involved them giving tickets or credit and then collecting the money weekly from those who'd bought clothes or furniture or wedding presents. They were trying to devise a new system whereby they weren't demanding that careworn housewives fork out for both rent and credit repayments on the same night. 'They don't answer the door,' insisted Desperate. 'And they cross the street when they see us coming.'

'We'll do better if we spread the burden,' agreed his friend. He took a pencil from behind his ear. 'We're supposed to be financiers. We need a better system.'

Leslie watched the fowl pecking in the aviaries, Mendelssohn's high notes repeating under his breath. *'Oh for the wings, for the wings of a dove . . .'* The names of families and streets and amounts of arrears owed drifted over him and then on upwards towards the sky. He thought about choir practice and had another vision of the stained glass at the church and the figure of the mother of Jesus holding out her arms to him in a welcoming way. Without wanting to, he pictured the twins again in their white dresses with wings, fluttering like holy doves. He felt a little sleepy, a little drunk on the warmth, the combined smell of bird dirt and Schnitzler's Brilliant, which coated the heads of his friends. He remembered the dirty words chalked on the wall outside their flat and then he pictured the twins again, but this time as his brother had described them, mouldering and rotting in coffins, deep within the earth, their flesh all gone. His stomach churned and he felt a little sick, as he had earlier in the day. I wish they *were* dead, he decided.

Suddenly his attention was caught by Ratty, who was talking about the twins. 'What about *those* little hot patooties?' he sniggered, rather unpleasantly. 'Can you believe it? Jailbait like that oughtn't to be allowed. It's not fair.' He took out a comb and needlessly slicked back his hair. 'Yum, yum, yum.'

Desperate shrugged. 'Hey, you're just a nonce, Schnitzler. What are you?' He laughed. 'A bloody nonce. Should be ashamed. They're just babies. Baby pussy.' He crouched down on his haunches, next to Ratty's chair.

Ratty grinned. 'They're not as young as they look.'

Leslie tried very hard not to listen. I'm *so* fed up with those twins, he thought. They don't even belong to this neighbourhood. I wish they'd just . . . I wish they'd just . . .

Desperate continued: 'When that Betty gets on the bash she'll do anything. She's like you, man.' He rubbed his fingers together. 'If she sees a pile of dough in it then she'll be there. D'you reckon you can make something from those pictures?' He paused. 'But you know Iris isn't happy. Iris reckons . . .'

Leslie was at once wide awake. He turned. 'What?'

Ratty shot a warning look. He shook his head and flapped one hand, silencing Desperate. He stood up. 'Shut it,' he whispered.

'What you on about?'

'Nothing,' replied Desperate, a little sheepishly.

Leslie turned to Ratty. 'What's he on about my mam for?'

'Nothing.'

'What's he mean?'

Ratty stepped quickly out into the lane and got into the

76

bike's sidecar. Following him, Desperate slung a leg over the machine.

'What d'you mean about my mam?'

'Work to do, people to see,' said Ratty, jovially, closing the door. '*Mazuma* to be made.' He pushed down the window. 'Don't do anything I wouldn't do, kid.'

Desperate saluted, winked, pressed the kick-start and with a roar they were off. Leslie stared after a cloud of blue exhaust and the ripple of litter disturbed in the gutter. He remembered the twins leaving his mother's front room that morning, after Shirley Bassey had finished her robust ballads. What on earth were they doing there? He pushed the thought away. '*Oh for the wings, for the wings of a dove,*' he sang, his voice successfully climbing up the octave, aware for the second time that the sentiments of the song were the exact opposite of everything he desired. '*Far away, far away would I rove. Oh for the wings, for the wings of a dove, far away, far away, far away, far away would I rove.*'

Unseen, unseeing, Sammy Schnitzler was inside, behind a curtain drawn against the sun, listening to the melody from an open window.

3

A couple of days later the weather was still hot and bright. Sammy Schnitzler drank from a glass of bicarbonate of soda and regarded Scotch Iris meaningfully. Pleased to see her, despite recent disagreements, he'd shut the door of his shop on her arrival and drawn down its blind, turning the sign to 'Closed'. A customer rattled the letterbox, but he ignored this, hearing the man curse before he moved away down the street.

'*Halevai*, your problems would be over, if only you'd marry me. God sits on high and makes matches below.' He was trying to sound reasonable rather than beseeching or angry. He was aware of having struck the wrong tone many, many times before.

Iris stood behind a barber's chair, regarding herself in the mirror, languidly fanning herself with one hand. She felt sleepy and depressed. She said nothing, she merely pressed the adjusting lever with her foot, raising, lowering, then again raising the chair. She yawned, covering her pretty teeth. Her chiffon scarf fell from her shoulders to the floor.

Sammy's moist eyes dropped to her dark pink stilettos, her diamond mesh stockings.

Easily, she spun the chair, collapsing into it with a sigh. Out of habit, she began reapplying her lipstick. It was cerise, to match her dress. Kissing her lips together, she smoothed the colour and returned the tube to her white plastic handbag, taking out a small glass medicine bottle. She swallowed a tablet, then tossed the bag aside. She picked up a tail-comb from the jar in front of the glass and began idly backcombing her blonde beehive. She plumped it up with her fingers in the usual way, then examined her dark roots, aware that they needed touching up. Scotch Iris was thirty-five, but she appeared younger. She was slim and small with a seductive, girlish manner. Sammy's gaze moved to her big eyes rimmed with pencil and mascara. They were unreadable. They were cold and hard, despite their beauty. He stared at her fingernails, which were long, pearly and exaggerated, their points predatory, if not cruel.

'I said your problems would be over, if only you'd marry me.'

'I heard you, so I did.'

'Well then, what have you got to say?'

'Change the record.'

'What?'

'I said change the record.'

Sammy turned to the gramophone. There was no music playing. He looked at her helplessly. 'I don't know . . .'

She turned around to face him. 'Are you going to lend me some fucking money or not?'

*

Scotch Iris lived in reasonable accommodation, in the scheme of things. She was half-way up the hill and had been a tenant of Sammy Schnitzler since before her second son was born, but she'd never given him a penny. She'd paid off her considerable debt when Geordie was six months old by submitting to sex with him every night for a week and pretending she'd liked it. Since then, she'd called at his house in De Grey Street on the first Thursday of every month, slipped between his camphor-smelling sheets for an hour and paid her rent in kind. As far as Iris was concerned, this was a satisfactory arrangement, especially as Sammy was also prepared to give her money on occasions and never pressed her to repay the loans.

From his point of view, the situation was less satisfactory. He regarded Scotch Iris as his girlfriend and he was saddened by her reputation, the scurrilous way her name might be mentioned by one of his customers, or by the visitors he'd sometimes observed entering and leaving her flat. He thought of her as misguided and needy, but felt that the regular and long-standing assignations between the two of them endowed him with some kind of a claim. He knew she'd been widowed by the war, a victim, as he was, of cataclysmic events played out on the European stage. He knew that, like himself, she was a tragic piece of flotsam washed up in this unlikely, alien neighbourhood. They had this in common and this created a special bond. But unlike him, she hadn't made a success of the succeeding years. She needed protection. She needed a firm, guiding hand.

Recently Iris had become sullen with him and very distant. She had changed and now she hardly ever smiled. She had begun swearing like a man, not in anger, but casually. Her face had got too thin and now she *never* agreed to waltz with him in his living-room, to the sound of his radiogram, allowing him to close his eyes briefly, feeling her slender back and shoulders, letting happy and far-distant memories of his youth rise briefly and delight him. But despite all this, Sammy loved Iris and love made him blind. Her delicate ankles and cheap scent made him faint with desire. More than anything, he wanted to rescue her from financial insecurity by turning her into respectable Mrs Schnitzler. She would wear a sensible quilted housecoat indoors, and in the street a nice tailored costume with gloves. He would buy her a decent three-piece suite, a washing-machine, even a refrigerator with an ice compartment. His plans were full and complicated, but his entreaties fell on deaf ears.

Recently he'd observed her on the arm of Mickey Robson, the local councillor, and this had made him speechless with anger. He knew that Councillor Robson was responsible for the demolition blitzkrieg of the surrounding streets. He was a modernizer, a damned socialist and an enemy of hard-working businessmen such as himself. Not only that, but because he stayed late at the Town Hall every night his wife had left him and now his beautiful, motherless little girls roamed these ruined streets like refugees, unloved, displaced and uncared for. As far as Sammy was concerned, Robson was a disgrace.

He knew that Councillor Robson lived way up past the park, a long way off in the semi-detached houses, and was unaware of the rumours, the gossip and the goings-on in Scotch Iris's notorious front room. He was tall and young and looked like Gregory Peck. He'd not known her long but he'd bought her a marcasite dress ring, which she sported on her engagement finger as if it was a real diamond. Everyone said that he took her dancing in the town. Sammy wanted to tell Robson that Iris was a no-good *nafke* whore but couldn't bring himself to say it. He wanted to tell her that this damned Gregory Peck was destroying the neighbourhood and was a hopeless family man, but he feared her cold eyes and her contempt. He swallowed his furious words along with his bicarbonate of soda and muttered curses. *Gey in drerd arayn*. Go into the earth and die!

'You should ask your fancy-man for money.' Sammy

tried to draw himself upwards, hold in his stomach. 'He's the one with the fashion *schmutters* and those . . . what you say? Those winkle-picker shoes. All I ever hear from you is money for this, money for that. I hope his head aches as much as my ear does, may his bones be drained of marrow!' He sipped from his glass and pressed his unsteady heart.

Scotch Iris stared at her own pinched reflection then transferred her gaze to his image in the mirror. The amphetamine was starting to buzz in her brain. Now she was beginning to feel in control. Anything was becoming possible. Deliberately softening her expression, she stood up and moved towards him, her arms open in a gesture of invitation. She stepped out of her shoes.

Sammy Schnitzler swallowed hard. He put down his glass, feeling a little wobbly. He fell to the floor as if in prayer and grasped Scotch Iris loosely around the knees. She leaned a little against him so that one of his saggy cheeks nestled against her thighs. With both hands she grasped the hem of her new cerise pink shift dress. Slowly, she wriggled and raised it past his face, above her stocking tops and suspenders. Sammy looked up at her imploringly as she pulled it above her waist.

*

Later, Iris met Ratty Schnitzler on the corner of Clumber Street. She watched him approach, unimpressed by his outlandish clothes, his nonchalant walk, the slouch of his shoulders, his air of owning the whole neighbourhood. I'm sick of this whole bloody family, she thought. These Schnitzlers. I wish I had nothing to do with either of them. I don't know which one gets on my nerves the most, so I don't, and that's the truth. Father and son both, they're

Jew-boy pains in the backside. She took out a tail-comb and backcombed a tuft of hair. She adjusted her weight from one high heel to another. 'Just give me the usual and don't mess me about,' she said sharply, as soon as the young man was within earshot. 'I'm not fucking *haggling*.' She looked up the hill nervously. Here was another disconcerting new gap in a terrace, as well as a fire from old timbers and an unusual view of the back lane beyond. Rubble was piled along the pavements and the air was dry with dust. A heavy ball on a chain was swinging and battering somewhere out of her line of vision. She had the disorientating feeling of not being at all sure where she was, of familiar boundaries shifting. The whole place is falling to the ground, she thought to herself. Involuntarily, she shuddered. She handed Ratty two five-pound notes, taken from his father an hour earlier. She frowned. 'All right?'

Ratty affected a conspiratorial smile.

'That's a lot of money, so it is.'

He took the notes and held them up to the light.

Iris snorted impatiently. 'Just *give* me the bloody pills, will you?'

'OK, OK, keep your hair on, baby.' Slowly, Ratty folded the money into his wallet. He whistled 'Apache' and looked about ostentatiously, as if expecting a police car to appear from around a corner.

Iris was impatient. 'Just *give them to me*, why don't you?'

Ratty took a small medicine bottle from inside his pocket, concealing it in the cup of his hand. He handed it over with a knowing smile. Iris grabbed it, unscrewed the top and swallowed two tablets. Out of their line of vision but close enough to observe everything, Constable

Henderson was half concealed around the corner of a back lane. He took out his notebook, made a pencilled entry, then, unseen, plodded away.

Wordlessly, Iris dropped the container into her bag, turned on her heel and minced off, her small hips swaying, her nylons rasping, self-consciously assuming Ratty's interested gaze.

He smiled at her departing figure but then looked elsewhere. He leaned against a lamp-post. Iris's charms did not appeal to him in any way. She was too old and she belonged to the past. Somewhere a fire engine wailed its way towards another demolition fire that was smoking up the distant sky. There was a crash and the roar of a lorry. The woman disappeared around a corner. Ratty smoothed the sides of his head, lit a cigarette and cupped it under his palm. His attention moved to the sharp outlines of the high-rise flats, taking shape behind his home. He held up his matchbox, positioning its rectangle within the modern symmetry of the distant block. It fitted perfectly.

*

That evening, there was a public meeting at the Wesley Hall. Councillor Mickey Robson was sitting on the stage within the main room, chain-smoking and nodding, a newspaper in his hand. He was accompanied by two tense-looking officials from the housing department and a stranger, a sleek, long-legged, sandy-haired man in a good quality double-breasted suit, who seemed relaxed and a little bored. In front of them, all the straight-backed pews were full and there was a low hum of expectant conversation. Here were a lot of Vickers workers who'd come straight off shift, as well as a handful of unwashed

pitmen from the Monty colliery and some local shopkeepers, although Sammy Schnitzler was missing. Also present
were a large number of women, some with young children
on their knees. People fanned their faces against the warm,
stuffy air and fidgeted. A couple of babies cried.

Scotch Iris was conspicuous and her chemical mood
was now one of nervous excitement. She sat in the second
row, head on one side, smiling flirtatiously and waving
up at Mickey whenever he caught her eye. She had
changed into a deep red imitation silk dress with a low
scooped neck and full, see-through nylon sleeves, gathered
at the wrists. She wore costume jewellery, white gloves
and white stilettos and her hair was piled up in a loopy
topknot, sprayed with lacquer.

Muriel and Maureen were out of control and acting
childishly. They chased each other around the room,
squealing and pelting each other with mint imperials.
Their father tried to shush them half-heartedly with
hand gestures, but they took no notice. He grinned a little
shamefacedly into the audience. The seated mothers
glanced at the twins, disapproving, glad their own restless
offspring were better behaved, feeling sorry for Mickey
because they knew his wife had abandoned him.

Through the rafts of cigarette smoke which drifted
around the crowd, motes of dust floated upwards from
the floor. These were caught like specks of gold in the
dying sun, which still managed to stream through the
windows. High above, the dim space within the steeply
pitched ceiling seemed stale with the trapped words of
a hundred years of public prayer and endeavour. It
weighed down the space inside the building, giving an air
of importance and permanence to the place. There was
something complacent about its dingy, cream-painted

brick, its fly-speckled lights, the plastic flowers in vases, the posted schedules for bible classes, Cubs and Brownies, the new piano covered over with a tablecloth. Here, the Wesley Hall stood firm, unaware of the advancing demolition gang. It seemed as secure as Methodism itself. However, Mickey Robson's sandy-haired friend in the good suit looked around, a little impatiently. He glanced at his watch. He knew the whole place would be down in a matter of weeks.

Laying down his paper, Mickey got to his feet and there was coughing, a scraping of chairs, then silence. The twins giggled loudly from the back then disappeared out of the door, deliberately letting it shut with a reverberating bang.

'Ladies and gentlemen,' Mickey said authoritatively. He was tall, dashing and handsome in his sports jacket, red tie and dark slacks. The women in the audience regarded him with shy interest. Most of the men felt intimidated by his manner. He had one hand in his pocket and the other gesticulated importantly. 'Thank you for coming.' He paused. 'You will all have received notification about phase two of the clearance programme in this ward. We are here tonight to listen to your concerns and answer your queries. It is with great pleasure I introduce to you the leader of the city council.' He paused and turned. 'Mr Newcastle himself, Councillor T. Dan Smith.' He clapped his hands, signalling the need for a polite ripple of applause. A toddler called out from the middle row, 'I want wee-wee!' and nervous laughter accompanied the embarrassed mother's exit from the room. Smith didn't smile. He stood up and moved around in front of the table to address the gathering.

*

Leslie and Geordie walked along Beaumont Street. The sun had begun to sink, turning the sky pinkish-blue above the rooftops. Leslie held his pack of cards in his hands and shuffled dextrously. The stiffened paper oblongs flew between his expert fingers. Earlier he'd noticed that his brother's face and arms were a little burnt from the sun and he'd smeared him liberally with calamine lotion, which now gave Geordie a chalky-white, unearthly look. The smaller boy seemed unaware. He was preoccupied with something. He walked in his usual strange way, taking small steps, his arms stiff at his sides. His head was down and he was muttering the same words over and over again. 'Delavel Road, Benwell Lane, Adelaide Terrace, Elswick Road, Westgate Road.' This was the journey of the trolley-buses that he had been observing all day. He knew the route, indeed all the routes of all the buses in the city, off by heart, as well as their numbers, fares and timetables. Of course, he'd never travelled on one. Like Leslie, he'd rarely left the streets around his home. 'Adelaide Terrace, Elswick Road, Westgate Road, Grainger Street, Monument.'

Leslie was used to this obsessiveness and it comforted him, because it meant that Geordie was calm. He put his cards back in his pocket. He looked at the tall crane and the skeletal block of flats in the distance, their metal structures a black and intricate tracery against the vivid backdrop behind. He linked his brother's arm. 'Monument,' he agreed. He thought about the letter from the council, the 'shifting' letter, in his shoebox under the bed, and his heart lurched.

As they approached the Wesley Hall they became aware of a long, expensive-looking car, parked outside. The twins were sitting on top of it. One of them was perched on the bonnet, the other on the roof. Geordie stopped and stared and Leslie regarded him anxiously. However, it was immediately clear to him that his brother was unaware of the girls. He was completely transfixed by the vehicle. It was rare to see any car at all in these streets, and this one was exceptional with its red glossy paintwork and immaculate chrome. Leslie knew that when Geordie was this interested in something he was totally unaware of people, even those as potentially disturbing to him as the twins.

'Jaguar Mark Eleven saloon,' muttered Geordie, his voice hoarse with excitement. The boys approached.

'You shouldn't be sitting up there,' called out Leslie, indignantly, unable to help himself. He felt enraged. These twins seemed to think they could do as they liked. He remembered the horrible words chalked up outside his front door. 'That car must belong to someone important.'

'Take a running jump,' responded Muriel.

'Yeah,' agreed her sister. 'Take a long jump off a short pier.'

Geordie walked around the car, scrutinizing its every detail.

The girls regarded him a little nervously. 'What's the dafty doing?' Muriel asked, pointing with the toe of her sandal. 'Who does he think he's looking at?'

Geordie crouched down, taking in the line of the head-lamps and radiator grille. The registration plate, Leslie noticed, said 'DAN 60'.

'Your George is filling his pants,' suggested Maureen, her voice uncertain.

'Get him away from us,' her sister demanded. 'Why's he all white, like that? He looks like a damned spook.'

'He's a vampire. He's the living dead.' The girl made an ugly face, poking out her tongue.

'Bugger off,' retorted Leslie. He was pleased he'd said this. He touched his brother's shoulder. More gently he said, 'Come on. Let's go in.'

The girls shrieked with derision. 'Bugger off, oh yes, bugger off, oh yes, yes, please, just *bugger off*, will you?' Muriel called out, in both high and low tones, imitating the unsteadiness of Leslie's breaking voice. 'Ginger, you're barmy,' hooted the other, 'you want to join the army!' They pretended to laugh hysterically, holding their sides. 'Is that a wig on Leslie's head or what?' screeched Muriel. 'Wiggy the ginger tomcat,' insisted her sister. 'It's been dead for weeks!'

Geordie turned and stepped back towards them, avoiding his brother's restraining hand. Leslie noticed that he was tense, his neck rigid.

Straight away silenced, the girls slid down off the car, clearly afraid. Leslie knew that glowing within the whiteness of his calamine lotion, Geordie's eyes would be glassy-green and strange. 'Go away!' one of the girls whispered. 'He's coming for us,' offered the other. 'Leslie! Get him away from us!'

Geordie spoke. 'Miss-us Angela Robson's on the other side of a great big sea,' he said clearly and without emotion.

'What?' The girls moved together and held each other.

'Miss-us Angela Robson met a new fellah on the ship. She's thousands and thousands and thousands of miles away.'

Maureen's lower lip trembled. She clutched her sister. 'Listen! He's talking about our mam.'

'Miss-us Angela Robson's Miss-us Angela Clark now. She's got a new baby with Mis-ter Clark. They're in Australia. And you know what? She's never, ever coming back.' Geordie paused, returned to himself and joined his brother at the entrance to the Wesley Hall.

Leslie stared at the twins. They were both crying, only soundlessly. They clung together as if they were lost. 'He said our mam's not coming back,' murmured Muriel. Her sister agreed. 'He said our mam's got a new baby.' Leslie pushed open the door, guiding Geordie inside. Well that serves *them* right, he thought. That's shut *them* up. The buggers.

*

Inside, the Leader of the Council was standing on the stage addressing his audience. Leslie and Geordie sat in the back row of the hard wooden pews. Leslie looked up. I'll be there tomorrow, he realized. On that stage. I'll be there singing in the youth club talent contest in front of a big crowd like this one. His heart somersaulted with anticipation and dread.

In front of them was a narrow shelf, used for hymn books, gloves and suchlike. Geordie hunched his back and ran his fingers up and down it, as if he were playing the piano, his eyes closed in concentration. The calamine on his face glowed like white stage make-up.

Leslie's mind wandered. He tried to imagine himself sweeping up the dust, or stacking basins at Adamsez. It seemed more unlikely than ever. He then tried, for reasons unknown, to picture himself on his hands and knees with a small brush, cleaning under the seats of a trolley-bus. In his mind's eye the bus was suddenly speeding along, crossing the river on its way to the place called Prudhoe.

Here, within the weedy crater of an old bombsite, he imagined an ancient, blackened hospital building with bars at the windows. From inside came the wails and lamentations of lunatics. This was Geordie's potential prison and the thought of it made him panicky. He pushed the thought to one side. Leslie distrusted his imagination and he was uncomfortable about the way it was working overtime at present. He focused his attention on the front of the hall and tried to understand what the speaker was saying. He realized T. Dan Smith was talking about the town centre.

'We will have a city in the image of Athens, Florence or Rome,' he declared, his voice carrying impressively, 'although I prefer to think of it as the *Brasilia of the North*.'

Leslie had never heard of Brasilia but he tried to summon up a view of ancient European elegance and gracious ruins at the far end of the trolley-bus line. It was impossible.

Smith raised both his hands in a supplicating gesture. 'I say no to apathy! I say no to philistinism!'

Leslie studied him, interested. He had the flushed cheeks that come with a heart condition but he was tall, even taller than Councillor Robson, and just as confident. Despite his size, he moved gracefully, his elegant suit demonstrating the perfect fit of bespoke tailoring. Leslie decided that he was behaving as if used to addressing a much bigger audience. His local accent was slightly overlaid with something else, a kind of assumed gentility and an indicator of a belief in his own superiority that he must have picked up on trips to London. He was forceful, authoritative, and his voice carried without being loud.

'This canny toon of ours will be the city of the future. We'll see an end to post-war torpor, complacency, to everything that's second-rate. No longer will we North-Easterners be humiliated by a lack of opportunity. No longer will we be seen as backward. We'll all *aim for the sky*. This will be a regional capital worthy of the name. We'll hire the very best architects, the very best designers. Newcastle will become the most outstanding provincial city in the country. And you, the people of this great city, you will *rally to the bigger idea*!'

Geordie was oblivious. He continued his imaginary piano-playing, eyes closed, hair tossing, shoulders bobbing, his fingers flying up and down, enraptured by the complicated sounds in his own head. His white arms and face glowed.

A man sitting in front of the boys turned round. He gestured towards the speaker. 'The mouth of the Tyne,' he whispered disparagingly, grinning at Leslie for a moment, before staring at Geordie, his smile fading.

Leslie nodded. 'Yes,' he agreed, trying to appear friendly.

After a few more minutes there was a chair-scraping, foot-shuffling restlessness growing in the audience. 'What about Scotswood Road?' a brave soul called out loudly, interrupting. 'Never mind the town, man. We know the Council's pulling it all down and rebuilding. What we want to know is, what about *us*?'

'What about our houses?' someone else agreed, picking up the cue.

'Hear, hear!'

'What about them who don't want to go? They get nothing but trouble at their doors.'

'Fires!' someone agreed.

'Broken windows!'

'There's those who's trying to force them out!'

At this, the Council officials at the back of the stage shook their heads vehemently.

'What's happening to Scotswood Road?'

'Yes, man. What's happening to Scottie Road?'

T. Dan Smith paused, looked down at the front row and coughed delicately, somewhat discomfited. He took out a folded white handkerchief and mopped his brow. There was a brief silence as he rearranged his thoughts. 'Scotswood Road?' he demanded incredulously. 'That grimy, unlovable, old-fashioned artery? My friends, it will become a thing of the past.'

There was a cacophony of shouts. 'Where we going?'

'When's this happening?'

'Not us!'

'Shame!'

'Says who?'

The speaker smiled and held up a hand, requesting silence. The protests subsided.

'I believe in efficiency,' Smith said defiantly, 'and I believe in planning. The property around here is poor, dilapidated and it is let at inflated prices. Many of you have no modern amenities and you are frequently over-crowded. This area has an excess of pubs and unhygienic shops. These streets here have got to go and they *will* go.' He paused.

There was a silence in the room as if the people felt personally criticized. Someone coughed with an indignant tone.

Scotch Iris had stopped listening to the voices of the meeting a while before. Her thoughts were completely elsewhere. Her fingers were clenched and her long nails were cutting into the palms of her hands. In her head she could hear the roar of the sea, the howl of a gale, feel a storm whipping her hair and clothes. But this particular evening there was no tiny matchwood fishing vessel tossing in her fantasy, no helpless fishermen, no struggling husband, the long-lost love of her life. Instead her terror was focused on a scene much, much closer to her current situation. She pictured the hillside of Elswick, not bathed in sunshine like today, but rather on a windy, cold, weatherbeaten night. Instead of the stoical ranks of terraces, corner shops and pubs there was nothing familiar. In Iris's vivid imagining, the bulldozers and gangs had been and gone and all that was left was a potholed slope, an emptiness of wailing wind, a wide open, unfriendly sky and no landmarks. Her fear created a fusion in her mind between the present day slum-clearance, memories of wartime Glasgow during the Blitz and that Godless night when her man had been taken away from herself and her boys. She was tense with fright. She opened her eyes wide, took a pill from her bag and discreetly swallowed it. She dragged herself back to the Wesley Hall and tried to concentrate.

T. Dan Smith continued. 'My aim is to redevelop slumland. It's not just a question of rehousing. Here you'll get parks, you'll get community buildings, you'll get modern shopping centres. And schools. You need new schools. The schools here are a disgrace.' He took a deep breath. 'If we can launch ships in the North-East we can launch human beings. And I'm going to make sure we launch our children into a renewed world where there are books, where there is art, where there is decent architecture, a proper university, music, libraries, culture . . .'

The man in front of Leslie stood up. 'Right man, but where are we *going*?' He sat down again suddenly, his cheeks burning. The audience turned around, stared, then looked back up at the speaker, expectantly.

Smith swallowed, then pointed. 'Hundreds of you families live in slums. More than ten thousand citizens in this town want council housing. They are crying out for council housing. But what is our problem here? There's no building land available within the city boundaries. Like you, when I first shouldered this responsibility, I asked my brother planners, I said to them, where are all the people to go? But unlike the Tories before us, *we* came up with answers. *We've* got courage and vision. In our new Planning Department, dare I say the first of its kind in the country, we've made some difficult decisions. Good decisions.' He paused, turned and took a drink of water from a glass on the table. His cheeks were even redder than before. 'Some of you will follow your neighbours to those pleasant new estates on the outskirts where there are trees, open fields and birdsong. You'll breathe clean air and have plenty of space to raise your families. Meanwhile, we'll get on with clearing this area and . . .' He brushed his hair back from his brow in a fey, mannered gesture. 'As soon as there's room, as soon as some new flats are finished some of you may be offered modern accommodation right here. Here in Elswick itself.'

Leslie thought about the skeleton houses in the sky behind Ratty Schnitzler's house on De Grey Street, so high that birds flew below the window sills. *Oh for the wings, for the wings of a dove* . . . He glanced at Geordie who was now slumped back on his pew, staring at the ceiling. A little dribble of saliva had escaped the corner of his mouth. Leslie took out a handkerchief and gently wiped it away.

'The war is long over. We are turning our back on the fifties and all that post-war stagnation, that failure of nerve. And make no mistake,' Smith continued, 'we are clearing away more than the Germans ever managed to do. We are building good, modern, well-fitted flats and our new developments will be as attractive as possible. Around the blocks there will be landscaped open space and sculpture parks. In the evenings, discreet floodlighting will carry the verdant greenness of the lawns and the dappled shadows of the trees out into the north-east night.'

There was a stunned silence in the room.

'We will stimulate interest in the arts and architecture *within the very fabric* of these estates. We will attract people to the area and, I assure you, they'll not just be investors and new industrialists. People will come to Elswick, make special journeys to Elswick to look, to wonder and to marvel. Not only will you be better housed, my friends, not only will you be safer, more comfortable, cleaner and warmer, *you will also be proud*! You will be *proud* to tell the world that you, yes, you are lucky enough to live in Newcastle's modern west end!' Smith paused, mopped his brow again, then smiled. 'Let me leave you with a poem,' he offered. 'This is a poem about cities, about cities as a whole, about places where people live and work and play.' He took a slip of paper out of his breast pocket. 'Cities are what men make them, whatever these cities may be, slothful, slovenly, sleepy ... progressive, beautiful, free.' He paused for effect. 'If the hearts of the builders are noble, at one with the day and the deed, they'll grow into greatness and grandeur, for thus it was ever decreed.' He raised one hand, as if making a vow. 'Though they cleave to the breasts of mountains, or nestle by rivers broad, cities are what men make them, on land that is given of ... God.' Smith stared at his audience for several, wordless seconds. '*Progressive, beautiful, free,*' he repeated. Then he turned to Mickey Robson and stepped back, indicating he'd finished.

A quiet hubbub broke out among the audience, which quickly rose in volume. The man in front of Leslie got to his feet and began applauding. His big callused hands slapped together like thunder above the voices. Gradually, along the rows, everyone else stood up, copying their neighbour, clapping enthusiastically. Women held babies aloft to get a proper look. People started cheering.

T. Dan Smith bowed modestly. A grinning Mickey Robson grabbed him, pumped his arm up and down, then enfolded him in an embrace. The officials from the housing department stood at the back of the stage, smiling at each other in relief. Residents broke ranks and a surge of people moved to the front, reaching up to the council leader on the stage. He bent down like an evangelist, holding out both hands to be shaken. The atmosphere in the room had become electric, festive, celebratory.

At the back, Geordie still lay back, staring at the ceiling. Leslie nudged him, pulled him to his feet and led him outside.

The girls were now sitting on a wall. It was getting dark. Geordie stared again at the Jaguar, which glinted in the gloom.

The twins ignored the two brothers. 'Is our dad finished in there yet?' Maureen asked a couple of women who'd followed the boys out.

'We want our tea,' agreed her sister. They both sounded subdued. 'We're cold and we're starving.'

Leslie linked Geordie's arm, crossed the street. At that moment Smith, Mickey Robson, Iris and the officials all emerged and were immediately surrounded by a throng of well-wishers pouring from the building. Smith was helped into his driving seat as if he were royalty and then a respectful gap widened in the crowd as he started the engine and eased the car up the hill. More cheers broke out as everyone waved him goodbye. Mickey slipped the twins a banknote and then left them. He walked up the hill with happy Labour Party members, Iris on his arm.

Leslie set off for Glue Terrace. He held Geordie's hand. The twins were right, he decided. It was colder. There was a nip in the air, which suggested autumn wasn't far away. The sky was now stained dark red, orange and purple. In the distance, demolition fires flickered again and there was a smell of burning. The moon glimmered from behind a cloud. A ship on the invisible river hooted and was answered by another. Geordie was walking slowly. He shivered without a jacket. They huddled together, like the twins had done, like two little urchins, one scruffy, the other exquisite, their feet dragging over the cobbles.

'Shall we go and see Auntie Ada?' Leslie felt guilty about his rudeness to her earlier in the day. He missed the security of her upstairs kitchen. He thought for a minute as they trudged along. He was not unaffected by the spirit of the meeting. 'That man in the posh suit might shift us to a new house,' he said gently. 'A house in the sky.' He thought for a moment. 'He believes in the modern world.' Leslie's feeling of rebellion had been partly dissipated. Maybe it'll be all right, he reasoned. The three of us will shift. Our mam will get better, that hospital in Prudhoe will forget about Geordie and we'll all be happy up in the sky with the birds. He squeezed his brother's hand. 'Everything's going to be all right.'

Geordie was at once lucid. 'That man in the posh suit's got a nice car,' he asserted. 'Carmen Red. Twin cam, three point four litre straight six engine. Four speed manual with overdrive. Thank you Leslie.' He stopped in his tracks, letting go of his brother's hand. He stared away from the sunset into the inky distance where it was truly dark. He was suddenly tense and knowing. His tone changed. 'That man in the posh suit's in a cell. He's wearing a uniform and eating his dinner with a spoon.' He hesitated then continued. 'He's locked up in a gaol with lots and lots of bad men.'

*

Sammy Schnitzler sat in his living-room listening to his new radiogram. A Siamese cat rubbed against his trousers and Ratty's old dog snored on the hearthrug. Rachmaninov's first piano concerto played loudly. The barber was wearing an ancient, stained smoking-jacket, buttoned over his paunch, although he didn't smoke and had never done so. An unread newspaper was folded down the side of his armchair. As the massive and emotional chords of the music rose and fell, fat, immigrant tears welled in his creased and world-weary eyes. He listened, trembling, with memories of Vienna. He thought of the gracious trees by the Danube, the elegance of the Ringstrasse, games of bridge at the Prukel coffeehouse and the comfort of their creamy *eispanner*. He remembered the hot, fresh *strudels*, the conversation, the urbane politeness of the waiters. He thought of the golden tones of the strings at the Philharmonic, the sophistication of the Opera House, the rhythmic sound of soldiers' boots, the crowds who'd cheered behind the big black car, picking up, kissing the very stones it passed upon as Hitler . . . No! He snapped his mind shut and returned to the present. Gently he pushed the Siamese away and stroked the old dog with his slippered foot. He sighed.

Sammy was having his supper, which consisted of a cup of warmed water and a plate of digestive biscuits. Apart from frequent glasses of bicarbonate of soda, this was the only food that had passed his lips since the middle of the war. He dunked a biscuit into the cup and sucked on it, sadly. He smoothed his sparse, oiled hair. Despite the earlier warmth of the day, the outside temperature had by now dropped significantly and his electric fire burned on both bars, smelling of charred dust after months of being switched off. Its little mirrored wheel turned before an orange bulb, giving the illusion of flickering flames.

In the window, in front of the closed floral curtains, Ratty's budgerigar hopped between its perches, tweeting and trilling along with the music. Sammy regarded it in a puzzled way. He disliked seeing creatures in cages but this bird's optimistic personality seemed to defy and contradict its life of imprisonment.

'Pretty Billy,' Sammy chirruped in response. 'Pretty Billy Billy Birdy.'

'Pretty Billy Billy Birdy,' his little feathered friend replied.

The piano music flowed, soared, groaned and crashed its way to its finale. Sammy wiped his lips on a napkin then dabbed his eyes. He got up, dusted his wide lap of imaginary crumbs, raised the lid of the radiogram and moved the stylus arm to start the record over again. The heart-rending melody began once more.

Sammy sat heavily and put his hand to his chest where there was angina pain that he chose to believe was disappointment. He considered his son, who'd left the house earlier that evening with soldier-boy, intending to sell bundles of kindling wood around the doors. He'd been whistling an awful tune, which all day seemed to jangle from his transistor radio.

'I know this guitarist,' he'd repeated, mysteriously.

Sammy didn't doubt it. He was sure his son knew all manner of unsatisfactory characters. He spent his life wheeling and dealing and hanging around dubious establishments with *arumloyfers* and lowlifes and individuals wanted by the police. He certainly wasn't interested in saving or investing or setting himself up in a nice little shop.

Sammy sighed. He'd asked his boy to stay indoors tonight in order to discuss the future. He'd disobeyed of course. He'd simply shrugged on one of his dreadful jackets, declaring, 'It's colder tonight, Pops. Folks'll be starting to think about fires.' Then he'd stepped into the hallway with sniggering soldier-boy, combing his too-long hair into what was vulgarly termed in Sammy's trade a 'duck's arse', as vain as a woman.

Sammy was dismayed by Ratty because he had no staying power. His only real enthusiasm was pets and caged birds. Other than this, he went anywhere, did anything that merely involved making a quick ten shillings in order to finance his bad habits. He wanted fast returns and fast gratification. He seemed to have no proper plans. As well as unreliably collecting his rents, keeping a big percentage, his son was employed by a department store, giving and collecting credit payments all over the area. This was a hit and miss endeavour, as most of his clients were short of money apart from on Fridays. He also embarked on small, ever-changing schemes that varied as frequently as his outrageous jackets. Sammy despaired of him ever settling to anything because he appeared not to believe in real hard work.

Pushing thoughts of Ratty aside, Sammy could not help worrying some more about his own business, the threat to his livelihood, the paltry compensation which would be offered by the council when they pulled down his flats. A quarter of his tenants had already gone and the rest were soon to follow. Not only that, he anguished, his barber shop was also under threat. For one thing, his customers were being dispersed like Jews. For another, before too long, he might expect the shop itself to fall to the demolition gang. He knew that resistance was futile. It would only produce short-term harassment like dog-dirt and fireworks through the letterbox. He sighed, rubbed the upper left side of his chest again, allowing his lonely thoughts to move to Iris. I'll win her over one way or another, he thought. Eventually. I'll wear her down. He tried to smile. Mrs Iris Schnitzler. Mr and Mrs Schnitzler of De Grey Street. Schnitzler the barber and his lady wife, Iris.

Returning home from work, Sammy had seen Scotch Iris on her way to the Wesley Hall, where he knew the communist vandal child-neglecter Councillor Mickey Robson was holding a meeting tonight. She'd waved to him but she hadn't stopped. She'd clack-clacked past on her high heels, her nose in the air. She looks like a dog's dinner when she's going out with him, he decided. A dog's dinner. A curious English phrase. What in the old country we always called an *oisgetsatsket*. An overdressed woman. Perhaps I'll go and see him and tell him all about all those visitors she entertains in that front room of hers. Maybe *that* will make him think again, I should live so long. He rehearsed his conversation with the councillor in his head. He brought to mind some choice English phrases, learned at an evening class years before. He concluded by going on the attack and remonstrating with him about his daughters. It's a disgrace, he imagined himself saying, not providing those two little angels with a proper, decent home. You shirker! You lax, remiss failure of a father! He pictured the girls in his mind's eye. They were picking their way through the ruins of the demolition sites, abandoned, motherless, their white skirts and hair ribbons fluttering, their pale limbs luminous against the rubble. The poor innocents had no one, no one in the world except enemies, predators and despoilers who were determined to rob them of their chastity. It was an outrage. Sammy blew his nose on his napkin, then lifted his arms. From his armchair he began mournfully, sorrowfully to conduct the second movement of the concerto. His eyes were closed and his heart ached. The music filled the room in a dizzying, disorientating manner. He became lost, the decades fell away, his mind strayed back to the Schonbrunn Palace in Vienna, the gardens, the glasshouses and the obelisk cascade. Here it was always autumn, a weak sun gilding the beauty of his city, a cold nip in the air presaging the bleak events that were shortly to declare themselves and ruin his entire world.

*

At ten o'clock, Leslie sat at the Scottish piano in the dingy kitchen of Iris's downstairs flat, practising his vocal scales. His voice soared and dropped, soared and dropped, then all at once croaked horribly. His throat was rough and exhausted. It's going, he thought. My beautiful voice is going for ever and ever and ever amen. He slammed down the piano lid and rubbed his hands together. He blew on his knuckles. I hope I can manage the talent contest. I don't want to make a charlie of myself in front of all those people. He thought about Mr Green. Everything's going to be all right. That was splendid, Leslie, he imagined the choirmaster saying. Splendid.

Geordie was sitting at the table drawing the Jaguar. He drew the outline, then the backdrop of the street and the Wesley Hall, omitting the twins. He began applying detail to the car, remembering with absolute precision the hubcaps, the line of the windows, the curved, seductive mounds of the classic styling. He drew the door handles, the wipers, the bumpers and then the ornate architrave of the Methodist building, the carved stone motto above the door 'In God We Trust'.

Leslie watched him for the moment. He turned on the electric light, which was the only one in Glue Terrace. He was trying to avoid looking at the unpaid bills on the mantelpiece. He tossed some kindling into the dead hearth. Cheerful Ratty had given him this, free, at the door half an hour before. 'Don't say I never give you anything,' the youth had insisted. Then he'd added, mysteriously, 'Have you seen those little twins? Are they here?'

'No they're not!' Leslie had responded crossly. 'Why are you asking me that?'

'OK, OK,' responded Ratty genially, climbing on to the back of his friend's bike. 'Keep your hair on!' The sidecar, Leslie noticed, was full of bundles of wood.

At the hearth, Leslie crumpled up some newspaper and pressed it down among the sticks. He threw on half a bucket of coal then lit the paper with a match. He held up his hands to the blaze. I shouldn't have been so rude to Ratty, he decided. He's a good friend. I was rude to Auntie Ada too. He felt guilty. 'I'll make some soft-boiled eggs,' he said to his brother. 'Do you fancy a boiled egg and toast fingers, Geordie?' He felt disconcerted by his own rebelliousness, the failure of his good nature. He felt unlike himself, unsettled, ill at ease. He tried to bring to mind the stained-glass Virgin from the church window, with her ever-open arms, but she refused to appear.

After a while the two boys sat quietly, dipping charred bread into the golden centres of their eggs. The fire had smoked a little because the chimney was cold, but at last it was blazing satisfactorily.

'If our mam marries that Coon-sill man from up the park,' Geordie said slowly but rationally, 'then those girls will be our . . .' He looked impassive. He paused. 'Sisters.' He licked yolk from his fingers.

Leslie was startled. This wasn't a prophecy. Geordie was in the here and now, meeting his eye. It was rare for his brother to venture this type of opinion. Leslie said nothing in reply, but imagined their mother at this moment, possibly in some dark rum and black nightclub, doing the cha-cha-cha with a lithe and energetic Mickey Robson. He refused to let his mind take him further. His mother was lost to him already, changed, horribly altered, unlike her old self. He didn't want to contemplate a future where there might be wedding bells with unacceptable twin bridesmaids, or men in white coats come to take his brother away, or even a removal wagon to shift them both to a high-rise above the clouds with 'modern amenities and pedestrian walkways'. 'I'll get a job,' he said instead. 'And even if we do have to move from here to some sculpture park or something, I'll make sure at least we're on the ground floor.'

'No!' said Geordie, forcibly.

'No?'

'No!' Geordie's hands shook and his lower lip trembled.

'Don't worry,' insisted Leslie hurriedly. 'We'll stay here.

I'll get a job at Vickers and you'll become a famous artist with your pictures hanging in London . . . and Manchester . . . and Sunderland.'

'Pictures in Sunderland.'

'That's right.'

'Sunderland.'

'Yes. I'm sure of it.'

'Sunderland. Pictures in Sunderland. My pictures.'

'That's what I said.'

'Sunderland.' Geordie picked up his eggshell and examined it as if he had never seen such a thing before in his life.

Despite the lateness of the hour, the tune of an optimistic ice-cream seller tinkled in the street outside. Again, with a rush of joy, Leslie recalled them both on the beach, years before, with Geordie running out of the sea and holding out his hand for a melting ice-cream, which he himself held up, which their mother had bought from a van. Geordie was laughing. They'd all been laughing. It was a magical moment. 'Do you remember going on that trip to Cullercoats?' he asked.

Geordie continued examining the eggshell, as if he was deaf.

Leslie took the photograph from his shirt pocket. 'Do you? Do you remember Cullercoats? Look. Here you are. Look at this.'

There was no response.

'Tell me you remember. Our mam was happy here. She was her old self, buying ice-creams, telling jokes. She took this photo of you.'

Geordie laid down the shell and stared at the wall. His shoulders stiffened. His green eyes were dense, unfathomable, glowing like gorgeous emeralds in the smeared calamine-whiteness of his face. He was making another prediction. 'That place you went to. For a job? Today? It's closed down. It's shut up. No more basins. No more lavvy pans. It's got broken windows. Nobody works there any more. It's bust. It's finished. Gone.'

After a while, Leslie put Geordie to bed and the youngster lay propped up, studying his trolley-bus timetables. The older boy went to the scullery to get a glass of water and as he returned he thought he heard voices coming from the front street. He stood in the hall. There was giggling and the tinkle of girlish laughter. Oh no, he thought. He put his hand on the latch but his heart was racing. He couldn't face another confrontation. They're out there, he thought, it's nearly midnight and they're up to heaven-knows-what kind of mischief. At that moment the letterbox rattled and, startled, he jumped backwards. A folded piece of paper fell on to the mat. Tentatively he picked it up. His name was on the outside. He opened it, relieved to discover it was nothing more than a note, pencilled in a childish hand. It read:

Your mams a Prozzie and a big Hore
Your mams been with evry man in elswick we know
Leslee, we will kill to deth that nasty George MacD with
    stones when we get him on his own

Leslie scrumpled up the paper and, in the dark kitchen, threw it on the dying fire.

*

In the middle of the night, the front door slammed noisily, announcing Scotch Iris's return. In the big double bed, in the small back bedroom, which they shared, both Leslie and Geordie turned over but did not waken. Geordie's slumbers were deep and dark but Leslie was dreaming about the Queen. She was dressed in an ermine-trimmed cloak and the Crown jewels, just as she had been at her coronation. In the dream, despite the cramped nature of their back kitchen, she skilfully manoeuvred her finery in order to serve both himself and Geordie tea. She brought in plate after plate of sandwiches, scones, cakes and orange jelly in little glass bowls. Leslie's mouth watered. Beyond the yard, bombs were falling and exploding in an air raid and there was the low, terrifying whine of fighter planes. 'We have this at the palace,' she confided, ignoring the mayhem outside. 'His Royal Highness the Prince of Wales is very fond of orange jelly.'

Eventually she sat down, still wearing her crown, and picked up their big chipped brown teapot, intending to pour. 'You two boys tuck in,' she said, kindly. 'You look like you need a good feed.'

4

The next morning Scotch Iris and her friend Betty stood outside a house on Rye Hill with the twins. It was eleven o'clock and the sun beat down without mercy. In the distance there was a roar of bulldozers and diggers, but this street, with its decaying but elegant Victorian villas, had so far been spared the planner's zeal. Here, each dwelling was a multitude of bed-sits, with a transient, unsettled population of gypsies, seamen, burglars and jazz musicians. Some dwellings had broken windows and rusty pram wheels in their gardens, others had closed curtains, smells of spicy food and blues rhythms beating from guitars and drums.

One or two cars chugged by on their way into town. A rag-and-bone man clip-clopped past, his cart laden with three old gas cookers. A group of half-caste children swung on a rope tied to the street lamp.

'The three of you should stop this,' said Iris, impatiently. 'This whole thing's gone too far. I don't like it. I've never liked it.'

'You're right,' agreed Betty. 'I think we should call it a day.' Betty's face was bloated and caked in orange panstick. Her dyed black hair was thin from too much perming solution. She leaned against a wall, as if tired and worn out from a life on the streets.

'You started it, Betty,' said Maureen, to Iris's friend. She poked out her tongue, rudely.

'It was your idea,' agreed Muriel.

'Well, it's time to end it,' argued Iris. She pushed her

sunglasses up into her bouffant hair and regarded the twins keenly. Her expression was pinched, displeased. 'It's not a game and it's dangerous, so it is.'

'We like the money.'

'It's easy.' The twins were defiant. They linked arms and stood their ground.

Iris raised her voice. 'Someone's bound to find out. And you'll both end up in one of those approved schools. So you will, both of you. An approved school. They lock you in and feed you on bread and water.'

Maureen bent down and adjusted the tops of her ankle socks. Muriel opened a packet of Smarties and tipped the tube into her mouth. She munched ecstatically. 'We'll tell our dad about the whole thing if you don't shut up.'

Scotch Iris froze. This was her greatest fear. 'You dare.'

Maureen picked up the cue. 'We'll tell him *you* made us. We'll say you forced us. We'll tell him it was all *your* idea, not Betty's.' She poked her tongue out.

Iris's pale face turned white. She took off her sunglasses, folding them into her shoulder bag, her hands shaking visibly.

'He won't take you to any nightclubs *then*, will he? He won't buy you any more of those rings or dresses or rum and blacks. No, I don't think so.' Maureen straightened up, hands on her hips. 'He'll go right off his rocker. He'll probably call the polis.' She paused. 'He'll get the army and the magistrates and . . . the nuns.'

'He'll get the air force and the navy,' added Muriel. 'He'll have you thrown in *prison*.'

Iris hesitated. She lit a cigarette, took two puffs, then tossed it to the ground and stamped on it.

Betty yawned and adjusted her tight skirt over her ample thighs.

'He'll probably kill you,' offered Muriel. 'That's what he said he'll do to our mam if he ever finds her. Strangle her. He'll definitely do you in. He'll kill you stone dead with his own bare hands.'

Agitated, Iris paced ten yards to the corner as if about to leave. Her high heels clacked and her bottom wiggled inside her lime-green capri pants. Muriel made as if to follow her, copying her walk in an exaggerated way.

Betty was calm. She chewed gum lazily and straightened her nylons. 'All right then. Shut up you two. Just do as you're damn well told for once and get it over with.' She adjusted her scuffed slingbacks and pointed to a house. 'Number sixteen. Top floor. Flat six B. Just another old wanker. A dirty old man. Don't let him touch you, mind. Just the usual. No more than the usual.' She paused, for emphasis. 'The usual, right?'

'Right,' agreed Muriel.

'Right,' echoed her sister.

Betty continued. 'He won't take long, he never does. And it's three pounds. Get the money first. If there's anyone else there, anyone at all, or if he so much as moves off the settee, you're both out of there. You hear me? Out. Pronto.'

'You *both* wait for us,' said Maureen.

'Pronto,' added her sister, liking the sound of the word. 'You *both* wait for us. Pronto.'

Scotch Iris stood apart. She looked drained, pinched and exhausted. 'I don't like this,' she said.

Betty gestured to a café up on Elswick Road. 'We'll wait for you. We'll be in the Fryer Tuck.'

The girls disappeared and the two women climbed the hill. 'They tell their dad and I've fucking had it,' muttered Iris. She glanced nervously at a patch of cleared land in the distance. It looked wide and frightening. She averted her eyes from the empty space, which reminded her of the boiling expanse of sea, in Scotland, all those years before when tragedy blighted her life.

Betty was unsympathetic. She said nothing.

'Their dad's the best thing that's happened to me in years. What am I going to do?'

*

Not far away, Mickey Robson sat in a small, whitewashed room where there was a grille over the glass that looked out on to a colourful, well-tended courtyard garden. The nun who had left him there had been tiny, bent and ancient and she'd shown him inside without speaking. He sat, fiddling with his tie, a little nervous, looking out the window where two novitiates in white bent over the flower-beds. They seemed feudal and pure. Bloody women, he thought to himself. He took a folded newspaper from his jacket pocket but didn't read it. Instead his mind strayed back to one of the final days with his wife. She'd been standing at the ironing board, pressing little frilly identical petticoats that belonged to the twins. She was a big woman who'd turned fat in her thirties. The delicate garments were like snow in her sausage fingers. There was a warm, domestic smell of hot cotton, of labouring female flesh.

'You've got them like babies,' he'd raged at her from the kitchen doorway, for no reason. He'd been drunk and out of control. 'They're not babies. They're nearly grown women. Why've you got them like bloody babies? What's it all about? Why?'

His wife had ignored him. Her bovine face was expressionless but he thought he'd detected contempt.

'Why've you got them like bloody babies? Eh?' He advanced and picked up a delicate garment. He'd swayed, a little unsteady on his feet. 'What's all this baby rubbish? Baby bloody clothes? They're not babies. What's it all about? Eh?'

There was no reply. The capable hands carried on ironing.

Mickey had raised a fist. It wasn't the first time. 'Bloody women!' he yelled, for no reason in particular, other than blind fury. He'd punched her in the side of her fat head.

Now, sitting in the cell-like room, Mickey took out his cigarettes and lighter, examined them, then returned them to his pocket unopened. He fidgeted with the folded newspaper then tossed it aside. After a long wait, the Mother Superior appeared. He'd been expecting a smooth-skinned, peaceful woman with the gentle air of Florence Nightingale or possibly the beatific television zither player, Shirley Abicair, for whom Mickey had a great deal of respect. Instead a cross, skinny individual confronted him with her lined forehead and National Health eyeglasses. She appeared irritated, even impatient. She kept adjusting her veil as if it were an encumbrance. 'Well?' she enquired, sharply.

Mickey stared at the outsize crucifix on her flat bosom and explained his dilemma. He mentioned his missing wife, the letter from the headmistress, his inability to control the twins. 'The other day they stole my wallet,' he confessed. 'Before that, they pawned my wristwatch.' He hesitated, realizing he was probably on the wrong track. 'I'm worried about their moral welfare,' he offered. 'I found some . . . some . . . some Durex . . . in their bedroom. I fear for their . . . their . . . chastity.' It was unusual for

Mickey to feel intimidated, as he wasn't afraid of anyone, but this woman was giving him the creeps.

There was a long silence. Somewhere in the bowels of the convent, a phone rang and there was the clack-clack of an angry typewriter. 'I'm afraid there's nothing we can do,' said the nun, eventually. 'We can't take them here. This isn't an orphanage. Especially as you're not even a *Catholic.*'

*

Mr Long ran the youth club at the Wesley Hall. He was known as Lofty Long because he was very tall and thin. His trousers were too short and the cuffs of his shirts were always frayed and everybody said this was sad but it was because he'd never married anyone.

The club was open to all between the ages of ten and eighteen, but the rules were flexible. Ratty and Desperate sometimes came along for the dancing, even though they were over-age.

Mr Long himself was very fond of the younger boys and took them camping as often as he could in the school holidays. Some of his favourites he even invited to his flat on Isabella Street, where they played draughts, ate chocolate biscuits and drank home-brewed ginger beer. Mothers never questioned these visits because Mr Long worked for the Ministry of Health and had a briefcase. Despite seeming a little down at heel, he wore a detachable clean white collar every morning. He was respectable. The boys themselves tolerated his attentions because it was such good fun to go out to the country in a gang and sleep in tents and cook food on campfires. They merely laughed about his wandering hands. Lofty Long's going to feel you up, they joked behind his back. Hey! Whose turn is it tonight? Better put your pants on back to front!

Mr Long was popular with all the teenagers who attended the club because he was good at table tennis and because he was prepared to spend funds on the Top Ten hit records, playing them on the club gramophone. Like Ratty, he was very fond of the Shadows. He'd impressed everyone, even Ratty, by his claim that he knew Hank Marvin personally, because although Ratty had been to school with him, he never actually *knew* him. Not to speak to. He'd just seen him in the cloakroom and so on. But Mr Long knew him properly when they both lived on Stanhope Street. He said that Hank Marvin had changed his name from Brian Rankin because he wanted to sound American and become famous. He was a brilliant guitarist. Not only that. Mr Long also claimed that he'd known Bruce Welch. He'd once played with both of them in a skiffle band when their regular double-bass player had a sprained arm. He couldn't actually play himself, he'd just stood there going 'plonk-plonk, plonk-plonk', trying to look as though he knew what he was doing. This was two years ago, before Hank and Bruce quit Newcastle altogether, went to London to seek their fortunes and got into the Hit Parade. He said if ever Cliff and the Shadows came to the Stoll, he might be able to get people in backstage.

Lofty Long's all right, everyone said. That Mr Long's OK, even if he has got bad breath. Meanwhile he turned a blind eye to smoking and necking in the club and the only thing he wouldn't allow was alcohol on the premises. He said he didn't want the Reverend John Wesley turning in his grave. That afternoon, the afternoon of the talent contest, Mr Long swept up the cigarette ends left over from the T. Dan Smith meeting, straightened the pews and removed the furniture from the stage. He took the tablecloth and the plastic flowers off the piano and lifted the lid. The Wesley Hall Bechstein was an above-average instrument, recently purchased by public subscription. He flapped a handkerchief over the keys. He closed the games room and the music room. He said all members who were not taking part had to sit in the audience and watch, because this was common courtesy.

Ratty and Desperate turned up early and lounged around on the battered settee in the office where the boxes of records were kept. Ratty sorted through the singles, inspecting the B-sides. He told his friend the story, for the umpteenth time, of how he'd been with Hank Marvin in the art room at school one lunchtime and the future Shadow had taken his banjo from out of its case and strummed a tune. 'I lent him some Sellotape,' he added proudly, suddenly remembering this detail.

'What for? For his banjo?'

'No. To mend his glasses. His glasses were broke and he mended them with *my* Sellotape! I lent it to him.'

Desperate took his army beret off and unlaced and removed his heavy boots, lighting a Woodbine. He scratched his scrotum and leafed through a film magazine.

'He was good at art,' Ratty concluded. 'He looked like an arty type back then. College scarf, beatnik hair. All that jazz. The art teacher bloody loved him.'

Desperate wasn't listening. 'That Audrey Hepburn's a skinny bint,' he said disapprovingly. 'No bazookas.' He showed Ratty the centrefold. It was a pin-up of Jayne Mansfield bending forwards in a low-cut evening gown. He whistled. 'Not like *that*.'

Gradually, the main hall filled. Anxious parents accumulated at the back, glancing at the clock while saying silent prayers under their breaths. They looked about, trying not to stare, wondering if it was true that a talent scout was here from Darlington. There seemed to be no strangers present. Geordie stood in a corner, reading a bus timetable. No one spoke to him and he seemed unaware of the crowd. Young people filled the seats, their eager, expectant voices soaring up, to be caught and stored in the high space above the rafters. Constable Henderson was at the back, relaxed and genial, his helmet on the window sill. There was excitement in the air, not dissimilar to that stirred up by T. Dan Smith, the night before.

Behind the scenes, girls changed into ballet frocks and colourful junior jazz band outfits and boys put on carefully pressed suits and bow ties, in preparation for magic acts or stand-up comedy routines. Here, there was a low buzz of anticipation plus a smell of hair lacquer mixed with Schnitzler's Brilliant. There was a ventriloquist's dummy propped up on a chair, a live rabbit in a box, a tuba, a xylophone and a pair of acrobats trying to limber up in a cramped corner. Leslie sat on a tea-chest. He felt apprehensive and a little sweaty. Although he'd removed his duffel-coat, he was nevertheless wearing his ordinary clothes. One of his socks stuck out through a hole in his plimsoll. He tried to think about his choirmaster. He imagined him sitting at the organ in the church, in front of the bejewelled stained-glass Virgin with her welcoming arms. That was splendid, Leslie, he heard him say. Splendid. That was splendid, Leslie. Despite running this scene through his mind several times, the boy felt that today Mr Green's words lacked conviction and he was less than adequately reassured. After a while he concentrated instead on a scene from *The Wizard of Oz*, which was his favourite film. He'd seen it seven times. He thought about the little girl singing *The Yellow Brick Road*. If that Dorothy can sing in a film in front of millions and millions of people, he told himself, then I can manage this. This is nothing compared to what she did. This is easy-peasy. The other excited children taking part smiled and reassured him. Someone gave him a toffee. 'You singing, Leslie, or you doing your card tricks?'

'Singing.' Leslie had no special, close friend except his brother but he was a popular boy with everyone.

'You'll be great, man,' they all said to him.

'Don't worry, you'll be great.'

'You're the best singer around here for miles.'

'Isn't he? Isn't he the best?'

'For miles and miles.'

'And miles and miles.'

At that moment the twins arrived and came straight over to where Leslie was sitting. 'Get our note, spotty-face?' Maureen asked this question in a loud, aggressive way. A nervous hush fell in the room.

Leslie swallowed. 'Note? What note?'

'Can he read?' enquired Muriel looking about. 'Does anyone know? Can stupid Les-lee here even read? We've heard he was the great big dunce of top class.'

The other children were embarrassed. They stared at the twins, uncomprehending.

'What note?' Maureen was scathing. 'You *know* what note. The one that said your Mam's a prozzie and a whore.'

There was a collective gasp from the children.

Muriel chimed in. 'The note which says we're going to

kill that precious dafty of yours, just as soon as we get the chance.'

Mr Long caught the tail end of this and quickly intervened. 'Come along now, boys and girls,' he ordered in a bossy voice. 'Let's get ourselves properly organized.'

The children broke up, formed new groups and betrayed their nerves by chattering noisily about their forthcoming ordeals on the stage. Leslie stood as far away from the twins as was possible. After a few more minutes, Mr Long appeared in front of the audience, now sporting an ancient, too-small dinner jacket with a carnation in its buttonhole. He made a speech about boundless enthusiasm and hard work. He was followed by two little girls, dressed as robins, who performed a dance duet. A nervous youth did a Tommy Cooper impersonation. The acrobats proved to be noisy without any backing music but their routine never faltered. There was more than one Shirley Temple and the rabbit appeared and disappeared before changing into a bunch of paper flowers. The applause after each act was deafening and was accompanied by cheering, whistles and the stamping of feet.

Just prior to the interval there was an overlong pause before the last of the first-half turns. People in the audience looked at each other, puzzled and a little concerned. Parents turned to Mr Long, seeking an explanation. He was just about to move backstage when the strains of the Shadows' 'Apache' crackled from the loudspeakers. 'Yes!' called out Ratty from the audience. 'Yes! Yes! Yes!'

The tune started to swing and, at once relieved, everyone tapped their feet in a jolly way, or beat their palms against their thighs. Muriel and Maureen appeared from behind the curtain at the rear of the stage. There was tittering in the audience, then, after a long moment, laughter. One of the twins clomped across the stage in an enormous pair of army boots which had been daubed with lime-green paint. She left partial green footprints behind her. The other was wearing an army beret pulled down low to her eyes. The regimental plume had been dipped in the same luminous colour. They began to perform a mock jive to the jaunty number, their faces daubed in make up, spots of paint staining their dresses and legs. The laughter among the spectators died away. There was a collective grimace, a shudder of embarrassment. It was clear that the twins were not trying to perform, or even entertain. It was suddenly apparent to everyone that they were making fun of the whole enterprise. They were mocking the show, indicating their contempt for the aspirations and pretensions of the other acts, the other children. They turned and bent down, revealing their bottoms, their matching flowery knickers. The music stopped and they faced forwards, curtsying ironically and grinning, revealing their yellow teeth. There was a spatter of nervous clapping, then silence.

A shout sounded from the body of the hall. 'Hoy! What the hell . . .!' Everyone turned to stare. It was Desperate Dan. He'd stood up and he was pushing his way out to the end of his row. 'Hoy! You two! You little bastards! What d'you think you've got there?'

There was consternation. One or two people tried to restrain him. Constable Henderson put on his helmet. Mr Long moved forwards, placing himself between Desperate and the stage. 'All right,' he said. 'Take it easy, take it easy. It's nothing. They're just kids. Take it easy.'

The twins remained, still smiling and holding hands.

Desperate tried to shove Mr Long aside. 'What the

hell d'you two think you're doing?' he shouted at the girls.

Maureen ran off, followed by her sister who was slowed down by the cumbersome footwear.

His voice was very loud. 'Who told them they could have my boots? My beret? Those bloody little bastards!' The soldier was in his stockinged feet and his beret was not rolled up inside his epaulette. The twins had borrowed his boots and his hat, taking them from the office. They'd ruined them with paint from the art cupboard in the games room. Several men including Ratty jostled forwards and restrained Desperate Dan.

'Who told them? Who said they could do that? Whose idea was it . . .?' Desperate was emotional. He was close to tears. 'Who said they could have them? My boots. They're bloody ruined!'

Parents looked at each other, astonished. Children stood up. One or two younger ones began to cry. There was a murmur of disapproval, of shock. Mr Long climbed on to the platform. He held up both palms in a placatory gesture. 'Friends. There will be a short interval of ten minutes. Refreshments are available courtesy of the Co-operative Women's Guild.'

Ratty had his friend in an arm-lock. 'Keep your hair on,' he muttered. He pushed him towards the exit, followed by the worried policeman. Desperate didn't struggle. Distraught, his head was down. Ratty was grim-faced. 'Mind your backs, please,' he called out, as if Desperate were a troublemaker or an out-of-control drunk. 'Mind your backs ladies and gents, *please*.' He pushed his bootless and hatless friend out into the street.

*

Sammy Schnitzler sat at the back of his empty shop, arms folded, legs apart surrounded by more newly filled bottles of Schnitzler's Brilliant. A pool of the greasy liquid was spilled on the floor and, in the heat, its scent was overpowering. Sammy's head was back and his mouth was open. He was asleep. Heavy snores reverberated into the saloon, through the open door and into the hot street outside, but there was no one to hear them. The very last 'afternoon' worker had already passed by on his way to Vickers, the last coal-blackened pitman had trudged wearily home from the early shift, about to turn day into night.

Sammy was dreaming of Vienna. He was a boy again and he was happy and secure, but there were no melodious violins welling above the spire of the Stephansdom. Instead, unaccountably, he was wandering alone in the Leopoldstadt district, only ten years old, without his nurse and without his brothers and sisters. Small, pampered and round, holding a tin soldier, he soon found himself lost. The streets were like a maze and here, everywhere lurked the furtive, threatening figures of orthodox Jews, new and desperate refugees from the Polish and Russian pogroms. They stood on the corners, looking poor, exotic and haunted. Sammy passed them by, deciding they were foreign, peculiar and possibly lice-infested. As he continued, his confidence deserted him. He wanted to go home. He stopped and stared into the face of a man with ringlets, a felt hat, a beard. Certainly, these Jews were nothing like his own prosperous, assimilated family, which generations before, along with others, had quit this area and moved to the nobler avenues of the inner city. Here they'd enjoyed plenty of money and respect and even though they spoke Yiddish, they very definitely *looked* the same as everyone else. In his dream, Sammy carried on walking through these ragged groups of the dispossessed, now for some reason handing out handkerchiefs, trinkets and gold coins. Suddenly, from around a corner, there was shouting and the screams of women. The clatter of army boots, breaking glass and the rat-tat-tat of gunfire followed these. Sammy stopped in his tracks, his heart pounding, paralysed with terror. Never in his young life had he ever heard such a commotion. The bearded man reappeared and at once gathered him up. The two of them were running down a dark alley and *shtetl* children were crying in doorways, accompanied by barking dogs.

Sammy stirred in his chair in the back room of his barber's shop, quit snoring, but didn't wake up. One of his ineffectual legs kicked. Crazily, his dream continued and the decades collided together. Head on, the small boy from the year 1920 met the unit of pounding and shouting Nazi soldiers. Unwittingly, the Russian immigrant Jew, the refugee, had carried him straight into the presence of the anti-Semites. Terrified, he looked into the angry eyes of his enemies, and all at once the twins, both of them weak and clinging, were at his sides. As helpless as dolls, their cynicism dispelled, they shivered and cried in their flimsy lace-trimmed dresses. Sammy knew he couldn't defend himself, let alone these girls. Powerless, completely vulnerable, he was unable to shut out the advancing uniforms, the swastikas, the distorted faces, the leather and jabbing guns, the hate.

*

Mickey Robson now sat in the lounge of a city-centre public house with Scotch Iris at his side. He was drinking a pint of bitter and chain-smoking Senior Service. He

123

looked handsome and big in his stylish narrow grey suit with a white shirt and red tie. He seemed depressed. She was jumpy and animated.

It was warm and the air was dim and cloudy with tobacco. Sunlight streamed in through window-panes and the opaque etched glass shone patterns on to the faded linoleum floor. There were few drinkers and the barman was reading the *Sporting Pink*. The racing results were droning on a wireless in the background and from the bar in the room next door there was the sound of a noisy darts game.

Iris had refused alcohol and ordered a lemonade, but unknown to Mickey she was high on amphetamines. She had just bought yet another bottle from Ratty Schnitzler, insisting, as she handed over another ten pounds, that they kept her slim. He'd just smiled. He wasn't interested in drugs himself but he knew enough about them to be sure that they bestowed her with temporary courage and temporary self-belief. This was the true reason behind her compulsion. He also knew that coming down off them was unpleasant. The only way to avoid these symptoms was to take 'downers' and go to sleep or alternatively take more 'uppers' to maintain the high. He'd sold her both kinds, taken her money with a shrug. Ratty didn't care. Addiction was good for business. 'It's just a question of meeting a need,' he'd once remarked to Desperate. 'Free market economics. Capitalism in its purest form.'

Now Iris's pupils were wide and her voice a little shrill but Mickey appeared not to notice. He frowned into his drink and swirled it around in the glass. He lit a new cigarette from the butt of the old one and sighed. He glanced at the headlines in a newspaper at his elbow.

Iris was looking very pretty. Her pouting cupid-bow lips matched her elegant fingernails and her eyelashes were caked as usual in black mascara. Her pert little chin jutted and diamanté droplets hung from her ears. She had several Fenwick's carrier bags at her feet.

Iris had been brought up in the Gorbals, the youngest in a family of twelve children. She'd never had any clothes except worn-out hand-me-downs until she left school and got a job of her own. She could still remember that first pay-packet, that first dress, the silky feeling as she slipped it over her head in the changing-room, the smell of it, the luxurious rustle of its skirts, the tissue paper and card-board box it was in, the sheer excitement of carrying it out of the shop.

Restless now, she picked up four beer mats and shuffled them like playing cards. She was complaining about the sales assistant in Fenwick's gowns and mantles. 'I knew her when she was plain little Sandra Laidlaw from Clumber Street. Skinny legs. Buck teeth. Laddered nylons. Before she got her fancy *ideas*. Before she got *above herself*.' She stared at Mickey. 'How did she manage to get that job, I wonder? A good job like that.' She paused. 'Hey! You're not listening.'

It had become clear to Iris that Mickey wasn't a talker. Despite his endless discussions in smoke-filled rooms with Labour Party members and the beery joviality of the pub afterwards, he wasn't natural or relaxed with her, or indeed with any woman. She decided he was comfortable only with other men. He didn't seem to like women all that much, except for the times when they were in bed together. He likes *me*, she told herself, repeatedly. He's a man's man, that's all. A *man's man*. She rather liked this

125

notion because it seemed like confirmation of his virility. Not that there were any problems in that department, of course.

He glanced up. He looked grumpy.

'What's the matter with you today?'

'Nothing.'

'Something's the matter, so it is.'

'Nothing's the matter.'

'Don't nothing me. Something's up.' She was loud. One or two men standing at the bar turned around.

'Sshh.' He drained his pint, went to the bar to buy another, then on his return confided, 'It's the girls.' His voice was low.

Scotch Iris was suddenly anxious. 'The girls?' She took a cigarette from Mickey's pack, flashed his lighter, inhaled, took another couple of quick drags then stubbed it out. 'What about the girls?' She smoothed her hair with both hands, then her lime-green capri pants. She undid a button on her blouse, revealing the tops of her breasts. Her gestures were rapid, nervous. 'What have they been saying? What've they been saying now?' Iris deeply regretted the connection between herself, Betty and the two girls. She would have given anything to stop it, but everything had slipped out of control. She was at a loss.

Mickey studied her cleavage then sighed again. He took out a handkerchief and blew his nose. 'Saying? They're saying nowt. That's the problem. They don't talk to me, except to ask me for money. I hardly ever see them. They do as they please. I can't . . . I can't . . .'

'You can't what?'

'I can't control them. I can't . . .'

Scotch Iris leant back in her seat, relieved.

'I'm not looking after them properly. That's the honest

truth.' He shook his head. 'They're a liability. They're beyond me. I don't know what to do.'

Iris ran her pretty fingers across the back of his hand. She said nothing. Of course it was still her dearest hope that Mickey might propose marriage, but she was more than familiar with the simple contours of male psychology and she sensed he wasn't yet ready. She realized that the idea hadn't yet occurred to him but it was far too early to start dropping hints. She knew she wanted him as a husband but she didn't want his horrible children and in any case she knew how to bide her time.

'They're out at all hours. Roaming the streets. I got a letter last month from their headmistress saying they never go to school.'

Iris was sharp. 'It's not your fault their mother left them. It's not fair. Can't *she* have them?'

Mickey sipped from his glass and grimaced. 'Their bloody mother? I don't even know where she is, these days. Do I?'

'What about their nana? Their aunties?'

'There's no one. No one at all.'

'What about . . .?' Iris stood up, adjusted her bra, then sat down again.

'What?'

'You know.'

'What?'

'You know what I'm talking about, so you do.'

'You mean a home?'

'Yes.'

'I've thought of it.' Mickey looked desolate. 'God knows. I've been that desperate at times. I've even asked the nuns at the Big Lamp. Asked if *they* could take them over.' He paused, remembering this morning's embarrassment. 'But

I've got to face it. I can't avoid it. They're my own kids. Mine. My own flesh and blood. I can't give them away. It wouldn't be right.' He looked at her imploringly. 'Would it?' He inhaled deeply. 'I mean, it wouldn't, would it?'

'You sure?'

'Sure?'

'Sure they're really yours? They don't look like you.'

Mickey stared at Scotch Iris, amazed.

She continued, quickly. 'Look. Before you know where you are they're suddenly off your hands. What about me? Nothing's for ever. Time flies. I've got two boys and they both look after themselves now.'

'My girls are only *thirteen*.' He paused. The girls had insisted on birthday presents a month or so ago. Maybe they were fourteen. Or were they twelve? He kept this doubt to himself. He was a little ashamed of not knowing. 'It's too bad. They'd have been sorted out properly with those nuns and a bit of discipline. I wish . . .' Mickey sighed and glanced at Iris, his eyes travelling over her small frame. There was no question that she would make a terrible mother for the twins. She wasn't the maternal type.

A loud cheer sounded from around the dartboard next door. The barman stood up and pulled a pint. A man in a white jacket and cap came through into the lounge with a tray of seafood hanging from his shoulders. 'Cockles anyone, please? Fresh mussels?'

Scotch Iris was jittery and bored. She didn't like the conversation moving away from herself. There was a long silence between them, then she said, 'I saw a smashing sundress in Binns. Orange and dark blue triangles with a little bolero. Only sixty-nine and eleven. It would go lovely with my navy-blue slingbacks.' She opened her white shoulder bag, took out a powder compact and began dabbing at her nose. She unscrewed a lipstick and applied it liberally. She smiled at Mickey and rubbed his sleeve. 'Cheer up!' she exclaimed. 'I don't like it when you're miserable!'

Mickey forced a grin. He finished his drink. He took out another cigarette. 'Let's go,' he said. 'Let's not risk my house,' he suggested. 'We don't want any interruptions. I've booked another room in the Station Hotel.'

*

After the break, the atmosphere at the talent contest in the Wesley Hall was less celebratory, more tense. People were offended by the twins' disrespectful behaviour and either puzzled or discomfited by Desperate Dan's outburst. To some extent, the show had been spoiled. Children sucked on lollipops, a little mournfully. Parents wished the proceedings would finish so they could get away. Mr Long announced the second half, clapping his lanky fish-like hands wholeheartedly, trying to drum up some support from the crowd.

A group of boys played brass marching tunes and they were followed by a tap dancer who slipped in a wet paint smear left by the twins. A couple more acts were met by polite applause. Then it was Leslie's slot. He came on to the stage shyly, his trousers noticeably torn in both knees. He stood facing the audience, at once embarrassed by their curious gaze. He gulped, visibly. These people had ceased to be friends, neighbours he spoke to every day of his life. Collectively, they now seemed hostile, frightening. He was used to singing in church, but this empty stage was far from the anonymity of the choir stalls, the candlelit darkness surrounded by the benevolence of God himself.

Again he tried to think about Mary, Mother of Jesus, in the stained glass, holding out her arms to him in an encouraging way. But here the lights were glaring, there was a sea of unfriendly faces and without an organ accompaniment he felt completely on his own. He swallowed and made his eyes go out of focus so that the hall was nothing but a blur. He tried hard to forget that he was being watched. However, in the silence he could hear whispered conversation, the scraping of feet on the floor, different individuals coughing.

He cleared his own throat nervously, then began singing. *Panis angelicus . . . fit panis hominum . . .* His stomach was hollow and empty. His voice sounded thin, strained. He felt his throat tighten and he struggled to take in enough air. His heart started to beat too fast and his tongue was instantly caked and dry, sticking to his lips. It felt huge. *O res mirabilis . . . manducat Dominum . . .* He climbed to the high notes, but with an unwanted croak creeping in on the very edges of the Latin words. Instead of coming strongly from low in his chest, the music seemed to emerge, trapped and small, from the back of his mouth, his voice audibly shaking. Before the end of every long phrase he ran out of breath and spoiled the sounds with an unscheduled gasp. He struggled and struggled and then disaster struck. His breaking voice plunged to a strangled baritone and heavy, lifeless, unmelodious sounds fell from his lips like dull stones. He felt colour surge into his cheeks. He stopped, started over again and persevered, managing to soar once more. *Pauper servus et humilis . . .* but with his vocal chords rebelling, his throat rasping like sandpaper, he was forced to quit again, midphrase, his mouth in a gormless 'O'. He looked down. His face was burning. Rows of surprised faces stared up at him. The stage felt at once enormous, like a wide-open prairie where he was the only single exposed human being. His heart contracted with fear. The palms of his hands were clenched and clammy and he felt sweat break out on his brow and upper lip. He wanted to run but he was rooted, frozen with humiliation. He tried to apologize but his voice was paralysed. Several seconds went by, as long as hours. His eyes filled with tears. There was tittering from backstage that sounded like it was coming from the twins. Mr Long got to his feet as if about to assist Leslie into the wings.

At that moment a dramatic chord sounded. For the first time that evening, below the stage, someone struck the keys of the piano. Attention was immediately distracted from the hapless figure above and people strained their necks, trying to discern who was sitting behind the instrument. Only a dark head was visible. Leslie crept to the edge and looked down. From his vantage point he could see that it was Geordie who had seated himself behind the Wesley Hall Bechstein. He almost smiled, comforted that his own ordeal was now eclipsed, but nevertheless worried and surprised by his brother's unfamiliar exposure.

At once, Geordie began a Rodgers and Hammerstein medley from *Carousel*. He launched first into a spirited rendering of 'June Is Busting Out All Over' before merging melodiously with 'When I Marry Mister Snow'. It was note-perfect, confident. The crowd, feeling safe, let out a collective sigh of pleasure. Leslie listened, transfixed, then slipped out of sight. It wasn't the first time he'd heard his brother play like this, but he knew it was the first time Geordie had ever attempted it outside the seclusion of their own gloomy kitchen. He was copying, with total recall, the exact notes of the music he had heard booming from a Russ Conway long-player on his mother's front room Dansette record player. His memory was faultless, phenomenal. His long fingers pranced up and down the keyboard without effort or hesitation. Leslie knew that the music itself meant nothing to Geordie. It was no more than a series of complicated patterns and formulae. However, to the audience this was as convincing as a professional performance. Without a pause he followed the first two numbers with 'If I Loved You'. Several men unselfconsciously joined in, supplying the necessary emotion, their voices sonorous and laden with feeling as if participating in a hymn. Geordie then straight away glided into 'When You Walk Through a Storm'. This appeared to be expertly judged. The entire hall gradually began to echo with a hundred fervent, uplifted contributions. They were united and grateful. *And don't be afraid of the dark* ... Geordie came to the end but then immediately began the number again. This time everyone present sang their heart out, giving thanks for the piano solo, for the event itself, for the children's talent and most of all for the spirit of their own community. At the end there was thunderous applause. Mr Long climbed the steps to the stage, wiping his eyes. He was about to make a speech. Geordie stood up, revealing himself as the pianist. He didn't smile but he bowed, stiffly. For a moment the tumult faltered as everyone identified the strange, undersized, beautiful boy, the outcast, the one they told their children always to avoid. But this was only momentary. Cheering started as Geordie moved towards the door, looking neither left nor right, impassive, elegant, aloof, detached, but possibly, just possibly, proud.

Leslie was still standing at the edge of the stage. With everyone's attention distracted away from his own disaster, he had almost recovered. I'm glad our mam's not here, he decided. He knew his mother had, at one time not so long ago, been proud of his singing. Geordie's piano-playing she'd always ignored. He swallowed hard. She'd have been a lot more bothered by *me* going wrong than she would've been pleased by *him* doing all right, he reasoned. I'm really glad she's not here. He felt a pang in his heart. He often felt this way about her these days.

For some reason he remembered the letter from the psychiatrist in Prudhoe and wondered if his mother actually wanted to get rid of Geordie. Could it have been her idea? The envelope was still hidden in the shoebox under his bed. It was next to the letter from the council, which was all about shifting. Before too long, he suspected, another one would arrive. Then another. Those authorities wouldn't give up.

At once, he had a vision of a thousand energetic letters bursting like confetti out from under his bed, through the open window, across the lane then out on to a demolition site. The new high flats stood like soldiers in the distance. Here the letters swirled and lifted like a flock of airborne gulls, high above the devastated earth, dancing to the sound of Geordie's melodious keyboard chords.

Leslie turned and looked about. He reined in his wayward imagination. There were clots of dust gathered in the corners where Mr Long's brush had failed to reach. I could get a cleaning job here, he thought, irrationally, I could get this place ship-shape with a tin of Vim and a mop. His heart was still beating a little too fast. He was pleased for his brother, glad he'd entertained the crowd in such an impressive way. I'll go and find him, he told himself. I'll congratulate him. It doesn't matter that I wasn't any good. We'll both go and see Auntie Ada and tell her about it. He pictured her warm upstairs kitchen, fragrant with the smell of delicious cakes.

At home he found his brother alone, back at his drawing. He was absorbed, uncommunicative. He refused to discuss the talent show. The tottering rooflines of Elswick were being immortalized, this time in pen and ink.

From his shirt pocket, Leslie took the precious photograph taken on the beach at Cullercoats. It was a little creased. He smoothed and studied it for a while. It made him feel better. 'Geordie, look at this.' He swallowed the remnants of his hurt pride. Never mind about that stupid contest he told himself. At least one of us did all right. *He* was splendid. He handed it across. 'Look.'

His brother took the snapshot, examined it, then passed it back. His face was unreadable, expressionless. He immediately returned to his sketchpad.

Leslie pressed the picture between his palms. 'Cullercoats,' he said aloud. We were all happy then. Tenderly, he kissed the image. Here was Geordie, younger, laughing, running out of the sea in his swimming trunks, his arms outstretched to take the ice-cream which he himself could be seen holding, at the edge of the frame. The sky and the sea were grey but of course in reality they'd been very blue and there was water splashing up around Geordie's feet. 'Cullercoats,' he said again. He returned the photo to his shirt pocket. It *will* be like this again, he told himself. Soon. Our mam will go back to being like she used to be and she'll take us there again. All together, with a picnic. We'll all be happy and laughing. Everything's going to be all right.

There was a heavy knock on the front door. Unwillingly Leslie answered it, opening it a mere chink, expecting to see one of his mother's clients or, even worse, the twins. It turned out to be Constable Henderson, beefy and smiling, and a dark-skinned man in a suit and a white shirt.

'This is Dr Kumar,' said the policeman. 'Is your mam at home? He wants to talk to the little laddie.'

'Why?' asked Leslie, suspicious and afraid.

The doctor smiled, revealing teeth as white and as perfect as his shirt.

The officer coughed. 'There's been more er . . . allegations . . . Those Robson twins have been down at the station again. They said . . .'

'I don't care what they said.' Leslie kept tight hold of the door. 'They're nasty little troublemakers with nothing better to do.'

The dark doctor interrupted. He had a refined accent that was both foreign and English public school. 'If I could just spend a few moments with young George . . . My colleagues at Prudhoe Hospital . . .'

'Prudda?'

'Yes, if I could just . . .' He stepped forward.

'That Prudda place where they lock people up?' Leslie straight away pushed the door. Constable Henderson tried to shove his boot in the crack but his reactions were slow. Leslie forced it closed and locked it. His heart was beating fast. It's started, he thought. This is it. They're coming for him and next time they won't be so polite. He was shaken. He bit the back of his hand. First a letter, then a visit, he thought. He didn't know what to do. He waited in the hall while determined knocking lasted for a minute or two. Then, to his relief, the pair went away.

*

Later Leslie left Geordie sleeping. Tired from his piano-playing exertions, he was curled like a baby on the big double bed, his mauve eyelids closed. His sweet and regular breathing disturbed a stray feather, on the pillow that supported his pretty head.

On entering the upstairs flat, Leslie took off his plimsolls and coat and apologized for his rudeness on his previous visit. Ada was sitting in her usual armchair. She smiled and nodded, as placid as ever. Relieved by her forgiveness, Leslie helped himself to rock buns and told her all about the talent contest. He praised Geordie's success and made a joke of his own sorry efforts. Neither of them mentioned the cause of their disagreement, the psychiatrist's threat to Geordie. However, it was now clear to Leslie that the appointment letter from Prudhoe Hospital, the one in the shoebox under his bed, had come from the very same doctor who, with Constable Henderson, had stood earlier on the doorstep downstairs.

A wind-up gramophone on the sideboard was playing a selection of well-known dance hits from the war. The fire was mercifully low in the grate and the window was wide open. The back of the building was in shadow and the room was dim and peaceful. Leslie could hear the big old grandfather clock ticking and its unwavering beat soothed him. He returned the smile of two grinning Toby jugs. Outside, an ice-cream van circled the terraces playing the same repeating melody. Leslie took out his Cullercoats photograph, kissed it, then replaced it in his pocket.

As usual, Ada was reading the notices in the paper, ringing the ones that concerned anyone she might know. 'Eeh . . . that Billy Wanless has gone and passed away,' she said to herself, pencilling furiously. 'My brother Jack knew him when he was at Vickers. He was a marvellous bowls player.' She pursed her lips. 'Unitarian. A decent man.' She licked the end of the pencil. 'He wasn't very old. Sixty-six. What a shame.' She held the paper and the magnifying glass close to her face, beginning another lugubrious column. Her double chins shook with emotion.

*

Below, almost silently and with extreme patience, Geordie was poking with his penknife around the edges of the sash in the back bedroom. He was loosening the grime which had stuck the window closed for years. Delicately he prodded and dug, until eventually the frame wobbled in its grooves. Then he painstakingly chipped away at the catch, freeing it from several coats of paint. After half an hour of careful effort he was able to push up the top pane, creating a gap big enough to wriggle through. He was unseen by Leslie and Ada who were above. He took his sketchpad and his pencil-case and he left the flat, crossed the yard and opened the gate into the back lane. He listened out for the roar and clatter of the demolition gang, studied the sky for clouds of dust. Then he nodded seriously, locating the gang six streets or so away. He set off in their direction.

*

'Have you had a letter from the Council?' enquired Leslie. 'About shifting?'

Auntie Ada pointed to the mantelpiece. 'Behind the clock,' she said.

Leslie stood up and extracted the single sheet. He glanced through it. It was exactly the same as the one sent to Scotch Iris. The one that was in his shoebox under his bed. Mentally, he compared them. They were identical. They both mentioned a 'one-bedroom unit'. 'What's a one-bedroom unit?' he asked.

Ada lowered the paper and bleakly met his eye. She looked dismayed. She shook her head. 'I don't know.' She laid down her magnifying glass. 'I don't like the sound of it.'

'They've offered my mam a one-bedroom unit too.'

'How are three of you going to fit in there?'

'You tell me. I think she's planning on going without us.'

Ada sighed heavily. She picked up a poker and jabbed at the dying embers in the hearth. 'These houses are coming down,' she said eventually. 'Tulloch Street's nearly down.' She paused. 'Hawes Street's down. Herbert Street's down. They're all coming down. We've all got to shift and that's all there is to it.'

'How long have you been here?'

She considered. 'Thirty year. Nigh on.'

'So what will you do?'

There was a silence. After a while she said, 'I suppose I'll go to the place in the town, down by the cathedral. Amen Corner. Like they've told me to. The housing people. I'll go and talk to them. I'll get the bus.' She paused. 'Then we'll just have to see.'

'See what?'

'See what they tell us to do.'

'We don't *have* to do anything. Do you want to shift?'

'I can't say I do.'

'Well then?'

Ada looked nonplussed. Leslie's new spirit of rebellion had surfaced once more, but not wanting to get involved in another pointless argument, he decided to change the subject.

The two of them had been sipping a companionable cup of tea. Leslie felt relaxed but not quite as peaceful as

he usually did when he was upstairs. The visit from the
doctor and the policeman had unnerved him. 'Auntie
Ada?'

'Yes, pet?'

'You know you said you'd teach me how to bake big
fancy cakes and meringues and suchlike?'

'Yes.'

'Will you then? Will you show me now?'

'What, now?'

'Yes, now.'

'All right then.' Auntie Ada paused for a moment then
heaved herself upright. She stoked up the fire to heat the
oven. 'Wash your hands.'

'I've washed them.'

'Wash them again.'

The two of them went into the scullery, setting to work
as a unified mistress and apprentice team, co-operating
effortlessly.

Later, after two halves of a Victoria sponge had been
slipped into the oven, Auntie Ada sat down in her armchair and once more took up her newspaper.

Leslie wound the gramophone. A burst of saxophones
filled the room.

'Will you remember that recipe?'

'Yes.'

'We'll give it twenty minutes. Then we'll ice it later on.
After it's cooled.' She tapped her foot in time to the music,
her massive bosom wobbling under her apron.

Leslie took out his photograph of Cullercoats once more
and showed it to Ada. She examined it under her magnifying glass, smiled wistfully and wiped away an invisible
tear. 'What a little rascal he is.'

'I'd better go and check on him,' Leslie said, sighing.

'Where's he got to now?'

'He's fast asleep. I locked him in.'

'Locked him in?'

'I've only just started doing it. I know it's awful, but it's for his own good. He keeps going off on his own, drawing the houses. He wants to get them all down on paper before they disappear. He's making a record of Elswick.'

'He's a funny one, your brother.' Ada's tone was affectionate. 'What'll he do next, I wonder? You should have brought him up here.'

'I would've done, but I told you, he's tired, he's fast asleep.'

*

Leslie went downstairs and entered the rear door. He checked the kitchen for Geordie, his eyes lingering on the unpaid bills on the mantelpiece. There's more of them to come, he thought, but he didn't examine them. He went into the back bedroom. His heart missed a beat when he discovered it was empty, with the window open. He's gone, he realized, alarmed. He's gone and got out. He just won't be stopped, the little terror.

Leslie stared at the row upon row of drawings lining the walls. There were buildings, cars and buses, all perfectly represented in pen and ink or pencil. More recent efforts were pinned on top of earlier ones, giving the impression of layers of work, accumulated over time. The wallpaper was all but obscured. Leslie picked up some clothing, folded it and laid it on a chair. He made the bed.

Trudging back upstairs he felt the weight of responsibility on his shoulders. 'He's gone out. Escaped. I'll have to go and look for him. He follows those workmen everywhere.'

Auntie Ada stood up and pulled a clean apron over her head, tying the strings. She lifted the two halves of the sponge cake from the oven and put them on a wire rack to cool. She was expecting her brother Jack for his tea. 'I've got a nice piece of cold tongue,' she said, arranging her straggly hair, glancing in the sideboard mirror. 'It's too hot for anything else. I've got tongue, some jersey potatoes and some lovely fresh tomatoes. Are you coming for tea? You and Geordie?'

Leslie paused. He stood at the table and pulled at the fringe of the green chenille cloth. A cool, refreshing breeze was now blowing through the curtains. The cake was waiting to be iced. The two halves had become a perfect golden dome. The grandfather clock continued its comforting, ancient rhythm. Everything upstairs was as it should be. 'Yes,' he said, realizing that this was the *only* safe place, for Geordie, for both of them. 'I'll go and find him.'

He moved to the window. The noisy children in the back lane had all disappeared inside. The ice-cream van had given up for the afternoon and the deep blue of the sky above the rooftop was bisected by the thin white vapour of an almost invisible aeroplane. He sighed. 'He could be anywhere.'

'You've got an old head on your shoulders. You worry too much.'

'No. Not *too* much. Nobody cares about him. You know they don't. Even if he does play the piano and make them all cry. Geordie's got no one looking out for him except me and I'm all he's got.' He met Auntie Ada's eye. 'Except for you, of course.'

'And your mam.'

Leslie was silent.

She smiled. 'You go and find him and bring him back

here for some cold tongue. There's plenty to spare.' She
smiled. 'And we can all have a piece of your lovely cake.'

'I need to ice it. You need to show me how to ice it.
I need to put jam in the middle.' Leslie thought for a
moment about his mam, wondering for an instant if she'd
like a slice of his Victoria sponge. She won't, he thought,
she's slimming. She says those awful pills are slimming
pills. With an effort he pushed Scotch Iris from his mind
and instead pictured the Virgin Mary in the stained-glass
window of the church, holding out her hands. She's holding out her hands for a piece of my cake, he decided.
She won't be on a stupid diet. They don't have diets
in Nazareth. 'Thank you for having me, Auntie Ada.' He
pulled on his old duffel-coat and plimsolls. 'Thank you for
showing me that new recipe.'

She smiled. 'Get along with you.' She picked up her
purse and handed him a coin. 'Keep the change, pet, but
get me a jar of that Heinz salad cream for the tea.'

*

Beyond Glue Terrace, outside and in the west, a pink glow
had appeared in the sky behind the factory. It looked fresh
and vivid above the soiled rooftops. The days are getting
shorter, Leslie decided as he climbed the bank, searching
for Geordie. The new high flats had grown even taller,
improbable silhouettes above the remaining old rooftops.

Calling in at a corner shop, he bought the salad cream,
then on impulse he asked for a single cigarette, matches
and three penny chews, one liquorice flavour and two fruit
cocktail. Trudging upwards, he sucked on the sweets and
thought about his need to get a job. I can't go on like this,
he reasoned. I can't spend my life running other people's
errands for ha'pennies. I must get work. He paused at a

crossroads, glancing left and right. He took a deep breath. Auntie Ada's Jack's coming, he remembered. He thought about the remainder of the day, comforted by forming a plan. First, I'll find my brother. Second, I'll go back and speak to Uncle Jack about a job at Vickers. Third, I'll ice my sponge. Fourth, the four of us, we'll all have cold tongue, salad with salad cream and cake. Maybe afterwards we'll even have a game of whist. He smiled to himself. Geordie was either very bad or very good at whist. Sometimes he wasn't interested and just threw any old combination on to the table. Other times, if he was in the mood, he remembered the numbers on every single card in play and he and Leslie were able to beat the opposing pair hands down. Leslie was reassured. Searching along the lanes he felt his optimism rise. Uncle Jack *will* get me a job, he reasoned. I'll be able to pay all those bills. He forced his mind away from the terrifying prospect of heavy machinery, molten metal, noise and the unknowable male rituals of manufacture and industry. He remembered the jolly foreman at Adamsez and talk about a sweeping brush. That's it, I'll be a cleaner, he told himself. I could sweep the floors in the offices and the canteen. He was suddenly confident. That's what I'll do. I'll tell Jack I want to be a cleaner at Vickers. He'll sort me out. I'll be responsible and willing and make myself very, very useful indeed.

He lit the cigarette. He held it in a manly way and tried to swagger like he'd seen Hollywood stars do, at the Majestic. He breathed in the smoke but it choked him. He tried again, then gave up. Feeling a little silly, he dropped it down a drain. Instead, he stood up straight and sang the opening bars of 'Panis Angelicus'. His voice, without breaking, rose easily, mellifluously above the semi-erased and beaten-up landscape of Elswick. It soared up to the high notes, sounding as pure and as poignant as a child's hope, as a child's faith, as a child's innocence. He sang the entire song and at last the final tremulous cadence, the final perfect high G, floated off lengthily into the dying afternoon. Wavering as he was on the very cusp of adulthood, Leslie's song dropped beautifully away. As it did so, without him yet knowing, in advance of his own awareness, it was finally and irrecoverably lost. In its place was the distant thump-thump of the Vickers steam hammer, just starting up for the evening shift, and over the top of this, a sudden roar and clatter and rumble of a falling building in the next street. 'Everything's going to be all right,' he said aloud, but at some profound level within himself this now sounded like a question rather than a resolve. He hesitated. 'Geordie!' he shouted eventually, 'Geor-die, Geor-die! Where are you? *Where – Are – You . . .?*'

5

Later, Leslie discovered Sammy Schnitzler sitting outside his barber's shop in the fading light, holding a broken umbrella. The disappearing sun was behind him, casting a long and grotesque shadow. He seemed absorbed, despondent. His small hands examined the distorted frame, turning it this way and that.

'Hello there,' said Leslie uneasily. 'Have you seen my brother anywhere?'

There was no response.

Always wary of his mother's landlord, Leslie gave him his best smile. 'I don't think anyone will be needing their umbrella, not in this weather!' He took out his playing cards. I'll show him a trick, he thought. Cheer us both up.

'Earlier I heard a ghost,' said Sammy, mysteriously, without raising his head. '*Sheyn vi ziben velten.*'

'A ghost, mister?'

'As lovely as the seven worlds.'

Leslie pocketed his cards, deciding to walk by. His property's coming down and it's all making him a bit touched, he concluded. I remember Ratty saying he's dead upset. I think it's maybe worse than that. He's going a bit funny in the head. I think I'll stay away from him.

Sammy looked up. The creases around his eyes seemed wet. His lower lip trembled. 'Where I come from,' he explained, 'there is a choir of boys whose voices are as lovely as the seven worlds. They sing at the Burgkapelle. They are called the Wiener Sangerknaben. The Vienna Boys' Choir.'

Leslie stopped in his tracks. 'Mr Green's told me about them,' he offered.

'Mr who?'

'Mr Green. He's my choirmaster.' Leslie remembered his own generous but solitary solo, in a street nearby, half an hour before. He was pleased he had been overheard. It almost made up for the disaster at the talent show. 'And that wasn't a ghost you heard. It was me.'

'You?' Sammy was astonished.

Without a second thought, Leslie began singing once more. His voice climbed effortlessly through the tones and semi-tones of the ordered pattern of E major, followed immediately by D flat minor.

Sammy stood up, dropping the umbrella. Even in the dimming evening light it was possible to see that his sallow skin had paled. He pressed his chest with his palm. Without another word he went back inside his shop and shut the door. He turned the sign to closed and pulled down the blind.

Leslie continued on his way. I think I'd best have a word with Ratty about his dad, he thought. Tell him that things are maybe worse than he thought. I think he's going all to pieces over the council taking away his barber's shop and all of his flats. I think his nerves have got very bad.

He paused on a broken kerb, staring along the remains of Marsden Street, a newly shattered terrace where clouds of disturbed plaster dust still hung in the air. A demolition man was now sweeping the cobbles, ineffectually, with an outsize broom. Another was shovelling smashed bricks into the back of a wagon. They were getting ready to go home for the day. Pathetic items stood pointlessly in the road. There was a wooden towel rail, a double-hooded pram, a hatstand. Where a house was left half standing, a

carpet hung from a collapsed floor and a bedroom fire-
place was suspended in space, the wallpaper next to it
torn, but still recognizable as a wreath of twining roses. As
Leslie watched, it was clear that all the resonating Elswick
echoes of his voice were undoubtedly extinguished.
They'd disappeared a while before, in the presence of
Sammy Schnitzler, exquisite note by exquisite note by
exquisite note. Without understanding why, he brushed
away a tear. Something had been irretrievably lost.

A limping cat emerged from the damaged front door
and crossed his path. It was white with dust and one of its
rear legs was broken and bloody and dragged along the
ground. Leslie bent down, horrified, but it spat then glow-
ered at him with furious eyes. It struggled away out of
sight leaving a trail of red in its wake.

Leslie shivered. The wrecked streetscape and the
closing day made him at once insecure. A spasm of fear
gripped his heart. Where *is* Geordie? he thought. Something's wrong here, something's happened. Things are in
pieces everywhere, things are falling to bits. Everything's
being broken up and I hardly know where I am. He
glanced at the western sky. It was an angry red now, with
clashing violet streaks. It's late, he thought. He approached
one of the gang and made enquiries. The man was kind
but said he hadn't seen Geordie for over an hour. 'That
strange lad? With the paper and pencil? He'll be away
home for his tea.' He wiped his brow. 'We're away ourselves.' He climbed into the front of the lorry. 'None too
soon.' His mate started the engine.

'I don't think so,' Leslie murmured, his words inaudible. 'Not home. No, I don't think he's gone home.'

The vehicle accelerated, bouncing over rubble, its tail
lights winking. Unaccountably, Leslie felt abandoned. He

watched the twin points of red until they disappeared. He wanted to weep. 'Come back,' he said aloud. A breeze wafted up from the river carrying an autumnal chill. He walked slowly along the street, fastening his coat. On the corner, the remains of a chapel tottered, its wooden panelling stacked together in pieces like fences. Pews were haphazardly piled on the pavement, the roof was gone, but the sign indicating the Sunday hymns was still in position, announcing the numbers sixty-one, one hundred, forty and fifteen. A few dusty prayer books were strewn about. Leslie continued. Outside another half-house there was a mangle and a broken chamberpot. He crossed a cleared area where the heaps of debris were piled tidily ready for disposal. There was already a deep, wide and dangerous chasm dug in preparation for the foundations of more high-rise flats.

He stopped. He had lost his bearings. Panicky and fearful, he retraced his steps back to Marsden Street and tried to orientate himself in relation to Vickers at the very bottom of the hill, where its expanse of buildings hid the river. It was not yet dark but the remaining light was peculiar and thin. The ruined street had a surreal quality with its jutting timbers, its abandoned belongings, its crazy, hopeless angles. It looked just like a newsreel from the war.

Leslie thought he heard a sound. He hesitated near the place where he'd seen the injured cat. There it was again. His heart lurched in his chest and he felt sweat break out under his shirt. It was not the mewing of an animal in pain. It was a nonsensical, half-human sound, a jabbering, a rapid chatter. It was a person's voice but it was making noises that bore no relation to language. He listened carefully. He was in no doubt. He had heard this before. It was Geordie and he was distressed.

Leslie picked his way through broken bricks, slates and glass. He disturbed a heap of lead flashings, put aside for collection. Dully, they teetered and fell. 'Geordie!' he called. 'I'm here!' Frantic, he stumbled against a door jamb, banging his arm. He entered the derelict hallway of a building, which was largely intact. The remains of the day glimmered redly through the bashed-in roof.

'I'm here! I'm here!' The image of the Virgin in the stained glass appeared in his mind. Please help me find him, he beseeched her. Please. Please.

Unusually, Geordie failed to answer. His normal response in a crisis should have been 'Me! Me! Me!'

'Where are you?' Leslie shouted. Then he paused, listening for the words.

Instead the terrifying, meaningless babble grew more desperate.

'What's the matter?'

Shaking with anxiety, his heart pounding, his mouth dry, Leslie moved from the front room to the back. This was bad. This was very bad. This was possibly one of the most disturbed states in which Geordie had ever been. He could take a fit. The older boy checked the kitchen and the space that had once been the scullery. There was no one. The voice filled his ears so that it seemed impossible to discern its source. 'Where – are – you!' He shouted as loud as he could.

There was a sledgehammer hole in the passage, giving access to the staircase leading to the neighbouring flat above. Leslie squeezed through and tentatively stepped on to it. The whole structure appeared insubstantial and half-detached from its moorings. The handrail was loose and useless. His heart now juddering with both fear and anticipation, he began to climb. The stairs moved slightly, sending a shower of plaster dust earthwards. This whole place is going to fall down, he thought. I'll be killed here. This'll be my grave. There was more movement under his feet, it was like being on a ship. He trembled. And poor Geordie's grave too, we'll both be lying crushed under a fallen-down house.

On the landing, closer to the gash where the sky penetrated, it was a little lighter. He looked in the front bedroom, Geordie's cries now filling his head like a demented prayer. There was no one. He passed into the rear. Here, to his enormous relief, was his brother. Leslie rushed towards him and gathered him up. He was shaking and babbling and tearing at his clothing. Foam bubbled on his lips. Leslie folded him in an embrace. He held him tight. 'Shush,' he murmured, rocking him, 'shush.' He squeezed him to make him feel safe. He kissed him, trying to instil some calm. 'Hush now,' he muttered, 'I'm here. You're safe.' Geordie felt damp with panic. 'Your Leslie's here. Your Leslie loves you.'

After what seemed an age, the tumult diminished. Geordie stopped shouting and began quietly sobbing. Leslie released him, staring into his white, beautiful face. His own heart was still beating madly and he had a sense of the unstable building cracking, toppling and leaning. I'm dreaming, he thought. This is a bad dream. 'What *is* it?' he demanded. 'What's the *matter*?'

Geordie's green eyes were fathomless pools. He pointed and whimpered. Hoping it would be nothing, Leslie strained his eyes then walked into the wrecked centre of the room. Something's really, really scared him, he reasoned, trying to calm himself now, but it's just something stupid. This place is almost falling down. Maybe he saw that cat. He moved a broken chair, stepped over a metal bedstead. In a gloomy far corner there was a dusty mattress. On it were what appeared to be two pale bundles. Leslie stared. 'What's that?' he said. He was reminded of laundry, stuffed into bags. He turned. 'It's nothing. The shifters have left stuff here that's all. Clothes, useless stuff.'

Geordie was still shaking but he was now completely quiet.

'Let's get out of here. Let's go home.'

Geordie pointed at the mattress again. He extended his arm and made slow jabbing movements with his finger.

The sky beyond the hole in the roof was now dusky and purple with a moon beginning to show. All was now silent outside except for a distant ship hooting mournfully on the Tyne. A breeze suddenly disturbed the window, which hung outwards, held only by its sashes. It creaked eerily. Leslie peered at the mounds. They were indistinct in the half-dark. He took a couple of steps towards them. He bent down.

Geordie whimpered again.

'No!' With a sharp intake of breath Leslie straightened. He felt his body shake.

Geordie began sobbing once more.

Leslie took a step backwards, pulling pointlessly at his duffel-coat. 'Oh, no!' He felt sick. He retched and clutched his stomach. After a moment, as if unable to believe his own eyes, he moved back towards the mattress and looked again. There, unmistakably, lay the twins, Muriel and Maureen. They were neatly side by side, on their backs, almost but not quite holding hands. They were like two sleeping angels on a tomb. Their pale limbs were bare, their skirts carefully covering their thighs, and their light-weight broderie anglaise blouses were buttoned up at the front, straining against, but concealing, their girlish breasts. Leslie rubbed his face with the back of his hand. They were not asleep. The twins were not resting. Their eyes were open but oddly opaque and sightless. Their mouths gaped. There was a dark gash in each of their necks. These didn't quite match, making them, for the first and last time, non-identical. Blackness had oozed behind their heads in a sickening stain darkening their hair, spreading out a little on to the mattress. Leslie swallowed hard. No, the twins were not asleep. They were not playing some prank of their own devising. They were not acting. They were not trying to trick him. There was absolutely no doubt. They were dead. Their throats were cut.

Dazed, bewildered, Leslie looked around. Near Geordie's feet lay his drawing pad, his jacket, his pencil-case. Leslie laid down the jar of salad cream, which he'd bought for Auntie Ada. He picked up his brother's belongings. He went back to the horror in the corner and tried to find a knife. He was looking for his brother's penknife. There was nothing. He stared at the twins again. Time stood still. He was aware of the creaking window, a faraway boat, chug-chugging on the river, his own heartbeat. He felt as if he'd been in this room for a very long time. In a peculiar way he realized that at this moment he was already used to seeing the girls lifeless. They had been alive but now they were dead. Dead. Definitely dead. Words came unbidden into his mind. *That's the end of them.* Their waxy faces did not show shock. They were blank, like puppets. They almost looked like they never had been alive, as if he'd only ever imagined them alive, as if they'd *never been*. He turned and stared into Geordie's face. It was unreadable in the half-dark. He'd stopped crying. As if he'd been given a signal, the smaller boy made for the door and quickly descended the stairs. Leslie followed, thinking about the way the structure moved and creaked, about the danger.

Outside it was almost night.

'Put your jacket on,' said Leslie automatically. 'It's cold.'

Geordie obeyed.

Suddenly two bright beams appeared from around a demolished corner.

'Oh, damn it!' Leslie tried to pull his brother back into the doorway. There was a small tussle and he dropped the pencil-case, spilling some of the contents. Geordie grabbed the pad and defiantly, side-stepping his brother's grasp, he moved out into the street. He was at once caught in the glare of two torches. He froze like a startled rabbit, his face white and strained and streaked with dirt, holding his sketchpad in front of him like a shield. He looks like a crazy person, Leslie thought, paralysed with fear. And now he's been seen. He's been seen by witnesses.

'How do,' muttered one of the men, as they passed by, unconcerned, their lights now streaming ahead in glaring triangles. They carried haversacks and their cloth caps were jammed on their heads. Their boots crunched. They did not pause or notice Leslie. They were shift workers from Vickers, returning home, using torches to light their way through the clearance site because there were no street lamps any more, no proper pavements, no reliable landmarks. Their footsteps ebbed away. Somewhere a cat mewed pitifully.

As they disappeared, Leslie emerged from the blackness clutching the pencil-case. 'Put your jacket on,' he said. 'It's cold.' He took his brother firmly by the hand. Now

Geordie had disappeared into a world of his own. He was blank, unresponsive. Marching quickly, Leslie pulled him towards the place where the land dropped downhill, back towards the ordinary, undamaged streets where there were lights and friendly smoke from the first burning hearths of the season, where safe people still lived normally, doing ordinary evening things, free from all horror, destruction and death.

Back at home, Scotch Iris was still out. Leslie decided not to go upstairs to Auntie Ada's for tea. It was too late and anyway, it would be impossible. He struggled to push from his mind the memory of the bodies on the soiled mattress. I won't think about it, he vowed to himself. *That's the end of them.* I won't think about it. *That's the end of them.* I won't think about it. *That's the end of them.* Acting automatically, he built up the fire with coal then, once he'd banked it to a high blaze, he got the tin bath out from the yard and filled it from the water-boiler next to the range.

Geordie sat at the table. He was expressionless and still.

Using a big enamel jug, Leslie added cold from the tap in the scullery until the bath was steaming hot, but bearable. He went into Iris's front room and without looking at the dishevelled bed, the clothes strewn about, the litter of cosmetics, he took a perfumed cube from a drawer in her dressing-table. In the kitchen, he unwrapped the paper, crumbled the flower-scented powder into the bath. The air was filled with lavender. He undressed Geordie, who was unresisting, then helped him into the water. 'Lie back,' he ordered. Carefully, using a sponge and a slab of Sunlight soap from the scullery, Leslie washed his brother as if he were a baby. He helped him from the fragrant warmth and rubbed him with a towel. He dressed him in his

154

monkey pyjamas and led him to bed. 'Go to sleep,' he said, turning out the light. Gently, he closed the door.

Leslie cleared away then tidied the kitchen. He made a pot of tea and found a packet of ginger snaps in the otherwise empty pantry. They were soft and stale but he dunked each one into his cup and sucked on it thoughtfully. He wasn't calm, his heart was beating in a fearful way, but he tried to work out what to do. *That's the end of them.* Geordie's gone and killed those blasted twins, he decided, again refusing to let the image of the bodies linger in his imagination. *That's the end of them.* I don't know how, but he's gone and murdered them. He searched through the half-empty pencil-case. There was no sign of the penknife.

He remembered all the stories and gossip about his brother, how it wouldn't go away, how it was repeated and repeated around the streets in shocked whispers or exchanged like cigarette cards, routinely, in the playground at school. Stories about the dafty torturing animals or the dafty peeing himself. More recently, of course, there'd been the accusation that he'd exposed himself to the twins in the back lane. Leslie had never witnessed anything like this. He'd always defended his brother, hotly denied the rumours, believing it to be untrue slander, the result of blind, cruel prejudice. Now, all at once, he was no longer sure. Maybe he did do those things, he wondered. Maybe he can be nasty and ... dirty. Just because I've never seen it doesn't make it impossible. He stared into the flames watching them lick and dance. Tears welled in his eyes then poured down his cheeks. He rubbed his face on the cuff of his shirt. This sudden doubt about Geordie was unbearable. He thought about some of the girls he knew from school and tried to imagine Geordie following them, unbuttoning his trousers. He tried to picture him trapping a dog in the yard, poking it meanly with a stick. These images were suddenly vivid. 'No!' he exclaimed aloud. 'No!'

He went back into the bedroom. He pulled the curtain aside, letting the gaslight from the outside lane enter the room. He stared at his brother, who was sleeping on his back, one of his arms thrown up above his head. He looked innocent, slim, long-lashed, pretty. His hair flopped over his face like a poet's. Leslie sat on the edge of the bed and wept.

*

The next morning, Desperate Dan sat outside in a corner of Ratty Schnitzler's yard, cleaning his boots for the seventh time. The sun beat down on the back of his neck, turning it bright red. He was still in immaculate battle-dress, khaki shirt and gaiters. Following well-rehearsed procedures, he'd already blancoed his webbing again and brassoed his buckles and buttons. Now, the combination of the effort with his footwear and the warmth of the weather made sweat stand out on his brow. He had barely spoken to anyone since the twins' outrage at the Wesley Hall, other than to curse, weep and repeat peculiar army insults which seemed to bear no relation to his current situation. He spat before polishing another hundred circles on his toecaps.

Ratty's elderly dog and one of his Siamese cats basked in the heat. Ratty himself was in his shirtsleeves and his third best drainpipe trousers, brushing out his aviaries and humming along to his transistor radio. When 'Apache' by the Shadows was featured he stopped, picked up his broom and played it, as if it were a guitar. 'Those boots are fine now,' he said encouragingly, striking a penultimate imaginary chord. There was no reply. 'Private!' Ratty called out in a jokey but peremptory way. 'I'm talking about your boots!'

Desperate responded automatically. 'Two, two, nine, four, seven, five, eight, five, Private Matthews D.' He straightened his shoulders. 'Sir!'

'As you like,' answered Ratty with good humour, resuming his task. He grinned at a couple of greedy sparrows, which were trying to squeeze under the netting in order to access the birdseed. He lifted the edge, letting them in. He was a little wary of his friend when he was in a grumpy mood. Because he came from a bad home at the bottom of the hill, with a shrewish, dirty mother, he could be unpredictable, even violent. And the twins' actions had really upset him. Ratty knew that the little blighters had somehow struck a blow against something important, something that was wrapped up inside Desperate's sense of self, his deepest feelings about his own value. He was also aware that his friend should have handed back his uniform to the army when he was demobbed. He definitely had no right to it as a civilian. Consequently, unless recalled, he could never replace the beret, which was completely ruined. Ratty also understood that the previous shine on Desperate's best boots, now devastated by paint-stripper, had taken him years to acquire. The current sheen of seven rubbings was a mere glimmer compared to the deep patina of before.

'These things happen.' He tried to sound consoling. 'If you think about those little floozies at that contest, they were wild. They'd have done anything to get attention.' Ratty emerged from behind the wire netting and fastened the gate. His trapped birds fluttered and pecked and chirruped. 'That big Betty went and ruined them.' His voice dropped to a murmur. 'Her and blokes like me.'

Desperate didn't look up. He spat and polished feverishly. 'If you don't swing that arm, laddie,' he replied, a touch hysterically, 'I'll tear it off, stick it up your arse and have you for a lollipop . . .' Talking to himself, rambling, he seemed very close to breaking point. 'And you, Private Matthews! Don't just stand there like a vulture that's about to shit itself!'

'It's the first signs . . .' Ratty faced him and tapped his friend on the head.

Desperate looked up. 'What?'

'It's the first signs of madness. Talking to yourself.'

His friend resumed his rubbing.

Ratty insisted. 'You're talking to yourself.'

Desperate shrugged.

'Here, have a look at these.' Ratty produced something from his trouser pocket. It was a small bundle of photographs. 'I've got more of those twins. See what I mean?'

His friend laid down his cloth and polish, took the pictures, flicked through them, then quickly handed them back.

Ratty laughed. 'I tell you, man, those two. I've never known anything like it!' He returned the photos to his pocket. 'I'm going to give these to some blokes in London. Soho. That's where they sell dirty books. He's offered me a good price.'

Desperate scowled with distaste.

'I've got good contacts with London, me. I'm extending my business interests all the time.'

His friend seemed unimpressed. 'That's more your kind

of thing than mine.' He picked up his cloth once more. 'Tying kids up? Handcuffs?' He thought for a minute. 'Mind you, that's nothing. I'm not even *saying* what I felt like doing to those damned girls the other day. I wanted to . . .' He made a jabbing, bayonet gesture.

Ratty was suddenly businesslike. 'Leave that polishing. We've got work to do.'

His friend eased one foot into a boot and began lacing it. 'What now?'

Ratty produced a piece of paper. 'I've got more addresses. These folks that's awkward about moving. The ones who say they won't go, who won't take the new houses on offer.'

'And we're going to try and persuade them?' Desperate squared his shoulders, trying to look tough. He grinned unpleasantly. 'Make them shift?'

'Something like that.'

'Like we did before?'

'Yep.'

*

Scotch Iris had come home late and now, only half aware that it was morning, she sat on the end of the bed in her untidy front room, the curtains closed. Shirley Bassey's voice blasted from the Dansette record player. It was stifling hot and almost dark. Clothing was strewn around and there was a smell of sweat mixed with 'Evening in Paris'. She was dressed in a black petticoat and her bare feet dangled. Her hair was drawn up into a tiny topknot, secured with grips, its unbleached roots revealed. A man lay next to her, a regular client, half covered by a sheet, smoking a cheroot. Iris sipped from a tumbler of whisky, pulled a grimace, then picked up the bottle and refilled the man's glass. She inspected her fingernails. The final song ended and there was a long silence between them.

Outside, there was the sound of children playing, the distant crash of falling masonry and the thump-thump of the steam hammer at Vickers. An ice-cream van went by, playing a tinkling tune. Thin strips of sunlight filtered in, around the edges of the shaded windows.

Iris stretched and sighed. 'No,' she said finally.

'What d'you mean, no?'

'What I say. No. It's over. It's finished. Because Betty says she's finished it so she has.'

The man pulled himself up to a sitting position. He was naked, he had a large stomach and in the half-light the tattoos on his arms were visible. 'We had an arrangement.' His voice was quiet but not without menace.

Outside there was a shriek and the sound of a small child crying. The ice-cream van passed by once more. Iris got up, switched the record player on again, turning the volume down low. She sat in a chair. She fanned herself against the heat of the room.

'I said we had an arrangement.'

Iris turned to him. She was fierce, her face pinched and angry. 'You had an arrangement with Betty, never with me. I *never* agreed with it. And if you must have chicka-dees like those two little twins, you'll have to go some-where else. They're off the team for good and that's that.' Her voice was raised. 'Betty's through with it all, so she is. Finished.' She paused, adopting a more measured tone. 'Look. They were never reliable, those girls. You didn't have any *say* with them. They weren't scared of Betty. They weren't scared of anyone. It was too big a risk. You never knew who they were talking to or what they were getting up to.' She paused. 'And you know who their *dad* is.'

The man drained his glass and relit his cheroot. 'I've heard you fancy your chances with *him*. The dad. It's being said. You *do*, don't you? Is that what this is all about?'

Iris picked up her handbag, opened a small glass bottle and washed down two purple hearts with a swallow of whisky. 'That's got nothing to do with this.'

'No?'

'No.' She was vehement again, even a little shrill. 'I never agreed with it. It isn't right, they are just bairns. And since ... now they're ...' She stopped, rubbing her eyes. 'They've bothered and blackmailed me and I don't know what else. Betty couldn't control them. They were out of control. Anything might have happened.' She stood up, paced a little, sat down again. 'What could I have done? They fucking scared me, to tell you the truth. They fucking *scared* me. They were wild. They were terrors. I wish she'd never started it with them. I wish ... I wish ...' Iris was almost shouting now.

'What?'

'They threatened me with their dad, with the law. I'm going to end up in bloody clink.'

There was another silence. The man leant over, picked the bottle up off the floor and refilled his glass. As the dim light from the window caught the side of his cheek, his bushy black sideburns were visible. He was about forty-five. He was the greengrocer from Elswick Road, the one who'd refused to look out for Geordie. 'It's a pity,' he said resignedly.

'Yeah, well.'

He held out a hand. 'Come here.'

Iris got up and crossed over to the bed. There was a faint sheen of sweat on her chest and on her face.

'I'll just have to make do with you then. Again.'

'I'm afraid you will.' She sat on the bed, then lay down on her back, on top of the covers. The man smiled and pulled down the strap of her slip. He bit her shoulder.

*

In the back bedroom next door, Leslie had found sleep to be impossible. His eyes wide open all night, he had heard his mother come in and he knew she had a visitor. He listened to the sounds from her record player, wishing she'd turn it off, wishing the man would go. His heart raced, his mind turning over and over the horrific events of the evening before. He got up and closed the door. Then, getting back into bed, he woke Geordie and began talking in a soothing way. Gently, he mentioned the derelict, half-demolished house. He asked his brother what had happened the previous evening. Geordie was silent but not entirely absent and he was very, very calm. Sleepily he yawned and rubbed his eyes. He lay back on the pillows.

'What did they say to you? Those girls? What did they do?' Inside, Leslie was far from calm. Over and over, all night, he'd kept thinking the same thing – *if only those men hadn't seen him*. If only those men with the torches hadn't come along just then and seen him. No one need have known. It could have remained a secret, a big mystery, an unsolved case for the police. But they saw him clearly and they're bound to know who he is. Everybody round here knows Geordie the dafty, from Glue Terrace. Everybody's wary of him, thinks he's strange. They'll go and tell the authorities, and then they'll all come and lock him up in gaol. For ever. It'll be even worse than him being locked up in a loony bin, because he'll be in a horrible cell with a bucket for a lavvy and a plank for a bed and no one to care for him. 'What did they say to you? Those girls. Tell me.'

Geordie didn't reply.

Leslie persisted. 'Did they . . . Did they call you names, Geordie?'

Geordie sat, drew up his knees under the covers and grasped them. 'No,' he answered, sounding sure.

'What happened?'

There was a long silence. In the next room, a Frankie Vaughan long-player was now sounding from Scotch Iris's record player.

'What happened, Geordie?' Leslie said again.

'I was drawing. I was drawing Marsden Street.' Geordie was in the habit of repeating phrases in conversations. 'Did those girls call you names, Geordie? No.'

Leslie was unconvinced. He persisted. 'Did they call you nasty names? Did they?'

'What happened?' The younger boy clasped his fingers together in a loose handshake. 'What happened, Geordie? I was drawing Marsden Street. Marsden Street. Not nasty names. No. Did those girls call you names? No.'

'I said *what happened*?' Leslie insisted. He was used to these convoluted dialogues with his brother and wasn't to be deterred. 'Yes, *what happened*. That's it. You tell me. Tell me now.'

Geordie echoed him. 'That's it you tell me. I said *what happened*?'

'I'm waiting.'

163

'I'm waiting. Tell me now.'

'Did – *they* – call – *you* – names?' Leslie spoke slowly and with careful emphasis.

Geordie pulled at the counterpane. He became a little agitated. 'I've already said "no". That's what I said. I just said "no". I said it already. I said "no" already, didn't I? I said "no"! I was drawing Marsden Street. *What happened?* Not names. No. Did those girls call you names, Geordie? Were you *listening* or what, Leslie? I said "no". Those girls call you names, Geordie? No.'

Leslie was patient. 'You were drawing Marsden Street . . .?'

'That's right, I was drawing Marsden Street.'

'And?'

There was another weighty pause.

'And?'

Geordie sighed. 'There was a cat.'

Leslie answered quickly. 'Yes, a cat. I saw the cat. Did you hurt the cat?'

'No,' answered his brother forcefully. 'I saved the cat.'

Leslie stroked his arm. 'Go on.'

'Marsden Street. I was drawing Marsden Street. Not names. A cat. A cat. Did those girls call you names, Geordie? I didn't hurt the cat. Not the cat. Not the cat. No. What happened? What happened, Geordie?'

'What happened after you saved the cat?'

For a while, the conversation welled back and forth in a similar vein.

'Did you hurt *anyone*?' Leslie ventured.

'The cat was under a jack rafter,' said Geordie finally.

'Trapped?'

'Trapped under a jack rafter, that's right. I saved the cat. I was drawing Marsden Street. I saved the cat.'

Loving Geordie

'You freed it.'

'I saved the cat. Good boy Geordie. Good boy Geordie, tell Auntie Ada. Go upstairs to Auntie Ada's. Good boy Geordie. I saved the cat. Yes. Yes, I did, yes. What happened, Geordie? I was drawing Marsden Street.'

'What happened to those girls?'

Geordie was silent. His eyes took on a distant, impenetrable quality and he tilted his head back and stared at the ceiling. He~~~~~~ his tongue out, licked his lips. He
~~~~~~~~~~~~~~~~~~~~~~~ght, looking through
~~~~~~~~~~~~~~~~~~~~~~~~~~~~ hill

Andrea Badenoch

'I know you saved the cat. Did you hurt the twins?'

'I was drawing Marsden Street.'

'And you went into the house. You saved the cat. Then you went upstairs. The twins were upstairs.'

'That's right, those girls were upstairs.'

'Did you hurt those girls?'

The record player next door was now silent. There was the sound of Iris's door opening then closing. A man coughed in the hall and then the front do slammed.

Geordie pushed th
the bed. H

became tense. He then sat up straig... the wall, looking far away, through time, up the ... to the West Road. A slow, mournful ballad wailed from the Dansette in their mother's room.

He's seeing something, Leslie realized. With a shudder, he remembered the earlier prophecies about the twins and coffins and graves with worms. He's seeing something in the future again. He drew up his knees, wrapped his arms around them, waited and was silent.

'Our mam's in a white room wearing a long white dress. Her face is pale and she's holding leaves. She's got leaves in her hair. She's with ... with ... She's with a man.'

Leslie was surprised. Sounds like a wedding, he thought, pushing the thought away. He knew it was pointless to interrupt. He sat patiently, but there was no more.

Geordie slowly came back to the present. He turned his green gaze on his brother. 'Breakfast,' he said.

Leslie was undeterred. He had to continue. I can't give up, he thought, desperately. I've got to try and find out. 'No breakfast yet. Did you hurt the twins?' he shook Geordie a little. 'Did you?'

'I saved the cat.'

...ne covers away then lay down flat on
...ie buttoned his pyjama jacket, concealing his chest. He smoothed his trousers flat. His face took on a wide-eyed, open-mouthed expression.

Leslie realized he was emulating the position of the twins in death. 'What did you do?' His voice was now less patient. It was beseeching.

'I couldn't save those girls.'

'What?'

'I couldn't save those girls. They were dead. I saved the cat. Not those girls. Those girls were goners.'

Leslie sat bolt upright. His heart started to race. 'What?'

'I was drawing Marsden Street. I saved the cat. I couldn't save those girls.'

'The twins were already dead when you went upstairs? Is that it? Is that what you're telling me?'

'I saved the cat.'

'Yes, I know.'

'I couldn't save those girls.'

'They were already dead?'

'Yes.'

'They were lying there dead when you found them?'

'Yes.'

Leslie let out a huge sigh. He punched the air. 'Thank

you Jesus!' he shouted, jubilantly. 'Thank you Jesus, God, the Virgin Mary, the Apostles and . . . *everybody*!'

Geordie was surprised. He realized he'd pleased his brother but was unsure why. He sat up and unbuttoned his jacket. 'I saved the cat.'

Leslie started crying with relief. Kneeling on the bed, he hugged Geordie and buried his head in his shoulder. 'I'm sorry,' he said, over and over. 'I'm sorry. I should never have thought . . .'

'I was drawing Marsden Street.'

Laughing and crying all at once and rubbing his eyes, Leslie got up and began rummaging in a drawer looking for clean underwear. He took off his pyjamas and joyfully slapped his boyish chest. He sang a triumphant and happy scale. 'La! La! La!' The Virgin in the stained glass popped into his mind and she was smiling, as cheerful as a winner on the football pools.

Leslie was intimate with the byways and cul-de-sacs of his brother's mental processes and knew he was incapable of lying. Even though he could see the future, he had no imagination whatsoever. He was able to talk only of what he *saw* and had no ability to invent or change facts. He couldn't manipulate reality or order it to suit his own purposes. Lying was a completely unknown concept to him. Leslie knew that Geordie had never told a lie in his life.

'Someone killed those girls,' he said. 'Not you. Someone else.'

'Someone else,' agreed Geordie. 'I'm sorry. I'm sorry. Someone else. I'm sorry.'

Everything's going to be all right, Leslie thought. 'Thank you, Mary.'

*

Next door, Scotch Iris was still in her underwear. Last night she'd been out looking for Ratty and more pills but she hadn't found any. All she'd managed to pick up was the greengrocer. Now, suffering from withdrawal, she felt awful. Sprawled on her dishevelled bed, she rubbed her damp brow with a corner of the sheet. Her handbag lay next to her, its untidy contents strewn about. She stared at the ceiling for some time. After a while she rolled over among the banknotes, used tissues, cosmetics and spilled sleeping tablets. She pulled herself up on to her elbows and tried to cry, but couldn't. Her shoulders shook but no tears came. Her pinned-up hair began to escape and hung around her face.

The morning sun shone on her window and the gloomy room was already hot. A man outside wolf-whistled and then rapped on the pane. Startled, Iris sat up on the bed but ignored the summons. She rubbed her eyes with both fists again, smudging her mascara. She felt tired and dirty and her head ached. All the muscles in her body tingled in the familiar, unpleasant way that signalled her need for amphetamines. She rummaged through the mess on the bedclothes and found a couple of the sedatives. She washed these down with the dregs from the whisky bottle then flung this across the room.

'Thirty-five,' she whispered. 'Thirty-bloody-five.' Too strung-out to cry, she was also too tired to be angry. She felt both hopeless and helpless. What's the matter with me? she wondered after a moment. What's the *matter* with me?

Scotch Iris had no understanding of the drugs she was taking and no real knowledge of the process of addiction. All she knew was that she needed the pills supplied by Ratty Schnitzler in order to get through these summer days and nights without going crazy. At the same time she blamed her misery on the fact that she'd recently turned thirty-five. These seemed like a lot of years chalked up for a woman in her situation and her profession. She knew that it was absolutely necessary to escape but there was no obvious way out of the bondage apart from marriage. Marriage to Mickey Robson. She thought about the twins, about their budding breasts, their stupid babyish dresses and little socks, about their threats. They'd threatened to spoil her chances. 'You deserve to be dead,' she muttered. 'So you do and nothing less. I hate you both. You both deserve to be dead.'

It had once been so different, so bright, so hopeful. Scotch Iris had met her fisherman husband in a Glasgow dance hall during the war. He'd been a shy country boy, out of his depth and awkward. He'd come to the big city to visit his brother who'd found work in the shipyards. Iris had liked him immediately, in fact she was later to declare that it had been 'love at first sight'. He'd approached her, nervous and tongue-tied, on a dare and they'd then danced together all evening. They married six months later and despite many warnings to the contrary, against the advice of all her family and friends, Iris had moved to his fishing village up on the west coast of Scotland where she was briefly and deliriously happy. Everyone had told her she'd be 'bored stiff' but she found she liked the little cottage with its own front and back garden. It was better than the grim and noisy tenements of home. She liked the scenery, she liked the sea. Most of all she liked, indeed she loved passionately, her new young husband who was so quiet and so kind and whose gentle accent sounded like the wind rustling through the wild gorse on the clifftops. Then the babies had made their contentment complete, until that fateful night when his boat fell out of the sea and there was nothing of him left to bring home and bury. Afterwards, when the storm subsided, the villagers had taken her out in a rowing boat and they'd all thrown flowers into the water. They'd floated for a while, sad and beautiful against the black, frightening depths. A priest said a few prayers over the choppy waves. A hymn was sung. There was little else they could do, except mourn.

Scotch Iris stood up, crossed the room to her dressing-table and sat before the mirror. She picked up a couple of jars then tossed them aside in irritation. Eventually she found her eye make-up remover. Using a ball of cotton wool she wiped the smudged mascara from around her eyes. She pulled the remaining pins from her hair and combed it with her fingers. She unscrewed a jar of cold cream and angrily rubbed some into her cheeks, squinting into the glass and examining the tell-tale fine lines that were beginning to appear around her eyes and mouth. Sleepy now from the pills, resting her face in her hands, she stared into the mirror. Her face was smeared in cream and her hair was tatty and in need of a wash. She looked old instead of glamorous. She thought of Mickey Robson, handsome in his narrow suit, his thin tie, his Chelsea boots with their fashionable pointed toes. 'What a sight,' she declared, addressing her own reflection. 'What a bloody sight you are, girl.' She rested her head on her arms. In a minute or so she dozed, but there was no peace. She dreamed of a massive tidal wave running up the Tyne from the coast. As it approached Elswick it got higher and higher. Small craft and quayside timber buildings were dashed to pieces as it progressed. It reached Vickers and flooded over the factory rooftops, surging blackly up the hill, unstoppable, demolishing the houses more quickly and more effectively than a thousand gangs of workmen with bulldozers and mallets. The buildings were flooded then pushed aside, as innocent people bobbed, screamed and drowned in the watery turmoil.

*

Mickey Robson was sitting with T. Dan Smith in his office in the Town Hall. He was greyish-looking today and the dark circles under his eyes made him look older than usual. Between them on his desk was an unrolled plan of the west end of Newcastle as it was intended it should look in two years' time. Most of it was coloured green with irregular circles that signified bushes and trees. The high flats were shown as squares and referred to as 'fifteen-storey point blocks'. Beyond the grey rectangles of the Vickers factory, which were largely unchanged, the Tyne was coloured an unlikely blue. The council leader was speaking to London on the telephone. 'I completely agree, Harold,' he said. 'That matches my thinking exactly.' Mickey yawned then grasped his forehead as if in pain. A uniformed tea lady brought in a tray of coffee and biscuits. Smith replaced the receiver. 'Harold Wilson,' he informed Mickey, rattling and arranging the cups.

Mickey was impressed. 'Of course,' he said, nodding.

'Filling me in on the Shadow Cabinet's draft strategy for the development of the regions.'

Mickey bit into a biscuit, chewed, then stared at it doubtfully. He suppressed a burp. 'Of course,' he agreed again, clutching his stomach and wincing.

Smith fussed a little with the teaspoons and napkins. He set great store by perfect table manners. In silence the two men drank their coffee. Mickey held his cup in both hands as if gratefully warming them, Smith was refined, prissy, with his little finger extended. Mickey took out a small bottle of aspirins and swallowed one.

'Heavy night?' asked Smith.

Mickey nodded. He tried to give a rueful smile but it appeared as a grimace.

Smith put down his cup and saucer, leaned back in his padded leader's chair, stretched then clasped his arms behind his head. 'Drink sends you to the devil,' he offered, his voice consoling rather than accusatory.

Mickey nodded once more.

'Take it from me. Drink is the enemy of success. Look at me. I don't smoke or drink. Why take up habits that merely stand in your way? That prevent you getting on?'

'You're right,' agreed Mickey. He'd already decided this morning, as on previous mornings, that he'd never touch another drink again in the whole of his life.

'My father drank,' Smith confided. 'It was the ruin of him. He was a fine man at one time. A miner and a good communist. But drink turned him into a wastrel.'

Mickey eyed him balefully. He was unsure how to respond.

Smith paused. He seemed to be collecting his thoughts. He eyed his colleague then stared at the carpet. 'If you don't mind my saying so, Robson, you could do with putting your house in order.'

Mickey raised his eyebrows.

Smith was a little uncomfortable. 'I've got three fine children. All of them at the very best schools that the region's got to offer. My eldest daughter intends making a career for herself as a teacher. My wife . . . my wife . . .'
He stopped.

'Your wife?' responded Mickey.

'My wife is a cultured woman. She likes theatre, ballet, good literature.'

'I see,' said Mickey, not seeing at all.

'What I'm trying to say, Robson . . . What I'm trying to say . . . is this.'

Mickey waited. There was an uncomfortable silence.

'Robson. You're a talented politician and a real socialist. I respect you. I see a future for you as . . .'

'As?'

'As my right-hand man.'

Mickey smiled wanly, taking another swallow of coffee.

Smith sat up straight, put down his cup with a clatter. 'I was at a party in London last week. A late-night do. Senior Labour Party people, Lords of the Realm. Businessmen. Even a member of the royal family. But there was too much drink. Way, way too much drink.' He paused. 'Someone thought it would be a good idea to show a . . . a . . . er . . . one of those blue films.'

Mickey laughed in a loud guffaw, them immediately stopped, realizing it was inappropriate.

Smith blustered. 'I left immediately. Of course. Immediately. There really is no place in politics for *that* kind of thing. I left immediately and made it clear to my host I was not pleased.'

'Certainly not,' Mickey agreed, hiding a smile with his hand.

'Robson, your girls. Your . . . your . . . fiancée. You need to do something about them.' Smith's words came quickly now and with relief. 'It's been noticed by certain people . . . Your daughters are running wild and they don't go to school. It's really very, very poor, I must say. Lovely young girls like that, wasting themselves, throwing away an education. And your, er . . . your fiancée.'

'I haven't got a fiancée.'

'Well, your *friend* then. Whoever she is . . .'

'Iris MacDonald?'

'Yes. Scotch Iris.' His mouth made a little grimace of distaste. 'I believe that is her nickname. She really isn't the right kind of woman for you . . . Not for you, Mickey.'

Mickey met his eye.

'You don't mind if I call you Mickey?'

'No, sir.'

'Never mind the sir. Call me Dan.'

'Right.'

'You shouldn't be out drinking and fooling around with *her* kind, Mickey. You should put your house in order.' He stared sternly at his colleague. 'In order. You understand?'

Mickey stood up, went over to the window, looked out, turned back again. Silhouetted against the light, he was at once elegant and attractive. 'I hear you,' he replied. He rubbed his eyes and tried to suppress a yawn.

'I sleep a mere six hours a day. I run a successful business. I'm very well off. I talk to Harold Wilson on the telephone every day of my life, which effectively means I have the ear of our future PM.' He paused. 'Do you know something? Do you know how I started? I started off painting "*Evening World*" on the fascias of corner shops. That's what I did. "*Evening World*", in paint, over and over and over again. Every day.' He sounded defiant. 'I was a painter's apprentice. I was a nothing. A nobody. Now I have the best painting and decorating business around these parts. Now I write poetry, now I eat in restaurants. Now I *lead this city*.'

Mickey had heard enough. He squared his shoulders. He was at once impressive and a little threatening. He didn't like criticism and he was afraid of no one. Resolutely, he changed the subject. 'You always make sure it's *your* decorating business that gets all the council contracts.'

Smith was startled, but he responded immediately. 'My firm is the best one for the job.'

'Is that why you're called "One Coat Dan?"' Mickey smiled. He was skilled at claiming the advantage and he rarely let anyone intimidate him.

However, Smith was an able adversary. He knew when to prevaricate and when not. Sizing up the situation, he was at once straightforward, speaking quietly and in a matter-of-fact way. 'People like me are expected to work full-time without salaries, without staff, without even postage stamps. I can't afford such a situation. So I make sure my business doesn't miss out. It's perfectly simple. I merely combine my desire to give public service with what's called . . . a piece of the action.'

The councillor was surprised by his leader's bluntness. There was a silence in which the two regarded each other. Still a little aggressive, Mickey then steered the dialogue in another direction. 'Scotswood Road,' he went on. 'We've got a small but stubborn minority of people who won't shift.' He pointed to the plans on the desk. 'Who don't want to shift. Not many, mind you. But a few.'

Smith took a deep breath. 'No one will be evicted. No one. This is a socially justified exercise. Everyone will be convinced. Everyone will see the greater good. *No one will be evicted.*'

'What about the ones who won't . . .'

Smith interrupted. His tone became declaratory, his voice a little too loud. 'So often people don't live long enough to see their personal vision become a reality. But I can see it. I stand back and see the landscape change before my very eyes. I can *feel that things are getting done.*'

'But what about . . .?'

'We are painting on a new canvas.' Smith's voice started to boom. 'There's not another city in England which can say that. Where *one can do just that* . . .'

'We're mixing people up,' Mickey interrupted.

Cut off, as he was, in mid-flow, Smith was discomfited. 'Pardon?'

'We're mixing people up.'

'You mean confusing them?'

'I mean we're mixing together the more well-to-do people from up the hill, from up by the park, the ones with upstairs bedrooms, inside facilities and all that, we're mixing *them* up with people from further down. The ones with netties outside, cold taps and no electric.'

'I'm not quite sure I catch your drift . . .'

Mickey was assertive. 'Look. It's something that's been bothering me. It's been bothering me more than those troublemakers who won't shift, because I can *deal* with *them*. This is something else. Another problem. But a trickier one. I'm worried that we're mixing together the better-off people with the ones who've got nowt. The ones *in work* with the ones who *never work*. You know that hill above Scotswood Road? It's graded. There's high, middle and low. Depending on which street you're in. And people like to know their place. They like being in among their own kind. People aren't *all the same*.'

T. Dan Smith looked impressed. He stared at Mickey, his brows knitted together. 'That's a very interesting point which you've just made. Very interesting.'

Mickey continued. 'Shove everybody together in blocks of flats, mix them all up with no attention to old neighbourhoods, the old pattern of streets . . . well I think we might be laying down problems for the future, that's all. They won't like it. People won't like it at all.'

Smith scratched his head. He leaned back in his chair, cupping his head in his raised hands. He smelled slightly of fresh sweat, Mickey noticed, mixed with rigorous carbolic. 'It's not a problem,' he said decisively. 'No.'

'No?'

'No. It's good to mix them all up. Can't you see, it'll raise the general level. The people from the bottom can only *benefit* from the influence of their betters. This is a wonderful social experiment, Robson. Sorry, I mean Mickey.' He paused. 'I say, let's really *mix them all together*. Stir them up. Let the great unwashed improve themselves. Give them facilities, give them decent neighbours, give them sculpture parks, give them the opportunity . . .'

There was a knock from outside.

'Enter!' called out Smith.

The door opened and two policemen stood uncertainly in the entrance. They were holding their helmets and looking downcast. One of them beckoned to Mickey. He stepped quickly from the room, then was led away down a gloomy corridor. The other briefly conveyed to the leader the awful news about the discovery of the bodies of the twins.

Smith sat down carefully. His face was flushed. 'Cause of death?' he asked curtly.

'We have reason to suspect foul play.'

The tall, sandy-haired man looked displeased.

At that moment there was a shout from down the corridor and a metallic sound which was actually a fire-bucket clattering down a staircase. There was a harsh male scream.

Smith moved towards the door.

'It's all right, sir,' the policeman said politely, holding up one hand in a detaining gesture. 'We have a doctor on duty.'

The telephone rang and the Leader returned to his desk to answer it. As he picked up the receiver he said to the officer, 'That will be all, Constable.'

The policeman retreated, replacing his helmet, grim-faced and respectful.

6

Leslie and Geordie were having their breakfast of a few leftover scones, which Auntie Ada had given them the previous day. The door opened and Scotch Iris came into the room. She'd managed to pull herself together and was now wearing a smart navy-blue dress with a matching sailor jacket. Her hair was excessively backcombed and stiff with lacquer and her newly applied make-up was heavy, hiding the ravages of the night. 'What are you two doing, not finished your breakfasts yet?' she asked. She was jittery, distracted, worried. 'This isn't a holiday camp. Why, that Geordie's still in his pyjamas.'

Her younger son stared at a patch of wallpaper to the side of her head. His face was at once composed into uncommunicative blankness. He didn't acknowledge her at all. Leslie said, 'We're nearly finished.' He scraped some jam off his plate and licked the knife.

'I'm off out then,' said their mother. She sounded weary. 'I'm expecting ah . . . um . . . a visitor. At half ten. Tell him I've gone out. Tell him I've been unavoidably called away. So I have.'

'Unavoidably called away,' repeated Geordie, still staring at the wall.

'That's right.'

'There's no food,' said Leslie. 'There's nothing in the pantry.'

Scotch Iris raised her eyebrows quizzically. It was as if the concept of the need for food in the house was completely alien to her. She regarded the remains of the scones with distaste.

'Give us some money, will you?'

'What?'

His breaking voice plunged low. 'You never go shopping any more. You haven't been shopping all summer. You've given up buying food. Give us some money, will you? For bread. Milk. Eggs.'

His mother opened her handbag and, tight-lipped, handed him a pound note. She seemed close to tears.

Leslie heard the door bang. He stared at the cash. He was still elated with the relief of discovering his beloved brother wasn't a murderer. 'We can go to the pictures with this,' he said. He had never before demanded money from his mother. He felt proud to have dared to do it and amazed that she had agreed so readily. It might not be so easy next time, he reasoned. I took her by surprise. He then felt a little ashamed of himself and the fact that he was glad she'd gone out. He fingered the photograph in his shirt pocket without removing it. He swallowed hard and rubbed his face with his sleeve.

'Unavoidably called away,' said Geordie.

Leslie went into the kitchen and filled the kettle for tea. 'First we'll go and see Auntie Ada,' he called out. 'I made a sponge cake yesterday. You can have some if you like. It looked smashing.' He lit the gas. The smell for some reason reminded him of the world outside, of the dreadful abnormality of everything, the demolition, the injured cat, the disappearance of familiar landmarks, the horror. Those twins are still dead, he remembered, his joy evaporating. He saw their bodies in his mind's eye and his heart lurched, unpleasantly. *That's the end of them.* They've been lying there dead, all night. They'll be cold and stiff and they'll be getting horrible flies and stuff on them. I wonder what's going to happen? He swallowed hard. I'm glad that my Geordie didn't do it, but it's still really awful.

The letterbox rattled in the hall. Leslie retrieved an official-looking envelope addressed to his mother. He opened it and immediately his spirits sank further. It was another letter from the psychiatrist at Prudhoe Hospital. He remembered the smart dark-skinned man who'd wanted to talk to Geordie. The flowery signature was no doubt his.

Leslie cleared the table and washed up, then he took the letter to the bedroom. He lifted down the dictionary from the top of the wardrobe and painstakingly tried to decipher the words. The doctor, addressing himself to Mrs MacDonald, 'referred to his earlier correspondence' and 'noted a missed appointment'. He offered an 'alternative date' and said he hoped 'that this would be convenient'. He added that he had been 'in receipt of a further report from the General Practitioner' and 'referrals from a variety of the welfare agencies involved'. He said that 'all parties had the best interests of George MacDonald high on their individual agendas' and that 'he looked forward to meeting her with a view to agreeing a mutually acceptable regime of rehabilitation in the context of appropriate residential care'.

Geordie came into the bedroom and began slowly dressing himself, concentrating hard on getting the garments the right way round.

When he felt he had understood its contents, Leslie folded the letter and put it in his shoebox under the bed, along with the original one and the information about shifting which had come from the council. What can I do? he thought. He went over to his unsuspecting brother and folded him in another embrace. 'I love you,' he whispered. 'Don't ever forget that.'

*

Scotch Iris had once tried hard to be a good mother, but the caring and domestic toil of the boys' childhoods seemed to have retreated into the recesses of a faraway past. Now she walked from the flat, disorientated, sweating, her limbs shaky, her mouth dry, thinking about the remains of those scones on the table. Old Ada must've given them those, she decided, for their breakfasts. There's no food in the pantry. She felt ashamed. I'll do something about it, she resolved. But first I'll find that young Schnitzler and I'll get hold of some pills to set me right. *Then* I'll go shopping, so I will. I'll cook a proper meal. We'll have a big dinner with meat and vegetables and pudding with custard. She felt giddy and sick at the prospect but her intentions were firm.

Scotch Iris had found it hard going at the welfare clinic when Geordie was a toddler. He wouldn't play with the other children and he could be difficult about sharing toys. His vacant stare, his dribbling, his refusal to listen or take notice, caused consternation at first among the other mothers, then whispering, then ostracism. They sat apart from her, on the other side of the fishtank. They told their own offspring not to go near Geordie. Iris knew they talked about her when they thought she couldn't hear, suggesting her way of life was the cause of her younger son's difficulties.

The nurses too had been hostile. They asked her if she played with the boy, questioned her about her mothering skills. They blamed her for his blank-eyed stare, for his refusal to be tested, to build bricks or arrange letters.

Because he would not respond to her, or even acknow-ledge her, they assumed she was an inadequate mother. 'I'm doing my best,' she'd insisted. 'He just won't look at me. He doesn't seem to hear me.'

'His hearing is unimpaired, Mrs MacDonald.'

'It's as if he's in a world of his own, so he is.'

They looked at her in such a way that suggested the boy *needed* to be in a world of his own, as if it were all her fault. After a year or two of this, Scotch Iris stopped going to the welfare sessions. She kept the boy clean, she fed him, she bought him presents on his birthday. She couldn't persuade him to speak to her or sit on her knee or play or look at picture books. He would only go to sleep at night if his big brother put him to bed and then climbed in next to him. He hates me, she thought privately. He misses his dead daddy. He's been damaged by his daddy falling out of the sea before he was even born.

When Scotch Iris sent her youngest boy to school, the teachers refused to keep him there. They sent him home with Leslie time after time. 'We can't have him,' they told her when she went to ask why. 'He can't be educated. He's mentally deficient.'

'He can do sums,' argued the young mother, 'he can read his alphabet, he can even play tunes on that old Scottish piano!'

'Yes, but he's not all there,' his spinster form mistress said with a nasty smile. 'Is he? He's not all there up top.' She pointed to her own head.

'You best take him home, my dear,' said the headmis-tress kindly, although as she said so she pushed Geordie firmly by the shoulders towards the door. 'He won't settle. There's nothing we can do for him. He's nothing but a dreadful nuisance to us here, when all's said and done.'

Andrea Badenoch

Afterwards, Iris trailed around, taking her beautiful boy to the vicarage and the doctor's surgery among other places. Everybody shook their heads. A long-faced woman with rimless eyeglasses came from an office in the town and filled in some forms, but then Iris never saw or heard from her again. When he was bigger she took him to the police station and to the nuns at the Big Lamp. No one was interested. She tried to get him into a Catholic school, a Church of England school and even a small, private school where the boys wore ties and fancy blazers. Nobody wanted him. In the end she gave up and his life was spent in the kitchen or in the back bedroom, drawing, saying bus timetables over and over aloud, tinkling the piano or dreaming to himself. When Leslie came home from school he took him outside or to see the old woman upstairs. Her life with him was so difficult that she was sorry to admit that she looked forward to the times when he was out from under her feet. And it was clear that this was a place where Geordie had no desire to be.

*

Later, Ratty Schnitzler lounged against a jukebox in a milk bar on the Westmoreland Road. He was wearing his best purple drapes, a white shirt and a black silk jabot. Today his greased quiff was spectacularly moulded and his crêpe soles raised his not inconsiderable height by at least two inches. As usual, the place was crowded and in among the sharp Italian suits and winkle-picker shoes of all the fashion-conscious young men he cut an anachronistic figure. However, his look was too studied, too unerring, too complete to be anything other than impressive, if not menacing. He looked dark and in the know. A few girls eyed him flirtatiously but he made a point of ignoring them. Casually, he flicked a florin and, barely moving, caught it on the back of his hand. Then he repeated the gesture. He seemed bored and disdainful.

After a while a tubby man in a tight sports coat and pork-pie hat appeared down some stairs. He beckoned to Ratty surreptitiously, glancing around with furtive eyes. In response, languidly and feigning disinterest, Ratty followed him up.

The upstairs office had a name on the door. It said 'Social Club Services Ltd.' It was a gloomy, small room, its window facing a brick wall across an alley. Here a sleek middle-aged businessman in shirtsleeves with silver arm bands sat behind a desk and talked on the telephone. He was smoking a big cigar. Ratty's appearance seemed to surprise him and he raised his eyebrows. He gestured to Ratty to sit but instead the young man leaned against a filing cabinet. The fat man positioned himself by the door. He was clearly a minder and his piggy eyes focused on nothing except the wall opposite.

'Mr Schnitzler, welcome,' the sleek man said after a minute, replacing the receiver. 'Thanks for your time.' He had a London accent and his manners and confidence spoke of power and influence.

Ratty nodded. He strolled over to the chair, turned it round and, in an easy gesture, sat on it back to front. He smoothed the sides of his head and his gold skull and crossbones cufflinks glittered. 'No problem like,' he replied, his local accent sounding very pronounced. 'So.' He paused. 'About these one-armed bandits . . .'

The conversation got under way. It was terse on Ratty's side, amiable and persuasive on the other. They discussed the installation of fruit machines in a number of clubs and pubs in the west end of Newcastle. It was clear that Ratty was to take charge of the management of these and make sure that any unwilling proprietors fell into line. He was to report directly to London and pay the takings into an offshore account. It became clear in the discussion that there was rivalry between this outpost of a London-based organization and a local Newcastle 'firm'. It was Ratty's job to try and squeeze the competition out of the picture.

'The Twins are very keen to make a go of this,' the sleek man said. 'They've got a lot hanging on this. It's to do with empire building. Newcastle's the furthest city in England away from London, so ... are you the man for the job?'

Ratty was nonplussed. 'The twins?' he responded, hesitantly.

'Yes?'

'Which twins?' For a crazy moment he thought that the businessman was referring to the Robson girls. These were the only twins he knew.

'Your new bosses. In London. The Kray brothers.'

'Oh, I see. They're twins?'

'Yes, they are.'

Ratty swallowed his discomfiture. 'You can depend on me,' he declared, standing up and offering his hand. 'Those London twins can depend on me. I'm their man.'

*

The gramophone played loudly in Sammy Schnitzler's hairdressing saloon. He stood in the back, stirring his vat of Schnitzler's Brilliant. He'd slightly overdone the perfume and the air was thick and heavy with a cloying, sweet odour. In his sink a new load of second-hand bottles were washed and ready for filling. A collection of replacements was awaiting a good soak, piled in a box near the door. They were washing-up-liquid bottles, beer bottles and lemonade bottles, some only half empty of their contents. Sammy was known to pay more for empties than was retrievable from the local pubs or grocery stores and his son's friend, that soldier-boy, had brought these to him the other day. When Sammy handed him five shillings the young man admitted he'd been around the demolition sites, taking them from the cupboards of abandoned homes.

Sammy sat on a stool and began siphoning his hair oil into the clean containers. Even above the music, he thought he could hear the noise of the bulldozers and sledgehammers drawing inexorably nearer. He sighed. He was a lonely man with no friends and had never practised his religion in England. Up until recently his social standing as a landlord and shopkeeper had more than made up for this, but now, as disaster and ruination loomed, he felt as valueless and as frightened as he had during the Nazi ascendancy in Vienna. Another fat tear moistened his eye. It's the war all over again, he thought. In so many ways his days felt similarly perilous, anarchic and without meaning. Destructive forces were blasting away everything familiar, everything he held dear. Carefully he wiped the newly filled bottles with a rag. He lined them up in neat rows, like soldiers. He pressed his hand over the pain in his heart.

The door to his shop rattled and the bell pinged. 'Come in! Come in!' Effusively Sammy welcomed a customer. It was Leslie. He sat him on a cushion in the barber's chair. After a few moments of sharp combing the boy watched as his red, wavy, unkempt hair fell to the floor in clumps.

He was aware that he was trying hard, and largely succeeding, in *not* thinking about the bodies on the abandoned mattress in the half-demolished house.

'It's been left too long,' Mr Schnitzler shook his fat cheeks disapprovingly. He snipped along the edge of his comb. 'A boy your age should be neat and tidy.'

'I have to get a job,' Leslie agreed, his voice plunging low, like a man's.

'A job?'

Leslie took a deep breath. The weight of his responsibility was burdening him like a heavy stone. 'Do you need an assistant here, mister?' He was hesitant. The thought of touching people's heads, the thought of their hair, their skin, made him a little queasy. 'I could sweep the floor.'

'Assistant? Assistant? I should be so lucky. I'm not even covering the overheads, my boy.'

Leslie sighed.

Sammy laid down his comb and scissors and moved over to the gramophone. An operatic long-player had just ended. Leslie watched in the mirror as the barber took the record up off the turntable and returned it to its cardboard cover. Carefully he picked out a replacement, dusted it then set it spinning. The sonorous sound of a cello welled like a wave through the warm air. Sammy stood behind the boy once more. 'So. *Vos vilst du zayn?* What do you want to be?'

'I don't know what, Mr Schnitzler. I'm sorry but I don't.' His voice trembled. 'I just don't.'

'You don't know? You don't know? What's the matter with you young people these days? You're like my son, God help him. A *leydikgeyer*. No trade. No profession. No ideas. No ambition.' He sighed theatrically and shook his head. 'You don't know? Well, I don't know, either.'

Leslie was indignant. 'Oh, your Ratty's got ambitions. He's got ideas all right. Ratty's going to have one-armed bandits in all the pubs and clubs on Scotswood Road.' Leslie was enthusiastic. 'He says they'll rob people blind and he'll make lots and lots of money. A hundred pounds a week maybe. He says I can go in with him when I'm eighteen.'

Sammy paused, both hands raised, holding his scissors and comb. He looked horrified. He glanced about, then out into the street as if fearing someone might overhear. 'You get a proper job, you hear me?' He was vehement. 'Never mind what my Ratty says. He's a bad influence. A Teddy boy. You get a proper trade and you look after your mother.' He considered a moment. 'You don't know? You don't know? What's your mother say?' He paused and lowered his voice. 'I must speak to her about these matters.'

Leslie felt his cheeks burning. He picked up a newspaper from the bench and pretended to read. He didn't want to talk about Scotch Iris. Just at this moment he didn't want to think about her. He was aware that Sammy Schnitzler was the family's landlord and he was more than suspicious of the nature of all his mother's business arrangements. He pushed all thoughts of her out of his mind. 'We might be shifting, any road,' he said, folding the paper and changing the subject. 'We might all be shifting.'

Sammy attacked the top of his head, his scissors snipping at double-fast speed. 'The wicked person fares well in this world,' he murmured mysteriously. 'The saint is in the life to come.'

'I went to a meeting about it,' Leslie continued, ignoring Sammy Schnitzler's enigmatic response. He winced as the blades nicked his ear. 'We might all be shifting out to the country. Or maybe up into that big skyscraper at the back of your house. We're all going to have inside netties.' He remembered his visit to Adamsez. 'And washbasins.' Then T. Dan Smith's ruddy face surfaced in his memory. 'And trees and lawns and art and sculptures.' He tried to picture this, but all he could bring to mind was the disturbing chaos of smashed streets and broken buildings.

There was a silence between them. On the gramophone, the sad cello reached its conclusion and there was a click as the mechanism switched off. Outside, the distant demolition gang could be faintly heard. The heavy steam-hammer down at Vickers thumped rhythmically. A horse and cart clop-clopped past. Leslie sank into a reverie as the tickly shears ran up the back of his neck. They felt nice. He was momentarily relaxed. I must bring Geordie in here, he decided. Geordie needs a haircut. Mr Schnitzler hasn't cut his hair for months and months and months. He recalled the previous occasion, his brother's anxiety, his fear of the scissors, his obstinate refusal to get in the chair. Miraculously, the barber had calmed him. He'd asked if he'd like to play the gramophone. Geordie had hesitated. Because he never went into his mother's room, he had no experience of her Dansette, of her long-playing popular records. Mr Schnitzler, with a curious understanding of his interests, had given him a recording to hold. He'd let him take it out from its sleeve and showed him how to hold it by its edges and how to polish it. He'd then guided him to the window where he'd told him to raise the smooth bakelite circle up to the light. At once, the shiny black concentric lines, the engraved symmetry, had entranced Geordie. He'd studied the disc for some time, turning it this way and that, observing the pattern, before being instructed on how to place it in the gramophone and set it going. He'd pressed the little lever several times, starting and stopping the stylus arm, watching it move back and forth. Finally, happy and satisfied, he'd submitted to a haircut. Mr Schnitzler was kind to him, Leslie remembered. He'd been patient and gentle.

His thoughts strayed back to the beach and the trip to Cullercoats. He saw again Geordie running to him, his feet splashing on the edge of the sea, his face delighted and sunny. He sighed. He took the photograph half out of his pocket, studied the edge of it, thought about showing it to Mr Schnitzler but then changed his mind. He returned it to his pocket. He looked in the mirror and was pleased. He now had a proper short back and sides. All his hair had been removed except a ginger trimmed thatch, high above his ears and eyebrows. He looked naked and rather earnest, but very clean. The barber blew on him, before tickling him with a special brush. Leslie smiled. 'Thanks, mister. That's better.' He took out his playing cards. 'Pick a card. Any card.' He shuffled them expertly, then fanned the pack.

Sammy Schnitzler met his eyes in the mirror, but he had a serious expression on his face. He ignored the playing cards. 'That Councillor Robson is a bad man,' he suddenly declared. He sounded heated again, emotional. 'A very, very bad man indeed. That whole Council is full of bad men. Trotskyists. Apparachiks. Collaborators. I can tell you something. Sir Winston Churchill did *not* win the war and keep this country free for the likes of *them* to ruin everything that is British. They should all go to Russia.'

Leslie put his cards away. He felt rebuffed. He wanted to get up, pay his half-crown and leave, but he felt trapped in the reflection of the barber's angry eyes.

'It's those poor little girls I feel sorry for.' Sammy dunked his comb in a jar of disinfectant.

'The twins!' Leslie was shocked. He knows! he thought. Already! He stepped down from the chair and faced Sammy Schnitzler. 'Why?'

Sammy picked up a dispenser of Schnitzler's Brilliant and squeezed some on to his palms. He sighed and considered his words. 'Those two babies run around these streets like ghetto orphans. Little angels, fluttering around the ruins, all motherless and abandoned. All alone.' Energetically, he rubbed his hands together. 'I've seen it before. I've lived through terrible times, my boy. Terrible times. You don't know the things I've seen. And I know what can happen to innocents like those poor lost girls.'

Leslie was out of his depth. He was embarrassed and could think of nothing to say. He edged towards the till. He left his money on its shelf and made for the door.

Mister Schnitzler was over-excited, trembling slightly. He advanced towards Leslie, hands outstretched, intending to rub the hairdressing oil into his scalp. 'Very bad things are happening to them. Bad men are everywhere. And who cares? Who cares? If God lived on earth all his windows would be broken.'

Leslie opened the door, escaped and let it bang behind him. He could hear Mr Schnitzler still shouting after him as he hurried off down the road.

*

Geordie was at the piano when the police knocked at the flat on Glue Terrace. He was playing Beethoven's 'Moonlight Sonata', which was note perfect, but rendered without emphasis or emotion.

Leslie peeped around a crack in the open front door.

It was evening. 'My mother's out,' he said hoarsely, his voice deep and mature. 'She's been unavoidably called away.'

The officer wedged his boot in the aperture. 'Open up, Sonny Jim.' He pushed and the boy stepped backwards, his heart at once beating fast and hard. It wasn't Constable Henderson. It was no one Leslie knew.

Later, when he was to try to remember the next twenty minutes, Leslie could recall only a scrimmage and a blur. They were the worst moments of his life, except perhaps for the time when his father's boat fell out of the sea, a subliminal disaster which he knew had occurred when he was only six months old. In the following days he tried frequently to bring to mind the exact sequence of events after the police arrived for Geordie, but it proved to be impossible. Try as he might, he could only experience a series of impressions. There was a crash of piano chords, a surge of uniformed bodies in the passage, unwelcome shouts, the smell of male sweat, and Geordie's astonished screams. At some point a harsh-faced Welfare woman came in, grabbed him and held his arm as tight as a vice, preventing him from going to Geordie's aid. 'You keep out of this, big boy,' she'd hissed like a snake in his ear. He struggled and tried to stamp on her foot but she overpowered him. 'Where's your blasted mam?' she'd said. She had a strange accent.

'Unavoidably called away,' Leslie answered automatically, breathlessly, still trying to escape.

The woman laughed, unpleasantly. 'I bet she is.' Her face, he noticed, was covered in spots. She pinioned his arms. Her breath smelled of drains.

There were loud voices in the kitchen and the sound of furniture overturning. Geordie began his terrified babble, his cornered-monkey gibberish, the same sounds that he'd uttered in the half-demolished house the previous evening. Leslie wriggled and sobbed with anger. 'Leave him alone!' he shrieked, clawing at the woman. 'You buggers! Leave my brother alone!'

Leslie remembered another jostle of people and for some reason, more determined piano-playing soaring above the chattering fear and the shouting and the sound of glass shattering. The woman's face was close, too close to his, and her fingers dug in, painfully. 'You're a wicked old cow,' Leslie spat in her face as she shook him. 'Let me go, damn you! Let me go!'

A police siren sounded outside and was then extinguished. Auntie Ada was calling his name in the street and then Geordie was bundled past, his jumper half off, muttering, a drop of saliva leaking from the corner of his mouth, his laces undone, his black hair dishevelled, pale, handcuffed and manhandled by two enormous officers. He seemed very thin and very, very vulnerable. He looked as if he were about to die of fright.

'Let me go or I'll *kill* you!' Leslie sank his teeth into his captor's fleshy arm. He tasted blood. Swearing, she released him and he dived out behind the gang of police, hitting the fresh, cool air of the street only to see the woebegone, ashen-faced stare of Geordie, goggling at him in betrayed disbelief through the windows as the vehicle moved away.

Leslie sank down on to the pavement, kneeling as if in anguished prayer. His heart was thumping in an agonizing way. The car was called a Wolseley, he noted, irrelevantly. A Wolseley. The world swam as he almost fainted. Oh no, he thought, oh no, oh no. Please help me Jesus. Mary. Everything was happening in slow motion. He watched the red brake lights of the departing police car, poised on the junction, for what seemed like a very long time.

Then something completely unexpected happened. As the car turned resolutely but unhurriedly out of the street, one of its rear doors swung open. Geordie rolled out fast, like a tiny acrobat, hitting the cobbles then somersaulting over and over. The car continued to accelerate as the boy jumped to his feet. Restrained by handcuffs, he began running in his stiff-legged, ungainly way, away from the police, away from the flat, away from his brother who was paralysed and open-mouthed with astonishment. The car jerked to a halt, stalling. Officers emerged, confused, gesticulating and shouting. A crowd of neighbours milled about, their faces distorted with surprise. There was a great deal of yelling. In an instant, Geordie disappeared. He was gone for what seemed to Leslie like ages before he or anyone else managed to gather his or her wits sufficiently to set off in pursuit.

*

Later, dull with shock, horrified, Leslie trudged around the lanes of his home searching for his brother. It had been another hot day, but as usual the night had given way to an early autumnal chill. His movements were predictable, habitual. He combed the area as he had done many times before, checking the occupied streets as well as the ruined, rubble-strewn areas. This is my fault, he kept thinking, irrationally. This is my fault. His mind was in turmoil. He was aware that this time he was not alone. Searchlights, torches, car headlamps and the ominous blue flashes that signified the Law bisected the dark, cool night. There was noise and upheaval, sniffer dogs, a fire engine and a great number of officers, all apparently anxious to find and bring to justice the dafty from Glue Terrace. It seemed to Leslie that a pitiless invasion force had taken charge. The uneasiness and upheaval of the summer was now pulled into sharp focus by the arrival of aliens in uniforms, symbols of the suspicion and distrust coming from the world outside. It was as if the rest of the city had sent its army into the devastation and chaos of the once symmetrical streets, in order to try to assert control. And this was despite the fact that it was exactly because of recent civic decisions and interference that control had become irretrievably lost. It was a kind of madness.

A few small children had forsaken their beds and ran about excitedly with pokers and sticks, but in general, the residents of the beleaguered streets stayed well indoors. To them, all of this was the last straw. Not only was the community being smashed to pieces, but also the unthinkable had happened. It was worse than the war. Elswick had been transformed into an unsafe, unpredictable, unrecognizable combat zone. Everything was in ruins. People sat around inside, drinking strong tea and talking quietly to their families. 'This used to be a good place,' they murmured. 'Once upon a time.' They were numb. They were in shock.

Back at Glue Terrace, Auntie Ada sat upstairs in her flat, but she was not reading the notices in the paper, in her usual way, ringing them with a pencil. Instead she rocked back and forth, wordless, her doughy face even paler than usual. She'd already told everyone in the street that she wasn't going to talk to the police and that she wasn't interested in their 'damned circus'. Scotch Iris was still missing, apparently unaware of the turn of events. Mickey Robson was drugged by a doctor. Sammy Schnitzler was sipping bicarbonate of soda and listening to

Chopin in his lonely living-room, tears wetting his cheeks. Ratty and Desperate were depositing excrement through the letterboxes of those on a special list – a list of residents who'd ignored the Council's request for them to sign up for new housing and who were therefore seen as trouble-makers who were refusing to shift.

Leslie trudged about, sick with anxiety and dread. His body felt clammy with sweat and his hands shook. He pictured his brother, trapped in a dank corner some-where, set upon by avengers and hungry dogs. He brought to mind the police and the smelly-breathed Welfare woman, now dragging poor Geordie into the Wolseley by his jumper and his hair. He saw prison bars, and a tiny, spartan cell. Here, the hapless prisoner was sitting on a plank bed, his head in his arms, his legs in irons. It was unbearable. He didn't do it, Leslie told himself. He didn't do it, he didn't do it. He didn't murder those blasted twins. He *said* he didn't do it and he never, ever lies.

A siren wailed and there was the nack-nack-nack of an army helicopter. It's like the war, he thought. It's worse than when the Luftwaffe was after everyone with their bombs. I wonder who *did do it*? Nobody liked those horrible twins. It could have been anybody because we've all stopped being like ourselves, here, this summer. We're all shaken up. Nothing's the same. Nothing's safe like it was before. Anything's possible.

Leslie climbed the steep gradient of Clumber Street and stared at a mound of uprooted cobbles, a toppled gaslight and an abandoned toy pram. In the distance, the new giant high-rise flats were black against the purple sky. The fear of change filled his heart. He took a deep breath. The world's falling to pieces. He was suddenly terribly weary. He tried to bring to mind the Virgin in the stained glass of the church, her generous outstretched hands and the way she always seemed to enjoy the singing of the choir. She glowed for a brief instant in the heavens above the high-rises but then immediately she disappeared. He thought instead of Auntie Ada's dim and quiet kitchen where there would be cake and the comfort of a friendly fire. I'll have a break, he told himself. I'll have a short rest and eat something. Then I'll start looking for him again.

As he retraced his steps to Glue Terrace, Leslie remembered again the happy day, one of the few occasions when he'd visited somewhere away from the narrow terraces of home. He pondered, letting the memory flood his consciousness. It was a relief to think of it, the trip with his mam, his brother and the youth club superintendent, Lofty Long. He let it linger in his mind. A special open-topped bus had come for everyone and they'd gone miles and miles and miles, all the way to the seaside. Leslie remembered that they'd gone on to the lower deck because he knew the rushing air upstairs would make his mother nervous. They'd sat on their own at the front behind the driver because the other children were avoiding Geordie. All around them were piled bags, which contained towels, swimming costumes, pop and picnics. Leslie took a deep breath and recalled the expanse of beach and the unbeliev-able colour of both sea and sky, neither of which had made Iris or Geordie afraid. There was something reassuring about the warmth of the sand, the stickiness of candy floss and the gentle shush-shush of the waves. He remembered big white birds cutting across the heavenly blue and the thwock of a cricket ball. He'd dug a hole and sat in it, watching some of the others swing up aloft in the four-seater shuggy boats, screaming, 'Higher, higher,' and then Geordie had run towards him, splashing through the shallows then up the beach, his face for once made beautiful by a smile. 'He's smiling!' he'd said to his mother as she took a photograph. 'He's really smiling!' It was amazing. Geordie was smiling. Remembering it now, Leslie sighed, nostalgically. This had been and was still the most completely happy moment of his life. He took out his photograph, fingered it in the dark then replaced it.

Passing along the remains of Isabella Street, Leslie saw Ratty and Desperate in the distance, standing next to the motorcycle. Automatically he took out his playing cards. He waved, but surprisingly they pretended they hadn't seen him. Leslie felt a lump rise in his chest then lodge itself in his throat. He stopped in his tracks, then waved again. His two friends were definitely ignoring him. They think my brother's a murderer, he said to himself. They're not my mates any more. He felt tears well up in his eyes. Not for the first time since his brother ran off, things were becoming too much. He wanted to lie down on the smashed pavement and cry. He wanted to disappear. He wanted to give up, crawl away, go to sleep for ever and ever. Instead he called out, 'Ratty! Ratty! Desperate! What're you doing?'

Ratty ignored him again. He seemed to be delivering something, pushing something through a letterbox.

Hurt, rebuffed, Leslie turned a corner, heading for home. He heard the motorbike roar away as if his two friends were in a big hurry. Everybody's changed, he thought to himself. Nothing's the same. Everything's falling to bits around here and I might never see my Geordie again.

The lower flat on Glue Terrace was all in darkness. Leslie pushed open the unlocked adjacent door, which led upstairs. Now Auntie Ada was as usual holding the newspaper, folded at the page which showed the Births, Marriages and Deaths. However, she still wasn't pencilling. She wasn't examining it with her magnifying-glass. Forlorn, she stared at him.

'Are those twins in the deaths column?' asked Leslie, abruptly. He took off his duffel-coat and plimsolls.

She shook her head. 'Not yet.'

He hesitated. 'Can I have another piece of my sponge?' He and Geordie had enjoyed some cake that morning. It seemed like a very long time ago.

Auntie Ada rested the paper on her wide lap. 'Of course you can. I put it in that tin in the pantry. The one with the roses on the lid.'

'Have you tried it? D'you like it?'

'It's lovely.'

Leslie cut himself a slice. They then sat for a while, the obvious question left unspoken.

'Where do you think he's got to?' asked Ada eventually.

'I don't know.'

*

Ratty Schnitzler and Desperate Dan were in Benwell, several streets away. They'd almost finished their night's work. A string of residents, who'd failed to answer the request to register for new council housing, would this evening find dog-dirt dropped in their passages or, in some cases, ignited fireworks.

'There's three left,' said Ratty, crossing out names with a crayon. 'There weren't that many tonight. Not as many as last time. Quite a few of those from last time took the hint.'

Desperate was astride his motorbike. 'I think people are more keen to go since that meeting.'

'What meeting?'

'The man from the council came to a meeting. My mam went. He told everyone the new flats will be fine and dandy. A lot who weren't convinced before have changed their minds since.'

Ratty shrugged. 'Have you noticed how the council's mixing everyone up? It doesn't matter which part of the hill you're from. You get shoved together into these new flats, regardless.' He kicked a stone, dismissively. 'It doesn't matter, though. 'Cos folks round here do as they're told. The council tells them to shift, so they shift. The council mixes them up, they stay mixed up. They're like sheep.' He held up his list of names. 'I reckon a lot of *these* can't read. That's the problem. They get their letters and they don't understand them. So they sit tight.'

Desperate looked dubious. 'I don't know anyone who can't read.'

Ratty fished in his pocket for a penny banger. 'Well, a bit of bother from us and they'll sharp take the trouble to figure out their letters and find out what's what. We're what's know as enforcers.' He frowned again at his list. 'One of these is Scotch Iris. She's not gone and registered. That's strange.'

'I don't think we should do *her*,' exclaimed Desperate. 'She's got enough trouble already. And that damned Leslie. That Leslie saw what we were doing, before. He *saw us*, man.'

Ratty stared at the pavement. His face was unreadable in the yellow glow from the gaslamp. 'Yeah,' he said eventually. 'Yeah, well.' He paused. 'That old lady upstairs from Iris. She's another one who's not done anything about it. She's taken no notice of the letter.'

Desperate spat expertly into a drain. He hesitated. He

knew old Ada well and she'd always been kind to him but he swallowed his finer feelings. Out of bravado he insisted, 'Right. Let's go and do *her.*'

Ratty lit the firework and shoved it through a door. 'Let's go and have a drink first.' Hastily, he jumped on the back of the bike and the pair roared off in the direction of the Crooked Billet, which was a public house on Scotswood Road. They stopped outside.

'Those girls had it coming, I reckon.' Desperate dismounted and smoothed the pockets of his battledress. It was the first time either of them had mentioned the murders. The subject had hung between them, unacknowledged.

There was a long silence. Ratty sat on the back of the bike, motionless and odd. He whistled a few bars of 'Apache'. There was uneasiness, an embarrassment. 'I wonder where that daft lad's hiding out,' he said finally, in a non-committal kind of way.

'We should join the hunt for him.' Desperate laughed, harshly. He tried to sound keen on the idea of unofficial guerrilla combat, but his manner was strained.

'I don't reckon he did it. He's just a little kid.' Ratty swung his leg over and stood up. He pressed the sides of his hair to his head in a habitual gesture.

'No, but it'll be great tracking him down and that.' Desperate dismounted, trying to look manly and effective. He shouldered an imaginary rifle.

Ratty shrugged, moving into the light of the pub doorway. He echoed a statement his friend had made to him, not too long before. 'Hey, that's more your kind of thing than mine.'

*

Leslie was sitting with Auntie Ada by the fire when the silence was suddenly shattered by a scream. It came from downstairs. Leslie jumped to his feet. There was another scream, then another.

'That's your mam,' Auntie Ada said. She struggled out of her chair. 'She's got back. She's heard the news. Come on.'

Leslie followed her downstairs. She pushed open the door to the lower flat and joined a group of neighbours in the kitchen. He stood in the doorway, reticent and apart.

Iris was sitting at the table, surrounded by a semi-circle of concerned women neighbours. One was stroking her hair. Another was offering a steaming cup. Leslie noticed that a drawing was lying there, almost complete. His mother was sobbing into a handkerchief. She saw Leslie and let out an extra-loud cry. He took a step back into the hall. Bruised by her recent disinterest, her summer of neglect, Leslie was suspicious. Maybe she's just doing this for show, he thought to himself. This isn't real. She doesn't care about anything since she's been taking those pills.

A woman lit a cigarette and handed it to Iris. She took it and puffed on it nervously. Her hands were shaking. 'She's a bag of nerves,' someone said, sympathetically. 'Here, drink your tea,' said another.

'My little bairn!' Scotch Iris cried. 'My poor little bairn. He doesn't know nothing. He doesn't know what he's about!'

'There, there,' said an elderly matron. 'There, there. You calm yourself, dear.'

'Why does all this trouble find its way to my door?' Her shoulders shook. Her crying suddenly became more hysterical. 'Where is he?'

'Shall I call the doctor?' asked one of the women.

Andrea Badenoch

'Maybe we should get her to bed.'

I hope she's not just trying to get attention, thought Leslie.

'Where are your nerve pills, Iris?' The woman turned to her friends. 'She takes nerve pills. I've seen her taking them. She's already under the doctor. She must be to get pills like those.'

'You calm yourself now.'

'Drink your tea.'

'Shush, now. Shush.'

Maybe she's play-acting, Leslie said to himself, bitterly. Maybe this is all for show.

Iris's cries were now high and rhythmic. Her eyes were tight shut and she rocked from side to side.

'It's all right.' Leslie said above the din. He stepped into the room.

Iris was immediately wide-eyed and almost quiet apart from a tiny mewing in her throat. Everyone turned to face him.

'It's all right. You can all go. I'll sort her out. I know what to do.' In the shocked silence his voice was deep and sounded very grown-up.

The neighbours glanced at each other, nodded and began to file out.

'Thanks for your trouble,' Leslie said politely. 'Thanks very much for your trouble.'

Only Auntie Ada remained.

'It's all right,' said Leslie again.

She looked uncertain.

'I can manage here.'

Iris was now calmer. She dabbed her eyes and drank some tea. She picked up her smouldering cigarette from an ashtray, puffed on it then ground it out. She replaced her cup in its saucer, accidentally slopping some on Geordie's drawing.

Leslie was assertive. 'I know what to do.'

'If you're sure, pet.'

'You go.'

Auntie Ada lumbered to the door. 'Knock up if you need anything,' she said kindly. 'Mind you do now.'

'I won't need anything.'

She disappeared, closing the front door behind her.

Leslie stood in front of his mother and looked at her, trying to gauge her true emotions. Iris met his gaze for a long moment, then lowered her head to her arms. She cried and cried. For the first time in a long time she was able to let go. Leslie stood watching and his own eyes filled. She's as scared and upset as me, he decided. This is real. She's beside herself. He felt guilty for doubting her.

'Where the fuck is he?' she said hoarsely. Iris looked up. Her make-up was running down her cheeks and her face was blotchy and red. 'Where is he?' she repeated. She sounded as lost as a boat in a storm.

Leslie could tell by her voice, by the wave of sadness and fear that moved from her to him and struck him like a draught, that his mother cared about Geordie. She cared a very great deal. He moved forward and allowed her to fold him in her arms. She's come back, he thought. She cares. She's come back from wherever it was she's been all summer. She's had a shock and she's our mam again. Thank goodness. He stammered, 'Geordie didn't . . .' He stepped back and took the photograph from his shirt pocket. Wordlessly, he showed it to her.

Iris stared at the picture of her youngest son, struggling to gain control of her voice. 'I know he didn't,' she agreed. 'Of course he didn't. Why's he getting the blame? He's only a baby.' She stood up, wiping her face with her sleeve. 'Oh God,' she muttered to herself. 'What have I gone and done?' She rummaged in her handbag for her pills.

'Don't,' Leslie said.

His mother looked at him. Her expression was one of understanding. She tossed the bottle on to the table and the little blue tablets spilled everywhere.

'Mam ... I never told you, and I know I should have . . .'

'What?'

'There's been letters about him. From Prudda.'

Iris was tight-lipped. 'What about?'

'They want him to go there. They want to lock him up.' Leslie hesitated. 'Did you ask them to lock him up?'

His mother's reply was immediate. 'Me? Of course not! I've spent my whole damned life trying to *stop* them locking him up. Those bastards at Prudhoe? What the hell do you mean?'

Despite everything, Leslie felt a warm rush of relief sweep over him like a wave.

7

Sammy Schnitzler moved his home-made cardboard sign to the very front of the window in his barber shop. It now rested in front of the discreet display advertisements for razor blades and condoms and declared, in careful, large copperplate, 'Umbrellas Mended'. He sighed as he man-oeuvred his portly body back into the shop. There hadn't been any rain for weeks. It was the wrong time of year for this sideline. Business was slack, all round.

He removed scissors and combs from the sterilizer and held them up to the light to check for stray hairs. He took a handkerchief from his pocket and dusted the framed photographs on the walls, which he'd cut from the *Hairdressers' Journal*. These showed effeminate-looking men modelling various styles called by improbable names such as 'The Kensington', 'The Ascot' and 'The Grosvenor'. Sammy had been pleased when, in response, some of his more adventurous customers had turned down the usual short back and sides in order to copy these creations, calling them instead 'that Tommy Steele on the wall', or 'that Perry Como over there', or 'that Tony Curtis by the basin'.

Sammy sighed again. He flicked his handkerchief over the bench, available for customers to wait in a queue. There hadn't been a proper queue for some time, he reflected. He spat and tried to clean the special chair that was slightly apart and reserved for pitmen who came in black and filthy, straight from work at the Montague Colliery. It was known as 'the Monty Chair'. No one had sat in it for days and days.

He placed Mozart's *Marriage of Figaro* on the turntable of his gramophone and turned up the volume. Then he stood in the open doorway, his hands behind his hips, leaning, his stomach protruding, in what was a habitual stance. There was a smell of dust in the air. The sun struck his face for a minute, then he went inside. He looked at the floor. It didn't need sweeping. He went into the back and changed from his best into his second-best white jacket. I'll make some more hair-dressing, he thought to himself. It'll give me something to do.

His imagination strayed to a memory from more than twenty years before. Unwillingly, he felt it form, grow, then bloom like a dark fungus in his conscious mind. He tried to suppress it, but this was impossible. In the back of the shop, he stirred an almost empty vat of Schnitzler's Brilliant then emptied in a half gallon of mineral oil. To this he added a measure of gum base and some golden dye. Energetically, he whisked these together. He poured in a little perfume. His actions could not dispel the thoughts that had come unbidden. He pressed his hand against his heart. The chaos of the demolition kept taking his mind back to his past.

When Sammy was a young man, he'd been a junior partner in a bank. It was a family concern, run for several generations by a succession of Schnitzlers, and was owned and managed by his father and two uncles. It was a profitable, respectable and secure life. Samuel, as the family called him, had grown up happy and privileged. He was being groomed to step into his father's shoes and he wore a smart suit, a stiff hat and a fresh flower in his buttonhole each morning. He lived with his wife and three children in an apartment in the Hofburg, a pleasant district near the Danube. In time, as an only son, he expected to inherit the family home in the Stephansdom quarter, an elegant, three-storey residence close to Blutgasse where Mozart wrote his greatest works. Here, a balcony looked out over a square and chandeliers twinkled from inside high baroque windows. A grand piano stood proudly in the salon and an immaculate Negro responded to visitors' peals on the doorbell.

Everything changed for Samuel and all the other Schnitzlers after Hitler's people began their work. First they were bled dry. Then they were moved. Finally, all was stolen, destroyed and lost. The bank was smashed up, the house looted. The family was ruthlessly torn apart. Their world collapsed and they had nothing left to hold on to, in some cases not even their very lives.

Sammy paused in his exertions. He stared down into the vat of hair-dressing. He remembered shouts and banging, rifle shots, breaking glass, the rough angry voices of the soldiers as they smashed their way through the apartment building in the middle of the night. He pictured himself jumping out of bed, tripping over his nightshirt and banging his shin, the searchlights in the street outside, the wide-eyed astonishment of the two older children as they were dragged from their beds and bundled up in quilts. He remembered the perilous drop from the fire escape, the way his wife's hair hung long and loose, her flapping gown, her struggle with the ascent to the roof, the baby in her arms. He saw himself clearly, returning, going back into the living-room, the enemy meanwhile pounding on the door with their rifle butts and boots. Fumbling with fear, dragging out the drawers of the bureau, he'd stuffed bank notes into his sleeves and grabbed a jewellery box. Back on top of the building they'd hidden in a water tank, cold as death up to their waists, hands clamped over the mouths of the little ones to stop them making a sound, listening to the screams of their unlucky neighbours as they were flung from windows or herded away in carts.

Sammy's fists were clenched around the ladle he used for stirring Schnitzler's Brilliant. 'One's good luck is another's ill fortune,' he said aloud. He rubbed his damp eyes with the back of his cuff. He took several deep breaths and the terror receded a little. '*Mit Got's hilf*, my past is all ghosts.' He stared into the pale yellow depths of his hair oil. Just ghosts, he thought. Nothing but ghosts. He turned to the sink where the used bottles were soaking. He ran the tap over them and rinsed a few, relishing the chill on his wrists. He felt clammy and uneasy. From all those years ago, lodged in his brain was his wife's anguished glance, as she climbed up to the rooftop. She was never to see her home again. At one time almost dispelled except for occasional nightmares, these memories had started to become more and more bothersome this summer. Every day they crowded in on him, unwelcome but insistent, like a clamour from *Gehenem*, from hell itself. It was as if all his years in England were nothing, as if the horror had been only yesterday. His hands shaking, he lined up a few clean containers. The Mozart long-player finished and the gramophone switched itself off. Outside, in the distance, there was another crash of masonry and the glass vibrated and chinked under his hands. It's like the war, he mused, feeling sweat break out on his body. Everything is falling apart. This demolition craziness, it's sending me back. It's sending me back to a time and a place I thought I'd never live to see again.

He took a drinking cup down from a high shelf and filled it with tap water. He went again to the door of his shop and stood once more in the sun. He raised the cup to the deserted street. A plume of dust, or maybe it was smoke, rose above the neighbouring rooftops. His extended arm cast a long shadow. 'To life,' he called out. The creases around his eyes were wet as he squinted in the bright light. 'To life!'

*

Tossing and murmuring, Leslie lay alone in the big double bed in the back bedroom in Glue Terrace. He had been awake nearly all night and now he slept late, sweaty and troubled, the bedclothes tangled and damp. He was dreaming of fires, of rubble, of dust and the wail of sirens. In his dream he stumbled through the shattered ruins of Brunel Terrace on his way to church. Ahead of him but mysteriously unreachable, no matter how fast he attempted to move, Geordie moved further and further away, even though his poor legs were imprisoned in irons and he was dragging a heavy chain. He was wearing a convict's suit made of sackcloth, such as Leslie had seen in films. Attempts to call out to him came to nothing. Leslie found himself curiously mute, with only dry rasps emerging from his throat. Thankfully, the scene suddenly changed and he was entering the peaceful, dim entrance of the church where he experienced the familiar smell of damp hymn books and roses. Once inside, he discovered light streaming through the stained glass, nearly too bright to bear. As he squinted upwards, the Virgin Mary stepped out of her window and moved daintily down a staircase made of smoke, which had miraculously appeared. She had small pointed feet and her blue dress trailed in a becoming way. Leslie moved towards her feeling at once calm and reassured. Close up, he discovered that she had a tiny cherry mouth and features that seemed painted on, like a picture in an art book he'd once seen at school. She smiled and beckoned. Leslie noticed that she continued to float above the ground but despite this he was able to follow her. They both returned to the space she had occupied in the window. She gestured and pointed. Outside, the battered Elswick streets continued to totter and fall, dust blocking out the sun. A straggle of displaced householders trudged away like refugees, clutching babies, suitcases and a few other pathetic belongings. Some seemed tense with shock, others were weary and resigned. As Leslie stared, a high, dark, derelict building with a tall chimney materialized in the far distance surrounded by a cloudy haze. He strained his eyes. It was familiar but he couldn't quite remember where or what it was. 'Your brother is in there,' the Virgin Mary explained. 'He is waiting for you.' She sounded rather posh, like an announcer on the wireless. At this moment, Leslie woke up.

Later, with this extraordinary dream still fresh in his mind, Leslie went outside and wandered about. He tried and tried but he couldn't remember the building, where it was, or for what purpose it had once been used. He trudged all the way up to the hospital, which was similarly grey and imposing, but this wasn't right. He went to the fire station and the police station but these were not the same as in the vision either, although they were the correct sort of size. If only I could find it, he thought. I'm sure that's where Geordie is hiding. He hurried off when he saw the Wolseley police car that had come for Geordie but not before noticing both Ratty and Desperate Dan sitting inside. Desperate looked very desperate, but Ratty was apparently chatting amiably to the two officers in the front seats, his long, sallow face resting casually in one hand.

Leslie hadn't eaten breakfast and he felt faint. He was too hot and his feet hurt in his plimsolls. He sat down heavily in the doorway of the Crooked Billet public house, took off his shoes and rubbed his sore toes. A couple of workmen stepped over him on entering, as if he were a beggar. He was grubby, troubled and pasty-faced and he looked like a homeless person or a neglected child of the type rescued by Dr Barnardo. His hands were shaking. I've got to find him, he thought. This is hopeless. I've got to get to him soon or who knows what might happen?

Shoppers and other passers-by eyed Leslie with a mixture of sympathy and wariness. He didn't offer to show them a card trick or even greet them in his usual friendly way and because of this, no words were exchanged. The murders had stabbed the community through its very heart, but although everyone was dismayed by what had happened, they nevertheless accepted that anything was possible in such strange times. The atmosphere on Scotswood Road was simultaneously electrically charged and disablingly static in an entirely new kind of way. Bulldozers roared hellishly in the distance. The cinema was down and the roof had gone from the entire corner that had previously housed both the Co-op undertakers and the bicycle repair shop. People were confused and not themselves. They were disturbed, as they had been during the war, but also somehow enervated and depressed. Both everything and nothing seemed possible and the normal rules no longer had any meaning. Unlike the Blitz, they were not linked together in a fight for victory, when they all faced Hitler together. Instead, they were oppressed and helpless and their only hope seemed to reside in getting away, starting a new future in the 'country' or 'up in the sky'. The old streets were in ruins. The twins were dead. Leslie MacDonald's apparent disintegration was an embarrassment. Geordie's disappearance was at once both shocking and mundane.

The beat policeman appeared in his helmet. 'Good morning, Constable Henderson,' Leslie said automatically, but not without nervously eyeing his truncheon. Since Geordie's bodged arrest, Leslie felt mistrustful of *all* law-enforcers, even this one, his very old friend.

The policeman regarded Leslie with an expression of concern. 'What you doing sitting there, son?'

'I've been looking for my brother and I'm tired.'

'We'll find your brother. You leave that to us.'

'If you lot find him, you'll lock him up in prison.'

Constable Henderson crouched down on his haunches and touched the boy's arm. 'What happened?' he asked gently. 'What did those terrible twins do to him then?'

'Geordie didn't kill those girls,' Leslie said simply. 'He said he didn't and that means he didn't. He never, ever lies.'

'Well, he's got nothing to worry about then, has he? Why did he run away?'

'Because he was frightened, because he was getting dragged into a car by people he'd never seen before, because he doesn't trust anyone apart from me and our upstairs Auntie Ada, because he doesn't *understand*.' He took the photograph of Geordie out of his shirt pocket and held it in the policeman's line of vision.

The officer nodded and stood up. 'If he's not guilty, then he'll be sent home again in no time. In no time at all. You tell him that, if you see him.'

Leslie stared up at him, dumbly.

'You want to show me one of your card tricks?'

'No.'

'All right then.' The big man was concerned. 'Where's your mother?'

'Don't know.'

The policeman hesitated. He wasn't used to Leslie being glum. 'You take care now.' Reluctantly, and glancing over his shoulder several times, he continued on his beat.

*

Scotch Iris had taken a trolley-bus into Newcastle city centre and she was hammering on the big carved wooden doors of the Town Hall. She beat at them with her fists yelling, 'Let me in, damn you! Let me in, God damn you all!' The entrance was locked up because this was a Saturday. The building was entirely empty of councillors, officials and clerks. Town-shoppers and city strangers stared and giggled. 'What's the matter with her?' they asked. 'Hey, look at that funny wifey. Has she gone off her rocker, or what?'

Iris was a mess. She'd been a mess since Geordie's disappearance. Her bouffant hair-do was a tangle of knots and her make-up was as smudged as an artist's palette left out in the rain. Her nylons were laddered and one of the heels had come off her spindly sandals. She'd made the journey into town in a state of intense anxiety. As the half-empty bus had careened across an old bombsite near the meat market she'd become mesmerized by the uneven, weedy open space, imagining that it was the Irish Sea. She'd held on to her seat and cried out in horror. That tiny line of earth and sky near the city had seemed like the end of the world, like a vast expanse of nothingness. Her disordered mind slipping back fifteen years, she thought she saw her husband's matchwood fishing vessel bobbing in tumultuous Scottish waves. She thought she heard him

Andrea Badenoch

call her name. She relived her desperate moment of knowledge just before his boat fell out of the sea. 'Who's going
to care for my boys now?' she'd demanded of the bus
conductor, hysterically. 'And who's going to look after
me?'

He'd shaken his head, sympathetically.

'I thought this war was finished. Isn't the war finished?'

'Yes, pet,' he'd murmured. 'The war's finished. We won
the war.'

Iris rummaged in her handbag. Her pills were, of
course, gone. Her thoughts focused on the present. 'It's not
finished up in Elswick,' she muttered. 'Nobody's a winner
out there.'

Half an hour later, furious at finding Mickey's office
closed, she kicked at the heavy oak doors of the seat of
local government as hard as she could. 'Let me in, you
deaf bastards!' she screamed. 'I want to see Councillor
Robson! I've got urgent business with Councillor Robson!'

A reporter from the *Newcastle Post* happened to be
passing, on his way back to the newsroom, which was
nearby. He stopped and spoke to her. He gave her a
handkerchief and a cigarettte. Scotch Iris sat down on the
steps, pretended to inhale and told him about her son,
who was missing. She told him the boy 'wasn't all there'
and that he was suspected of murdering the twins. She
dabbed at her eyes but now she was unable to cry.

'The Angel Twins?' asked the hack, sensing a story.
It was high summer, there wasn't much news, and the
deaths of the two girls had already created a flurry of
national interest. A sub-editor with an eye for a cliché
had dubbed the girls the Angel Twins and this had
stuck. The BBC had covered the story, as had the *Express*
and the *Mirror*. Several newsmen from other dailies were

rumoured to be at present propping up the bar in the Station Hotel, asking directions to Elswick. In their minds the girls had not been thirteen. Encouraged by descriptions of the pair in their habitual frills, flounces, hair ribbons and white ankle socks, their copy in the newspapers suggested that the unfortunate victims had been little more than babies.

Iris told the kind young man her life story. At some point he summoned a photographer. A small crowd began to form, sensing scandal. Without caution or constraint, she told him about Geordie's problems, about his drawings, about her purple hearts and about her plans to marry Councillor Robson. 'I've got to speak to him,' she insisted. 'I've got to tell him that my lad didn't do it.'

'And you're engaged to Councillor Robson?' the reporter asked, scarcely able to believe his luck. The father of the Angel Twins? T. Dan Smith's right-hand man?' He stared at Iris's wrecked face in disbelief.

Iris showed him her marcasite dress ring, worn on her wedding finger.

'You've been having ... you've been having ... an affair?' He handed her another lit cigarette, which she accepted with trembling fingers.

'He's been getting his leg over regular for the last four months, if that's what you mean.' Iris was out of control again. She puffed on the cigarette a couple of times. 'Just like all the rest of them. The fuckers.' She stood up and ground the butt under her shoe. She turned her back on the assembled and growing audience and hammered again on the locked doors of the Town Hall with her little fists. 'And now the bastard won't even *let me in*.'

*

At the police station on Scotswood Road, Ratty and Desperate Dan were being interviewed in separate rooms. Desperate was being asked by a burly sergeant about his right to wear the uniform of Her Majesty's armed forces, now that his National Service was complete. Nervous, he kept getting up and standing to attention but every time he did this he was told by the amused officer to sit down again. The atmosphere changed and became more serious when he was questioned about the twins. Desperate insisted that he hadn't seen the girls since the night of the talent contest, when they had ruined his boots and beret with paint. He admitted to having what he called 'a paddywack' at the time, but he insisted he'd never confronted them over it, never threatened them, never even seen them.

'But you were angry?'

'Yessir.'

'You were furious with them?'

'Yessir.'

'You told your young friend Schnitzler that you wanted to kill them? That's what he's informed *us*.'

Desperate hesitated. Sweat stood out on his brow and he bit his lip. 'Only in a . . . in a manner of speaking, sir.'

'Yes?'

'Well I said I wanted to kill them, sir, that's what I said, but I didn't mean I wanted to *kill* them. Not *kill* them, as such. I just meant . . .'

'You just meant?'

'Well, sir. I just meant . . . I just sort of meant . . .'

'Yes?'

Desperate was at a loss. He wanted to cry, but of course this was impossible. He leapt up again, and with a great deal of noisy stamping, began running through his drill.

The policeman was now impatient. He banged on the table with his fist. 'Stop it, laddie!' he yelled. 'Will you just stop it! You're *not* in the bloody army now!'

Desperate stood at once to attention, quiet, almost motionless, his head erect but with his eyes tight closed. His face was as creased as a distressed baby's. One rigid knee trembled visibly.

The Sergeant turned to a constable standing by the door. 'We've got a right one here,' he said. 'A *right* nutter. Lock him up good and proper. Make sure you get his belt and laces. This one's potty enough to top himself.'

*

Along a corridor, Ratty flicked a half-crown, caught it on the back of his hand, then flicked it again. His thin legs were extended in a relaxed posture, his crêpe-soled shoes appearing huge within the tiny room. He yawned. His transistor radio played quietly in his lap. A detective-inspector was writing in a notebook. This officer was mousy-looking and a little deferential. He had a wispy bald head and pen-pusher's shoulders. Ratty was describing his business dealings, his connections with London, his plans. He was grandiose and self-regarding. 'Ultimately,' he confided, liking the sound of this long word, 'I intend making a fortune. Then I'll move to Gosforth where I'll open an animal shelter. But that's for the future, of course.' He was wearing a new claret-coloured drape-coat and the dress-shirt with rows of ribbon-trimmed nylon ruffles down each front. Confident and chatty, he was behaving as if this conversation was a polite exchange between equals, a necessary diversion, the details of which could be quickly finalized and drawn to a conclusion. He smoothed the sides of his hair and chewed gum. The radio started playing 'Apache' by the Shadows. Ratty turned it up. 'I used to go to school with Hank Marvin,' he confided.

The officer's manner changed. 'Turn that thing off! Where do you think you are? A blasted fairground?'

Surprised, Ratty obeyed. He shifted his position to a more upright posture.

'Can you tell me about your relationship with Iris MacDonald?'

Even more startled, Ratty placed his radio on the floor and bit the backs of his knuckles. However, he recovered his composure in an instant. 'Keep your hair on,' he said. 'Mrs MacDonald is a tenant of my dad and a family friend.'

'I believe you have been supplying Iris MacDonald with amphetamines. These are prescription drugs that you have obtained illegally.' The Detective-Inspector's voice was terse and staccato. He'd been on the telephone all morning trying to prevent Scotland Yard from coming north to take over his case. Remembering this again now, he was all at once in a bad mood.

Ratty now drew in his legs entirely and sat up straight in his chair. 'That is a lie and a defamation and totally and completely untrue.'

The policeman was silent for some time. After an uneasy pause he looked Ratty straight in the eye. 'So that's how it's to be, is it, sonny Jim?'

'Pardon?'

'That's how it's to be. Lies, evasion, lack of co-operation.' He sighed. 'I see.' There was a protracted and uncomfortable silence. He smiled in a frosty, unfriendly way. 'I *see*.'

Ratty considered. 'It's my public duty to help you in any way I can.'

The officer clicked his fingers and motioned to a uniformed constable. He didn't take his eyes off Ratty. His voice sank to a low, uncompromising hiss. 'You're a wide boy and a *bloody foreign four-by-two*. You're a sheeny crook and a nonce. You might be from here, but you don't belong here. Not *here*. And I'm going to lock you up.' These words, spoken quietly and without particular menace, sounded more aggressive, more abusive, more shocking than if they'd been shouted. Despite the weather outside, the atmosphere in the room was at once freezing cold. Ratty was white, immobile, as if carved from ice.

The Detective-Inspector sniffed. He was handed a folder and with his manicured hands he extracted a packet of photographs. His wedding ring glinted as he spread the contents on the table between himself and Ratty. They were black and white snapshots, inexpertly printed, showing the twins half naked and tied up with rope and handcuffs in a variety of pornographic poses.

Ratty gulped, his prominent Adam's apple juddering in his throat. 'Where . . .' he croaked. 'Where . . .'

'These were supplied by your good father,' said the officer. 'The barber. I believe he found them under your bed.'

*

Weary and much too hot, Leslie had wandered as far as the limits of Benwell, then back again. He called to see Auntie Ada, hoping to be given a glass of ginger beer, but unaccountably her door was locked and there was no answer to his poundings on the knocker. Tears of frustration and tiredness ran down his cheeks. I want my mam, he thought. I want my Auntie Ada. *I want my mam.* He went indoors but Iris was out. He drank a glass of water from the cold tap in the scullery and sat down at the untidy table. He eyed the unpaid bills nervously. He tried not to think about the letters in the shoebox under his bed. His mother's pills were still scattered on top of Geordie's drawings. He tipped them off on to the table and examined the picture. It was a perfect rendition of the corner of Tulloch Street and De Grey Street, showing the flats rising spectacularly in the distance. It was the first time, as far as Leslie knew, that his brother had attempted to draw one of the new buildings. He had managed it extremely well, conveying the contrast between the low and dilapidated Victorian architecture and the high, fresh, clean, modern lines. There was a stain in the centre of the paper, where the previous night Iris had spilled her tea. Leslie smoothed the drawing under one hand, then leant his head in his arms. He wanted to go to sleep, but he was too anxious. After a while, his shoulders shook and he made small sounds. He was weeping in a babyish way that he'd not done for years and years. Once he'd started he couldn't stop.

*

Sammy Schnitzler closed his empty shop and walked up the hill. He passed several news reporters and photographers who eyed him speculatively, but he avoided meeting their gaze. No one seemed to want to talk to them, he noticed. They were hanging around looking bored and out of place. One of them was knocking on doors. A small boy shot stones at them from his catapult.

Sammy entered the cemetery and passed through the flower-strewn Christian graveyard where one or two elderly women tended the plots of loved ones. A youngish woman holding a bunch of antirrhinums and pushing a baby in a pram nodded to him courteously. She was one of his tenants.

'Good morning, my dear,' Sammy said, relishing the respect. He was about to walk on.

She was embarrassed. 'I'm sorry I still owe you for three weeks. I've been a bit short. If you can just wait, I've managed to borrow . . .'

He paused and smiled, affably. 'You just pay what you can, my dear. Just pay what you can.' Feeling cheered by his own largesse, Sammy continued, using a customer's umbrella as a walking-stick. He twirled it in a jaunty way. The sun beat down upon him, casting a shadow. He climbed again, too warm in his stiff collar, his tie and second-best suit. He mopped his brow with a handkerchief.

He reached his destination and opened a rusty wrought-iron gate. This led to an enclosed, shady area, where the gravestones were back to back, cheek by jowl, many drunken and cracked with age. Here there were no flowers, no grass verges neatly mown, no angels, no unnecessary ornamentation. He was in the small Jews' burial ground, an austere and foreign-seeming place, the tightly packed inscriptions all carved in Hebrew. Separate, railed off, exclusive, it was at the top of a slope known locally as Miser Hill.

Sammy was suddenly very weary. It was cooler here but there was nowhere to sit. He was only dimly aware why he'd come, knowing that it was just something he did occasionally, something that provided him with a small, tenuous link with his past. He had no relatives buried here, indeed he knew none of the families represented, most of which had long since moved to other, more prosperous parts of the city where they'd settled and built new synagogues. This tiny enclave was now an anachronism, a neglected place of moss, stained hieroglyphics and old bones turned to dust.

Raised voices could be heard in the distance. Sammy glanced in their direction. In the road, a woman with a rolled-up newspaper was threatening a reporter in a green trilby and his sidekick photographer. They backed away from her, comically. Her voice was shrill, her language colourful. Sammy sighed. They don't like strangers around here, he thought, his eye skimming over the ranks and ranks of dead who'd lived in a place which they'd never been able to call their own and who'd finally been brought here, if not to rest, at least to lie in the earth undisturbed.

He read some names. Hannah, daughter of Josiah, Rebecca, mother of Jabez, Ezekiel grandfather of Ruth and Isaac. These were Jews unlike himself who'd lived their entire lives here in England, whose predecessors had no doubt come to escape some conflict or persecution in Europe but whose own sons and grandsons had been lucky. They'd missed that recent genocide, that immense destruction, played out in three tragic acts across the water, that tale of spite, of undoing, of terrifying climax with loss piled upon loss, piled upon loss. Sammy felt that they were fortunate, these long-dead skeletons sleeping in English soil. They hadn't suffered like *he'd* suffered.

He turned his back and left the sad, unkempt place, the last refuge of outsiders. Outside, the sun shone and the colourful Christian mounds looked as festive as a carnival. Carefully, he placed one fat foot in front of the other as he made for home. Unbidden, a religious voice, a soprano, echoed in his mind. I never knew that the older boy was a singer, he said to himself. I never knew that Iris's boy sings like one of the Wiener Sangerknaben. Leslie's pure notes sounded for another ghostly moment. The memory of the song frightened him, so he tried to put it aside.

Sammy Schnitzler's wife hadn't survived long once exiled from her home. She was delicate and she had a weak chest. The hours they'd spent hiding from the soldiers, waist high in the water tank, had made her ill and then there was the dodging and scurrying and moving, the eating of garbage and of course the winter cold. She simply became more and more frail. Her milk dried up and the baby was weaned, in Sammy's opinion, much too soon. She had a wracking cough followed by fever and chattering teeth. She died in an empty attic, one night, somewhere near the Alserstrasse. Sammy found her there, covered in a pile of reeking blankets. The baby boy was asleep next to her, unaware that she had passed over. The other children were dozing, arms around each other, in a corner. He himself had come back, almost cheerful, with a cooked turnip and two chicken legs given by a jeweller and former customer of the bank, but he was too late to force any morsels between her lips. She was cold and stiffening and *he'd had to leave her there*. That was the most terrible thing. He'd taken the three children and climbed down the rickety stairs and abandoned her. He had no choice. She was a religious woman and she had no grave, no funeral, no stone setting, no kaddish, in fact nothing at all to assist her to heaven, to enable her to sit in the presence of God. Sammy had never made peace with himself about this. It tortured him daily, like an unhealed wound.

'*Hashem in himel*,' Sammy murmured now as he quit the cemetery. '*Hashem in himel*. God in Heaven. Please forgive me.' He didn't consciously visit the Jews' burial ground seeking atonement. In his mind his motives were not entirely clear, but somewhere deep in his heart the place reminded him of all that was proper and ordered and devout, such as his poor wife had wanted. It was away from the godless chaos that had been Vienna when he was a young husband unable to make things right, unable to protect his family. It was a small example of *how things ought to be*.

Unfortunately, even here, now, just down the hill, this modern council was ruining everything. They were as bad as the Nazis. Sammy Schnitzler sensed a reprise of anarchy and collapse and fearsome threats and it was drawing closer to him, declaring itself more forcibly day by day. *Hashem in himel. Hashem in himel.*

*

Mickey Robson was hosting a press conference. Surprised by the interest of the media and feeling somewhat under siege, the Chief Inspector had hastily organized a few chairs and tables and encouraged the Councillor to venture out from the 'secret location' where he was being 'comforted by friends'. As details were being finalized, T. Dan Smith surprised everyone by arriving in the chauffeur-driven Daimler usually reserved for the Lord Mayor. By this time, the police station was thronging with people and its staff struggled to cope. Ordinary enquirers were abandoned in a musty reserve waiting room somewhere in the basement, and ordinary suspects and prisoners, including Ratty and Desperate, were kept locked up without any breakfast or lunch.

Mickey was red-eyed and hollow-cheeked. He was chain-smoking and arrived in a dirty shirt. A helpful sergeant lent him a clean collar and a tie. Dazed, he joined the Council Leader in front of a battery of cameras and clamouring journalists.

The story of the 'Angel Twins' was about to grip the popular imagination. To the surprise of everyone in Elswick, they were becoming front-page news. An old school photograph of the two girls, released by their bemused headmistress, was at this moment rolling off every press in Fleet Street. It was a flattering shot, showing them aged ten, or thereabouts, but looking younger, their hair a mist of blonde curls, their faces smooth and babyish, their small and identical features both unworldly and pleading. Their eyelashes cast shadows on their cheeks and their rosebud mouths were closed, concealing their discoloured teeth. To the newsmen, it was an image of innocence, and it had been horribly defiled. It was about to rock the nation. 'Dead Angel-Girls Horror,' screamed the headlines. 'Slum Babes Slasher On Loose,' 'Angel Twins Murder Shock,' 'Tragic Cherubs Maniac Slaying.'

Smith was photographed with his arm around his grieving colleague. He made a few comments relating to 'sadness', 'heaven' and 'justice' and then departed. Afterwards, Mickey rambled on a little, explaining that the whereabouts of the twins' mother was unknown, that the girls had been 'his life' and that he was, along with the Leader, responsible for the clearances in the area. 'We're building the Brasilia of the North,' he said, irrelevantly, quoting Smith. He looked vague and dishevelled and for a moment seemed to be under the impression that he was expected to talk about the aims of the Planning Department. He was, everyone decided, a little drunk. When he was bombarded with questions from enthusiastic reporters, he nearly broke down. He was assisted from the room by a uniformed policewoman who took him into the canteen and gave him a cup of tea. She flirted with him but he was unaware of her giggling attention. Later he was smuggled from the rear of the building, covered in a car rug. He collided noisily with the dustbins but escaped without further harassment.

Outside the front of the police station, Scotch Iris had been told to wait. She'd managed to fix her make-up and she was holding a roll of papers that were a selection of Geordie's drawings. Several newsmen had mentioned large sums of money, but she was less interested in these than the chance to talk. Disorientated without her pills and almost half-crazy, Iris thought that telling her story would help her to get both Mickey and Geordie back. She seemed to believe that the pitiful nature of her situation could be reversed by publicity, that somehow public sympathy for her plight would signal a change in her fortunes. Once the press conference appeared to be over, she was grabbed by a young man from the *Mail* and bundled into a taxi. Iris's look was defiant and was recorded by a jostling bank of flashbulbs.

*

Leslie had finally fallen asleep at the table, his head in his arms. He awoke to hear a pounding on the front door and shouts coming from the back lane. He went to the window and saw two men scaling the wall of the yard. One was carrying a camera. Hastily he drew the kitchen curtains and turned the key in the lock of the front door. He was scared. He realized that these people wanted to interview him, but he was sure that he had absolutely nothing to say to them. He felt ashamed about having fallen asleep when he should have been out searching for Geordie. 'Please go away,' he called through the letterbox. 'Just go away. I'm just nobody. I'm *nobody*. I haven't even got a job.'

Eventually the banging and shouting ceased and all was quiet on Glue Terrace. The reporters went off to file their stories before adjourning to the Crooked Billet. Thankful, Leslie decided he had prevaricated for long enough. On impulse he went into the bedroom and changed his shirt, leaving it on the bed. He was worried about the reporters. I don't want them to think I'm a scruff-bag, he decided. They might put it in the paper and our mam will be ashamed. He went into the scullery and washed his face at the sink.

Next, after a certain amount of rummaging in the cupboard under the stairs, he found his old school satchell and some apparatus left over from a camping trip he'd once taken with the youth club and Lofty Long. This was a primus stove, a tin mug and plate, a billycan and a torch. He also retrieved Geordie's pencil-case and sketchpad. He stripped the blankets off the bed and folded them neatly, leaving everything ready in the hall. To his relief, Auntie Ada's door was now open again so he went upstairs.

'Where've you been?' he greeted her. 'There's been men here with cameras. Our mam's gone off somewhere and I still haven't found him.' He wiped his feet on the hooky mat. 'I think I know where he is, but I can't remember the place. Where've you been? Can I have some cake and a glass of lemonade?'

Ada was sitting in her coat and headscarf and her fire was unlit. She looked as if she was waiting at the doctor's. Her doughy face was sad and thoughtful.

'You're not away out again, are you?' asked Leslie anxiously. He took off his plimsolls and went to wash his hands.

She sighed.

'What's the matter?'

'The world's gone mad,' she replied, enigmatically.

Leslie helped himself to food and drink in the scullery. 'Where've you been?'

She sighed again, heavily. 'I've been doing as I've been told. Like the letter said. I've been to the housing place on Amen Corner, next to the cathedral, down the town.'

Leslie was startled. 'Today? Why?' He stuffed a ginger-bread man into his mouth.

'Because they're open seven days a week, morning noon and night. You should see the queues! I tell you, it's a madhouse down there.' She hesitated. 'I had a firework through my letterbox.'

'What happened down there? What did they say?'

Ada paused. She looked desolate. 'They've offered me a one-bedroom unit.'

'Oh no!'

Ada was upset. Her voice trembled. 'I've said no to Westerhope. I've said no to Newbiggin Hall. I've said no to Fawdon. Why would I want to go to any of those places? I ask you! Can you believe it? I've lived here in Elswick for all of my life!'

'What's going to happen? What about me and Geordie?'

Ada hesitated. 'I think I'd better speak to our Jack.'

'What's Uncle Jack going to do about it?' Leslie felt irritated. He understood that Uncle Jack was a Vickers foreman, but this wouldn't necessarily cut any ice with the Council.

Ada could not imagine a subject over which Jack would have no influence, so she ignored this question. She was depressed and unsettled. She began unfastening her headscarf. 'I haven't baked a single scone,' she admitted. 'What's the world coming to? I haven't had a cup of tea all day. I stood in a queue for hours. They lost my papers.

They sent me to different rooms. *And* I waited nearly an hour for a bus back.'

Leslie sat in his usual chair. He drained his lemonade and wiped his mouth on the back of his sleeve. 'I think I know where Geordie is.'

Ada stood up and took off her coat. 'I can't stop thinking about the poor little mite. I've been worrying about him all day.' She hung it on the back of the door and pulled her apron over her head. She smoothed it over her wide hips and tried to settle herself. She held out a match to the ready-laid fire. There was a small burst of cheerful flame.

Leslie described the building in his dream. 'I think he's in there. Don't ask me why, I just think he is. Where can it be?'

Ada responded immediately. 'In the old baths and wash-house? It's been closed for nigh on a year.'

Leslie jumped to his feet, spilling crumbs from his lap. 'Of course!' he cried out, excited. 'You're right. Of course!' He stepped over and hugged Ada.

She was flustered. 'Away with you,' she exclaimed, but she was pleased. 'If he's there, you know you've got to tell someone. It's no good him hiding in there. It'll be full of rats and mice and creepy-crawlies.'

Leslie judged the situation. 'I will,' he lied. 'But he'll need something to eat and drink. First. Before I tell the polis.' He knew there was no point in revealing his true plans. Ada was in awe of all authority and that was that.

Ada looked doubtful.

'I'll have to give him something to eat and drink before I do *anything*.'

Ada could see the sense in this. Feeding people was her life. 'All right then.'

In the scullery, Leslie began filling a shopping bag with

food. He took a tin of home-made cakes, a bottle of milk, crackers, sugar, tea, biscuits, cocoa, Tizer and half a loaf of bread. He took a small piece of cheese and a packet of raisins.

'Steady on,' said Ada, 'you're clearing me out of house and home!'

It's not *me* who's doing that, Leslie wanted to say, but he held his tongue.

*

Within half an hour Leslie had left with his bags, blankets and Geordie's sketch pad and pencil-case. To his relief, the reporters had all completely disappeared. It was getting dark and the streets were deserted. The search parties of the previous evening seemed to have melted away. A fire engine sounded in the distance, no doubt on its way to the distant glow in the sky, which would be another demolition fire out of control. There was an autumnal nip in the air again and Leslie shivered. He walked along Scotswood Road staring at the parallel lines of gaslamps, evenly spaced, surrounded by their pale yellow haloes. They're very beautiful, he thought. He was feeling optimistic, brave, a little light-headed. Everything's going to be all right, he told himself.

PC Henderson was plodding along, a hundred yards ahead, on his evening round. Leslie stepped into the entrance of a shop, in order to wait for him to go. I'll hide for a minute, he reasoned. I don't want to have to try to explain these bags.

'Hello there,' said a voice in his ear. He spun round. Someone had followed him into the doorway. A familiar face stared into his own. Startled, Leslie clamped a hand over his own mouth to prevent himself from calling out.

He took a step away, tripping slightly and staggering. His heart raced and he felt chilled all over.

'Don't be frightened, my boy. It's only me. Your hairdresser.' It was Sammy Schnitzler. His lugubrious face was pale in the poor light, his features exaggerated. He stood too close and his breathing was slightly laboured.

Leslie was afraid.

'I've been following you. Where are you headed with all your belongings? Palestine? Or could it be South Africa? You're a clever boy, aren't you? But you'll never get through. You got false papers? There are soldiers everywhere. Take my word for it. Everywhere.'

Leslie wanted to push past him and call out to the policeman, but it was too late. PC Henderson would be out of earshot. 'I've got to go,' he muttered.

'The trains have started leaving from Franz-Josefs-Bahnhof. You're supposed to report there. Everyone's reporting there. It's official. Everyone's being crammed in with their suitcases. Like animals. Even the old people. I've seen it with my own eyes. Whether they like it or not, everyone's being sent off to Poland. In cattle wagons.'

'Our mam's been looking for you,' said Leslie, feeling inspired. 'She's at the flat, waiting for you.'

Sammy seemed not to hear. He regarded Leslie in an intense and disconcerting way. His breath was still noisy and rhythmic.

'Our mam's been *asking* for you.'

'A wise person knows what he says, a fool says what he knows.' Sammy's tone was guttural, hoarse. He was a short man but he was wide. He was blocking the doorway.

'I need to go, Mr Schnitzler, sir.' Leslie remembered a recent encounter when his joyous music had so discomfited the barber in the street that he'd rushed inside his shop and locked the door. 'I'm sorry but I haven't got time to stand here and chat.' He took a deep breath, filling his chest with air. Without further warning he broke into song. *'Oh for the wings, for the wings of a dove . . .'*

The effect was immediate. Sammy Schnitzler stepped backwards in surprise and out of the confined space. Under a street lamp he cast a distorted shadow. He held his hands to his ears.

Leslie carried on. *'Far away, far away would I rove, Oh for the wings, for the wings of a dove . . .'* Struggling with the bags, he forced the notes out. His voice was strained but echoed down the quiet street. He felt it plunge lower in its new and disconcerting way, but he carried on. *'Oh for the wings, for the wings of a dove . . .'* He moved as quickly as he could away from the doorway, resuming his route to Geordie. After a few moments he stopped singing. He glanced behind him. Sammy hadn't moved but he was watching. He hurried, then looked back again. The barber appeared comical and stout from this distance, rather than threatening. I'll be afraid of my own shadow next, thought Leslie. I'm becoming as touched and weird as everyone else around here.

He turned a few corners and reached his destination. This was on the very edge of the area he defined as 'home'. Here the streets were all pulled down, but the demolition had taken place a while before and there were no vehicles, tools or machinery. All was in darkness because the gas-lamps were smashed or flattened. It was a terrible scene. Leslie shuddered. The cobbles were partly uprooted, leaving small craters in the road. He thought again of windy bombsites he'd seen left over from the war, but there was no breeze tonight, no movement of air. All was still and motionless and quiet. The river was invisible and silent, the sky was featureless, all distant lights seemed like pinpricks in a universe of dark. Leslie stared at the abandoned building. It had a gable roof and a tall chimney. Its windows were cracked or gone and the lead had been stripped. A pile of timber was stacked at one side. He can't be *here*, he decided. He advanced towards the front. There were two doors; one had led to the public baths, the other to the wash-house. Carved into the stone above each lintel was an inscription. One said 'Cleanliness is next to Godliness.' The other read 'The Health of the People is the Highest Law.'

Leslie pulled himself together. I've got to go in, he thought. At that moment there was a glimmer just out of his line of vision. He looked upwards. There was an unearthly glow in the sky. It was the Virgin Mary and she was floating above the pointed end of the roof. She was surrounded in an aura of what he decided must be celestial light, but she was too far away for him to be able to tell if she was smiling. Leslie blinked and in a split second she faded. In less than two seconds she'd disappeared entirely.

8

Scotch Iris sat on a wall outside Mickey Robson's respectable semi-detached house, which was up the hill and
beyond the park. She stared at a light shining from the
small bedroom above the front door. The curtains were
open, showing that there was no one inside. Visible on the
wall was a poster of the Shadows doing their famous
'Shadows Walk'. A couple of sad-faced toy bears leaned
on the window sill alongside an old doll with only one
arm. The rest of the house was in darkness. Despite this,
Iris believed that her former lover was inside and that he
was refusing to answer her knocking.

Earlier, the newsmen had taken her to the Station
Hotel where she'd been plied with spirits. Iris was not a
drinker, so now, as well as suffering disorientation from
the withdrawal of amphetamines, she was also inebriated.
The whisky had made her aggressive and noisy. 'Come on
out, you bastard!' she shrieked again. 'Come out and stop
hiding!' She picked up a stone and threw it at the window,
breaking the small top pane. Shards of glass rained down.
'You fucking shite-heed! I want to talk to you! Come on
out, why don't you!'

A neighbour poked his head over the hedge. 'If you
don't shut up, I'll call the polis!' The people in this area
were not used to disturbances of any kind.

Iris responded with some colourful epithets.

Others appeared, from up and down the road, clad in
their dressing-gowns. 'Who is it, Davy?'

'What's the trouble?'

236

'Someone after Councillor Robson.'

'He's not there, is he?'

'Try telling her that!'

'She's drunk!'

'It's that Scotch Iris. She's from over Elswick.'

'Call the polis.'

'This is a decent neighbourhood.'

Iris stood up, staggering slightly. She looked older than usual and dishevelled. Her clothes were stained and there was blood on one knee.

'What a state!'

'What's she want with him? He's got enough trouble at his door.'

Iris tottered towards a lamp-post then caught hold of it in order to steady herself. 'He thinks he can ignore me now,' she declared, loudly, 'he thinks I'm not good enough for him now. Doesn't he? Doesn't he? The bastard. Where's he hiding? He can't do this to me. *Come on out!*'

A woman ventured beyond her front garden on to the pavement. She was wearing slippers and, over her nightgown, an old coat. Her hair was in rollers and her expression was fierce. 'Davy!' she yelled. 'It's all right. I've called the polis on the telephone and they're coming. They're sending someone. They're on their way.'

*

Leslie pushed open a side window and with some difficulty wriggled through. Inside, he sniffed and wrinkled his nose. There was a smell of mouldy damp and staleness, underlain with the faintest memory of Sunlight soap. It was completely dark. He felt inside one of his bags, found the torch and switched it on. There was an immediate scurry of rodents fleeing from the beam. He shuddered.

237

He shone the light around. This was the place where the housewives of Elswick had come for more than a hundred years to do their weekly wash. The rows of old sinks were still in position, with their troughs and washboards, all draped with swathes of cobwebs. Plaster was heaped up on the stone floor, where the ceiling had, in places, fallen in. An overhead pipe dripped into a fetid pool and there was still, even after all this time, an occasional dull clank-clunk that suggested ancient plumbing stirring uneasily. A faded packet of Daz, stiff with moisture and age, leant abandoned against a rusty tap. Leslie tried to summon up some courage. Surely he's not in *here*, he thought. This is a terrible place. This place is probably *haunted*.

He forced himself to walk into the adjacent room. Here the old wooden drying racks were dismantled and heaped up in a corner. His heart leapt into his mouth as there was a sudden violent flapping, a clatter and a collapse of dust. A pigeon, he told himself. I disturbed a pigeon. There was more scurrying of rats, this time from behind the ancient boiler. Somewhere he thought he heard foot-steps. 'Geordie?' he called out tentatively. 'Geordie? Is that you?' He hesitated. He tried to bring the vision of the Virgin Mary to mind. 'Help me,' he whispered, but she refused to come. There was no glow of light, nothing to suggest her interest. I suppose this isn't her kind of place, he reasoned. It's too nasty, too dirty. But of course she might be still outside somewhere, on the roof or in the sky.

Moving cautiously he negotiated a corridor. There were dead offices on either side, concealed by opaque windows. He emerged in the main entrance hall, behind the heavy, sealed front door. The old glass-fronted booth was still in position, where people had once paid to come in. Cautiously, Leslie passed into the swimming baths. He sniffed,

238

expecting the whiff of chlorine that he remembered from his own few reluctant immersions, but all he could detect was mustiness and mouse-droppings and decay. He shone his torch and its beam appeared puny and desolate. Around the perimeter of the space were cubicles, their wooden doors ajar, missing or broken. The pool, of course, was empty. Without water the empty space beneath his feet seemed smaller and less significant than he remembered. A lot of tiles had become detached and lay in the bottom in disconsolate piles. There were slimy stains and some rotting fabric, which might have been old curtains. Archie Watson drowned here, he remembered. He pictured the boy's blue face, his sightless stare when the attendant had pulled him from the deep end. In those days the pool had been smooth, clean and deadly. Now it held different terrors. There was a scuttling, the creak of a half-closed skylight, a draught. Leslie shuddered. 'Geordie!' he whispered urgently. 'Geordie!' He sounded loud and there was a horrible, eerie echo. Orrr-dee. Orrr-dee. He felt clammy with fear. 'Geordie! Are you here?' Orrr-dee. Ooo-eer.

There was no response. He quit the pool and went back into the main entrance. Stone steps curved upwards. With more courage than he had known he possessed, Leslie began his ascent. Upstairs, above the wash-house area, were lines of small rooms containing bathtubs. Leslie and Geordie had always stayed at home and used the tin bath in front of the fire, but his mother had at one time come here on Ladies' Nights for what she referred to as 'a damned good soak'. Leslie shone his torch into each partitioned area. The big tubs looked much as they had always done, apart from dust, cobwebs and neglect. The brass fittings still shone a little. The pattern of vine leaves was still visible on the blue and white ceramic walls. There was broken and abandoned furniture. Tentatively, he opened each door. It was very dark, very quiet. 'Geordie! Are you here?' His small point of light travelled about, nervously enquiring, a little shaky.

A small voice piped up. 'Geordie's a good boy. Geordie's a very good boy.'

Leslie spun round, ecstatic with relief, locating the white, wide-eyed face of his brother, instantly dazzling him. He ran over, fell to his knees and took him in his arms. He rocked and hugged him. 'Thank goodness,' he repeated over and over again, 'thank goodness. You're safe, thank goodness.' Geordie felt small and cold, but also whole. He was real. He had survived.

'Geordie's a good boy. He saved the cat.'

'Hush,' whispered Leslie. 'Hush.' He kissed his brother's cheek.

Geordie led him into the small bathroom where he'd been hiding. He was still wearing handcuffs.

His fingers shaking, Leslie fumbled with the bags before tenderly wrapping the fugitive in blankets. Struggling with the torch, he tried to unpack the food.

'The light,' offered the younger boy.

'What?'

'The light.' He pointed. Above, just discernible, there was a gas mantle. 'Geordie's got no matches.'

Leslie dragged a chair to the centre of the space, climbed up, thrust his hands through the cobwebs and fiddled with the small metal knob. There was a faint hiss. He struck a match and there was an instant pop and a wash of pale illumination from the filthy but ornate glass shade. He climbed down. 'I can't believe the gas is still on.' He looked around. Geordie had found himself a jug and a cup. 'You've got clean water?' Leslie noticed that he'd also made himself a little nest from a pile of mildewed towels. He was grubby and scared. Peering from the folds of his blanket, his green eyes were like saucers, but he appeared unharmed. 'I'll give you something to eat. I'll sort you out. You want some cake?'

The two boys picnicked in companionable silence. Geordie was starving.

'What we going to do?' Leslie said eventually, clearing away.

There was no answer.

'You can't stay here.'

Geordie's response was to cower away, huddling like a small hibernating mammal in his folds of fabric. Gratefully he clutched the sketchpad and pencil-case Leslie had brought to his chest.

Leslie felt unequal to the problem 'I suppose you could stay till this all blows over. Until they get the person who did it.' He took his brother's hand. He made his voice sound serious and forceful. 'That evening. When you found the twins. Did you see anybody else hanging around? Was anyone else there?' He paused. 'Any bad men?'

Geordie opened his pad. His drawing of Marsden Street, the same one that he'd started immediately before finding the dead twins, was unfinished on the top. Wordlessly and despite his chained-together hands, his pencil flashed and scribbled and scored across the page.

Leslie watched attentively. In the previously empty street, a lorry took shape before his eyes. It was drawn in great detail, its number-plate clear, its wing mirror delineated, its engine grille, its single wiper. 'Yes, I know the workmen were there. I saw them leave. Was there anybody else?'

Geordie appeared not to hear. He was engrossed in his drawing. The outline of the broken-down terrace gained more details on either side of the vehicle, narrowing to show perspective, the missing doors and windows of the houses becoming shaded, like dark caverns. The cobbles of the road were added to form a textured foreground. 'Those girls were goners,' he offered after a few minutes.

Leslie tried again. 'Did you see anyone else? There were the dead girls, the cat, the gang of men. There was you. Who else?'

'You.'

'Who else apart from me?'

'You.'

'Yes, me. Who else?'

'Our mam.'

Leslie was surprised. 'You saw our mam there?'

'And you. You were there, Leslie. Those girls were goners.' Using the side of the pencil lead, he made smudges, depicting clouds in the sky. They were high and scattered, suggesting afternoon, suggesting sunny weather. There was a long pause. 'Geordie saved the cat. Geordie saved the cat. Geordie's a good boy.'

'Are you sure our mam was there? Where was she going?'

'Are you sure our mam was there? Where was she going? You saw our mam there?' Geordie picked up the torch. He held it in front of him directing the beam forward.

Leslie understood. 'Yes, there were two men with torches. Later on. As we were leaving. It was dark then, wasn't it? They were on their way home. They saw you and told the police. I know about *them*. Was there anybody else? Was anybody there *before you*?'

Geordie began sketching again. In the very bottom corner of the page, he drew a circle. In the centre of this he drew a smaller circle, then, in the very middle, he drew a tiny circle.

'What's that?' asked Leslie. 'A wheel?' It looked exactly like the wheel of a motorcycle, disappearing off the edge of the page. 'Is that Desperate Dan? Desperate and Ratty, on the motorbike?'

Geordie didn't reply. Leslie took the drawing, folded it and put it in his pocket. I'll take this home, he thought. It might be useful. At that moment there was a sudden crash from downstairs, like a door closing. Geordie froze. Leslie leapt to his feet and on to the chair. He extinguished the light. He jumped back down and huddled close to his brother. They trembled together. 'Shush,' murmured Leslie.

'Those girls were there,' whispered Geordie. 'I couldn't save those girls.'

'Shush.'

Leslie's heart was in overdrive. There was a new, warm smell in the space now, created by the gaslamp. The illumination would have been visible from outside. I left footprints on my way in, he remembered. I walked through that puddle. I might have been followed. Did I leave the window wide open? He waited for what seemed like an age. There wasn't another sound. 'Let's go to sleep,' he said eventually.

Geordie was tense, his body stiff. His mind was in the future. 'Geordie's in a big flying machine,' he whispered. 'Geordie's high in the sky with a man with a dark brown face.'

Leslie said nothing. He waited, but there was no more. After a while he listened to his brother's steady breathing.

He was asleep, but rummaging and restless in his covers. Eventually, settling, he curled up against the older boy's chest like a little dormouse in a children's story book. Leslie held him tenderly.

*

The next morning, Scotch Iris's friend Betty turned up at the police station, as instructed. She looked as blowzy as usual, wearing a tight imitation-leather skirt, her breasts propped up within a boned sun-top, her thick panstick make-up too orange and badly applied. She was no stranger to the desk Sergeant, who greeted her with a wry smile.

Brought in for being drunk and disorderly the night before, Scotch Iris had taken the opportunity to talk. She'd talked and talked. Then she'd been sent home. Now, in the interview room, the Detective-Inspector looked at Betty disapprovingly, before studying his notes. 'So,' he said. 'Are you clear? You understand the procedures?'

'I don't have to do this,' Betty answered, sulkily.

'You'll do as you're told.'

'Oh, I will, will I?'

'Yes. I think so.'

'How are you so sure?'

The officer leaned back in his chair, frowning. He was not an impressive-looking man, but his manner was force-ful. 'Because, you *fat tart*, I'll have you up for corrupting minors. And it'll be all over and done with a lot quicker than one of your punters can have a wank. That quick, right?' He paused. 'You're looking at a custodial sentence, not some twopenny-ha'penny fine this time around, Betty. You think I won't pursue it? I've got the evidence. I've talked to enough of those sick lowlife bastards already.

You were the procuress. And you, my dear, have *broken the law.'*

Betty was indignant. 'I don't see how. Not one of them ever touched those girls. Not one of them. Never. Nobody ever laid a finger on them.'

'The twins were exposed to lewd acts. To licentious behaviour. They were used in the pursuit of immoral earnings. They were well under age.' He paused. His voice was Arctic cold. 'And they're dead.' He stared at the woman, meeting her scared eyes. 'We can press charges.'

Betty became a little shrill. 'I never had anything to do with that. Not their murder. Not me. I never did. What are you saying? What are you saying I did? I never . . .'

'We may find . . .' the Detective-Inspector interrupted, 'we may find that someone from your personal rollcall of perverts harmed young Muriel and Maureen Robson. We may discover . . .' His voice became low and snake-like, 'that you introduced them to their killer.'

Betty looked sweaty and ill. Her fat neck wobbled as she gulped for air. She said nothing. Then she whispered. 'It was their idea. Those girls were terrors. It was all their idea. They were money mad. They wanted money to buy those long-playing records. You know. "Apache." The Shadows and all that.'

The policeman exploded. 'They were thirteen years of age! They were just bairns!'

Betty hung her head.

There was a silence. The clock on the wall ticked. The policeman picked up a photograph from the desk between them and held it by its edge, as if it carried horrible germs. It was an enlarged version of one of Ratty's snapshots of the twins. It showed them lying together on a floor somewhere, holding hands, their clothing disarranged, their

245

small breasts and their pubic hair exposed. Their socks were rucked on their thin legs, their round-toed sandals seemed childish. They were both wearing an excess of make-up and one of them smiled impudently at the camera. Their pose was not unlike the position in which they had been found in death.

'It was just play-acting,' muttered Betty.

The Inspector stood up. He motioned to a constable by the door. 'Right,' he said, decisively. 'The line-up's ready. You come with me. You tell us who took this photograph. This ... damned pornography. You point out the man responsible.'

*

Inside the abandoned public baths, Leslie organized some breakfast, did a few card tricks and then left Geordie as comfortable as possible. He told him not to venture outside. 'I'll be back,' he reassured him. 'I'll come back with more food. We'll use that little stove to make some tea, heat up some baked beans. It'll be just like camping!'

He set off towards home, his mind racing. It was another hot day. He was relieved to have found his brother, but the scale of his predicament overwhelmed him. He can't stay there, he thought. Someone is bound to find him. And they're probably going to pull the whole building down any day now. I've got to get him out and into a place where nobody knows him. He considered. He remembered the letters in the shoebox under his bed. I've got to get him *away* from here. He stopped and stared at the Bath Hotel, which was a public house on the opposite corner. That's it, he thought, suddenly excited. I'll get him into an *hotel*. A proper hotel that is, not a pub like this one. And not here. It'll have to be in the centre of Newcastle somewhere . . . I know, I'll get him into the Station Hotel in town. They must have bedrooms because that's where people stay when they've been on trains. No one will know us. No one will bother us.

Leslie had never been inside an hotel in his life. He felt unsure of what went on inside such establishments, apart from what he'd seen in films. He had a vague idea about sandwiches on silver trays, American accents, uniformed people called bellboys and, of course, lifts and telephones. It'll be great, he decided, suddenly enthusiastic. We'll both stay in an hotel. He hesitated. Of course, I'll have to get a job to pay for it all. We can't just stay in an hotel for nothing. I wonder how much it'll cost?

At the bottom of the hill, in the most run-down, disreputable street in the area, where the demolition men had yet to arrive, Leslie saw Desperate Dan tinkering with his motorcycle in one of the tunnels that led through to a back lane. He remembered the fact that Ratty and Desperate had ignored him recently, that Geordie had drawn what looked like a departing motorcycle wheel near the crime scene and that the capture of the real murderer would let his brother off the hook. He watched as Desperate tightened a nut in the engine. The youth stared back for a moment, unsmiling, then resumed his work with the spanner. I wonder, thought Leslie. The idea was unthinkable but he forced himself to think it nevertheless. Desperate hated those twins, he recalled. They ruined his boots and his beret. Maybe . . . just maybe . . .

He approached. 'Hello there.' He was trying to sound friendly.

'No,' said Desperate tersely, 'I *don't* want to see a card trick.' Desperate had not recovered from his ordeal. For the first time in his life he'd been unable to please someone in authority. The police Sergeant had been unimpressed and had remained so, even when he let him go. 'Off you go, Private Droopy Drawers,' he'd said, smiling in a sarcastic kind of way. 'Go and play tin soldiers and stay well away from *me*.' Desperate was traumatized by his experience at the police station. He was finding it difficult to collect his thoughts.

Leslie decided not to prevaricate. *Be like that then*, he thought. If that's the way you want it. Not for the first time recently, he decided to abandon his normal warm and generous manner. 'My brother saw you near that house where the girls were found,' he said simply. As he spoke, Leslie was aware that he was becoming a harder person. 'He saw you riding away.'

Desperate laid his spanner on the kerb and met the younger boy's gaze. He'd gone white. 'I was collecting bottles,' he croaked, swallowing hard, trying to clear his tightening throat. 'I was collecting bottles for Mr Schnitzler. From around the empty houses.' He hesitated. 'There's no law against that.'

Leslie sensed his discomfort. 'You were in that house,' he said, 'weren't you?'

'I . . . I . . .' There was a pause. 'No! I wasn't.'

'You were in the house where those twins were done in.'

'I wasn't. I've already told the polis everything.'

Leslie could tell he was afraid. 'In that case it doesn't matter if I go and see them, then. Does it? It doesn't matter if I tell them he saw you there.'

Desperate stood up. He was much taller than Leslie but his manner was cowed. Brave and fearless in the army, he was unable to cope with the complexity of recent events. He tried to summon up some aggression. 'Your brother's a dafty. Who's going to listen to him?' He straightened his battledress. 'They think the dafty *did it*. You know that, don't you, kid? That's why they tried to take him prisoner and cart him away in their car.'

'It wasn't just my brother who saw you,' Leslie lied. 'I saw you too. Quite a few people saw you actually. And I'm going to tell Constable Henderson.' He turned and walked away. He was conscious of Desperate's eyes boring into the back of his skull. At the corner he turned around. 'Where's Ratty?' he called out.

Desperate stared at him and his expression was piggy and narrowed. 'The polis think the dafty did it,' he shouted in reply. 'They need to find the dafty. They want to arrest him and lock him up.'

*

Outside Taylor's paper shop, Leslie read the headlines on a *Newcastle Post* newsboard. ANGEL TWINS ARREST SHOCK. Underneath in smaller writing it said 'New Lead'. He felt in his pocket for coins then went in to buy the newspaper. There was the usual picture of the girls on the front page, looking innocent and beautiful. They weren't like that at all, he remembered. They were skinny and spiteful and their hair was tatty and they had nasty teeth.

He wasn't a good reader, but he leant against the wall and puzzled his way through the print. He discovered that Ratty was being held in custody. This meant the polis were keeping him inside. His heart raced. He was both horrified and elated. Not Ratty, he thought, but almost simultaneously it occurred to him that Ratty's misfortune might be Geordie's salvation. He read on. Apparently the twins had been involved in something called gross indecency and it was Ratty's fault. Ratty was in possession of something called an obscene article. Also involved was his mother's friend Betty. This was less surprising. Towards the bottom of the page Sammy Schnitzler was quoted as saying that he'd 'disowned' his son. Leslie understood enough of what this all meant to realize that Ratty had done some dirty stuff and was in deep trouble. He turned the page. Here, in the right-hand corner, there was a picture of the tall sandy-haired man who had come to speak at the Wesley Hall. Leslie recognized him immediately. Mr Newcastle himself. He had been interviewed about this turn of events and he said that he condemned all perversion, salacious behaviour and moral corruption. Leslie was unsure of the meanings of these words but he realized it was something to do with the way Betty and his mother earned a living. He was only surprised that the twins had played a part in it all, but this explained their presence at the front-room party in Glue Terrace. He felt slightly sick. Maybe Geordie can come home, he thought, but when he turned the next page he received another fright. Reproduced in a grainy way were two of Geordie's drawings. SUSPECT BOY'S MIRACLE GIFT said the caption in bold type. The article described the fact that Geordie had never been to school, that he had a learning age of four, and commented on the astonishing brilliance of his art work. Leslie was pleased for a moment, but when he read on he discovered that his brother was still wanted as 'a key witness'. Worse, the journalist described how Geordie had been observed at the crime scene and suggested that he'd been 'a prime suspect'. Leslie folded up the newspaper and stuffed it in his pocket. Nothing's changed, he told himself. They're still looking for him. And fancy saying he's only *four*. How stupid can you get? He's fourteen. What are they on about? As he turned the corner into his own street he realized that his mother must have given his brother's drawings to the press. This made him furious for reasons that he couldn't explain.

The flat was empty but Scotch Iris had clearly been home. Leslie noticed that the pills, which had been sprinkled on the kitchen table, had now disappeared. I should have thrown those buggers away, he thought. She's probably eaten them already. He felt depressed. We won't *get her back* as long as she's taking them. She won't be our proper mam, our Cullercoats mam, as long as she's swallowing those purple hearts.

The kitchen was untidy and the unpaid bills leered at him from behind the clock. He went into the back bedroom, but it no longer felt right without Geordie. He saw his shoebox sticking out from under the bed and kicked it out of sight. He looked in the mirror, combed his short thatch with his fingers. He rubbed a smudge of dirt from his cheek with his cuff. There's nothing else I can do, he told himself. It's the Station Hotel, it's prison, or it's Prudhoe. I've got to save him and get him out of Elswick. Leslie was on his way once more to try and get a job.

*

By sheer persistence, Scotch Iris had managed to force a meeting with Mickey Robson. After her splash in the newspapers where she'd talked graphically, if not crudely, about their relationship, his solicitor had advised him to have a word. Reluctantly he'd accepted a telephone call from her in his office at the Town Hall. She was feeding pennies into a phone box somewhere near the meat market and Mickey was puzzled by the background moans and shouts, which were in fact frightened cattle being unloaded from a wagon.

'Where are you?' he asked, dismayed.

'I'm in the frigging Ritz, London,' said Iris. 'I'm having tea and bannocks with the bloody Duke of Edinburgh. What d'you mean, where am I? You shite-heed bastard. Where the fuck are *you*?'

Mickey agreed to meet in an out-of-the-way pub on the Quayside. It was a place frequented by sailors and others merely passing through. He was sure that here he wouldn't bump into reporters or anyone he knew. Coming straight from a planning meeting, he was dapper and groomed although his face was greyish from lack of sleep.

He was horrified when Scotch Iris appeared. Now wiped almost clean of make-up, her complexion was shiny and haggard. She had a black eye from a fall and one of her front teeth was broken. She was wearing a plastic rain cape, lent to her after she'd been picked up drunk outside Mickey's house. The words 'Newcastle United F.C.' were emblazoned on both the chest and back. It had once belonged to a linesman at St James's Park and had somehow ended up in the squad car after a football match. The police officer had given it to her because she'd been shaking. Mistakenly, he'd thought she was cold.

Iris seemed oblivious to the transformation in her appearance. On her feet she was wearing a pair of carpet slippers. She looked like an itinerant or a plonkie. Her former lover barely recognized her. She flopped down at his table. 'Giv'us a tab,' she said, grabbing a cigarette from his packet, lighting up and pretending to inhale.

The meeting did not go well. Mickey tried to be calm, he said it was better for them to stay apart until 'things quietened down'. Iris repeated and repeated that Geordie was not responsible for the deaths of his daughters. 'And neither am I,' she added defiantly and rather loudly.

'Neither am I, even though I hated the little whores, so I did.' She was teetering on the brink of total loss of control. Since that morning she'd been back on the amphetamines but by now all her judgement was gone and she'd effectively overdosed an hour before. She twitched and fidgeted. 'Geordie didn't do it,' she said for the thirtieth time. 'There's *no reason* to finish with me.'

Other drinkers in the bar kept trying to look at her sideways while appearing unconcerned. The landlord rolled up his sleeves, ready for trouble.

'We can go somewhere. Start a new life. We don't have to get married if you don't want to.' Iris saw this as a huge concession. 'We could go down south. To Nottingham, maybe. How about the Isle of Wight?'

Dismayed by her persistence, her irrationality, while struggling to cope and still emotional from shock and grief, Mickey drank four pints of beer in under half an hour. Finally, pushed to the limits by Iris's repetitions, accusations and crazy suggestions, he lost control of his temper. This wasn't what he'd been told to do. He'd been advised by his solicitor to 'reason with the troublemaker', or offer her money, but by now he'd forgotten about these intentions. Without warning he thumped the table with his fist, juddering his glass. 'Bloody women!'

Startled, Iris moved her chair backwards with a sudden jerk.

'Can't you see, it's all your fault?' he shouted. 'Bloody women!'

She stared at him, the wind gone from her sails, her mouth open.

'If it wasn't for you I would've been there for them. I would've been a better father to them.' He was yelling in her face, spittle hitting her cheeks. He carried on like this for a while. Then, very drunk, he slumped forwards, muttering, maudlin, desolate. He covered his hands with his face. He swayed a little in his seat. Everyone in the pub was staring. Someone who'd been listening attentively throughout got up and went outside to a nearby phone box.

Iris said nothing. Her hands shook. She looked pathetic. He doesn't love me, she thought to herself.

Mickey continued. Uninhibited by beer, his mood changed again. He blew his nose on a folded handkerchief from his breast pocket. His emotions had finally found expression. Quietly now, rationally, but vehemently and articulately, as if he was in a Labour Party meeting, he said some terrible things to Iris about her way of life and her values. He blamed her for everything. He said she'd tricked him and led him astray. He said she'd introduced the twins to Betty and therefore led them into vice and consequently to their ends. 'You *did* kill them,' he concluded. 'Even if it was indirectly. And I hold you res ponsible. Yes, *you*. If you were a man, I'd kill you with my own bare hands.'

*

Leslie set off for the tannery. Like Adamsez Sanitary Wares, it was also beside the river but in the opposite direction. Again he tramped past the massive and endless Vickers yards, heading for somewhere smaller, somewhere less frightening, less alien where he might be able to make some sort of a contribution. He knew that Richardson's Leather was a closed shop. This, Ratty had told him, meant that all the people who worked there were from a few families. They all lived together in special houses at the side of the factory. Their employers owned these dwellings. It was hard to get a job at Richardson's if you weren't born and bred in this little enclave. However, Leslie thought it was worth a try. Leather seemed like a very ordinary kind of thing. It was simply a matter of processing skins, turning them into something useful. There can't be too much to learn about leather, he reasoned. It wasn't scary, noisy and massive like Vickers with its complicated metal, its machinery and its crash of engineering. The tannery didn't resound day and night with heavy hammers and drills. It didn't have huge cranes loading steam loco-motives and printing presses on to waiting foreign ships. Most importantly, it wasn't exclusively male. Ratty had told him that women washed the hides and made the glue. It's probably a small, friendly concern, he told himself, even if it does stink to high heaven.

When he arrived in Crucible Place there was a bell tolling from the roof of the factory and people were coming out of their houses, going back to work after their dinner break. Leslie felt suddenly shy and awkward. He didn't recognize anyone. He tagged behind a couple of girls who were wearing overalls and whose hair was tucked beneath turbans. To his dismay, one of them turned to him and asked him what he wanted.

'I've come about a job,' he stuttered. The girl was young and pretty although her skin was unhealthy, as if she didn't see enough daylight.

She smiled. 'You better come with me, then.'

Right next to the factory they walked past a row of greenhouses filled with tomatoes in pots. Then they passed into a dim shed.

'Have you got an appointment with Mr Alaric? Or with Mr Frank?'

Leslie shook his head. He knew she meant the Richardsons and that this pair of brothers ran the company. They were both tall and gaunt and had long beards because they were Quakers. They were against drink, swearing, cinema, and dance halls. The boy held a hand over his nose, pretending he was about to sneeze. The smell was overpowering and truly, truly awful. I'm going to be sick, he thought. There was a very uncertain feeling developing in his stomach.

'You get used to it,' said the girl, undeceived by his subterfuge. 'Watch out!'

Leslie turned abruptly. The floor was slippery and he almost lost his balance. He realized that the area was dotted with open, unguarded pits and inside these, greasy-looking skins were submerged. Piled up around the sides were hundreds of hides, some of which were hairy with bits of fat and meat attached. A dense cloud of flies buzzed about. Leslie retched but tried to disguise this as a cough. The deeper he penetrated the shed, the worse the odour became. He breathed through his mouth. Please God don't let me be sick, he prayed. *Please.*

'Come on.' The girl led him up a rickety staircase and into the brick building. Here the air was less thick, but sunlight beat in through the windows and Leslie's head still swam. He felt beads of sweat break out on his face. That's the worst stink I've ever smelt in my entire life, he decided. That was absolutely horrible. He now risked taking a proper deep breath. It steadied him a little. Just then he saw a real crocodile nailed to the wall at the end of the corridor.

The girl knocked timidly on a door. She followed his gaze. 'We see to crocodiles,' she offered. 'We see to goats, seals, sheep and snakes.'

'Really?' said Leslie, unsure how to respond.

'We see to leopards, tigers and lions. But not that much.'

'Lions?'

'We mainly see to cows. That's what you smell. We see to hundreds of cows. They come up from the meat market twice a day.' She knocked again. 'You know something? We make the best patent leather in the world. It's used for dancing shoes. It's as shiny as shiny with no cracking. It's a *secret* formula. I don't know it. None of us know it, not even the finishers. Only Mr Frank and Mr Alaric know it.'

'Gosh.'

'This is Mr Frank's office.'

Leslie felt almost recovered. Automatically, he took out his cards. 'Do you want to see a . . .'

'Put those away!' The girl was horrified. 'The devil's picture book!'

Hastily, Leslie concealed the pack.

'Mr Frank and Mr Alaric *do not allow* cards. They dock your pay.' She knocked again. 'I'm afraid Mr Frank's not in.'

'I'll come back later,' Leslie lied.

'You're not one of us, are you?'

'No.'

'Mr Alaric sometimes takes strangers on, but not too often. Mr Frank said only the other day we don't need shavers at present. Boys generally shave. We need a flesher, but you're too young for fleshing.'

Leslie felt queasy once more. 'I'll come back,' he repeated. 'Thanks for your trouble.'

'It's been no trouble.'

Leslie hesitated. He felt unwilling to go back into the shed. 'Right, then.' He filled his lungs. 'I'll be off.'

'Can you see yourself out? It's straight back that way.' The girl pointed. 'Just follow your nose.' She added this without irony.

*

Sammy Schnitzler wanted to talk to Scotch Iris. He stood outside the door of her flat in his best suit and bowler hat, anxious and sweating slightly. I've got to get her away, he kept thinking. There's nothing left for us here. We'll start a new life. I've got to get her right away. It's not as if I haven't got money saved. My mother's diamonds are hidden inside the soles of my shoes. He tapped both feet, almost happy in the knowledge. '*Gold shaynt fun blote,*' he muttered. 'Gold glitters even in the mud.' He knocked repeatedly on the door. He had a key but he was unwilling to use it. His mind was restless. We've got to get away before it's too late. He listened to the roar of the demolition wagons approaching, the thud of the ball on the chain as it battered against Cannon Street. Dust obliterated the sun again and there was the rumble of Vickers tanks out on test. 'Answer the *door*, why don't you!'

In response to the noise he was making, Ada appeared from upstairs. She was surprised and disconcerted to see her landlord on Iris's step. 'Oh, Mr Schnitzler, sir,' she stuttered, 'Mrs MacDonald's not here, with all the trouble and one thing and another. Come up. Come up, sir, and have a nice cup of tea.'

Pleased by her deferential manner, Sammy took off his hat and agreed. 'You always keep this place very nice,' he complimented her as they climbed the stairs. 'Very nice. Very nice indeed. I wish all my tenants were all so hygienic. So concerned.'

'I do my best,' Ada puffed.

'Perhaps I'll get the electric put in,' he offered. 'Mrs MacDonald has the electric. For you, I could do the same.'

Upstairs, he settled himself in her armchair. A small fire burned, despite the hot weather. There was a smell of baking scones and the clock ticked in a soothing way. He stared into the hearth, as if forgetting where he was.

'The council are putting me out,' Ada informed him without ceremony. 'I had to go to Amen Corner, down in the town. They're putting me in a one-bedroom unit. They want me to go to Westerhope! Or Fawdon!'

He looked at her bleakly.

'I haven't been to either of those places since before the war. Why would I want to shift *there*?'

'There's nothing I can do,' Sammy replied. 'It's out of my hands.'

'I've lived here since I was first married. I've lived in these same two streets all my life!'

Sammy's face was long and mournful. 'The twins are dead. All is in ruins.' He took out a handkerchief and blew his nose.

Ada ignored this. 'What am I going to do?'

'People are leaving for Poland,' her landlord answered mysteriously. 'They have no choice in the matter either.'

'Shifting to *Poland*?'

'My cousin's boy has managed to escape to Chicago.'

'*Chicago*?' Ada's mouth dropped open. Speechless, she busied herself in the scullery with the kettle and crockery, then returned. 'Have a fairy cake, Mr Schnitzler.' She'd got out her best china and silver apostle spoons.

He held up one hand, in refusal. 'I'll have a cup of hot water,' he said. 'Plain hot water. And do you have any McVitie's Digestives?'

They sat together for a while. 'I'm concerned to locate

Mrs MacDonald,' Sammy said eventually. 'I believe her youngest boy is suffering injustices.'

'That boy is her cross,' Ada replied, then corrected herself. 'I mean that boy is both a burden and a blessing.'

'*My* boy has turned out a *knaker*,' Sammy confided. 'Poland's probably the best place for him.'

Ada poured more plain hot water into his cup. She had read about Ratty in the newspaper but the details embarrassed her. She said nothing. 'I'll tell Mrs MacDonald you called,' she said eventually. 'I'm sure she'll be very touched by your concern.'

Sammy drained his cup delicately and handed it to her on its saucer. 'That is very pretty china,' he remarked, 'but china doesn't travel well.'

Ada sighed.

He stood up. Absent-mindedly, he felt in his pocket for change.

'You're my guest,' she said, surprised.

He stared at her as if he'd forgotten where he was. 'Ah,' he said, trying to collect himself. He pressed his hand on his heart. 'Thank you, my dear. Yes, very kind. Thank you.'

*

Leslie, feeling dismayed about Richardson's, but too restless and disconcerted by events to do nothing, had caught a trolley-bus into town. It was a rare event for him to leave Elswick. On a city-centre street he felt intimidated by the traffic and amazed by a glass-fronted shop which was selling luxury goods. He stared in, noticing plain, pared-down furniture made out of blond wood. That must be the latest thing, he thought. It's probably what you have when you live in quality apartments in the sky. There was a lamp with a plastic shade, a plain, hard-looking settee with six small red cushions all the same and a television set in a cabinet. On the pretend wall were an electric clock shaped like a sun and two paintings. One was of a foreign-looking lady with a blue face. The other was even stranger. It looked as if a baby had been allowed to throw colours at it randomly, then let them run together.

Leslie sighed. He walked to the Station Hotel and stared up at its impressive façade. Here there were revolving glass doors and a doorman with a uniform. This will have to do, he thought to himself. I'll get Geordie sorted out and living in here just as soon as I can. We'll both live here. We'll get our dinners brought up to us on trays. We'll drink cocktails, go up and down in the lift. Everything's going to be all right.

He enquired directions to the Town Hall. Here, he slipped inside when the porter's back was turned. He asked a lady with a tea-trolley the way to the Council Leader's office and, surprised, she gave him directions. Forcing himself not to think about what he was doing, because to do so would be to lose courage, the boy located the room, knocked firmly on the door and, without waiting for a reply, entered.

T. Dan Smith was sitting in his shirtsleeves, eating a sandwich. He was also talking on the telephone. Eyebrows raised, he motioned Leslie to sit.

Leslie sat on the edge of a chair. He glanced about. The office was tidy but rather featureless apart from a photograph of a family in a real silver frame. They were all positioned in such a way that they smiled at both the occupant and any visitors who might seat themselves on the other side of his desk. The whole lot of them had come straight from the hairdressers, Leslie decided. The wife

261

had a neat perm. The children were wearing the uniforms of impressive-looking schools. They grinned in a way that suggested security, electric blankets and regular balanced meals.

When the Leader replaced the receiver, he turned to Leslie with a friendly smile. 'What can I do for you, son?' he asked.

'I've never talked to anyone on one of those things,' Leslie offered, pointing to the phone. His prepared speech had deserted him. He swallowed hard, then blurted out his words. 'I saw you in the paper, mister. And you were at the meeting. In our Wesley Hall. I'm from Elswick, me. My brother Geordie's wanted by the polis.'

Smith made a steeple with his fingers. He was patient and relaxed. He was behaving as if ginger-headed, scruffy boys sat in his office every day of his life. 'Tell me all about it,' he said kindly, 'since you're here. You tell me all about it. Take your time.'

Leslie started by trying to describe his brother. 'He's never been to school, but he's not daft. He's starting to go out a lot by himself. He's clever in his own way, you see. He can play the piano. He's an artist.'

'Those are very valuable attributes,' Smith agreed, solemnly.

'He's just different from other people. That's all. But he's a lovely person.' Leslie paused, collected his thoughts then told the entire story, starting with the injured cat and finishing with Geordie hiding out in an empty building. 'I'm not saying where, mind,' he concluded. 'But it can't go on much longer.' He felt better for having got the secret off his chest. All at once he felt warm and confiding. The Council Leader was regarding him steadily and with great interest.

'Geordie didn't do it, mister,' Leslie repeated. He hesitated. 'That Ratty Schnitzler probably did it,' he added. 'He's a Teddy boy.' He felt like a betrayer, but he had to do what was necessary for his brother. 'That Ratty Schnitzler's a . . . He's a . . .'

'I know about *him*,' responded Smith, with an expression of distaste on his lips. 'The Detective-Inspector is keeping me fully informed.'

'I just thought . . .' offered Leslie.

'You thought?'

'Folks call you Mr Newcastle.'

Smith smiled. 'So I believe.'

'Well, all things considered and seeing as you said you've the interests of the people of Elswick close to your heart, I just thought . . .'

'Well?'

'I thought you might call off the polis. Tell them to leave my Geordie alone.'

Smith pursed his lips in his usual prim way. He offered Leslie a sandwich from a special plastic box. His wife had obviously prepared these that morning. The boy took one. It was ham and tomato and very delicious. He munched enthusiastically.

'Are you hungry?'

'Yes, mister, I am.'

Smith handed him the entire lunch. 'Here. You eat this. I'm watching my waistline.' He stepped outside the office for a moment and coughed loudly. 'Gladys!' he called down the corridor. 'Bring my young visitor a cup of tea.'

Leslie finished the food while Smith phoned the police station. The boy listened carefully to the conversation and was grateful that he was not mentioned, nor the fact that he knew where Geordie was hiding.

Smith put down the receiver. 'Your brother's wanted for questioning,' he said. 'If you think about it, he's a vital witness. He may have important information at his disposal. It really is his duty, it's the duty of both of you to help in any way you can. And really, when all is said and done, one's duty is really the most important thing. Yes? We are all responsible for everyone else, are we not? This is a serious matter and a terrible tragedy for the whole city. Only this morning I was discussing it with our future Prime Minister.'

Leslie was disappointed. The encounter felt like an anti-climax. He stood up, dusting crumbs from his duffel-coat. He didn't meet Smith's eye. Absently, he took out his playing cards and shuffled them, staring at a row of books on the wall. One of these was called *English Choral Music*. 'I'm in a choir,' he murmured, by way of taking his leave. 'I'm the treble at St Stephen's.' He turned to go.

The Council Leader was immediately animated. To Leslie's intense surprise, he blocked the door. Detaining Leslie with a flood of words, he explained that he too had been a choirboy. He said that his mother had been a very musical woman who'd married beneath herself and that she was courteous and cultured, encouraging her son in every way. 'I always wanted to be a boy soprano,' he allowed, 'it would have made her *so happy*. But it was not to be. I was in the choir though. I was in the choir for years and years. I *love* music.' He took hold of Leslie by both arms. 'And you. *You* are a boy soprano!'

Leslie stepped back and cleared his throat. He put his cards away. He took a deep breath and began singing.

Panis angelicus
fit panis hominum;

Loving Geordie

> *dat panis caelicus*
> *figuris terminum;*

The notes emerged from his lips like pearls, forming, growing, shining, then dropping, contained in the small room like luminous and precious treasures. His voice poured forth effortlessly. There was no uneasy cracking. Pure, harmonious, the devotional cadences soared and swooped, as heart-breakingly beautiful as the prayers of heaven's own cherubim.

> *O res mirabilis!*
> *manducat Dominum,*
> *pauper, servus et humilis.*

T. Dan Smith was transfixed. His body, his face, were rigid with both shock and pleasure. As Leslie finished, he blinked rapidly, forestalling tears. 'Unbelievable.' He took out a handkerchief and blew his nose. 'Unbelievable. And you're an Elswick lad,' he whispered. 'Well, it just goes to show. An Elswick lad ... It's like I've always said ... It really ... just goes to show.'

*

Scotch Iris wandered along the footpath on the quayside, swaying a little, talking to herself and stumbling on loose cobbles. Stunned by Mickey's rejection and harsh words, she was unsure where she was or what she was doing. In her slippers and outsize raincape she looked like a drunkard or a mad person. Conscious of people's curious gaze, she abused everyone in sight. Her language was rich, but her articulation poor. She shook her fist at a pair of clerics on their way to the cathedral. She tripped on the kerb and nearly fell into the river causing the

265

master of a passing coal barge to hoot in a derogatory way. She wasn't angry, she was confused. Confused and in despair.

Beneath the High Level bridge, she paused and rubbed her eyes. She shook herself, as if trying to clear her mind and body. Angry phrases from her encounter in the pub kept demanding her attention, despite her attempts to push them away. She examined her own hands as if she'd never seen them before. She twitched and fidgeted. She tapped her teeth with her nails, tugged at her hair. Details of her life, both recent and not so recent, pressed in on her consciousness. She thought about her brothers and sisters, whom she hadn't seen for seventeen years. She thought about her rougher clients, about Sammy Schnitzler's damp embraces, about Betty, about the dead twins. She thought about Leslie, his beautiful singing voice and all the ways in which she had let him down. She thought about her youngest son's stony stare, his inability to love her. She remembered her long-lost husband and the gentle way he had at one time stroked her skin.

She turned to the wide sweep of open water and stared at it in horror. It was grey and forbidding and smelled of the coast. A couple of gulls flapped and cried. There was little wind, but a draught blew from the shiny surface of the rushing high-tide stream as it swept along, hurtling eastwards all the industrial detritus and muck of Elswick, towards the sea. Scotch Iris considered her life and a series of unwelcome sensations crowded in. She felt like a failure. She felt disappointment, loneliness, a sense of wrong decisions piled up, one on top of another. She felt weakness and the steady erosion of hope. Her life felt like the bottom end of a short and dismal cul-de-sac. It was dark, utterly pointless and too painful to bear. For some reason, her elder son's voice began resonating in her mind. *'Oh for the wings, for the wings of a dove . . .'*

The torrent churned and rushed past, gurgling and mocking. The Tyne seemed broad and fathomless and as terrifying as the wild explosion that had claimed her husband's fishing boat in the middle of a Scottish storm. She thought, it's just what I deserve, so it is, and she stepped off the path, at once falling, slipping into the current without even a splash. The water claimed Scotch Iris in a few seconds. She disappeared.

Despite many workers on the quayside that day, five boats in the vicinity and several pedestrians up on the bridge, no one noticed. There was no drama, no cries, no rescue attempt. No one was aware and no one saw her die.

9

Leslie was used to Scotch Iris's absences because she would sometimes spend days on end away, but it was strange being at home without Geordie. He found it unnerving, being in the flat on his own. He felt self-conscious. He was used to doing things for his brother, but had never given any thought to looking after himself. It felt odd, almost unnecessary. He used the same cup and plate without washing them. He crawled in and out of his side of the bed without undressing and without bothering to straighten the covers. He lived on cups of tea and cakes from upstairs.

He went to see his brother several times, taking more supplies and some candle ends, which he decided would be safer than illuminating the entire room with the gaslight. He also took the timetable of trolley-buses, which Geordie was in the habit of reading, committing the details to memory. Today, as he made his way to the public wash-house, he searched the sky for the Virgin. The sun was bright and dazzling and the vision didn't appear. She prefers darkness, Leslie decided. It's because she's a spirit. Spirits are the same as ghosts. They like the dark.

Inside the abandoned building, safe in his nest of blankets and towels, Geordie was quiet and thoughtful. Still handcuffed, he'd done several new drawings of the streets of Elswick, all from memory. His remembered work, Leslie noticed, not for the first time, was just as accurate as drawings done from life. It was as if a photograph had become imprinted on his brain. Nothing was ever missing from his recalled observations.

Leslie told him about his trip to the leather works and how it had been too smelly to bear. He described everything he had seen. Geordie listened without responding.

'Mr Schnitzler's in the police box,' he said eventually.

'What?' Leslie realized after a moment that his brother's mind had again moved away from the present and that he was seeing things that had yet to happen. He waited for the moment to pass, not paying much attention. He tidied the drawings and straightened the makeshift bed.

'Ratty Schnitzler's in the police box too. You're there. Constable Henderson's there. The police box is crowded with folk ... And that poor old Mr Schnitzler ... he doesn't look very well.'

'Right,' said Leslie, soothingly. 'Right.'

Geordie quickly came back to himself and the present. The older boy made sure he was comfortable, then left him, treading carefully down the stairs before struggling through the small window, out into the sunny, half-demolished street. He looked to the left and right, but believed he was unobserved. Above the tall chimney of the wash-house, for a tiny split second, he thought he saw the Virgin Mary beckoning urgently. Her dress fluttered and her dainty hand gestured rapidly. He thought she seemed anxious. He blinked and she'd gone, too ephemeral to hold her own against the glare of the summer sky. He set off for home.

A solitary figure watched from the corner of the Bath Hotel. He stood rigid, his eyes following the boy. A newspaper was folded under his arm. He didn't move a muscle until Leslie was out of sight. His eyes then swivelled to the abandoned building opposite. He was very focused and for a long time he didn't stir. Eventually he sniffed loudly, hawked then spat. He stepped briskly out on to the ruined pavement. It was Desperate Dan. He was as smart as ever, his short back and sides plastered down with Schnitzler's Brilliant, his uniform immaculate, his boots shiny. He'd seen everything he needed to see. He proceeded at a quick march in the direction of the police station.

*

Leslie was very fond of Auntie Ada and he trusted her, but he knew there was no point in confiding in her about Geordie's hiding-place. She was too law-abiding. She would simply fret and nag him about the need to tell the police. She believed in his brother's innocence, of course, but she thought that all policemen were like PC Henderson. She believed that they would behave fairly and let him go after questioning. Leslie had no such confidence. After a lifetime of observing prejudice and suspicion directed at Geordie, he believed that the younger boy's difficulties in expressing himself would, as far as the authorities were concerned, merely damn him straight to hell. Leslie had not told Auntie Ada that he'd found Geordie in the public wash-house and he felt guilty about her continued anxiety and the way she kept peering out the window or listening for footsteps on the stairs.

All he could do was hope that someone else would be charged with the murder because that would end the matter. He thought about poor old Ratty, locked up in the police station. He remembered his friend's cheerful grin, his love of animals and the fact that he'd always been kind. I wish Ratty had stayed away from those horrible twins, he thought miserably. I wish he hadn't started all that dirty stuff with them. I expect they made him do it. Leslie sniffed and wiped his nose on his sleeve. But still, he reasoned, I hope he *is* sent to gaol by the judge because then Geordie can get his handcuffs off, come home and things will get back to normal. He sighed. But what's normal? A sudden wave of panic gripped his heart. We're going to have to shift, he reminded himself, I don't know what'll happen with our mam and those awful pills, there's bills to be paid, doctors writing letters from Prudhoe *and* I've got to get a job. He thought about the smell at the leather works and an unpleasant queasiness returned.

Upstairs, he discovered Auntie Ada, as usual, engrossed in the newspaper, but not with her columns of Births, Marriages and Deaths. She held her magnifying glass over the front page, studying it in detail. 'Would you believe it!' she exclaimed. 'Well I never!'

Leslie peered over her shoulder. In today's local edition, more of Geordie's art work was reproduced. In one corner was a recent pen and ink rendition of a pair of trolley-buses, but larger and filling almost the entire page were detailed pencil drawings of Clumber Street, showing the same scene both before and after the demolition gang's activities. A VANISHING STREETSCAPE said the headline, and underneath it declared 'Missing Suspect's Unique Skill Triumphs'. At the bottom of the page, to Leslie's astonishment, there was a thumbnail photograph of Geordie. Leslie stared. It was the picture taken on the beach at Cullercoats, smiling up at his ice-cream, smiling properly, looking really pleased.

'What!' demanded Leslie, loudly. He grabbed the newspaper from Auntie Ada's hands. There was no doubt. It was the same photograph that he treasured, the only one ever taken of Geordie when he'd been happy. He dropped the newspaper and slapped his chest. His pocket was empty. Where did I leave it? He rummaged in his coat. *Oh no!* It was in my other shirt. He remembered he'd changed his shirt and left the old one on his bed. I don't believe it, he thought. She hasn't done any washing for months!

He flung the paper on the floor and rushed downstairs. He rifled through the dirty laundry, on the floor, on the bed, piled up on chairs. He found the old shirt. The precious photograph had gone. His mother had given it to the newspapermen. 'Oh no!' he whispered aloud. 'Oh no!' Tears sprang to his eyes. He sat at the table, trembling with indignation, then went next door to Iris's room. *Where is she?* he thought. The front of the flat was messy and bleak. Leslie felt a wave of anger and resentment towards his mother. He leaned in the doorway, his mind racing. I'll get a camera, he told himself. No. I won't do that. No, I'll take him to one of those studios in town. That's right, I'll get him into the Station Hotel, get him settled, then I'll take him to that place on Neville Street. There's a photographer's studio on Neville Street. I've seen it there. It's got weddings and suchlike in the window. I'll get a big photo of him done, smiling and happy, and it'll be in a huge gold frame. I'll hang it on the wall of the Station Hotel. He hesitated. After I get a job, of course. After I get my first wage packet. He was shaking. Those newspapermen paid our mam for those drawings, he decided. And the photograph. He was, of course, wrong about this. But he was furious in his assumption. What does she think she's doing? She'll do *anything* for money. He felt both disgusted and betrayed.

There was a knock on the front door. Reluctantly, Leslie got to his feet. He discovered the dark-skinned stranger, in a white collar, tie and suit. He had a flower in his buttonhole. Oh no, Leslie thought. It's that Prudda doctor. He took a deep breath and then said, as instructed, 'My mother has been unavoidably called away.' He felt afraid.

'I'm Dr Kumar,' the man said, having already placed his elegant shoe on the threshold, preventing the boy from slamming the door. He was very polite and he smiled affably. 'As you may remember from my previous visit, I'm from Prudhoe Hospital. May I be so bold as to ask . . . can I come in?'

Leslie led him inside. 'My mam's not here and my brother's not here.' He remembered his manners. 'Please sit down.' He cleared a pile of drawings and dirty washing off one of the kitchen chairs. Unsure where to put it, he dropped it all on the floor. 'I know what you want, but nobody's going to lock my brother up. Not the polis. Not you. No one. So you're wasting your time.' He paused. He sounded desolate. 'Any road, he's *buggered off*, hasn't he? He's not here.'

The stranger attempted another smile. His teeth were very white against his dusky complexion.

He's an Indian, Leslie thought. A Brown Indian, not a Red Indian. He's nicer than he sounds in his letters.

'I've talked to the police,' offered Dr Kumar.

Leslie scowled.

The doctor was undeterred. He was used to difficult children, they were his job. 'Your brother denies murdering those girls, yes?'

Leslie was adamant. 'Of course he does. My Geordie wouldn't hurt a fly.'

'And what has he said about it?' The doctor examined his nails, which were long and shapely. He polished them on his lapel.

'They were already dead when he found them in the house.'

'And you believe him?'

Leslie took a deep breath. 'Look, Dr whatever-your-name-is, my brother didn't do nowt. He said he didn't do nowt, so he didn't. Right?' He paused. 'Right?'

The man nodded. 'Right.'

Leslie was very agitated. He paced back and forth. 'My brother doesn't tell lies. He's not like other boys. He doesn't make things up. He *can't* make things up. That's part of the way he is. He told the polis he didn't do nothing when they came for him. He was shouting it out when they yanked him through the door.'

'I know.'

'You know what?'

'I know he didn't do it.'

Leslie hadn't expected this. He was dumbfounded. *'What?'*

The doctor leant forward. Leslie caught a sweet whiff from the carnation in his jacket. 'Your brother is autistic. He has no fantasy life, no imagination. If your brother describes coming across those girls already dead, then that's what happened. He has no powers of invention. He speaks as he finds.'

Leslie was silent for a moment, letting this sink in. After a while, he felt a faint lightening in his heart. 'You've told the polis?'

'I have.'

'Did they believe you?'

'They listened.'

'So now they think he did nowt? Is that right? Are they saying he did nowt?'

'They want to question him, find out what he saw. But

274

no, they don't think he did it. Or at least, I think it's true to say that since my recent chat with them, they've got *very* open minds.' He opened his briefcase and took out a folded newspaper. 'The police are great respecters of psychologists, I find. They hold our profession in high esteem.' He coughed modestly, unfolding the paper. It was a copy of *The Times*. He opened it and revealed several reproductions of Geordie's drawings. THE LOST COMMUNITY, ran the headline. 'This article describes your brother as the best child artist in the country. Experts have examined his drawings. They say his sense of perspective and eye for detail are absolutely brilliant. Apparently they'd be astounding in an adult, let alone a young boy. His talent is referred to as "remarkable", "inspired" and "uncanny".' The doctor regarded Leslie keenly. 'There's mention of an exhibition. A tour. There's a clamour from different galleries.' He picked up some of Geordie's drawings from the floor and leafed through them. At once he became animated. 'He never draws people, does he?'

'No. Never.'

'Only buildings?'

'Buildings, cars and buses.'

'That makes sense. That makes complete sense.' He examined more sheets. 'The whole of London is talking about it. People are mad for this work. Quite mad. This is astonishing talent. Quite astonishing. I've seen the work of other savants, but this . . . this is absolutely magnificent.' He stood up. 'You go and get your brother,' he added quietly. 'You go and get him and bring him to me. I'd like to make a study . . .'

'I don't know where he is,' Leslie lied, without hesitation. He knew he needed time to think. 'I haven't seen him for days.'

The doctor ignored this. 'You bring him to me,' he repeated. 'I see a *great deal* of potential here.'

*

Desperate Dan stood to attention in a corridor of the police station, his eyes fixed on the military-style epaulette of a uniformed sergeant. He had just spilled the beans about Geordie's hiding-place. In addition, he'd repeated his earlier allegations about Ratty's interest in the twins and his plans to sell the dirty photographs. 'To a nonce down London way,' he'd insisted. 'Soho or somewhere.'

Now he was confessing to his and Ratty's harassment of non-shifters. The words poured out of his mouth, gratefully, in a torrent. He told the officer about the fireworks and the dog-dirt. He mentioned Ratty's list, the names of those residents holding up the demolition gang by their refusal to go.

'And who set you up to this, sonny?' asked the Sergeant, almost kindly. He sensed Desperate's need for approval.

'That Councillor Robson,' replied Desperate without hesitation. 'He's in the pay of the contractors who want the job done quick. He's also got some deal with the builders. Something about land values and . . .'

'Yes?'

'Something called vacant possession. I don't know. He's in it up to his neck. He awards the contracts from the Council. He's being paid by everybody.'

'These are serious allegations, son.'

Desperate's straight back became ramrod stiff and his fists were clenched. 'Councillor Robson paid me and Ratty Schnitzler to scare people. To be something called . . . enforcers. I'm very sorry about it, but I'm doing my duty now, sir. It's late in the day, I know, but I'm doing my duty now. I always do my duty.'

'You're a good lad.' The Sergeant patted the young man's arm.

Desperate's relief was demonstrated by his rapidly blinking eyes, a twitch in his cheek muscle. 'Thank you, sir. Thank you very much. Thank you, sir. Thank you.'

As the Sergeant hurried away, Desperate remained at attention, but simultaneously he let out a silent fart and a deep and relieved sigh.

*

Lofty Long was playing a new single on the record player in the office at the Wesley Hall. He half-lay on the battered sofa, his feet propped on a pile of film magazines, humming along to the catchy tune. The disc had only recently been released. Previously unknown, the young male singer Johnny Hurricane had made the 45 r.p.m. recording, which was a simple, but deeply-felt ballad called 'Angel Twins'. It had entered the hit parade at number three. The artist sang with a syncopated break in his voice, reminiscent of Adam Faith.

> *My angels, my angels*
> *You're above us in the sky, my angels*
> *No one can hur-rurt you, no one can har-arm you*
> *You're in heaven where you cay-ame from*

Lofty felt closely connected to the glamour and new-found fame of the singer because he'd known the twins. He reckoned this song was as good as 'Apache'. As he listened, he remembered his own brief taste of stardom, on the stage with Bruce and Hank before they left Newcastle and formed the Shadows. Johnny Hurricane might

277

be friendly with Hank Marvin and Cliff Richard, he pondered. They might all come up here together and play the Newcastle Majestic. I'd be guest of honour. This was a pleasant idea. He sang along, crooning enthusiastically, and after the record had finished he played it again. His mind roamed across the possibilities of after-show parties, backing groups with pretty boys in sequinned jackets all holding pink Fender Stratocaster guitars. He smiled. I'd better prepare myself, he decided. I'll get that Schnitzler's dad to give me a modern haircut. I'll take my trousers to the tailor and get them narrowed.

When the three strangers arrived, demanding to know if he was the youth club superintendent, Lofty got to his feet, grinning. For a crazy moment it seemed as if their matching dark suits and London accents meant they were in the music business. 'What can I do you for?' he enquired magnanimously. 'You like this "Angel" number?' He turned up the volume on the record-player.

The new men from Scotland Yard wasted no time. In their view, the local force had been in error, if not gross dereliction, for not calling them in sooner. This was, after all, a double murder, it was a case involving two beautiful little girls and it was already a national scandal, with questions being asked in the House of Commons. The media had got hold of it and were baying for justice. The police had been made to look like complete idiots, because of these local turnip-heads, and that meant it was *their* job to get a result.

The burliest of the three ignored Lofty's cheerful, outstretched hand, side-stepped behind him and pinioned him in an armlock. He kicked the record-player, sending the stylus noisily skidding. The second man hit him with a knuckle-duster on the jaw. The third delivered a blow to his lower abdomen that made him briefly pass out. They manhandled him into the main hall, just below the stage, and pummelled and kicked him for quite a while. His breath was knocked out of his body in short sobs. His bladder released its contents. His head bounced on the lino. He was bloodied, battered and three of his ribs were shattered. Eventually, after he'd stopped begging for mercy, they let him fall against the Bechstein piano. He smeared the keys red as discordant notes drowned out his groans.

It was established later, at the station, that Lofty Long had an alibi for the entire day and evening in question. He'd visited his mother in Chester-le-Street where at least seven people could vouch for him. However, the previous evening, several boys, all youth club members, had made giggling allegations, prodded by their anxious mothers. The goings-on in summer camps had been uncovered by relentless questioning from WPCs. 'It was just a game,' one boy said. 'Who cares? It didn't mean nothing,' added another. 'Old Lofty,' sniggered a third. 'He's a nancy but he doesn't mean nowt. Does he? He's canny.'

Lofty Long left the area that night. He was a broken man. His eyes were blackened and his face was covered in dressings. His chest was strapped together under his shabby suit. He disappeared without saying goodbye to anyone. He caught a trolley-bus, then a train. He took only a cardboard suitcase and under his arm a large photograph of Alma Cogan wearing a shiny fishtail evening gown, which had been both autographed and framed. Because his flat in Isabella Street was scheduled for demolition, it was left abandoned and unlocked. No one touched his stuff at first, out of bewilderment, affection and respect, but after a day or two, a man took his bicycle and a mother whose husband had just left her penniless helped herself to his groceries.

*

The officers from Scotland Yard released Ratty Schnitzler on bail after charging him with 'possessing an obscene article with intent to publish it for gain'. An hour later, they located Mickey Robson at the Town Hall. He was dictating a letter. He could tell by their suits and their thin lips that they meant business but he thought they merely wanted him to assist with enquiries. As they surrounded him and urged him with aggressive body language towards the stairs, he called out to the typist that he wouldn't be 'two ticks'. For once a little intimidated, he acknowledged the salute of the porter at the main exit. 'I won't be long, Harry,' he shouted. He found the Londoners surprisingly hostile and disrespectful. 'I'm the father of the murdered girls,' he insisted, amazed by their manner as they pushed him into an unmarked car. 'I'm T. Dan Smith's right-hand man.' Despite his protestations, he was locked up with no explanation. They took his belt and shoelaces and left him to sweat and curse in the airless, waterless, dingy cage only recently quitted by Ratty. There was nothing to eat. There was nothing to read except a few old names scratched into the dirty paint. There was no window and no company. The only other basement cell was empty. Mickey was forced to think about his dead daughters once more because here there were no distractions, no paperwork, no wheeling and dealing, no instructions to be given, no phone calls to make. The twins stood together in his mind's eye, swinging their held hands, smiling, their little faces angelic and sweet. He tried to dispel them but he couldn't. He heard the tinkle of their laughter. It was unbearable.

It's their mother's fault, he thought. He clenched a fist and punched the air. It's that bitch Scotch Iris's fault. She made me what I am. I'll see that whore in hell. I'll kill that bitch stone dead with my own bare hands. Bloody women! He stood up and paced two steps, his shoes slopping up and down. He had to hold on to his trousers. He reached the wall, paced two steps back and then sat down again. He looked at his watch. He'd been imprisoned half an hour but already it felt like more than half a day, more than half a week, more than half a lifetime.

*

Leslie was sitting upstairs in Auntie Ada's flat when PC Henderson came for him. The tall friendly Constable wiped his feet and took off his helmet. He accepted a cup of tea and a cake. Ada fussed around, unnecessarily giving him a cushion for his back, a pouffe for his feet and banking up the already too-warm fire. Leslie did a couple of card tricks. Auntie Ada told Leslie that she'd arranged for her brother Jack to take him to Vickers to see about a job.

'Jack'll fix you up,' agreed the policeman. 'Jack's a big man at the factory.'

Leslie felt apprehensive but said nothing. He took out his playing cards, shuffled them and offered them to the officer. They ran through the familiar routine.

The three of them discussed the warm weather, Leslie's growing accomplishments with sponges and icing, then Geordie's exposure in the press. They discussed this at length, without anyone mentioning his disappearance. The policman agreed that Geordie was a very good artist, but that too much attention was a bad thing.

'There's enough going on round here without all this,' Ada stated.

'He doesn't like people bothering him,' Leslie agreed.

'He's in enough trouble already,' the policeman concluded. He bit into his cake.

There was a long silence. The unmentionable had been breached.

'He's been missing too long,' Ada murmured, worried and upset.

'He's done nothing wrong,' Leslie insisted.

'We've got him at the station,' PC Henderson informed them quietly, wiping his lips with the back of his hand and slurping the dregs of his tea.

Leslie jumped to his feet.

'You need to come with me, Sonny Jim,' the officer added. 'There's these new boys up from London. Scotland Yard. Bully boys, I call them. They've sent me here to get you.'

Leslie was frozen with shock.

'Don't worry. No one's going to hurt you. I'll make sure they don't. I've told them I know you. I've told them you're a good lad.' He put his cup on the table, sighed and stood up.

Ada reached out and touched Leslie's arm. She wasn't usually physically demonstrative, but she was emotional and shaky. 'They've found him!' she breathed, clearly relieved. 'Everything's going to be all right! He's safe with the polis!'

PC Henderson put on his helmet.

Leslie said nothing. His heart was filled with foreboding. I'm going to lose him, he thought. Because even if they let him go, that posh Dr Kumar will get him and lock him up in Prudda and force him to draw stuff for *galleries*. 'Hang on a minute,' he exclaimed. 'I've just got to go downstairs. I need to get something.'

*

Out in the street, on his way to the police station, Leslie noticed the headlines scrawled on boards outside the paper shops. 'Angel Twins – Local Artist Boy Held', 'MP's Fury Over Police Twins Blunder', and 'Smith Denies Corruption Smear'. His feet dragged like lead weights. He fumbled with his pack of cards in his coat pocket. He was aware of a funny pressure behind his eyes which felt like a dammed-up reservoir of unshed tears.

Constable Henderson was trying to be cheerful. He whistled a few bars of 'Apache'. 'Where's your mam?' he asked.

'Don't know.'

'When did you last see her?'

'Can't remember.'

'We need your mam at the station.'

'You better find her then.'

'Where is she?'

Leslie sighed. They turned on to Scotswood Road. He kicked a loose cobble into a pile of dusty masonry piled at a half-demolished corner. Todds Brothers department store and the whole of Maple Street were down. The green-grocers and the bread shop were down. Shirley's Hair-dressing and Beauty for Ladies was down. Above it all, the indifferent sun was hazy behind a cloud of dust. In the distance, the demolition gang's wagon roared and there were shouts of warning from the men as yet another wall collapsed. The tall crane in the distance twirled like a mother beside its thrusting charges, the brand-new flats that were climbing even higher into the sky.

As well as this, the heavy hammer inside Vickers thumped like a muffled heartbeat. Boats hooted on the invisible river. A swarm of workers appeared on the hill, signalling a change of shift. Everything is changing, Leslie thought, but so many things stay exactly the same. He was depressed. He wanted everybody to stop doing the things they'd always done. He wished they'd stop going to work, stop buying things in the few shops that were left. He wished the boats would stop coming, that the buses would stop running. Everything's *falling apart*, he mused. Why are people behaving normally? He wiped his face with his sleeve. Why is it so hot? Why did those damned twins have to go and get themselves killed?

There was a sudden nearby roar and the stutter of an engine. Desperate Dan pulled up on his motorbike alongside. He met the boy's eye. 'I'm sorry,' he said. He seemed upset.

'Sorry for what?'

Desperate made no reply. He turned the handlebars, kick-started the machine and rode away. Leslie watched him, puzzled.

'Come along, son,' said the policeman. 'Let's get this over with.'

*

Inside their house on De Grey Street, Sammy and Ratty Schnitzler sat together in the small front room. The curtains were closed, and in its cage near the window the budgerigar sat quietly and uncertainly on its perch, unsure if it was day or night. The radiogram played Ravel's 'Pavane pour une Infante Defunte', with its volume turned low.

Sammy sipped from a glass of bicarbonate of soda. One hand rested against his chest, as if he were in pain. He leaned back in his chair staring at nothing. Ratty sat on a low wooden stool, his head in his hands. His drape coat was over his knees and his brocade waistcoat was unfastened. A cut on his cheek oozed a little and his quiff was flattened and unsculpted. He sighed. 'Pops, I've said I'm sorry and there's no more I can say.' He waited, then offered more placatory words. 'I've told you. I'm not proud of myself. But they've let me go. I'm free. That's the main thing.'

'There's no freedom. No escape,' said his father, mysteriously.

'I'll leave here, if you want me to. If you still disown me, I'll go. I don't want to bring shame on you, on the Schnitzler name.' He sounded repentant but then his tone changed. 'I've got money. I've got the chance of a flat above that coffee bar. The building's owned by that firm running the fruit machines racket.'

'What about your animals? Your birds?'

Ratty was silent. The mournful, melodious music rose and fell. 'Nothing's the same,' he said eventually. 'I'm going to have to find a home for all of us. The birds, the dog, the cats. You. Me. Everything's changing. Soon this house will go. The old life here's over.'

'True,' agreed Sammy. His lower lip trembled. 'The old life here is over. All dead, deported, dispersed. Where *is* your mother's friend Esther? Where's she gone? There's only you and me left, my boy.' His voice was faint, his thoughts disconnected. 'Where's Uncle Isak? And where're his sons, your fine cousins? What happened to Stiebitz the jeweller? And Arnsteiner *der tsondoktor?*'

Ratty raised his head and stared. He'd been aware for

some time that his father's mind was, on occasion, muddling the events of the war with the current disruptions in Elswick. There were a lot of similarities, he knew, and previously he'd both ignored and excused the confusion. 'Dad, this is nineteen-sixty,' he said gently. 'We're in England. The war's over. We're safe here.' As he spoke, the music drew to its melancholy conclusion and the radiogram switched off. A siren sounded outside, in the distance.

'No, not safe,' answered Sammy. 'We're not safe. Nowhere's safe. And the world is full of troubles. Full of troubles. And each person feels only his own.'

Ratty stood up and went towards the radiogram.

'Not that awful pop music,' said Sammy immediately.

Ratty selected a classical long-player and set it in motion. The sweet strains of Albinoni filled the cramped room.

'Not too loud,' demanded Sammy, snappishly.

Ratty turned the volume down to its minimum.

'We were a prosperous family,' sighed the older man. 'But *gelt tsu fardinen iz gringer vi tsu halten*. It's easier to earn money than to keep it. As my dear mother used to say.' He unfastened his tie, settled further back in his chair and began talking. The half-drunk glass of bicarbonate rested on his belly. His face was pale and unhealthy and his sad jowls hung in folds. Ratty sat down and listened. Uncharacteristically he was concentrating on his father's words. He wasn't about to rush off in his usual way and set up some deal. He was chastened and did not, just at this moment, relish the idea of facing the outside world. He took off his shoes and socks and studied his bare toes. Sammy's reminiscences flowed over him like the sorrowful voice of a rabbi at prayer.

Sammy described his parents' home with its wide

marble staircase, its chandeliers, its renowned library and its polished silverware. He spoke of his toy hobbyhorse, his tin soldiers of the Emperor's army and his sister's doll's perambulator. He told how their nurse tested their fragrant bathwater every evening with the skin of her elbow and how famous writers and musicians attended his mother's salon. It was an exotic and privileged world, about as far away from Elswick as the other side of the moon.

His parents, he said, lost their wealth slowly at first, after the Anschluss, and then quickly and all at once. Their assets were seized, they were made homeless, and soldiers stole their piano and paintings before setting fire to their furniture in the street. His mother's fur coat was dragged from her back as she was herded with other older women into the enclosure of a former dog track. His father, once the confidant of ministers, was made to scrub the pavements on his hands and knees, with a bucket and a little brush. 'Scrub, scrub,' said Sammy. 'Scrub, scrub. Like this.' He made some small gestures. 'He was spat upon by passers-by.'

Sammy was lost in the past. He described the November night when he himself was forced from his home. He talked about the water tank on the roof where they'd all hidden up to their waists, himself, his wife, their two daughters and the baby boy, shivering and mute as their neighbours were rounded up, shot or defenestrated. He described their subsequent wanderings, the people who'd tried to give them shelter, the trains departing for work camps in Poland, the semi-starvation and the bitter winter when there was no fuel to be had. He told how he'd sold their clothing but no one would buy the diamonds hidden in the soles of his shoes. His mother's jewels. Everyone he approached said it was too risky. He had no contacts left.

There were informers everywhere. He had diamonds but no bread. No milk. No firewood. His poor wife, Ratty's mother, shivered and coughed up blood all the time.

The younger man listened. He had heard some of it before, but not much. Not this much. He absorbed the details, pulling on his long fingers, cracking his knuckles. He had no real memory of any of this, except one or two dark shadows.

Ratty had grown up in the North-East of England and he had no sense of his old religion or his culture, but something remained. He had turned his back on his past, but he nevertheless carried a half-forgotten hunger, a dull sense of loss and emptiness. He realized, as he listened to his father's pain, that it was this barely conscious feeling of deprivation that had driven him all his life. It was why he was so restless, so dissatisfied with what he had. It was why he was determined to succeed, not to become respectably comfortable like Pops, but *properly* moneyed, *very* powerful, *entirely* in control. It was why he looked only forward to the future. All at once he saw his own motivation and the reasons behind it. He was going to *get on*, and nothing was going to stop him.

This business with the twins had been a bad mistake, one that he definitely wouldn't repeat. He'd lost sight of himself. But he'd recover. The authorities had locked him up but then, incredibly, they'd turned round and let him go. He was all right. He'd got away with it.

Sammy continued. His voice murmured against the recorded background of weeping strings. He moved on from his own experiences and described all that he'd read in the post-war British press about the camps. He mentioned the *News Of The World*, the *Sunday People*, experiments, gas chambers pretending to be showers and piles of confiscated Jewish bags, Jewish shoes and Jewish hair. Then he talked about the Council pulling down his houses and his barber's shop. He described Scotch Iris kissing Mickey Robson under a street light on Clumber Street, her hand inside the waistband of his trousers. Occasionally his tenses slipped and he spoke as if the Nazis were, at this moment, outside his front door in De Grey Street.

'But we got away,' insisted Ratty quietly, respectfully. 'We came here. We're safe in England. Pops, remember *this is nineteen-sixty*. Keep your hair on, OK? So we've got to move from this dump, but we've done worse before, haven't we? You've just been talking about it. This is nothing. It's *nothing* compared to the bad old war days in Vienna. We'll go to Gosforth. Jesus Christ, we'll get a nice big place among the nobs with a real garden for the aviaries and all the animals. We could get a pony. We could get a goat. Pops, listen, we could even get a car. It'll be all right. We can *start again*.'

Sammy Schnitzler wasn't hearing. His eyes were glazed with memory and the notion of starting over was one he could no longer comprehend. He talked about the journey they'd made, which had taken nearly three years. He described crossing a guarded border with baby Ratty fastened inside his overcoat. He described swimming across a river, the boy strapped to his back, struggling through a raft of sewage with rifle shots ringing in his ears and causing splashes all around. He talked about a priest in France and a woman who claimed to be a Countess. He mentioned stealing a chicken and trying to cook it over a damp, inadequate outdoor fire and how they'd both eaten it half-raw anyway, but it was all right because the Talmud says you can stomach anything if you've no choice in the matter. Finally he described how he lay with him lying inside an airless wooden box on a train, believing it might possibly become their coffin.

Ratty pulled on his socks and his crêpe-soled brothel-creeper shoes and stood up. He pushed his arms into his jacket.

Sammy sighed. 'God gives with one hand and he takes away with the other.' He closed his eyes.

Gently, Ratty took the glass of bicarbonate of soda and placed it on the sideboard. He turned off the radiogram. Sammy was now snoring quietly. The young man regarded his sleeping father with affection as he considered what to do. It was pointless moping around here. He would just have to face it out. A visit to the office above the coffee bar seemed in order, he decided. Those twins, he remembered, those *Krays*, they said I'm their boy. And they're real hard men. They're not going to give a lousy stuff about a couple of stupid, dead little girls, *all the way up here*. The whole thing will be nothing to them. He smoothed and adjusted the clinging legs of his drainpipes. So much for those damned *Angel Twins*. He started whistling the new Johnny Hurricane tune from the Hit Parade.

Admiring himself in the hall-stand mirror, he rescued his Teddy-boy hair, giving it appropriate height and volume in readiness to face the world. He sniffed his armpits, took a can of air freshener from the hall-stand drawer and sprayed inside his shirt. I'll get myself well in on this one-armed bandit racket, he decided. And I'll look after Pops. He's frightened by what's going on outside. Everything's falling apart for him, again. Ratty fastened his brocade waistcoat and stroked it with his palms. After all, he reasoned, Pops saved me from the stormtroopers. Now it's *my* turn.

*

Geordie sat in the corner of a bleak interview room, rocking from side to side, his eyes unfocused and sightless, his legs entwined round the chair, his freed arms wrapped tight around his chest. He looked small, exquisitely beautiful and lonely. A WPC was with him, but she was reading a magazine. A uniformed officer guarded the door.

Leslie rushed over and held his brother gently, but he could tell immediately by his stiff unresponsiveness that all was far from well. 'What have you done to him?' he burst out. 'What have you done to my brother?'

The WPC looked across and yawned. She didn't reply. PC Henderson had disappeared.

After a while the Detective-Inspector came in. He reorganized the chairs, so that Leslie and Geordie sat opposite him at a table. The WPC left and the uniformed Constable sat down in her place. He said nothing and stared into space as if the proceedings had nothing to do with him.

The Inspector cleared his throat. Just as he was about to begin, one of the three bully-boy newcomers from Scotland Yard opened the door. His colleagues were behind him in the corridor. He looked at Leslie and Geordie and gave a thumbs-up sign. 'So ... you got the scruffy one too!' he exclaimed, winking. He withdrew, shutting the door firmly.

'Don't be afraid,' the Inspector insisted, gently. 'We just need to get to the bottom of things.'

Leslie knew that Geordie was in his own world and that today this wasn't a happy place. Leslie himself was bitter and angry. Suddenly, he was shouting, his voice high and uncontrolled.

'I've been looking after him all his life!' he exclaimed. He held Geordie's hand. It felt cold and dead. The younger boy seemed unaware of his surroundings. He started rocking again and his teeth chattered. 'See what you've done!' Leslie insisted. 'Just look at him!'

'I know you want to protect him,' said the policeman, kindly. 'To shield him.'

'We need your help,' said the officer. He was making an effort to be kind. 'We need to know what you know. We've tried talking to your brother but we can't get through.' Slowly, patiently, he went through his own version of the events of the fatal evening when Leslie had found Geordie in the half-demolished house. 'We found a bottle of salad cream,' he added mysteriously.

Leslie realized he had little choice but to co-operate. He continued to be aggressive but he told the absolute truth. He mentioned the injured cat, the unstable stairs, the mounds on the mattress that he'd thought were old washing. He said several times that Geordie had come across the girls by chance when he was trying to save the cat. 'They were already dead. They were *already dead*!'

'And the knife?'

'What knife?'

'We found a penknife. A penknife saying 'A Present From Cullercoats'. Your friend Mr Long has confirmed that you bought one similar to it, two years ago, on a youth club trip to the coast. You bought it for your brother. To sharpen his pencils.'

Leslie was impatient, indignant, frustrated. 'His pencil-case got spilt, didn't it? On the floor. Nearly everything fell out, including the knife, I expect.' He thought for a moment. 'I bet that knife didn't have any blood or nothing on it. I bet it was clean. It just fell on the floor, that's all. It just got left there by accident'

The officer was impassive. 'All I can say is, a knife was found at the scene. A knife similar to one believed to be in the possession of George MacDonald.'

'Oh, yeah?' Leslie made a fist with his free hand. 'All I can say is, I found *Geordie* at the scene. He just happened to be there. Doing his drawings. Saving a cat. And he did *nowt* wrong. Right?' Leslie was furious. 'Right, Mr Swanky pants? You heard that? You got that? You listening? He did *nowt!*' Leslie wanted to cry. 'You're all buggers! All of you!'

The interview dragged on, the questions and answers batted back and forth. Geordie said nothing, but made the occasional incoherent sound. Leslie maintained his series of denials. They were getting nowhere.

'There were other people there,' Leslie offered, eventually.

'There were two witnesses who saw you and your brother leaving the scene of the crime. Earlier, there were workmen at the site. They saw you and your brother, separately, outside the property. We've spoken to them all at length.'

Leslie took a deep breath. 'Our mam was there. Desperate Dan was there, maybe with Ratty Schnitzler.'

The Inspector raised his eyebrows.

Leslie took something from his coat pocket. He let go of Geordie's hand and handed over the drawing of the street in question, which showed the wheel disappearing off the edge of the paper. 'That's the place. And that's what he saw that day, before it got dark, before he went in and tried to save the cat. You see that wheel? That's

Desperate's motorbike. That means he was there, possibly with Ratty Schnitzler. Geordie said he was there. He doesn't make things up. He saw him there.' Leslie paused. 'You see? You see it?' He proffered the page. 'There were loads of people there. Not just Geordie. That's proof. Loads of people.'

The inspector examined the drawing without much interest. 'I can't see a wheel,' he commented. 'You mean this here?' He pointed to the circle in the foreground and shrugged. 'It's a very good drawing. I *can* see what all the fuss is about.' He smiled. 'Within the art world.'

Leslie stood up and pointed. 'That's the wheel, man, there! Are you blind or what? That's a wheel! That's a motorbike wheel!' He sat down.

The officer handed back the drawing. He was unimpressed.

With a start, Geordie seemed to emerge from his reverie. He grabbed the page and stuffed it inside his jumper. 'Mine!'

Leslie took hold of his hand once more. He tried to make eye contact but Geordie's face had now taken on the other-worldly expression it adopted when he could picture something beyond the immediate. He stared into nothingness. Leslie gripped his fingers tightly. He knew he was seeing shadows from the future.

The policeman shuffled his notes. He coughed, about to say something.

'Sshh!' insisted Leslie.

'No one's there now,' Geordie offered, after a moment. 'The windows are bust. The skins are gone, the glue vats are gone. That girl's got married and left. Mr Frank and Mr Alaric are both dead. There's a sign on the wall and it looks like it's been there ages. It's all stained and rusty.

It says 'F. and A. Richardson Limited, Elswick Leather Works, For Sale or To Let.' Even the houses are empty and nailed up. Even the greenhouses.' He paused. 'No more smelly tanning.'

The policeman addressed Leslie. 'What's he talking about?'

Leslie shrugged.

The officer turned to Geordie. 'You saw a motorbike?'

The younger boy appeared vacant once more, as before.

The officer sighed. He clearly thought it was impossible to communicate meaningfully with Geordie and he also realized that as much as possible had been obtained from Leslie. He laid down his pen and stood up. He motioned to the Constable. 'That just about covers it,' he muttered, 'for the moment.'

The burly young policeman advanced and firmly took hold of Leslie's arm.

'What are you doing?' Leslie felt himself being propelled from the room. He struggled. 'What's happening? Where am I going?'

'You're going home,' said the Inspector. 'Hopefully, we've located your mother. George is staying here with us.'

'No!' Leslie yelled. 'No! I'm not leaving him! I'm not going without him!' He wriggled and kicked. 'You buggers!'

The Constable was strong and he ignored Leslie's protests as if he were a fish threshing on a line.

'Let me go! Leave go of my arm!' Leslie was manhandled from the room. He screamed and fought as he was escorted to the main desk of the station. He heard the door lock, closing off the corridor leading to Geordie. 'You *buggers!*' He stopped struggling, seeing it was hopeless. Out of breath, distressed, but still in an iron grip, he slumped against the counter. His heart was beating overtime.

The duty Sergeant came out from behind his desk and said something to the Constable, quietly, in his ear. He released the boy at once. Both men looked grim. 'Never!' exclaimed the Constable, quietly.

'It's true.' The Sergeant shook his head in a resigned way. 'It's been confirmed.'

The junior officer gawped. 'Jesus wept, who's going to tell him?'

*

Leslie was taken to the morgue in the police Wolseley. It was the same car, he noted as he climbed inside, that had attempted to capture Geordie from Glue Terrace.

Leslie had never been in a car before and as they waited for a driver, he sniffed the unusual petrol smell and felt the smoothness of the leather. It was new and exciting, despite everything.

The indifferent WPC who had sat with his brother earlier joined him on the back seat. She tried to talk to him but he ignored her. Then, as the vehicle eased slowly up Scotswood Road, Leslie decided he was like a star in a film. I should be crying or something, he told himself. My mam has just been pulled out the river. I should be sitting here looking like an orphan, and people ought to be pointing at me and staring. They ought to be saying, there goes that poor Leslie, the orphan, and I ought to be sad.

The engine purred and he held on to a little strap below the window. As it was, he just sat there, doing nothing, feeling nothing, because he was too shocked to react. He could locate no emotion inside of himself, except a residue of anger left over from before. He watched the familiar world go by as if it were in slow motion, a leaden feeling in his chest. No one seemed to notice him as he cruised past. He saw Ratty Schnitzler swaggering past the Crooked Billet, a free man. He saw a swathe of workers in cloth caps crossing the road, his own progress in the car impeded by a traffic policeman holding up his hand. It was the end of another shift at Vickers and the factory disgorged its tired workforce up the hill to the remaining houses. It's teatime, Leslie thought. I'll go to Auntie Ada's for my tea. Poor Geordie can't come with me. I hope those buggers give him something nice to eat in his cell.

He went with the policewoman into a special building beside the hospital. At the front it was like a church with pews, kneelers and velvet drapes but they went straight through this part into a clinical room at the back. This was tiled from ceiling to floor in white and it had sinks and taps. It smelled sterilized and germ-free and reminded Leslie of a public lavatory. A silent man in a white coat and white rubber galoshes wheeled in a trolley, which was covered up. He drew back the sheet.

'Is this your mother, Iris MacDonald?' asked the WPC.

Leslie couldn't see. He took two nervous steps forward then stood on his tiptoes.

'Take your time,' she said.

He gasped. His mam was lying very still and pale. She looked nothing like herself of course, because she was dead. Her hair was still wet and it was trailing river slime. She was wearing a long white hospital gown smeared at the waist with more green. Suddenly Leslie remembered the occasion when Geordie had seen into the future, not so long ago, when he'd said that their mam was in a white room, in a white dress with leaves in her hands and hair, and that she was with a man. Geordie had predicted all of this. It had come true but not in the way that Leslie had imagined. 'Yes,' he replied. He had a strange, woozy feeling in his head and he struggled to keep his balance. 'Yes, that's her.' The words of a sacred song came into his mind, but he was too shocked to sing. *'Panis angelicus,'* he whispered. *'Panis angelicus.'*

*

Later, after eating his tea at Auntie Ada's, Leslie decided to sleep upstairs. She took him into the smaller back room and made up the single bed using warm, scented flannelette sheets and pillowcases from the airing cupboard, fluffy blankets and a wine-coloured eiderdown. She filled two hot water bottles, a rubber one for him to cuddle and a stone one to heat the end of the bed where his feet were to go. She pulled the flowery curtains together and left a small nightlight illuminated. She hesitated at his side after he climbed between the soft covers. She touched his arm. In the half-light her doughy face was serious and concerned. 'You call me if you want anything,' she assured him. 'I'm just next door.'

Leslie lay on his back staring at a pattern of cracks in the ceiling, which reminded him of the map of a country he could no longer name. It could be India, he decided.

This room was seldom used but nevertheless smelled deliciously of lavender. Roses climbed up the wallpaper. Inside this bed he was as warm and comfortable as he'd ever been. Our mam's dead, Leslie told himself, for the umpteenth time. Our mam's dead and Geordie's locked up in gaol. He felt very alone.

Later, Leslie dreamed again about the Queen. She was

holding Geordie's hand on the beach, although she was as regal as usual, wearing a sapphire tiara, a sash and a trailing cloak. The three of them were on a trip at Cullercoats and nearby a crowd of children from the youth club played cricket with Lofty Long. The Queen spread out a blanket, sat down in her finery and unpacked a picnic from a plastic shopper. The sky was very blue and the distant waves hush-hushed in a satisfying way. I'll have a cheese sandwich, please, Your Majesty, Leslie said politely. He felt very honoured. However, instead of opening the lunch packet the Queen turned to Geordie and from the bottom of the bag, like a conjuror, she miraculously produced an ice-cream. He looked at it, then glanced at Leslie. He smiled. He took the ice-cream from her, grinning his thanks, then, after a moment, he laughed with delight.

'He's happy,' cried Leslie, surprised. 'Look at him. He's really happy!'

'Of course,' said the Queen, in a measured way. 'Happy? Of course he's happy.' She paused. 'Have you both come far?'

10

Ratty Schnitzler strolled down Scotswood Road, a newspaper under his arm. He held his head high and his gait was languid. He occupied the middle of the pavement and his crêpe soles creaked. He whistled 'Apache'. Housewives avoided his eye. Outside the Crooked Billet a drunk saluted him, unsteadily, and he nodded back. His thumbs were hooked over the waistband of his drainpipes and his full-skirted coat was pushed back behind his narrow hips. He looked unabashed by his recent experiences but this was, of course, a front. Ratty was of the belief that the way one acts determines the way one is appreciated and then, as a consequence, the way one ultimately feels. He knew that if he behaved like the Crown Prince of Elswick, respect would surely follow.

He stopped outside a pub called the Hydraulic Crane, which locally was known as the Toll Bar. He glanced at his watch. A little early, he opened the local paper and perused the headlines. He was pleased to see that his own release and the charges he still faced had disappeared from the news, but Geordie's frozen smile, captured on the beach at Cullercoats, stared from the front page, grainy and a little blurred. So they've found the poor little blighter, Ratty mused. They've pulled him in. I don't suppose they'll get any sense out of him. He studied the picture. He looks happy here, for a change. That won't last long. They'll probably shut him up in Prudhoe with all the other headcases, and it'll break his brother's heart. Ratty sighed. He felt sorry for the two boys, but the most important thing was that *he* was off the hook. If the dafty from Glue Terrace had to take the heat, well so be it.

He turned the page. There was an article on Councillor Robson's detention on corruption charges and a string of denials from both the Planning Department and the Leader of the Council, all of which seemed to be falling on deaf ears. The heavy boys from Scotland Yard had apparently invited up a bunch of smoothies from the Met's Fraud Squad and they weren't messing about. Ratty grinned. He wasn't worried about his own small role in Mickey's manipulation of the housing clearances. He knew Robson would deny everything all the way to Durham gaol. Either that, or T. Dan Smith would fish him out of hot water. Ratty was, in truth, rather relieved that his job of intimidating the shifters was now over. After all ... fireworks and dog-dirt ... they'd always seemed a little crude, a little juvenile, for a man of his talents.

On the next page were reproductions of Geordie's drawings. There was one showing the semi-collapse of Tulloch Street and another detailing a peculiar and brand-new view of the Tyne from the top of the hill, from a spot where river water had previously been invisible. Ratty examined these with interest. Blimey, he thought, that kid can draw! I never knew it, but these are cracking! He scanned the article, discovering that there was a great deal of London interest in the boy prodigy. Ratty leaned against a lamp-post and scratched his genitals. Maybe the kid needs a manager, he mused. Not that I know anything about art. But I *do* know what I like. He realized his own incarceration and temporary sense of disgrace had blinded him to what had recently been happening in the neighbourhood. It seemed that Elswick was big news! Suddenly the dafty from Glue Terrace was some kind of Leonardo da Vinci and the police had the very same boy-genius walled up in the nick. Not only that, the dead twins, the same ones that people thought Leonardo might have killed, well, they were the reason behind a load of crazy and hysterical national grief. It was wild.

Ratty started humming the Johnny Hurricane number.

> *Uh-oh angels,*
> *uh-oh angels,*
> *my angels you're say-afe*
> *from haarrm*

He glanced towards the back of the newspaper. Coincidentally, there was Johnny the Man himself. He was grinning too cheesily, Ratty thought, with his big cleft chin and dago eyes. His eyes skimmed the article. Johnny had knocked the Shadows off the top of the Hit Parade! Ratty dropped the paper in disgust and kicked it into the gutter. He looked at his watch once more. At that moment a van appeared and drew up. The driver flung open the rear door. Inside were four one-armed bandit machines. Ratty gestured towards the Toll Bar. 'Get this one in here,' he said, tersely. 'And make it snappy. I'm a busy man. I haven't got all day.'

*

In the streets and back lanes of devastated Elswick, people stood around in small groups, showing each other newspaper articles and shaking their heads in bewilderment. They looked up at the hot sky and the unrelenting sun, both hazy with brick dust, plaster and smoke. They shook their heads, sniffed the tainted air, talked quietly of the dead girls, of their imprisoned father, of Geordie's talent and the suspicion hanging around him. They talked about the laddie's mother, Scotch Iris, cold in the morgue, dead from drowning. She was no better than she should have been, of course, but it was still terrible. Terrible. No one mentioned Ratty. He was old news. There was too much to take in, too much to understand, too much disintegrating and falling down for anything to be possible other than static waves of excitement, followed by enervation. They fanned themselves with their folded newspapers, consoled each other, ran over and over events in shocked monotones and then went back indoors. No one knew what to do. They were besieged, threatened, confused and afraid. They were as insecure as they'd been during the war, only it was worse because now it wasn't clear who was the real enemy.

The heavy ball, swinging on the end of a chain, crashed into the public wash-house, not once or twice, but scores of times. It battered and battered and the solid Victorian structure, once founded on the purest of ideals, gradually succumbed to the inevitable. Ornate tiles were revealed, then loosened. They cascaded like petals. The roof caved in, the high chimney toppled, the cubicles imploded into the pit that had been the pool. A bulldozer pushed rubble into mounds and grimy men struck at stubborn stumps of brickwork with their mallets and pickaxes. A blizzard of dust was carried on a light breeze, making dirty everything that surrounded this former high-temple of cleanliness. The aspirations of one strong municipal authority had been superseded by the aspirations of another.

*

Auntie Ada remembered that today Leslie was meant to be meeting her brother Jack at Vickers to be 'shown the ropes'. 'Don't bother going,' she said in a concerned way, waking him with his breakfast on a tray. 'You won't be feeling like it. Stay here. You can stay in bed if you like.'

Leslie's night in the soft and fragrant spare room had left him relaxed and calm. However, as he opened his eyes he sensed that this peace was over. Reality straight away dawned and his rested imagination at once recalled his poor brother and his dead mam. 'I'll go,' he said, sitting up. 'I've *got* to get a job. I'll go and see Uncle Jack. I'll sort myself out.' He picked up a toast soldier and dipped it into his boiled egg. I'm responsible and willing, he reminded himself, taking a bite. The bread was crisp, the egg perfect. He tried not to think about Geordie's isolation, about his mam in the morgue, about the factory at the bottom of the hill and his terror of its noise, its machinery, its super-masculine workforce and its unremitting, grimy confidence.

Later, his cropped hair smoothed down with water but wearing his usual plimsolls and duffel-coat, Leslie tried to keep his mind on the moment. It was another hot morning. A hand-built bogey crammed with a group of small boys careened down the slope of Clumber Street, swerving wildly. The daredevils all screamed with excitement. Happy days, reflected Leslie. They'll all have to get a job sooner or later. He peered into a pram parked outside an open front door. A small baby in a blue sunhat stared at him solemnly. Leslie winked. He'll have to get a job, sooner or later, too. There's just nothing else for it. He remembered a phrase of Uncle Jack's. He'd said that the workers of the North-East 'keep the country running'. I suppose I owe it to the Queen, Leslie acknowledged, remembering his dream. She expects us all to do our bit for England.

He walked down Water Street then passed through

double gates, entering the tunnel to Vickers' Elswick works. This allowed men access underneath the railway line. He paused. The alley was known as Curds and Cream Way. It seemed a strange name given that it was a blackened, cobbled walkway, lined from floor to curved ceiling with a complication of cables and pipes, some lagged with filthy cloths or rubber housing. Leslie hesitated. *Curds and Cream Way.* If only it was as nice as it sounded. At the far end, towering brick structures opposed him, alongside the giant sheds, which were the workshops. He could hear the screech of metal on metal, whirring and clanking, muffled male shouts. His heart quickened. Here goes, he told himself. There was no turning back. A man's gotta do what a man's gotta do. He felt like a solitary cowboy facing a shootout in a Saturday afternoon matinée, only worse, because he wasn't playing the hero. He wasn't even the bad guy in the black hat. He was merely an extra, a walk-on, a random and unimportant stray from a crowd scene who'd somehow lost himself on the set. He didn't have a six-shooter or a palomino stallion, his voice wasn't even properly broken *and* he had freckles and red hair. He felt close to tears.

Uncle Jack was waiting inside one of the entrances. He smiled a little thinly. Unlike his sister, he was spare, with hollow cheeks, narrow lips and a nose as long as a toboggan run. He shook Leslie's hand. Despite the heat of the morning, his fingers were icy and damp. He wore the white coat of a foreman, buttoned a little too neatly, and around his neck hung protective goggles. 'Our Ada has recommended you,' he said in a neutral way. 'She said you'll be sure to keep your nose to the grindstone.' He hesitated. 'That's how I got where I am today, by keeping my nose to the grindstone.'

Leslie almost produced his playing cards, but stopped himself. He also swallowed the automatic response: a comment on how long Uncle Jack's nose must have been *before*. He followed the foreman into the workshop, listening to talk about Lord Armstrong and the seventy acres of engineering shops and foundries. Jack had to raise his voice above the noise. 'There were eighteen thousand workers here during the last war,' he yelled, proudly, 'and even now, we're still the biggest firm on Tyneside.' He put his mouth close to Leslie's ear. 'D'you know something, lad?' he shouted, 'there hasn't been a war anywhere in the world, for the last hundred years, where *we* haven't made the armaments. Guns, ships, shells,' he insisted, 'shot, fuses, carriages and mountings. Tanks.' He gestured with one sure hand. 'And that's the thing about wars! Wars carry on happening! There's always been wars and there always will be wars. You see, our Lord Armstrong, he had *the vision*!'

Leslie tried to concentrate. The vision. He looked nervously at the high glass roof of the building, but there was no sign of the Virgin. Some of the overhead panes were still coated with blackout paint against the air raids of the forties. He thought of the war and the devastated streets of Elswick, now engaged in its own private blitzkrieg with bulldozers flattening its buildings instead of enemy planes. Leslie knew that the very same demolished houses had been built for Lord Armstrong's workers, a hundred years before. He felt confused. The scale of the place as well as its glorious history was as daunting and overwhelming as his worst nightmares.

At floor level, the 'shop', as Uncle Jack called it, was

lined with ranks of workbenches where men in stained blue overalls stood at machines. The noise was deafening. The air was mineral and thick with the smell of oil. 'This is general engineering,' mouthed Leslie's guide. 'Come on. Follow me.'

Leslie glanced along the lines of operatives. A couple of young men nudged each other and laughed. Someone familiar avoided his eye. He recognized this fellow as one of his mother's regular visitors. Another, older man waved. The boy smiled balefully in response. It was someone from the choir. Leslie reflected that the blessed peace of St Stephen's, with the jewel of Mary depicted in the stained glass, seemed a long, long way away, even though it was only up the road.

As in a dream, Leslie traversed the heat treatment shop and the tender shop, then the foundry. Sweat broke out on his body and brow, from fear as much as the temperature of the place. The cavernous dark space was like nothing except the devil's princedom he'd once seen pictured on a Sunday School tract. In the gloom, molten metal fell from a height as if the sun itself had dissolved and dropped out of heaven. Smoke and steam billowed then eddied. The men seemed dwarfed on the ground and minute up on the gantries, like tiny ants among the swinging cranes, the chains, the hoists, the rattling overhead belts, the fiery furnaces and ovens. Just then, somewhere close, in another part of the works, the heavy hammer started up and the ground shook as if about to open and consume them all.

Geordie's locked up, Leslie suddenly remembered. Our mam isn't *ever* coming home. He pushed the thoughts aside. He rubbed his eyes and fixed his attention on Jack's white back, directly ahead. Let me out of here, he prayed.

They passed through several more shops. Leslie's head

was reeling with details. He thought he might faint. Meanwhile Uncle Jack, clearly very keen on horsepower, cylinder heads and vertical steam boilers, kept on shouting and gesticulating with enthusiasm. Finally they came to a lofty and complex metal structure as impressive as anything T. Dan Smith might imagine in his sculpture park. It was almost as tall as the roof. 'The Doxford crankshaft,' insisted Leslie's guide, as boastful as a curator.

The boy wiped his face on his sleeve and said nothing.

'Come on, lad, let's go and have a cuppa.' On the way to the canteen, Uncle Jack explained that post-war, the company had diversified into tractors, printing presses and special equipment for the Coal Board. 'Anything from a pin to a battleship,' he declared. 'We've got the skills, we've got the machines, we've got the cranage. Yes. Anything from a pin to a battleship.' He went on to outline the system of apprenticeships. He mentioned football and gymnastics, the seven-thirty morning shift, Black Time, night schools and the option of starting Leslie as a postboy. 'That's a dogsbody, mind, but it'd be only till you're sixteen.'

Leslie's mind was racing. There were so many possibilities. He would have to decide on whether he wanted to be a fitter, a turner, a miller, a driller, a slotter, a grinder, a setter, a moulder, a plater, a plumber, a welder, a riveter, a gauger, a presser, a borer or a toolmaker. None of these seemed likely, attractive or even possible. I want my Geordie, he thought. I want our mam. I want our Auntie Ada. He looked around to see if the Virgin Mary was offering any support, but she was nowhere to be seen.

In the shopfloor canteen, which was as big as an aircraft hangar with trestle tables, two giggling girls served them mugs of tea. They pointed to a blackboard showing the day's menu. Someone had rubbed a few letters out and instead of 'Meat Rissoles', the fare on offer was 'Meat R..soles 'You don't *have* to be mad to work here,' sniggered the prettier of the two, 'but it helps.'

Leslie tried to smile.

Afterwards, just before the boy took his leave, Uncle Jack, so keen to convince his charge of the exciting possibilities on offer, showed him the drawing office. He opened the door and indicated men wearing suits, collars and ties. Leslie noted that they sat at strange tilted desks, manipulating pens and wooden measuring devices. Glancing over and realizing that they had visitors, a sleek young wag in winkle-picker shoes, his hair wet with Schnitzler's Brilliant, slipped off his stool, clapped his hands and announced, 'All those who can't tap dance are queers!' At once, on cue, every man in the room got to his feet and began hopping and shuffling like Fred Astaire, even the old men, the ones who were at least sixty years old. They tapped and twirled, serious-faced and stiff-backed, pattering their shiny shoes up and down on the linoleum.

Leslie withdrew, aghast. 'Thank you very much for your trouble, Uncle Jack,' he muttered, backing down the corridor. 'But I have to be getting home.'

*

A deferential secretary showed the Chief Superintendent of Police, immaculate in his uniform and decorations, into the office of the Council Leader. T. Dan Smith sat behind his desk, his fingers forming a steeple, as if he were at prayer. His head was held at an arrogant angle, he didn't smile and he delayed just a fraction too long before rising to shake the hand of his visitor. 'It's been a while, Alec,' he said, mildly. 'I haven't seen you since Race Week.'

A tea lady came in with a tray then departed, a little flustered. Smith poured, taking his time with teaspoons, napkins, sugar tongs. An uneasy silence developed, which the officer finally broke by getting straight to the point. Bluntly, he outlined the case against Mickey Robson, which he described as 'cut and dried'. He detailed cash payments from developers, handed over in brown envelopes by a now-terrified solicitor's clerk. At length and with vehemence, he mentioned intimidation, corner-cutting, slush funds and backhanders, as well as a lot of back-scratching. He said Smith's 'right-hand man' was 'as bent as the proverbial'.

'The proverbial?' Smith's tone was ice.

'The proverbial five-bob note!' The officer picked up his cup without its saucer and glugged his tea. He threw his head back and swallowed gratefully. Despite this, his mouth remained dry.

His poor manners received a cold stare from his host. As if setting a better example, Smith himself picked up his cup with care, and, as once instructed by his genteel mother, out of place in her cramped colliery house, years before, he held his saucer in one hand while extending the little finger of the other. He sipped delicately.

The policeman helped himself to two biscuits, staring at them glumly. He hadn't expected to feel out of his depth. He was, after all, *right*.

Smith put down his cup with a well-bred chink, turned and stared out over the Newcastle rooftops, his lips pursed. A master in the art of quiet domination, he said nothing for a while. He allowed the atmosphere to stiffen and chill. The telephone rang once but the call was clearly diverted. Eventually he declared, 'You know, Alec, this is a *crusade.*'

'I'm sorry?'

'I said this is a *crusade*.'

The policeman gathered his wits. 'Crusade or not, man, you can't break the law.'

'To whom are you referring?' Smith's reply was as quick as a razor. His ginger eyebrows shot up.

The policeman examined his biscuits again then returned them to the plate. He coughed. 'I'm speaking generally.'

Smith was adamant. 'I knew nothing about Robson's activities. Let us be absolutely clear. Nothing. I disassociate myself entirely . . .'

'I wasn't trying to suggest . . .'

'Entirely. I categorically deny . . .'

'I never meant to imply . . .'

'. . . any wrong-doing on my part. I absolutely categorically deny . . .'

'Of course.'

'Of course.' Smith puffed out his cheeks as if blowing up a balloon, then sucked them in. He drummed his fingers on the desk, flicked through a pile of papers then slapped them down with the palm of his hand. These small and not particularly aggressive gestures seemed to carry a great deal of menace. There was another long and tense pause. 'You must be aware, Alec,' Smith continued, in a gentle tone, 'your lot did *nothing* about the slums.'

'My lot?'

'The Tory Party. The Tories did nothing, all through the fifties. Homes fit for heroes? I think not, Alec, I think not.' He stared accusingly. 'All that post-war energy. *Your* lot frittered it away.'

The Chief Superintendent looked a little bemused by this conversational departure. Not only bemused but also ill at ease.

'What you have to realize Alec, my friend, and you *are* my friend, are you not?'

The older man stared. His body had become rigid with discomfort.

'What you have to realize is this. I believe in change. Not just protest, but *change*. I believe in change with all of my heart. I'm determined to make a difference. I believe that's what I was put on this earth to do. To *make a difference*. And I believe in using the Council's power to bring about that change, to make that difference.' He hesitated. In softer tones he added, 'Alec, my friend, we have ten thousand families in this fine city of ours, waiting to be rehoused. We have an acute shortage of land. We have the money, waiting to be spent.' He became more insistent, more intense. 'This is a massive experiment and *it's going to work*. I'm going to make sure that it works because my goal is change and my goal is to make a difference. Do you understand? Do you, Alec? Do you appreciate that we're talking about the social and economic regeneration of the whole of the North-East of England?' His cheeks had become flushed. He pressed his hand against the left side of his chest.

The senior police officer said nothing.

'This is a socially justified exercise.' Smith stood and glanced again out of the window. The sky above the chimney-pots was a clear, unblemished blue.

The policeman looked up at him. He'd forgotten how tall the fellow was. He'd forgotten about the hand-made suits. He swallowed hard. 'I haven't come here to talk about . . .'

Smith wheeled round. 'You've come here, Alec, to put obstacles in my path. Obstacles, obstructions, impediments and stumbling blocks.' His voice was a little raised, but this was clearly calculated. 'I won't have it. I won't be diverted. This city has been humiliated by lack of opportunity, murdered by mediocrity. Those days are over. Both literally and metaphorically. Over. I'm not just aiming high.' He pointed at the clear heavens. 'I'm aiming for the sky.'

'I was only trying to say . . .'

'I *know* what you're trying to say, Alec. I know what all you Tories . . .'

The officer was indignant. He grasped his cap in both hands and shook it. 'I don't see how the way I vote has any influence over . . .'

'I know what you are trying to do to me. You Tories. You're trying to stop me. But you see, Alec, what you don't seem to realize is, *I won't be stopped!*'

'I came here about Robson.' The policeman raised his voice. 'About Robson!'

Smith met his eye and held his gaze until the other man looked away. 'I've been on the telephone to London,' he answered quietly. 'As I said. This is a socially justified experiment and there are to be no scapegoats, no fall-guys, no casualties. Harold Wilson agrees. My very good friend Hugh Gaitskell agrees. You'll discover that the Commissioner of the Metropolitan Police Force agrees. *He's* a Labour man, believe it or not. And we want no trouble, no diversions, no departure from the glorious goal of *change*. We are the great modernizers. We believe in cleanliness and efficiency. In opening up avenues, in the potential of the ordinary man. *We*, Alec, we are the future.' He smiled, without warmth. 'And not only that. Robson's off the hook.'

'What?'

'You heard. I need him. He's completely necessary to

me and he's off the hook. All charges will be dropped. Soon.'

The Chief Inspector looked baffled and embarrassed. He stood up, brushing imaginary crumbs from his lap.

Smith advanced, showing him the exit. There was a complicated manoeuvre of chairs and footwork. The subject was boldly altered. 'Alec, have you seen that Mac-Donald lad's drawings? In the quality press? Aren't they marvellous?' He threw open the door in a flourish. 'And I happen to know that his *brother* sings like an angel. That's the thing about the slums, Alec. You see, slums grind the people down. That's why they've got to go. Who knows what treasures we might discover there?'

*

Leslie carefully spread jam over four symmetrical sponges, two pink, two yellow, before assembling them into a perfect Battenberg. He smeared the surface then adhered a rolled-out strip of marzipan icing to the rectangular whole. He pressed it together, gently but expertly. The pale clammy exterior, fragrant with almonds, proved to be the perfect foil for the dainty, light-as-air cubes within. He knew the result was an aesthetic triumph on a plate. He stood back and admired his own efforts. I'll take this for Geordie, he decided. He knew that Geordie was fond of Battenberg although he'd never been known to eat more than one piece. Perhaps there'll be other prisoners, he reflected, picturing a row of cells similar to those he'd seen behind sheriffs' offices in the cinema's Wild West. Unaware of his mother's ex-lover's confinement, he imagined hungry Mexicans and cattle rustlers. Maybe I'll be allowed to share it around, he wondered.

Auntie Ada appeared in the doorway of the scullery.

She eyed the cake with approval. 'Come here a minute,' she suggested after a moment, indicating the two chairs by the hearth in the kitchen.

Leslie sat down with a couple of scones and a piece of Swiss roll.

'You haven't told me how you got on.' She meant at Vickers.

Leslie hesitated. 'Uncle Jack was very kind,' he said, a little lamely. He began eating, hungrily.

'Is he going to start you?'

Thoughtfully, Leslie chewed. 'I suppose so.' He looked depressed.

'It's not what you want, is it, pet? Tell me. You didn't like it, did you?'

'No.' Leslie surprised himself with the directness of his reply. In an instant he realized it was true. 'I didn't like it. No, I didn't, Auntie Ada.'

'What didn't you like?'

'I didn't like *anything*.'

'Oh dear.'

Leslie was suddenly guilty. 'Uncle Jack went to a lot of trouble. I don't want to be . . . I'm sorry.'

'I've been thinking. With your poor mam . . . gone and the little'un . . .'

'Locked up.'

Ada sighed. 'All locked up. Poor little mite.' She hesitated. She was a woman of few words. 'I've been thinking . . .'

'What, Auntie Ada?'

'I've been thinking about what I'm going to do with you.'

Leslie eyed her apprehensively.

'Why don't you . . . ?' Her soft face quivered.

'What?'

Ada answered in a rush. 'Why don't you get a job with a baker?'

Leslie was nonplussed. 'A baker?'

'Why don't you get apprenticed at something you like, something you're good at?'

'You mean ...'

'I mean get yourself a trade, just like Jack says, but in a bakery. You know. Bread, stotties, scones. And not just them either. You'd find yourself doing fancies, florentines and cream horns. Eclairs. For Gosforth. They do all of *them* sort of things for the rich folks over there.' Ada smiled. She knew she'd touched on a subject close to the lad's heart. 'What about apple turnovers? Chocolate Viennas? Marmalade slices?'

'I never thought ...'

'No, I never thought neither, up until now. But before, I came in, I looked at that Battenburg and I just ... I just ... *thought.*'

Leslie was silent. He finished his lunch and said nothing.

'There's at least two bakeries round here. There's one on Westmoreland Road. There's another one opposite the library.'

Leslie stared into the fire. He looked just as sad and preoccupied as he had before but a small candle had been ignited in his soul. It glimmered and flickered. He'd never been in a proper bakery but he could picture the queues in one of the adjoining bread shops. This was where heaped-up buns were twirled into paper bags and brown, granary and burnt-tops were shoved thankfully into shoppers. This was where there was a delicious smell and the endlessly satisfying machine, small and uncomplicated, trundled into its heart a line of delicious fresh loaves, producing an equally rapid succession of perfectly sliced white rectangles, ready for deft tissue wrapping. He tried to imagine the bakery behind the scenes and he saw mountains of dough, of sugar, of glistening currants. He pictured giant bowls of icing, a multi-tiered wedding cake.

'You don't have to work at Vickers. Or Adamsez, or Richardson's . . . There's no law says you have to work at any of those places.'

The boy at once realized that this was true. The effect was liberating.

'You're right, Auntie Ada, there's no law . . .'

'You could learn to be a baker.'

Despite everything, Leslie grinned. He remembered the words of an old nursery rhyme from his childhood, chanted by his mam as she buttoned his clothes in the mornings. *Patta-cake, patta-cake, baker's man. Bake me a cake as fast as you can.* 'Leslie MacDonald,' he pondered aloud. 'Leslie MacDonald, baker's man, bake me a cake as fast as you can.'

*

Later, when Leslie arrived at the police station, he demanded to see his brother. 'You can't keep him here,' he insisted. 'I've just been talking to my friend Constable Henderson in the police box. He says Geordie should be with the Welfare. He said he's very concerned. Why's he not with the Welfare?'

The desk Sergeant seemed tired. He'd spent most the day, so far, repelling journalists, two of whom were dozing on a bench nearby. One of them had a camera.

Leslie noticed them and made an effort to lower his voice. 'I want to see my brother. I've brought him half a cake.'

'Come with me,' said the Sergeant in a resigned whisper. He led Leslie, not to underground dungeons, or even a cell with bars, but to an ordinary room with curtains, a teapot on a table and several easy chairs. Dr Kumar was there, looking very different, wearing cricket whites and a pair of sunglasses pushed up into his thick black hair. The usual WPC was perched on the window sill filing her nails and looking bored. Geordie leant forward over a coffee table, pretending to play the piano. He was oblivious to everyone in the room, as his fingers raced up and down imaginary keys, his upper body bobbing and ducking with apparent passion. There was no sound. The music was all in his head.

'Does he often do this?' Dr Kumar asked Leslie.

'No,' he replied. He felt a little relieved. He knew from long experience that piano-playing meant that Geordie's mood was neutral rather than distressed. Quietly, he enquired, 'has anyone told him about our mam?'

'I told him,' said the WPC, yawning widely. She stretched both her arms above her head. 'He didn't say nowt.'

Geordie continued his imaginary arpeggios, his diminuendos, his octave transpositions.

'He had a poor relationship with your unfortunate parent, yes?' Dr Kumar had taken a notebook and pen from his attaché case.

Leslie stared. 'Who?'

'Your mother.'

'What d'*you* know about it?' As these words emerged

from his lips, Leslie realized they sounded rude, but he didn't regret them.

'I understand,' replied Dr Kumar patiently, 'that your brother never communicated effectively. That he was alienated from his mother. May she rest in peace.' He began writing.

'You understand bugger all,' said Leslie. He took a slab of Battenburg from the pocket of his duffel-coat and unwrapped it. He produced a knife and, resting on the coffee table next to his brother's flailing hands, severed a neat slice. He wafted it under his nose. A faint smell of almonds sweetened the air.

Geordie stopped his pantomime, his eyes met Leslie's and he immediately took the cake.

'Amazing,' said Dr Kumar.

'I told you,' said Geordie to Leslie after a moment, 'our mam is in a white room, in a white dress with a man. Her face is all white.'

'You were right,' agreed Leslie.

'What's he saying?' interrupted the psychologist.

'Our mam is dead,' continued Leslie keeping his gaze fixed on his brother. 'And you know something? She loved us both. Very, very much.'

Dr Kumar insisted, 'He has no concept of death.'

'Those girls are goners,' muttered Geordie, contradicting the doctor, his mouth full of cake. 'That cat is a goner. Probably. It was pretty smashed up. Our mam is a goner in a wedding dress. Geordie's a good boy, isn't he, Leslie? Leslie?'

'What did he say about those twins?' The policewoman jumped to her feet. 'I'll go and get the Sergeant!'

Geordie watched her depart. He gave the doctor a cold

stare then took hold of the corner of his brother's duffel-coat.

'I went to Vickers,' Leslie said to the younger boy, deciding it might be best to speak and act normally. 'I went with Uncle Jack to have a look round. But Auntie Ada, she thinks I ought to serve my time as a *baker*. Have you got your paper and pens?' He touched his brother's arm. 'Have you done any drawings? Have you got your trolley-bus timetable, or has some bugger pinched it?'

'He's stopped drawing,' said Dr Kumar. 'No doubt the result of trauma and disruption to his routine. The psychologist Blennerhasset said, I believe in nineteen-fifty-six, that autistics respond negatively to . . .'

Geordie turned to him. 'Why are *you* wearing white?' he asked. 'Are you getting married or what? Are you planning on being a goner too?'

Dr Kumar fell to his knees. 'He spoke to me!' he was very excited. 'He spoke! At last!' He shuffled next to Geordie. 'I – wear – white – because,' he intoned slowly and carefully, as if speaking to a toddler, 'I play cricket, George. *Cricket*. Do you know what cricket is? There are two teams and one team bats while the other . . .'

Leslie stood up. He held Geordie's hand for a moment. 'I'm going to try and get you out of here,' he said quietly. 'This is a complete madhouse. I don't know how, but I'll do my very best to get you out of here.'

Geordie seemed as if he were about to agree, when his bright green eyes were at once glassy and strange. He became stiff and intense, staring into the abyss of the future.

Leslie waited. Dr Kumar, appreciating the abrupt change in atmosphere, was silent, his pen poised.

Geordie spoke. 'Where you went, Leslie, to those

Elswick works. With Uncle Jack. They've all been pulled down. The Elswick works are goners. There's something new beside the river. With trees, and stuff. And there's a sign. It says ... it says bus-i-ness park.'

'What's he saying?' asked Dr Kumar in a whisper. 'What's he ...'

'Ssshhh!' insisted Leslie.

'The Toll Bar's gone. Burnt down. And the Scotswood works have gone,' Geordie continued, his voice slow and other-worldly, ''cept, 'cept ... for a very little place. It's much littler and sort of ... clean. It looks like ... an ice-cream factory.' He slumped back in his chair and stared at the ceiling. His eyes were like dark pebbles and his chest rose and fell as if he'd just made a big effort.

Leslie bent down and kissed him. Geordie seemed not to notice.

Dr Kumar followed Leslie to the door. 'What's he talking about? You must tell me what he's *talking* about!'

'He sees into the future, man,' Leslie muttered, indifferently. 'He's always done it. Since he was a bairn. Me, I don't take no notice of him. Sometimes he's right but usually he's dead wrong. I mean ... Vickers! Vickers isn't going anywhere, is it?' He quoted Uncle Jack. 'Vickers is the biggest employer on Tyneside!'

*

Towards evening, Desperate Dan stepped out from his mother's hovel at the bottom of the hill. He was followed by a tirade of abuse, a saucepan and a wellington boot which narrowly missed his head. He looked pale and tight-lipped but his actions and manner were outwardly calm. He closed the door, silencing the outburst. He straight away shouldered his kitbag, adjusted his battledress, pulled at the front of an imaginary beret and turned his back on the decrepit, run-down alley where he'd lived, apart from his time in National Service, for all of his young life. He set off at a quick march. His heart was palpitating wildly but to any observer he appeared in control. This was one of the things he liked about being in uniform – the way it enabled him to conceal his feelings, to adopt an expressionless resolution, to refuse emotional blackmail.

Like Lofty Long, he intended catching a bus then a train. Unlike Lofty he wasn't in retreat, in disgrace, planning on a life with his mother. Quite the opposite. Instead he was advancing towards Catterick Camp, where he knew he was expected. He had ten shillings and a travel pass both provided by the army. Despite his mother's hysterical objections, Desperate had enlisted as a real soldier.

That afternoon, he'd read in the newspaper that the conflict in Malaya was over. This seemed to be a significant and life-changing piece of news. Firstly, it invalidated his mother's anxieties about torture at the hands of 'slant-eyes'. Secondly, it convinced him that his endless wait for call-up into the reserves might be fruitless. They might *never* send for him. With no war being currently waged, his state of ready anticipation might drag on for ever. It became clear to him that to further his one true desire, he must take the initiative, sign up, make a career of it, commit himself for years. So this is what he had done, this very day. He felt light, excited and liberated. Now, at last, he could get out of his sorry home. He could get out of the guerrilla conflict in Elswick, with all the devastation of a poorly organized battleground. He could get out of Ratty's dodgy and nefarious rackets. He could escape his bad conscience, the sordid and shameful events of the summer that had resulted in humiliation at the hands of the police. All of this was past. He was joining the forces, taking refuge in Her Majesty's barracks. He only wished he'd done it before. He could barely wait to experience his second taste of discipline, predictability and the freedom of not having to think for himself.

Earlier, he'd sold his motorcycle and called on the old lady, Ada, to say goodbye. She'd given him half a Battenberg cake and a pound note. He felt terribly guilty about the firework that had been posted through her letterbox. 'I'll miss you,' he said. He meant it. He promised to write.

'I'll send you my new address,' she'd assured him, 'just as soon as I shift.'

Now he advanced steadily up the hill towards the trolley-bus stop, looking neither left nor right. He was no longer desperate. He was focused and defined.

*

In the evening Leslie went to the practice at St Stephen's church, aware that he hadn't been for a while. He was late and he slipped in noiselessly. Already resounding from the chancel to the nave and up into the vaulted splendour of the ceiling, the song 'Oh for the Wings of a Dove' was melodious and heart-breakingly poignant. The choir's certainty, amid the dereliction of the rubble and smashed streets outside the churchyard, was to Leslie, at some deep level and despite everything, somehow resonant of security, of continuation, of England's resolute heart. He swallowed his grief and his worries. They *need me*, he realized, struggling out of his duffel-coat and into his cassock. I hope I'm going to be all right. I hope my voice doesn't let me down. He joined the front row of the choir stalls, took a deep breath and produced his best sound, allowing his virtuoso treble to climb, then float and hover like a soaring bird above the anthem, pure, effortless and worshipful. He kept control. Nothing unexpected happened. He didn't falter.

The *a cappella* reached the climax of its crescendo then died away. In the moments afterwards there was a protracted silence in which the air around them, the very fabric of the building, seemed to thrill and vibrate, then there was calm. 'That was splendid, Leslie!' exclaimed Mr Green. 'It's good to have you back. Splendid!'

The Virgin Mary beamed down from her home in the stained glass, casting coloured motes that shone even brighter than the altar flowers. Leslie smiled, feeling calm for the first time in many, many days. Everything's going to be all right, he thought.

Sammy Schnitzler stood in the vestibule, his ear to the chink in the double oak doors. His eyes were damp. He sniffed the cool churchy smell, which was a mixture of roses, damp, old hymn books and Christian holiness. He shuddered. He looked unusually dishevelled, his tie at half-mast, his stiff collar wild and unanchored, his hair disorganized, his trousers dusty and stained. In his hands he carried a spade.

As the song ended, he turned to study the parish noticeboard. Here, there were details of services, flower rotas, Sunday School and Confirmation classes. Sammy took two press-cuttings from the pocket of his waistcoat, smoothed them out carefully and pinned them up. One was the now-famous photograph of the 'Angel Twins'. The other was a brief news item, describing the discovery of the body of Iris MacDonald in the Tyne. It said that the police did not suspect foul play and that an inquest would be held in due course. Sammy moved back to the doors and leaned against them, listening.

Inside, their mood charged by Leslie's unexpected appearance, the choir turned to the musical score of 'Panis Angelicus'. Mister Green spoke of tonality, timbre and ternary form. Now he too was feeling uplifted. He raised his arms to ready everyone. 'Give it your very best,' he insisted. 'This is about faith and love. It's about *belief*.'

There was muted coughing and rustling of paper. All of the choir was Elswick people and they felt determined to triumph. They knew that the choirmaster was not referring to organized religion in the strictest sense. He was talking about them, their families and their community. The brief ensuing silence was broken by the organ, sonorous and grave. They waited. Solo, Leslie filled his chest, opened his heart and began singing.

This time, doubt did not creep into the boy's consciousness and thus the possibility of failure was entirely dispelled. As sure and as precise as a heaven-thrust lark, his voice rose to meet the challenge.

> *Panis angelicus*
> *fit panis hominum;*
> *dat panis caelicus*
> *figuris terminum;*
> *O res mirabilis!*
> *manducat Dominum*
> *pauper, servus et humilis.*

The altos came in, as thankful as a prayer, then the tenors and basses, all binding and supporting the whole and providing a swell upon which Leslie's glorious treble could pilot, then quiver, then glide. The boy felt the music leave his body without effort, without thought, without design, as if he was a mere conduit for something bigger than himself, something *other*. His eyes met those of the glass Virgin and he sensed that for this moment she was inside as well as above him. At last, he felt not only close, but part of her. She'll look after me, he realized at that instant. She'll help me care for Geordie. His soul was filled with joy.

Sammy listened to the final cadences, aware of their soft echo reverberating through the stone and coloured glass of St Stephen's, into the pale evening. He sighed, as heavy-hearted as a refugee. He turned and picked his way through the gravestones, dragging both his feet and his spade. The light was fading, but in the distance a demolition fire suddenly flared and lit up the sky. The dual lights of a vehicle bisected the gloom, there were shouts from the gang and small explosions, as masonry was shovelled into the back of the wagon. A fire engine sounded on the main road and Sammy was puzzled by the skyline. A second skeleton block of flats had just sprung up next to its almost-complete neighbour, behind his house on De Grey Street. Straight-edged like contemporary works of art, the pair were elegant and aggressive, nurtured by a still-swinging crane. Further away, the other surprise was that the public wash-house seemed to have disappeared. Sammy stared, shook his head and tried to re-orient himself in relation to the river. He was confused. Feeling both emotional and exhausted, he sat on a wall. Where am I? he asked himself. If this is the Hofburg Quarter, then where is the Prunksaal? Where's the monument of Prince Eugene on the Heldenplatz? Why does nothing look the same?

The choir filed out of the church, cheerfully, bidding each other good evening. Mr Green, in high spirits, shook Leslie's hand. There was a certain amount of back-slapping and jocularity. Everyone began to disperse, setting off for home. Suddenly, the boy noticed Sammy Schnitzler, in the half-dark, in a corner of the churchyard, by himself. He looks like a ghost, he thought, feeling concerned. Leaving the path to the gate, he went across. 'What are you doing, mister?' he asked. Surprised by the barber's untidy appearance, he enquired, 'Have you hurt yourself?'

Sammy jumped visibly, then gave the boy a frightened stare.

'Why are you sitting here all by yourself?'

Sammy rubbed his eyes. 'I was listening to you,' he said. 'I was listening to the Wiener Sangerknaben. The Vienna Boys' Choir.'

Leslie smiled, mistakenly thinking he'd received a compliment. 'Nah, we're only the *St Stephen's* choir, mister. St Stephen's in Elswick.'

'What?' Sammy looked genuinely puzzled.

Leslie sensed that all was not well. 'I tell you what, Mr Schnitzler. I think you should go home.'

Sammy raised both fists above his ears and shook them. 'Home? I haven't got a home. I wander the back streets looking through the dustbins of restaurants. How can I feed my family? How can I keep them safe from murderers dressed up as soldiers? Where can we *hide*?'

Leslie was nonplussed. 'Perhaps I should go and find Ratty. Is Ratty at home?'

'Ratty? Who is this Ratty?'

'Ratty's your *son*, mister.'

'My son? My baby son is sleeping with his mother.'

Sammy stood up, shouldering his spade. 'Where? Where? *Vos iz dos?* Don't ask me any questions, my boy. *Freg mir nit keyn kashes!'*

Leslie felt out of his depth. 'I think I'd better find Constable Henderson,' he murmured to himself. 'He'll know what to do.' Louder he said, 'What are you doing with that spade?'

Sammy shrugged and stood up. He sounded all at once resolute and determined. 'With this? You're asking? You want to know? I'm burying the Angel Twins, of course.'

The man and the boy left the churchyard of St Stephen's and set off across a rubble-strewn patch of wasteland, gouged and scarred by the wheels of lorries, as potholed as a bombsite. Evening had slipped into night and there was an end-of-summer chill in the air. Here no street lamps were left standing and they negotiated the rough terrain by the light of the moon and nearby bonfires. A siren wailed in the distance. On the skyline the dark purple heavens glowed through the framework of the perfectly symmetrical, defiant modern flats, their now immobile crane towering like a giant insect. Leslie felt a little uncertain. I've lived here all my life, he reminded himself. How can I get lost?

The portly middle-aged man moved with surprising agility. Leslie struggled to keep up, panting slightly. He could smell woodsmoke and coal from people's hearths, mixed with dust, destruction and the faint breath of the river. I'll find Ratty, he thought. I'll find Constable Henderson. Poor Mister Schnitzler thinks he's in Europe or somewhere. He thinks it's the war. He's gone completely round the bend.

*

Loving Geordie

After the time when his family were robbed of their fortune, but around the same time that he was driven from his comfortable apartment in Vienna, Sammy Schnitzler's family comprised a wife and three children. He had twin girls aged eight and a new-born son. The baby was sickly and his mother, through stress and malnutrition, was unable to produce enough milk. Sammy could see that his wife had become thin and pale and weak with fragile lungs and although he tried to pretend otherwise, he knew she wouldn't last the winter.

The weather was harsh, with freezing rain and persistent wind, and clutching their pathetic bundles they moved from one temporary refuge to another. Sometimes they slept in abandoned buildings, in half-demolished attics where they could see straight through the damaged roof to the angry sky, or in damp basements, or in burnt-out shops. They tried to find friends and family but more often than not these had disappeared or their situation was as precarious as their own. Sammy searched for firewood and food, completely at a loss. Nothing in his life had prepared him for this. In a very short time he had descended from the heights of privilege and comfort to a mere subsistence, to a hopeless clinging-on at the very margins of life. Ironically, he was living like a dispossessed *shtetl* peasant in one of the finest and most sophisticated cities in the world.

Few options were open to him and they were all unattractive. One evening, huddled next to his wife and infant in a malodorous blanket, in a stable somewhere south of the Schonlaterngasse, he counted the possibilities on his dirty fingers. He could surrender himself and his family to the authorities and perhaps be shot. He could surrender himself and be separated from them all, before being transported somewhere distant and terrifying, in a cattle truck. He could carry on as he was, hoping to find help with a cousin, a friend, a well-wisher or perhaps with someone prepared to trade his diamonds. This was his current policy but it seemed to be leading nowhere. The only other alternative was to escape. He stared at the other-worldy, pale face of his wife, listened to her laboured breathing and realized she wasn't going anywhere. He fingered the tiny hand of the baby. It was so small it could possibly be smuggled out of the city inside his coat or maybe in a suitcase. It was too weak to cry and draw attention to itself. It probably wouldn't make it but then, by the same token, it wouldn't necessarily hamper things. The baby could take its chances with its wretched father. But what about the girls?

These sorry days, the twins were less and less with their mother, more and more fending for themselves. Always together, small, dainty and proficient in both the harpsichord and embroidery, the Schnitzler girls now rummaged through refuse and stole from market traders. They had learned to pick pockets. To their father's despair, they had even been seen in the indiscriminate company of licentious and dissolute men. Fair-haired, pretty and not obviously Jewish, they lived like street children, like slum-dwellers, like Strassenkinder.

How could he leave the city incognito, how could he slink away, disappear, escape, find a new and far-flung safe haven, *with the girls*? He loved them as much as he loved life. Therein lay his dilemma.

*

The memory of his twins that Sammy Schnitzler carried with him across war-torn Germany, France and Belgium to England and the present day was etched into his memory like a diamond drawn over glass. It was of the two girls, near the Reitschulgasse, hand in hand, their pale dresses fluttering, scrambling through the remains of a recently burnt and desecrated synagogue. They looked tiny but bright against the sorry ruin. Smoke still rose from charred timbers. Anti-Semitic graffiti was still visible on a half-collapsed wall. Black dust smeared their girlish limbs and one of them carried a stolen duck, plucked and dangling comically from twine around its legs. They played in among the rubble, tossing the bird to and fro, shrieking and laughing, indifferent to the cold, oblivious of the danger of the toppling structure and of the building's significance in relation to their family's plight. They were wild, out of control, irreverent. In a few short months they had forgotten their deportment, their manners, their obedience to their parents. Now they swore, they thieved, they went with men, possibly even with soldiers, for money. They were surviving, but they were corrupted, feral and savage.

Out of sight, Sammy watched as they piled floorboards on to the remnants of a fire, creating a small blaze. They tossed holy, rolled-up scriptures on to the flames, and proceeded to cook the fowl, rather than bring it back to their starving mother. Sammy remembered this particularly – the fire, the sizzle of duck flesh, their greedy, self-satisfied faces. He'd called out to them, '*Zol dir Got bentshen.*' May God bless you.

The subsequent scenes were less clear in Sammy's memory. He recalled his anger at the twins' selfishness, but more importantly he had felt dishonoured and betrayed by them. It had also seemed that he, himself, had failed to direct and control them in fundamental ways, resulting in their transgression against all his old values and aspirations. More than anything, however, he was aware that soon, maybe in a few days, after his wife passed on, he would be leaving this hostile, terrible Vienna. Ahead of him was a long journey of subterfuge, concealment and camouflage. He did not know where it would end. Although he could take the baby, it was impossible to take the twins and remain invisible. Equally, it was impossible to leave them because to do so would be merely forsaking them to a life of shame and degradation.

Sammy had joined the girls at their fire. He had eaten a duck leg, even though it was burnt. At the same time, clearly and triumphantly, from the Burgkapelle nearby, the sound of the Wiener Sangerknaben, the Vienna Boys' Choir, bloomed outlandishly in the late afternoon, as lilting and as perfect as a Nazi's gramophone recording. Their voices rose and rose and rose. Then above them, impossibly high, as high as a wind-borne bird, soared the fortunate and privileged cadences of their gifted treble, their very own boy soprano.

The dispossessed father listened to the choir. It was confident and secure. Meanwhile he took his giggling pair into an empty, smashed-up apartment nearby. The singers reached their crescendo. Despite loving the twins, despite wanting to return them to their old lives and keep them safe and pure, despite being as entranced as ever by their identical faces, Sammy slipped out his penknife and cut their delicate throats.

*

Leslie accompanied Mr Schnitzler as far as Cannon Street, at which point the barber began to slow down and appear less certain. 'Where am I?' he muttered. He started speaking under his breath in the curious foreign language he sometimes used and which made no sense to anyone but himself. He looked at his spade as if he had never seen it before. 'Who are you?' he asked the boy. He pressed his hand against his heart.

'I know the way,' announced Leslie, determined to get help. 'Come with me!' He took the man's arm and steered him towards Scotswood Road, the main thoroughfare. To his enormous relief, a light burned in the police box. It looked like a beacon of hope in the darkness. The door was open and Constable Henderson was inside. As they approached, he was pouring himself a mug of tea. His helmet was on the table and he'd removed his boots. An electric bar burned cheerily.

'Mr Schnitzler's having a funny turn,' announced Leslie.

The genial officer offered the barber a seat. 'Have you been in an accident?'

Sammy laid down his spade, entered and accepted a glass of hot water.

'You get yourself warmed up,' said Constable Henderson. He noted the man's uncharacteristic dishevelment, the fact that he clutched his chest and that his face had a strange bluish hue. The policeman picked up his telephone.

'I'll go and get Ratty,' Leslie offered.

'I lost my way,' muttered Sammy, as the boy hurried off. He leaned forward towards the fire. 'But I can't leave my wife and my girls unburied. I thought I could, but I can't. I have to go back. I'll dig the graves myself, if I must. I have to *right this wrong*.' He produced something from his jacket pocket. It was a carton of powdered baby formula. 'I got this from the Welfare, this morning,' he said. 'They were very kind. But what do I do with it? Do I mix it with milk, or with water?'

*

Ten minutes later, Leslie ran to keep up with Ratty through the quiet streets but after a minute or two he was left behind. The youth loped along, his frockcoat rising and falling, his crêpe-soled brothel-creeper shoes almost silent on the pavements. Leslie was soon out of breath and sweaty so he slowed down to a walk. Ratty's very worried, he thought. He's in a panic. He knows there's something wrong with his dad. When the boy joined him at the police box, the youth was on his knees, holding and rubbing his father's hands between his own. Constable Henderson was talking on the telephone.

Leslie stood by, uncertain. Ratty was *crying*. Sammy's eyes were closed and he was slumped on his stool. He was a ghastly colour and he gripped his chest with both hands as if trying to tear out his own soul. 'What's happening?' Leslie whispered, frightened.

Sammy groaned, his breaths rushing in and out as if they were his last.

'He's having a heart attack,' said Constable Henderson. 'I've sent for an ambulance.'

Ratty turned to Leslie, his saturnine features distorted by grief. He'd lost his know-it-all sneer, the self-important way he held his head. He looked young, bewildered and horrified. 'Pops killed the Angel Twins,' he said, shakily.

Leslie stood, shocked and wordless.

The policeman dialled another number then continued to mutter tersely into the telephone. He replaced the receiver. 'Help is on its way,' he told them.

'He thought they were his own daughters,' Ratty continued. 'He's all mixed up.'

Sammy groaned again, but faintly. His cheeks were the colour of ashes.

'His own *what*?' asked the policeman, his manner now bluff, professional, forceful.

'His own twins. He had twins. My sisters. I never knew them. They died in the war.'

'Oh, I *see*,' said the policeman, understanding very little.

Leslie's throat was so tight with emotion he could barely speak. 'Mr . . . Mr . . . I mean your dad . . . He killed Maureen and Muriel?' He was dismayed, but at the same time relieved. They've got to let my Geordie go *now*, he thought.

'Pops killed them,' repeated Ratty, on the verge of losing control. 'I don't know why, but he did. He's sure that he did. In that bust-up house, where you and your brother found them both. He says he did it. With a razor from the shop.'

'How . . . how do you know?' gasped Leslie.

'He said so,' said the policeman, sounding matter of fact. 'Just a minute ago. He admitted to the crime. First to me, then afterwards, quite clearly a second time, to his lad here. I cautioned him then he said he had to do it because . . .' He opened his notebook and read aloud slowly. 'Because of Councillor Robson, Iris MacDonald's friend Betty and a number of very bad men. Because of a burnt duck in a fire, a ruined synagogue and a boy soprano. That's what he said. He said all that more than once. *Because of a boy soprano.* It doesn't make any sense but I've written it all down. Every word.' He paused. 'Not the *foreign* stuff though. I didn't even try to write any of *that*.'

Leslie remembered the afternoon of the twins' murder. He'd been singing in the street and Sammy had heard him. Later, the barber had told him he'd heard music, but he'd thought it was a ghost. He'd been frightened and confused and all mixed up. He'd thought he was in Vienna, in the war. That's when he did it, Leslie realized. After he heard the singing.

The boy grasped the side of the police box, to steady himself. He tried to piece everything together. He considered Geordie's depiction of Marsden Street, the house where the girls had met their end. When questioned, he'd added to the image and drawn what looked like a disappearing motorcycle wheel. Leslie's mind now turned this over with a jolt. 'Of course!' he exclaimed aloud. He now realized it wasn't a motorcycle wheel after all. Geordie saw Sammy Schnitzler at the house, he reasoned, and afterwards, when questioned, he'd drawn a *gramophone record*! Unwilling as ever to portray a real person, he'd represented Mr Schnitzler as an object, and the obvious thing to choose was the intriguing Bakelite disc he'd been allowed to handle in the barber's shop, the last time he'd been to have his hair cut. 'Geordie saw him,' he muttered. 'He was there.'

Ratty was sobbing gently, nothing like himself. 'Yes,' he agreed. 'He was there.'

Sammy Schnitzler opened his eyes, blinked and stared at the policeman's uniform. 'So, the *Schutzstaffel* have arrived.' He leaned his head back against the wall of the police box. 'So. I'm caught. And I thought I might, even yet, get to England.' Eyes now half closed, he looked from one face to another. He was barely conscious. 'You know,' he murmured, 'I thought I might even find *peace* in England.' His hands dropped from his chest to his lap. His face was no longer grey, it was now as white as paper. 'From fortune to misfortune is but a short span, from misfortune to fortune is a long way.' He turned to Ratty. 'Take my shoes,' he murmured. 'There are diamonds hidden in my shoes. They are yours.' He paused, then whispered, 'Goodbye, my boy.' He closed his eyes.

Elswick, Newcastle upon Tyne, June 1963

Still wearing his dusty boots and his floury overall and cap, and with his white-stained haversack on his back, Leslie stepped from the lift on to the fifteenth floor of his block of flats, his key in his hand. There was an altercation taking place a floor or two below, with men shouting and swearing and a woman, or possibly a child, wailing and crying. Doors banged and a bottle smashed on the concrete steps. He ignored this noise in the same way that he ignored a pile of rubbish abandoned on the landing. He moved towards his front door.

Leslie was taller and considerably more stout. He'd spent the day making fruit scones, but not in a small tin tray, next to a coal fire in Glue Terrace. Instead he'd been in a proper bakery, where batches of 'product' were stirred in chrome vats and then shoved in and out of a giant electric oven by the hundred. Leslie was happy. He was doing well. Tomorrow he would be making quantities of icing for lemon drizzle cakes and the smell would be heavenly. The next day he was to help out with weighing on the small granaries. He loved watching the flour slide easily down the metal chute, as smooth as a river, followed by measures of rolling, tumbling seeds and bran.

He worked hard and he was keen to learn. He'd even overcome his fear of machinery and could operate the dough mixer. His cheerful disposition had made him everyone's friend and he no longer did card tricks to gain approval. He was respected as a member of the team.

He opened the door. Everything's all right, he reminded himself. 'It's only me!' he called out, his voice deep and manly.

Auntie Ada was the same, sitting in her usual armchair next to the fire. However, the blaze consisted of mechanical flames flickering round a little red light and the heat came in the form of warm air, from a vent above. A modern, pale, tiled hearth contained her pretend fire. The newspaper photograph of Geordie, somewhat old now, and yellowed, showing him on the beach at Cullercoats, was framed on the mantelpiece. Behind Ada's chair there was an electric wall clock instead of the old grandfather pendulum and a small table with a telephone in a knitted cosy. The floor was covered in wall-to-wall nylon carpet and there was a new three-piece suite, made of leatherette. Pride of place was given to a television set. Ada was reading the Births, Marriages and Deaths as usual, pencilling against the names she recognized. 'Hello, dear,' she said, mildly. 'Take your shoes off. Wash your hands. Put the kettle on.'

'Is he back yet?' enquired Leslie about his brother. The room was full of clear, shimmering light from the enormous picture window, which framed the sky.

'Any minute now.'

Geordie had stopped making predictions and there was no piano here for him to play, as the flat was too small. However, he was still drawing. He was going to art school in the town, three days a week, accompanied by Dr Kumar. He wasn't locked up in Prudhoe. He had his own room, next door to Leslie, who was next door to Auntie Ada, in a high-rise three-bedroom unit, miles up in the air with the birds. He was learning to use paint and there was some talk of life drawing, although so far he still showed no interest in portraying people. He had grown his hair rather too long and his excited tutors said he was a phenomenon. His first exhibition, initially shown in London, was still touring the world. He had been on television as well as in several aeroplanes and he'd travelled twice in T. Dan Smith's red Jaguar. A month before he'd even shaken hands with Prince Charles. Despite all this he was very unchanged. He was no taller, he was still as beautiful as a girl, and he said very little to anyone other than Leslie and Auntie Ada. He never mentioned his mother, his flight in handcuffs or his ordeal at the police station. He trusted Dr Kumar, but treated him with a manner that could only be described as disdain.

Leslie filled the kettle in the tiny kitchenette, and plugged it in. He crossed the small living-room and peered out over the dizzying drop. He hummed a song, his voice low and tuneless. *'Oh for the wings, for the wings of a dove . . .'*

Far below, on the ground, Vickers disgorged a shift of workers. They looked like grey ants crossing the bleak empty carriageway that at one time, not so very long ago, had been Scotswood Road, the heart of a community and Leslie's home. Now it was entirely featureless, without shops or houses, and its adjoining swathe of empty hillside, the top, bottom and middle all merged, was cloaked in planners' green. Verdant, neat and soulless, it was impossible to tell that at one time, not so long ago, here an endless succession of terraces had plunged, clinging to the slope, smoke-stained and populated, the homes of thousands of North-Easterners.

Leslie glanced over the roof of the Vickers Elswick

works and let his gaze fall on the expanse of grey river. His mam's soul wasn't in those watery Tyne depths, he was sure. He turned and smiled down at St Stephen's church, still standing despite everything, all alone and very small beneath the tower blocks, its resolute steeple pointing up to heaven. Leslie hadn't been to the church for a long time but he knew that Mr Green was still energetically conducting, still encouraging hope in the hearts of his singers. He felt sure this was his man's new home. Somehow, miraculously, she'd become merged with the jewel-like, generous Virgin who still hovered in the window, as bright as a dream, her arms outstretched, welcoming all comers. He also knew that above the choir stalls, above the altar, his stained-glass mother-figure remained preserved and smiling, for ever at peace.

He heard the kettle boil, he heard the voice of Geordie, reciting his trolley-bus timetable in the hall outside their new front door. Auntie Ada had dozed off, her head lolling above her newspaper. 'I'll get it,' he said, as the electric bell sounded like an organ peal. 'And I'll make the tea.'